She could not be that naive . . .

"I fear you have sadly overestimated my noble virtues, Miss Faringdon," Simon said bluntly. "I did not come down here to Hampshire to foster a shadowy metaphysical connection with you."

The glow went out of her eyes in an instant. "I beg your pardon, My Lord?"

Simon gritted his teeth and retrieved her hand. "I came down here with a far more mundane goal, Miss Faringdon."

"What would that be, sir?"

"I am here to ask your father for your hand in marriage."

The reaction was not at all what he had expected from a spinster with a clouded past who should have been thrilled to hear an earl was going to speak to her father on the subject of marriage.

"Bloody hell," Emily squeaked.

Simon lost his patience with the strange female sitting beside him. "That tears it," he announced. "I think what is needed here, Miss Faringdon, is a means of cutting through all that romantical claptrap about love on a higher plane that you have been feeding yourself all these months."

"My Lord, what are you talking about?"

"Why, the darker passions, of course, Miss Faringdon." He reached out and jerked her into his arms. "I am suddenly consumed with curiosity to see if you really do enjoy them. . . ."

Bantam Books by Amanda Quick

Ask your bookseller for the books you have missed

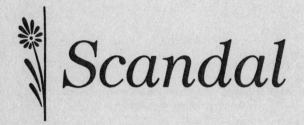

Scandal

AMANDA QUICK

BANTAM BOOKS

2009 Bantam Books Mass Market Edition

Published in the United States by Bantam Books, an imprint of The Random House Publishing Group, a division of Random House, Inc., New York.

BANTAM BOOKS and the rooster colophon are registered trademarks of Random House, Inc.

Originally published in hardcover in the United States by Bantam Books in 1991.

ISBN 978-0-553-59283-2

Cover art: copyright © 1991 by Brian Bailey

Printed in the United States of America

www.bantamdell.com

2 4 6 8 9 7 5 3 1

This one is for some very good friends:

Suzanne Simmons Guntrum
Stella Cameron
Ann Maxwell
Linda Barlow

My thanks.

Chapter 1

The daughter was the key to his vengeance. He had understood that for months now. Through her he would have his revenge on the entire Faringdon clan, for of the four men who owed him for what had happened twenty-three years ago, Broderick Faringdon owed him the most of all.

She was the means by which he would regain his birthright and punish the one who had stolen it from him.

Simon Augustus Traherne, Earl of Blade, brought the big chestnut stallion to a halt amid a stand of bare elm trees and sat silently staring at the great house. He had not seen St. Clair Hall in twenty-three years but to his brooding eyes it looked much the same as it had the day he had left.

The gray light of a late winter sun caused the stone walls of the hall to gleam with the cold sheen of gray marble. The country house was starkly graceful, not a sprawling architectural jumble as so many similar residences were. It had been built in the Palladian style that had been popular in the last century and it had an air of grave and remote dignity.

The house was not as massive as some, but there was an unshakable, if chilly, elegance in every line, from the tall, stately windows to the wide staircase that led to the front door.

While the house had not changed, the landscape in which it stood definitely had, Simon noted. Gone were the austere, aloof vistas of endless green lawn punctuated with the occasional classical fountain. In their place were flower gardens.

A great many flower gardens.

Somebody had obviously run amok putting in flower gardens.

Even in the middle of winter the softening effect on the house was obvious. In the spring and summer St. Clair Hall's cold gray walls would rise from amid a warm welter of brilliant flowers, cascading vines, and fancifully trimmed hedges.

It was ludicrous. The hall had never been a warm, inviting sort of house. It should not be surrounded by bright, cheerful gardens and hedges cut in silly shapes. Simon had a hunch he knew who was to blame for the outrageous landscaping.

The chestnut pranced restlessly. The earl absently patted the stallion's neck with a leather-gloved hand. "Not long now, Lap Seng," he muttered to the horse as he tightened the reins. "I'll have that lot of Faringdon bastards out soon enough. After twenty-three years, I will finally have my revenge."

And the daughter was the key.

It was not as if Miss Emily Faringdon was an innocent young chit fresh out of the schoolroom. She was four and twenty years old and, according to his hostess, Lady Gillingham, the young woman was well aware she had precious little chance of contracting a good marriage. There had been veiled references to some sort of scandal in the lady's past, a scandal that had blighted any hope of a respectable alliance.

That fact made Emily Faringdon extremely useful.

It occurred to Simon that he had spent so many years living amid the strange cultures of the East Indies that he no longer thought quite like an Englishman. Indeed, his friends and acquaintances often accused him of being enigmatic and mysterious.

Perhaps it was true. Revenge, for example, was no

longer a simple, straightforward concept for him, but rather one involving exquisite care and planning. In the Eastern manner, it required the destruction of an entire family, not just one member of it.

A decent English gentleman of noble birth would never have dreamed of using an innocent young woman in his quest for vengeance. But Simon found he had no problem with the notion. None at all.

In any event, if the rumors were true, the lady was not all that innocent.

Icy satisfaction settled deep inside Simon as he rode swiftly back toward the country house of his hosts. After twenty-three years of waiting, St. Clair Hall and vengeance were at last within his grasp.

Emily Faringdon knew she was in love. She had never met the object of her affections but that did not lessen her certainty in the least. She knew from his letters that Mr. S. A. Traherne was a man with whom her soul communicated on a higher plane. He was a paragon among males, an insightful man of refined sensibilities, a man of vision and intelligence, a man of strong character.

He was, in short, quite perfect.

It was unfortunate that the odds against her ever meeting him, let alone of developing a romantic liaison with him, were infinitely worse than the odds in a game of hazard.

Emily sighed, put on her silver-framed spectacles, and pulled S. A. Traherne's letter from the stack of letters, newspapers, and journals that had arrived with the morning post. She had gotten very adept at spotting Traherne's bold, graceful handwriting and his unusual dragon's head seal during the past few months. Her extensive correspondence and wide variety of subscriptions always resulted in a great deal of mail stacked on the huge mahogany desk but she could always spot an S. A. Traherne letter.

She used the letter opener with great care so as not to damage the precious seal. Every part of an S. A. Traherne missive was very important and worthy of being stored forever in a special box Emily had bought for the purpose.

She was gently breaking the red wax seal when the library door opened and her brother sauntered into the room.

"Good morning, Em. I see you're hard at work, as usual. Don't know how you do it, sister dear."

"Hello, Charles."

Charles Faringdon gave his sister a brief peck on the cheek and then sank gracefully into the chair across from the wide desk. He gave her the careless, engaging smile that was a hallmark of the Faringdon men as he crossed his elegantly clad legs. " 'Course, I don't know what we'd all do if you did not enjoy burying yourself in here and poring over all that nasty, boring correspondence."

Emily reluctantly put S. A. Traherne's letter down on her desk and unobtrusively placed the latest copy of the *The Gentleman's Magazine* over it. Traherne letters were private and personal items, not to be left lying out in the open where they might draw the casual interest of some other member of the family.

"You appear to be in excellent spirits," she said lightly. "I assume you have recovered from the discouragement of your recent gaming losses and plan to return to town soon?" She peered at her handsome brother through the round lenses of her spectacles, aware of a familiar mixture of irritation and affection.

Emily loved Charles, just as she loved his twin, Devlin, and her easygoing, gregarious father. But there was no getting around the fact that there was a certain strain of irresponsible, devil-may-care casualness in the attitudes of the Faringdon men which could be extremely trying at times. Even her beautiful mother, who had died six years ago, had frequently complained of it.

Still, Emily had to admit that, with the rather glaring exception of herself, the Faringdons were a handsome bunch.

This morning Charles was magnificent as always in his riding clothes. His coat had been cut by Weston. Emily knew that because she had just paid the bill for it. His breeches were perfectly tailored to show off his excellent build and his boots were polished to a high gloss. Emily could almost see her reflection in them.

Tall, with hair so fair it looked like gilt in the sun and with eyes as blue as a summer sky, Charles was a typical Faringdon. In addition to the features of a young Adonis, he also had the Faringdon charm.

"As it happens, I am quite recovered," Charles assured her cheerfully. "I leave for London in a few minutes. Fine day for riding. If you have any instructions for Davenport, I'll be happy to convey them. I'm bound to beat the post back to town. Got a wager with Pearson on the matter, in fact."

Emily shook her head. "No. Nothing for Mr. Davenport today. Perhaps next week when I get the news of the plans for the summer bean crop from my correspondents in Essex and Kent I will make some decisions."

Charles wrinkled his handsome nose. *"Beans.* How can you possibly concern yourself with such things as bean production, Emily? So bloody boring."

"No more boring than the details of iron manufacture, coal production, and wheat harvests," she retorted. "I am surprised you do not exhibit a bit more interest in such matters yourself. Everything you enjoy in life, from your beautiful boots to that fine hunter you bought last month, is a direct result of paying attention to the details of such things as bean production."

Charles grinned, held up his hands, palms out, and got to his feet. "No more lectures, Em. They're even more boring than beans. In any event, the hunter is a spectacular animal. Father helped me choose him at Tattersall's and you know father's excellent eye for bloodstock."

"Yes, but it was an awfully expensive hunter, Charles."

"Think of the horse as an investment." Charles gave her another quick kiss on the cheek. "Well, if there's no news for Davenport, I'm off. See you again when I need a rest from the tables."

Emily smiled wistfully up at him. "Give my regards to

Papa and Devlin. I almost wish I were going up to London with you."

"Nonsense. You always say you're happiest here in the country where you've got plenty to do all day." Charles strode toward the door. "In any event, it's Thursday. You have a meeting of your literary society this afternoon, don't you? You would not want to miss that."

"No, I suppose not. Goodbye, Charles."

"Goodbye, Em."

Emily waited until the library door had closed behind her brother before she lifted the *The Gentleman's Magazine* off of S. A. Traherne's letter. She smiled with secret pleasure as she began to read the elegant scrawl that covered the foolscap.

> My Dear Miss Faringdon:
> I fear this note will be quite short but I pray you will forgive my haste when I tell you why that is the case. The reason is that I will very soon be arriving in your vicinity. I am to be a houseguest at the country home of Lord Gillingham, whom I understand to be a neighbor of yours. I trust I am not being overbold when I tell you that I am hopeful you will be so kind as to afford me the opportunity of making your acquaintance in person while I am there.

Emily froze in shock. *S. A. Traherne was coming to Little Dippington.*

She could not believe her eyes. Heart racing with excitement, she clutched the letter and reread the opening lines.

It was true. He was going to be a guest of the Gillinghams, who had a country villa a short distance away from St. Clair Hall. With trembling fingers Emily carefully put down the letter and forced herself to take several deep breaths in order to control the flood of excitement that was washing over her.

It was an excitement shot through with dread.

The part of her that had longed to meet S. A. Traherne in the flesh was already at war with the part of her that had always feared the encounter. The resulting tension made her feel light-headed.

With a desperate attempt to hold fast to her common sense, Emily forced herself to bear in mind that nothing of a romantic nature could possibly come of such a meeting. In fact, she stood to lose the treasured correspondence that had become so important to her these past few months.

The terrible risk involved here was that while he was ruralizing in the neighborhood, S. A. Traherne might hear some awful hint about the Unfortunate Incident in her past. His hostess, Lady Gillingham, knew all about that dreadful stain on Emily's reputation, of course. So did everyone else in the vicinity of Little Dippington. It had all happened five years ago and no one talked about it much now, but it was certainly no secret.

Emily tried to be realistic. Sooner or later, if S. A. Traherne stayed in the area long enough, someone was bound to mention the Incident.

"Bloody hell," Emily said quite forcefully into the stillness of the library. She winced at the unfeminine words.

One of the disadvantages of spending so much time alone here in the great house with only the servants for company was that she had picked up a few bad habits. She was, for example, quite free to curse like a man when she felt like it and she had gotten in the way of doing so. Emily told herself she would have to watch her tongue around S. A. Traherne. She was certain a man of his refined sensibilities would find cursing very objectionable in a female.

Emily groaned. It was going to be very difficult to live up to S. A. Traherne's high standards. With a guilty twinge she wondered if she might have misled him a bit about her own degree of refinement and intellect.

She jumped to her feet and walked over to stand at the window overlooking the gardens. She honestly did not know whether to be overjoyed or cast into the depths of despair by Traherne's letter. She felt as though she were teetering on a high precipice.

S. A. Traherne was coming to Little Dippington. She could not take it in. The possibilities and risks staggered the imagination. He did not say when he would be arriving but it sounded as though he might be here within a short time. A few weeks, perhaps. Or next month.

Perhaps she should invent a hasty visit to some distant relative.

But Emily did not think she could bear to miss this opportunity, even if it ruined everything. How awful that it should be so terrifying to contemplate a meeting with the man she loved.

"Bloody hell," Emily said again. And then she realized she was grinning like an idiot even though she felt like crying. The tangle of emotions was almost more than she could stand. She went back to the big desk and looked down at the remainder of S. A. Traherne's letter.

> Thank you for sending along the copy of your latest poem, *Thoughts in the Dark Hours Before Dawn.* I read it with great interest and I must tell you that I was particularly struck by the lines in which you explore the remarkable similarities between a cracked urn and a broken heart. Very affecting. I trust that you will have had a positive response from a publisher by the time you receive this letter.
>
> Yrs ever,
> S. A. Traherne

Emily knew then she could not possibly rush off to visit a nonexistent relative. Come what may, she could not resist the opportunity of meeting the man who understood her poetry so well and who found her verses *very affecting.*

She carefully refolded S. A. Traherne's letter and slipped it into the bodice of her high-waisted, pale blue morning gown. A glance at the tall clock showed that it was time to get back to work. There was much to be done before she left to meet with the members of the Thursday Afternoon Literary Society.

Emily did not find the latest rejection letter from the publisher until she was halfway through the stack of correspondence. She recognized it immediately because she had received a great many others just like it. Mr. Pound, a man of obviously limited intellect and blunted sensitivity, apparently did not find her poetry *very affecting*.

But somehow the news that S. A. Traherne was soon to be in the vicinity softened the blow enormously.

"Damn, don't understand why you would want to attend a meeting of the local lit'ry society, Blade." Lord Gillingham's shaggy eyebrows rose as he regarded his houseguest.

He and Simon were standing in the court in front of the Gillinghams' villa waiting for the horses to be brought around.

"I thought it might be amusing." Simon gently slapped his riding crop against his boot. He was getting impatient now that he was within minutes of meeting Miss Emily Faringdon.

"Amusing? You're an odd one, ain't you, Blade? Expect it's all those years you spent in the East. Don't do to spend too long living among foreigners, I say. Gives a man strange notions."

"It also provided me with my fortune," Simon reminded him dryly.

"Well, that's true enough." Gillingham cleared his throat and changed the subject. "Told the Misses Inglebright you'd be attending. You'll be more than welcome, I imagine, but I should warn you, the society's nothing but a pack of aging spinsters who get together once a week and rhapsodize over a bunch of damn poets. Women are very, very inclined toward that sort of romantic nonsense, y'know."

"So I've heard. Nevertheless, I find myself curious to see how country folk are entertaining themselves these days."

"Suit yourself. I'll ride over to Rose Cottage with you and introduce you, but after that, you're on your own. You won't mind if I don't hang around, will you?"

"Of course not," Simon murmured as a groom led the

horses forward. "This is my odd notion and I am quite prepared to live with the consequences."

Simon vaulted lightly into Lap Seng's saddle and cantered down the drive alongside his host. The anticipation he was feeling was growing stronger, gnawing at his insides. He fought to control it. He prided himself on his ironclad self-control.

Simon had little doubt of his welcome from the Misses Inglebright and the group of poetry-reading spinsters. He might not be handsome in the style made popular by Lords Byron, Ashbrook, and others, but he was, after all, an earl.

That simple fact, Simon was well aware, combined with his enormous wealth and power, was fully capable of erasing a multitude of defects in a man's physical appearance as well as obliterating a wide variety of assorted sins, lapses in judgment, and various character failings.

The ladies of the Thursday Afternoon Literary Society had no doubt been thrilled to learn the Earl of Blade wished to attend their humble salon.

Rose Cottage proved to be humble indeed. It was a tiny little house, situated off a short lane not far from the village, surrounded by a tiny little rose garden.

Two small, gray-haired women of indeterminate years stood at the gate greeting three other women who had just arrived on foot. They were all bundled up against the cold in worn, aging cloaks and pelisses that were uniformly drab in color. Their old-fashioned bonnets were tied tightly under their chins.

Simon surveyed the ladies standing at the gate as he rode up with Lord Gillingham. He got the immediate impression he was about to confront a flock of nervous gray pigeons. He swore softly to himself, wondering which of these dull birds was Emily Faringdon. He experienced an odd sense of dismay and realized he was also somewhat surprised.

Somehow, from her letters, he had not pictured her as one of these severe, middle-aged females. He had been expecting a young woman who bristled with brash energy and overindulged romanticism.

Five pairs of wary eyes peeped out from under the unfashionable bonnets. Not a one of those gazes appeared to belong to anyone under forty. Simon frowned. He had been positive Miss Faringdon would be far younger. And prettier. The Faringdons were known for their looks as well as their feckless ways.

"Good afternoon, ladies." Gillingham removed his hat with an air of gallantry and smiled jovially. "I have brought along your guest for the afternoon. Allow me to introduce the Earl of Blade. Just recently returned from the East Indies, y'know. Wants to see what's up in lit'ry circles back here in England."

Simon was in the process of removing his curly-brimmed beaver hat, steeling himself for the task ahead, when it suddenly struck him that there was no sign of welcome in any of the five pairs of eyes that confronted him.

His own eyes narrowed as Gillingham ran through the introductions. There was no doubt about it. The ladies of the Thursday Afternoon Literary Society were not thrilled to see him. In fact, he could have sworn he saw annoyance and suspicion on their faces. One would almost think the good ladies of the society would prefer he not be there at all.

Gillingham quickly finished the formalities. "The Misses Inglebright, Miss Bracegirdle, Miss Hornsby, and Miss Ostly."

The women all responded politely, if unenthusiastically, to the introductions. There was no Miss Faringdon, Simon realized. He could not deny he was relieved but it also complicated the matter. He hoped she was merely late in arriving.

"Kind of you to join us today, my lord," Miss Bracegirdle, a tall, bony woman with a long face said quite coldly.

"Yes, indeed," the older of the two Inglebright sisters declared primly. She sounded as if she would much rather he had gone hunting instead. "How nice of you to take an interest in our little country society. I fear you will find us quite uninteresting, however. Not at all like the brilliant salons in London."

"No, no, not at all like London gatherings," Miss Ostly,

plump and dowdy, chimed in quickly. "We're quite behind
the times here, my lord."

"I have encountered no particularly brilliant literary salons in London," Simon said smoothly, curious at the recep-
tion he was receiving. Something was not as it should be
here. "Merely a few groups of chattering ladies and dandies
who prefer to discuss the latest scandals rather than the
latest works of literature."

The five women glanced uneasily at each other. The
younger Miss Inglebright cleared her throat. "As it happens, we occasionally slip into such silly talk ourselves, my
lord. You know how it is in the country. We look to city folk
for the best gossip."

"Then perhaps I will be able to provide you with some of
the latest *on dits,*" Simon retorted, half amused. They were
not going to get rid of him that easily. He would leave when
he chose.

The women glanced at each other, appearing more uncertain and annoyed than ever. At that moment the sound
of a horse's hooves clattering down the lane caught everyone's attention.

"Oh, here comes Miss Faringdon now," Miss Hornsby
said, showing signs of genuine excitement for the first time.

The elusive Miss Faringdon, at last. Simon glanced over
his shoulder to see a dappled gray mare cantering toward
the small group. Something went taut in his gut.

The first thing he noticed was that the woman on the
mare's back was riding astride rather than sidesaddle. The
second thing he realized was that this was certainly no gilt-
headed Faringdon. Bright red curls were flying about wildly
beneath a jaunty straw bonnet.

Something sparkled on the lady's face. Simon was deeply
intrigued. Emily Faringdon was wearing a pair of silver-
framed spectacles. The sight of them held him riveted for a
few seconds. No other woman of his acquaintance would
have been caught dead wearing spectacles in public.

"Miss Emily Faringdon," Lord Gillingham confided in a
low whisper. "Family's pleasant enough, I suppose, but
they're all gamesters, the lot of 'em. Everyone calls 'em the

Flighty, Feckless Faringdons, y'know. With the exception of Miss Emily, that is. Nice girl. Too bad about the Unfortunate Incident in her past."

"Ah, yes. The Incident." Simon recalled the gossip he had gently pried out of his hostess. It had been extremely useful information. Although he did not yet have all the details, he knew enough about Emily's past to know he had a powerful tactical advantage in the campaign he was about to launch.

He could not take his eyes off Emily Faringdon. He saw with amazement that there were a handful of freckles sprinkled across her small nose. And the eyes behind the sparkling lenses were quite green. Incredibly green.

Lord Gillingham coughed discreetly behind his hand. "Shouldn't have said anything," he muttered. "Happened when she was barely nineteen, poor chit. All in the past. No one mentions it, naturally. Trust you won't, either, sir."

"Of course not," Simon murmured.

Lord Gillingham straightened slightly in the saddle and smiled kindly at Emily. "Good afternoon, Miss Emily."

"Good afternoon, my lord. Lovely day, is it not?" Emily brought her mare to a halt and smiled warmly at Gillingham. "Are you joining us this afternoon?" She started to dismount without assistance.

"Allow me, Miss Faringdon." Simon was already out of the saddle, tossing the reins to Gillingham. His eyes skimmed quickly, assessingly over Emily as he strode forward. He was still having trouble believing he had run his quarry to earth at last. Every Faringdon he had ever seen had been tall, fair-haired, and inordinately handsome.

Looking at Emily now, Simon could only assume that some mischievous fairy had slipped a changeling into the Faringdon nursery twenty-four years ago. Emily even looked a bit like an elf. For starters, this particular Faringdon was no statuesque goddess. She was much too short, very slender, and had no bosom to speak of. Indeed, everything about her appeared to be slight and delicate, from her little tip-tilted nose to the gentle curve of her hip, which was nearly indiscernible beneath the heavy fabric of her old-fashioned, faded riding habit.

Sunlight glinted again on the lenses of Emily's spectacles as she turned her head to look down at Simon. He found himself pinned beneath that inquisitive green gaze. It was a gaze that fairly glittered with a curiously refreshing blend of lively intelligence and good-natured innocence.

Simon decided in that moment that Miss Emily Faringdon was going to prove anything but dull. A bit unfashionable, obviously, but definitely not dull. She was just like her letters, after all, he thought. The lady was an original.

Simon reached up, his hands closing about Emily's small waist. She felt lithe and supple under his fingers. Strong for her size, too. And full of feminine vitality.

Damnation. He was growing aroused just touching her. Simon frowned and instantly regained control of himself.

Gillingham started hasty introductions but Emily was not listening closely.

"Thank you, sir," she said a bit breathlessly as she started to slide down off the mare. Her attention was on her bulging reticule, which she had attached to the saddle. "Blade, did he say? Gracious, we are certainly not in the habit of entertaining earls on Thursday afternoon."

"My given name is Simon. Simon Augustus Traherne," Simon said deliberately. "I believe you know me as S. A. Traherne, Miss Faringdon."

Emily Faringdon's mouth dropped open in shock and her large eyes widened in obvious horror behind the lenses of her spectacles.

"S. A. Traherne? No, you cannot possibly be Mr. Traherne." She jerked backward out of his grasp as if burned.

"Have a care, Miss Faringdon," Simon snapped as he saw the mare's head come up in sudden alarm.

But his warning came too late. Emily's booted foot accidentally struck the rounded belly of the mare. The poor animal took offense at such ill treatment and danced sideways with a nervous movement. The reticule banged against the mare's flanks.

Emily's spectacles started to slide off her nose. She tried to push them back in place and struggled to control her mount at the same time. But she was already halfway off the horse and when the mare snorted again and made another abrupt, sidling movement, Emily began to slide inevitably downward.

"Good heavens," shrieked Miss Bracegirdle, "she's falling off the horse."

"I say," Lord Gillingham began in obvious concern.

One of the Misses Inglebright rushed forward to make a wild grab for the mare's bridle.

It was the last straw as far as the mare was concerned. The animal heaved its front half upward, pawing at the air with her hooves.

"Bloody hell," Emily muttered as she lost her balance completely and fell straight into Simon's waiting arms.

Chapter 2

Emily wished the floor of Rose Cottage would open up beneath her chair and swallow her whole. She was mortified. She was humiliated. She was in the throes of excruciating emotional anguish. She would have given anything to be able to succumb to a fit of the vapors. Unfortunately, her sensibilities were not quite that delicate.

Above all, she was furious. It was absolutely intolerable that the great love of her life should have snuck up on her and caught her so woefully unprepared for such a momentous occasion.

She took a sip of tea to calm her nerves, listening as the ladies of the local literary society made a desultory effort to discuss the latest articles in a recent edition of the *Edinburgh Review*. There was a distinct lack of enthusiasm attached to the project.

The cup rattled in the saucer when Emily replaced it. The sound made her realize how strained her nerves were. At this rate it was just a matter of time before she spilled tea all over the carpet.

"I suppose I should not have been surprised by the review of Southey's latest effort." Simon's cool, deep voice cut through a fluttering conversation on John MacDonald's rather tedious work, *A Geographical Memoir of the Persian Empire.* "As usual, the editors are entirely off the mark in their comments. They simply do not know how to take Southey. Of course, they do not seem to know how to take Wordsworth or Coleridge, either, do they? One would think they had a vendetta against the Lake poets."

The weak discussion, which had had a difficult time getting started in the first place, promptly ground to a complete halt. Again.

Simon sipped his tea and glanced around the room expectantly. When no one spoke, he tried valiantly to restart the conversation. "Of course, what can you expect from that lot of Scotsmen who call themselves reviewers? As Byron pointed out a few years ago, the *Edinburgh* critics are a petty, mean-spirited lot. I'm inclined to agree. What does your little group think?"

"You are referring to Byron's verses entitled *English Bards and Scotch Reviewers,* my lord?" Miss Hornsby managed to inquire politely.

"Correct." Simon's voice crackled with impatience now.

Miss Hornsby blanched as if she'd been bitten. One or two of the other members of the literary society cleared their throats and looked at each other nervously.

"More tea, my lord?" Lavinia Inglebright demanded bravely as she seized hold of the pot.

"Thank you," Simon said dryly.

Emily winced at the earl's obvious annoyance and frustration as the conversation trailed off into nothingness once more. But she could not resist a fleeting grin. Simon's thoroughly chilling effect on the Thursday Afternoon Literary Society was amusing in some ways.

It was rather like having a dragon in the parlor. One knew one ought to be extremely polite, but one did not know quite what to do with the creature.

Seated in a place of importance near the hearth, S. A. Traherne appeared to take up all the available space in the tiny, frilly, feminine room. In fact, he overwhelmed it with his overpowering, subtly dangerous masculinity.

Emily shivered with a strange excitement as she studied

him covertly. The earl was a big man, hard and lean and broad-shouldered. His strong thighs were clearly outlined by his snug-fitting breeches. Emily sensed Lavinia Inglebright casting anxious glances at the dainty chair in which the earl sat. Poor Lavinia was probably afraid the fragile piece of furniture would collapse. Social disaster loomed.

Now, the earl sitting amid the ruins of Lavinia Inglebright's chair would be an interesting sight to see, Emily told herself. In the next breath she decided she must be getting hysterical. Would this interminable afternoon never end?

She stifled a groan and squinted a little, trying to locate the nearest table, where she could safely set down her rattling cup and saucer. Everything was a colorful blur without her spectacles. She had, of course, whipped them off and stuffed them into her reticule as soon as the earl had set her on her feet. But the damage had been done. He had seen her in them.

After all these months of secret hopes and anticipation, she had at last encountered the great love of her life and she had been wearing her spectacles. It was simply too much to be borne.

Nor was that the end of the disaster. Blade had also seen her riding astride instead of sidesaddle. And he had caught her wearing an unfashionable bonnet and her oldest riding habit. And of course she had not bothered to dust powder over her freckles before leaving St. Clair Hall this afternoon. She never bothered with powder here in the country. Everyone around Little Dippington already knew what she looked like.

Dear lord, what a fiasco.

On the other hand, Simon Augustus Traherne, Earl of Blade, was quite perfect, just as she had known he would be. It was true that she had been somewhat taken aback by the coldness of his strange, golden gaze, but a certain cool glitter was only to be expected from a dragon's eyes, she told herself.

Nor could she hold the unexpected harshness of his fea-

tures against him. It certainly was not Blade's fault that
there was no hint of gentleness or softness in that bold nose,
high cheekbones, and grimly carved jawline. It was a face of
great character, Emily thought. A face that reflected enormous strength of will. An exceedingly masculine face. The
visage of a paragon among men.

How unfortunate he had turned out to be an earl. The
gulf between them was now much wider than it had been
when he had been simply S. A. Traherne.

The cup and saucer in her hand clinked precariously as
Emily leaned forward.

"Let me take that cup for you, Miss Faringdon."
Simon's strong, warm fingers brushed hers as he deftly removed the saucer from her grasp.

"Thank you." Emily bit her lip and sat back. Her mortification knew no bounds now. Obviously she must have been
about to set her cup and saucer on someone's lap, possibly
on *his* lap. *Bloody hell.* She sent up a desperate prayer for
escape from this waking nightmare.

"I suggest you put on your spectacles, Miss Faringdon,"
Simon murmured in an undertone as the ladies began to
argue halfheartedly about the fairness of the *Edinburgh* reviews. "No sense going about half blind. We are old friends,
you and I. You don't need to worry about fashion around
me."

Emily sighed. "I suppose you have the right of it, my
lord. In any event, you have already seen me in them,
haven't you?" She fumbled in her reticule for her spectacles
and put them on. Simon's grimly hewn face and oddly chilling eyes came into sharp focus. She realized he was studying
her very intently and she thought she could read his
thoughts. "Not quite what you expected, am I, my lord?"

His mouth quirked in brief amusement. "You are even
more interesting in person than you are in your letters, Miss
Faringdon. I assure you, I am not in the least disappointed.
I only hope you can say the same."

Emily's mouth fell open in astonishment. She closed it
quickly. "Disappointed?" she stammered. "Oh, no, not in
the least, Mr. Traherne, I mean, my lord." She blushed,

reminding herself she was twenty-four years old and not a silly schoolgirl. Furthermore, she had been corresponding with this man for months.

"Good. We progress." Simon sounded satisfied. He took another swallow of tea and something about the twist of his mouth made it subtly clear he did not approve of the blend.

Determined to behave like the adult she was, Emily forced herself to participate in the labored conversation that was going on around her. The others had finally managed to develop a somewhat uninspired discussion of the influence of the Lake poets and Emily did her best to assist the effort. The earl sipped tea in silence for a while.

Emily was feeling much more her normal self when, out of the clear blue sky, Simon put down his teacup and dropped a bombshell into the small parlor.

"Speaking of Byron and his ilk," the earl said calmly, "has anyone here had a chance to read Lord Ashbrook's latest piece, *The Hero of Marliana*? I thought it rather a poor imitation of Byron, myself. Which is certainly not saying much. Fellow simply is not as interesting as Byron, is he? Lacks a solid sense of irony. But there is no question that Ashbrook is quite popular in some circles at the moment. I am curious to hear your opinion."

The impact of the seemingly innocuous comment was immediate. The Misses Inglebright gasped in unison. Miss Bracegirdle's mouth trembled in shock. Miss Hornsby and Miss Ostly met each other's eyes across the room. Emily looked down at her hands, which were folded very tightly in her lap.

Even Simon, for all his cool sophistication, looked slightly startled by the leaden silence that descended on the parlor. This silence was quite different from the others that had preceded it. Those had been awkward; this was downright hostile and accusatory.

Simon glanced around with an expression of mild concern. "I take it you have not had a chance to read the Ashbrook epic, then?"

"No, my lord. We have not." Emily averted her eyes, aware of the fierce heat in her cheeks. She reached for her cup and saucer again in a desperate effort to occupy her trembling fingers.

"No great loss, I assure you," Simon said languidly. His golden eyes were dangerously curious, those of a dragon who had spotted possible prey.

The ladies of the Thursday Afternoon Literary Society suddenly came to life. As if the mention of Ashbrook's name had galvanized them into action, they took complete charge of the conversation. Their voices rose loudly, filling the parlor with a long, prosy discussion of a recent work entitled *Patronage* by Maria Edgeworth. Even the *Edinburgh,* which normally fawned on Miss Edgeworth, had had difficulty finding good things to say about it. The ladies of the Thursday afternoon salon tore it to shreds.

With a cold, unreadable smile, Simon leaned back in his chair and let the discussion rage around him. "Forgive me," he murmured to Emily. "I seem to have said something unfortunate."

Emily choked on her tea. "Not at all, my lord," she got out between quick gasps for air. Her eyes watered. "It is just that we are not very familiar with Lord Ashbrook's works here."

"I see." Simon reached over and quite casually slapped Emily between the shoulders.

Emily rocked beneath the force of the blow and then caught her balance and her breath. "Thank you, my lord," she managed.

"Anytime." With a sardonic tilt to his mouth, the earl rose to his feet. Instantly another hush fell over the parlor, this time a distinctly hopeful one. He raised a brow. "If you will forgive me, ladies, I must be on my way. I told Lady Gillingham I would be back early. I trust I shall have the great pleasure of meeting you all again. I assure you, this has been a most informative afternoon."

There ensued a few minutes of polite chaos as Simon was hastily shown to the door of the cottage. He bowed politely and walked down the little path to the gate where his stallion was tied. He mounted, tipped his hat, and cantered off down the lane.

Relief immediately swamped Rose Cottage. As one, the other five women turned toward Emily.

"Thought he'd never leave," Priscilla Inglebright muttered as she flopped down into her chair. "Lavinia, pour us all another cup of tea, will you?"

"Certainly." Her sister lifted the pot as the others resumed their seats. "Such a shock when Lord Gillingham sent word that Blade wished to visit today. One could hardly refuse. Gillingham told me the earl is an extremely powerful man in London."

"Blade is well enough in his way, I suppose," her sister said, "but he hardly fits into our little group."

"Hardly." Miss Hornsby sighed. "It was rather like having to entertain a large beast that had somehow wandered into the parlor."

"A dragon," Emily suggested softly.

"A dragon is a very apt description," Miss Ostly agreed at once. "Blade is a rather dangerous-looking man, is he not? There is something about those odd eyes of his that makes one extremely cautious. Very chilling, those eyes."

"We should be quite flattered that an earl came to call and I am sure we all are, but, quite frankly, I am enormously relieved to have him gone. Men like that do not suit little country parlors such as ours," Priscilla Inglebright declared. "So exhausting having a man like that underfoot."

"His family used to live in the neighborhood at one time, I believe." Lavinia frowned thoughtfully.

Emily was startled. "Are you certain?"

"Oh, yes. It has been more than twenty years, now. Priscilla and I had only recently moved here. The earl's family owned a fair amount of land around here, as I recall." Lavinia suddenly broke off with an odd expression in her eyes. "But, as I said, that was twenty years ago and I really do not recall the details."

"Well, I must say, it was especially disconcerting to have him show up today of all days," Miss Hornsby remarked. "Here we have been waiting this age for a report from Emily and we had to spend the last hour discussing the latest literary reviews. Extremely frustrating. But now at last we can get down to business." She turned faded, expectant eyes on Emily. "Well, my dear? How did it go?"

Emily pushed her spectacles more firmly onto her nose and picked up her reticule. She felt much more clearheaded now that S. A. Traherne was gone. "Ladies of the Thursday Afternoon Literary Society, I am pleased to bring good news." She fumbled around in the reticule while she spoke, drawing out some papers. "The navigable canal shares we bought have been sold at a respectable profit. I received Mr. Davenport's report in the morning post. He has already taken the drafts to the bank and deposited them in your account."

"Oh, my," Miss Bracegirdle said, her eyes glowing. "I might just be able to afford that little cottage at the foot of the lane, after all. What a relief to know there will be a roof over my head when the last of my charges goes off to school next year."

"This is so exciting," Miss Hornsby declared. "Just think, Martha," she added to Miss Ostly, "we are well on our way toward securing a decent pension for ourselves."

"Just as well," Martha Ostly retorted, "seeing as it has become quite clear neither of our employers is going to be bothered to supply us with one. What a relief not to have to contemplate an old age spent in genteel poverty."

"At this rate, Lavinia and I will soon have enough money to open our seminary for young ladies," Priscilla Inglebright said happily. "It seemed like an impossible dream for so long and now it is almost within our grasp."

"Thanks to Emily," Lavinia Inglebright added with a warm smile for the youngest member of the group.

"I shudder to think what would have become of all of us if you had not suggested this marvelous plan to pool our money and invest in shares and funds, Emily." Miss Hornsby shook her head. "I, for one, was dreading having to become the companion of one of my aging relatives. They're a miserable lot, my relatives. Every last one of them. Make one grovel for every scrap of charity."

"We are saved and we owe it all to Emily," Miss

Bracegirdle said. "And if there is ever any way we can repay you, Emily, you must tell us at once."

"You have all repaid me a thousandfold by being my friends," Emily assured them earnestly. "I will never forget what you did for me after I made a fool of myself five years ago."

"Nonsense, my dear," Miss Bracegirdle said. "All we did was insist you continue to attend our little Thursday afternoon group as usual."

And thereby made it clear to one and all that the decent folk of Little Dippington were not going to ostracize the Far- ingdon girl simply because of the Unfortunate Incident, Em- ily thought with a rush of affection. She would always be grateful to the ladies of the Thursday Afternoon Literary Society.

Lavinia Inglebright got to her feet, eyes sparkling. "Do you know, I believe this calls for a celebration. Shall I fetch that bottle of claret we have been saving, Priscilla?"

"A lovely notion," Priscilla exclaimed.

Simon was obliged to walk his stallion aimlessly among the trees for the better part of half an hour before his quarry had the grace to appear.

The earl fumed silently. Matters had not gotten off to the smooth start he had anticipated when he had arranged to attend the Thursday afternoon salon. Obliged to stage a strategic retreat, he had decided to lay in wait for Emily as she rode back to St. Clair Hall.

He had fully expected the literary society meeting to break up shortly after he took his leave but obviously the good ladies of the group had finally found something to talk about after he'd gone. He was getting damn cold, although it was an unseasonably warm afternoon. There was no get- ting around the fact that it was late February, after all.

Lap Seng whickered softly and pricked up his fine ears. Simon stopped pacing and listened. In the distance he heard the sound of a horse trotting down the lane.

"About time," he growled as he remounted. Then he

frowned as he heard Emily's voice lifted high in a cheerful, off-key song sung at full volume.

"What good is a man, now, I ask you, kind ladies?
If we had any sense, we would send them to Hades.
They say there's a use for each creature, e'en leeches,
But to discover the use of men, my dears,
A woman must look in their breeches."

In spite of his foul mood, Simon found himself grinning. Apparently the members of the society had gotten into something a bit stronger than weak tea after his departure.

He tightened the reins and urged Lap Seng out of the trees and into the center of the road. He was ready a moment later when Emily's dappled gray came bouncing around the bend.

Emily did not see him at first. She was concentrating too intently on her bawdy song. Her spectacles sparkled in the sunlight and her red curls bobbed in time to her tune. Simon was seized with a sudden desire to know what that mass of fiery hair would look like if it were unpinned and allowed to fall around her shoulders.

"Damn it to hell," he muttered under his breath as he waited for Emily to realize he was directly in her path. The last thing he wanted to do was find himself physically attracted to the woman. He needed to keep a clear head for what he intended. Cold-blooded revenge required cold-blooded thinking.

"Good afternoon, Miss Faringdon."

With a startled expression Emily brought her horse to a shambling halt. "My lord, what on earth are you doing here?" Her face was flushed and there was anxious alarm in her elfin eyes. "Did you lose your way? The Gillinghams are directly over that little rise. You merely turn left at the stream and go straight up the hill."

"Thank you," Simon said. "But I assure you, I am not lost. I was waiting for you. I had begun to fear you had taken another route home."

She looked at him blankly. "But you said you were expected back early at the Gillinghams."

"I confess that was an excuse to enable me to leave early. I received the distinct impression my presence was having a dampening effect upon the good ladies of the literary society."

Emily blinked owlishly. "I fear you are right, my lord. We are not accustomed to entertaining dragons—" she looked horrified and immediately tried to recover, "I mean, *earls* on Thursday afternoon."

"A dragon, hmm? Is that how you see me, Miss Faringdon?"

"Oh, no, my lord," she assured him quickly. "Well, perhaps there is a faint resemblance about the eyes."

Simon smiled grimly. "What about the teeth?"

"Only the smallest degree of similarity. But it does not signify, I assure you, my lord. You are exactly as I had pictured you from your letters."

Simon exhaled slowly, holding on to his patience with a savage grip. "Would you care to walk with me for a ways? We have much to discuss."

"We do?"

"Of course. We are old friends, are we not?"

"We are?"

"Correct me if I am mistaken, Miss Faringdon, but I had the impression we have been corresponding for several months."

She was instantly flustered. "Oh, yes, my lord. We most certainly have. Definitely." Emily's red curls bounced beneath her bonnet as she nodded her head in swift agreement. "I feel I have known you for ages."

"The feeling is mutual."

"The thing is, I never expected to actually meet you in person."

"I see. What do you say to a stroll down by the stream?" Simon dismounted and strode determinedly toward her, leading Lap Seng.

She looked down at him with unconcealed longing. "I

should like that very much, my lord, but I fear it would not be quite proper."

"Nonsense. Who will see us? And even if someone did notice us together, he can hardly complain too loudly. After all, we have just been quite properly introduced at a local meeting of the literary society."

Her momentary hesitation vanished immediately. She gave him a glowing smile. "You are quite right, my lord. I must tell you, I can hardly believe we have finally met. It is the culmination of all my hopes."

She started to slide down off the mare and Simon reached up to assist her. This time she did not lose her balance and tumble into his arms. He realized he was a little disappointed. A part of him wanted to feel that soft, lithe, feminine body against his own hard one again.

"I am sorry for catching you unawares this afternoon," he said as he led the horses into the trees. "I had hoped to surprise you. I know how you like surprises."

"That was very thoughtful of you," she assured him. "I do like surprises." She paused. "Most of the time."

He smiled wryly. "But not always."

"It is just that I would have liked very much to have been looking my best when we met," she admitted. "You cannot imagine how I have been agonizing over this event since I got your letter this morning. I assumed I would have weeks to prepare. Not that it would have made all that much difference, I suppose."

He looked down at her and realized she only came to his shoulder. She was small but there was an entrancing, airy grace about her movements. "You must allow me to tell you that you are in excellent looks, Miss Faringdon. Indeed, I was charmed the moment I saw you."

"You were?" She wrinkled her nose, clearly amazed by this pronouncement.

"Absolutely."

Her eyes gleamed with pleasure. "Thank you, my lord. I assure you I was equally charmed. By you, I mean."

This, thought Simon, was going to be almost too easy.

"But I would not have willingly upset you or the ladies of the literary society. You must forgive me."

"Yes, well, you see, we had not actually planned to discuss poetry or the latest reviews today," Emily explained as she stepped lightly along beside him.

"What were you intending to discuss?"

"Investments." She gave a vague little wave of dismissal.

He glanced shrewdly at her. "Investments?"

"Yes. I realize that must strike you as terribly dull." She looked up at him anxiously. "I assure you that today was rather unusual. I had some excellent news to report in regard to the investments I have made on my friends' behalf. They are all most concerned with their pensions, you see. One can hardly blame them."

"You are seeing to their future pensions?"

"I have some ability in financial matters, so I do what I can. The ladies you met today have all been very kind to me. This is the least I can do to repay them." She gave him a reassuring smile. "But I promise you that normally we devote ourselves to a lively discussion of the latest books and poetry. Why, just last week we were involved in the most intense analysis of Miss Austen's book, *Pride and Prejudice.* I was going to write you a letter on the subject."

"What did you think of the novel?"

"Well, it is all very pleasant in its way, I suppose. That is to say, Miss Austen is certainly a very fine writer. Wonderful gift for illuminating certain types of character, but . . ."

"But?" He was curious in spite of himself.

"The thing is, her subject matter is so very commonplace, don't you agree? She writes of such ordinary people and events."

"Miss Austen is not Byron, I'll grant you that."

"That is certainly true," Emily agreed in a rush of enthusiasm. "Her books are quite entertaining, but they lack the exciting, exotic qualities of Lord Byron's works, not to mention the spirit of adventure and the excess of passion. The literary society just finished *The Giaour.*"

"And enjoyed it, I take it?"

"Oh, yes. Such marvelous atmosphere, such remarkable

adventures, such a thrilling sense of the darker passions. I adored it fully as much as *Childe Harold*. I cannot wait for Byron's next work."

"You and most of London."

"Tell me, sir, have you heard precisely how the *G* in Giaour is to be sounded? Hard or soft? We spent a great deal of time discussing the matter last Thursday and none of us could be certain, although Miss Bracegirdle, who has an excellent command of ancient history, believes it should be soft."

"It is a topic which has not yet been resolved, to my knowledge," Simon hedged. He had not yet had a chance to read the poem and had no plans to do so. He had only dipped into romantic literature and poetry long enough to bait his trap. Now that the trap was about to close, he did not care if he ever read another epic poem of passion and adventure. He had far better things to do with his time.

"Not that it matters greatly, I suppose," Emily assured him tactfully. "About the *G*, I mean."

Simon shrugged. "I imagine it does to Byron." They had reached the stream and were now safely out of sight of the lane. He turned automatically and began to head to the right, moving upstream.

Emily lifted the skirts of her faded riding habit with an artless grace that somehow imbued the aging costume with more style than it actually had. She glanced around curiously at the landscape. "Excuse me, my lord, but you appear to know where you are going. Do you remember this path from when you lived in the neighborhood as a child?"

Simon slid her a sidelong glance. Of course, she had been bound to learn that bit of information fairly quickly. "How did you know my family had a home here?"

"Lavinia Inglebright mentioned it."

"It has been a long time since I lived in this neighborhood," Simon said cautiously.

"Still, it is the most amazing coincidence, is it not? Just imagine, my lord, you began corresponding with me initially because you discovered quite by accident that I shared your great interest in romantic literature. And then we learn that you used to live near Little Dippington as a child. And now we have met. Most incredible."

"Life is full of strange coincidences."

"I prefer to think of it as fate. Do you know, I can just see you as a small boy running down here near this stream, perhaps with a dog. Did you have a dog, sir?"

"I believe I did."

Emily nodded. "I thought so. I myself come here frequently. Do you recall my poem entitled *Verses on a Summer Day Beside a Pond*?"

"Quite clearly."

"I wrote them as I sat beside that little pond up ahead," she told him proudly. "Perhaps you recall a line or two?"

Simon took one look at the hopeful expression in her green eyes and found himself desperately wracking his brain to recall a few words of the sweet but otherwise forgettable poem she had carefully set down in one of her recent letters. He was vastly relieved when his excellent memory came to his aid. He made a stab at the first two lines.

> "Behold yon pond where drops of sunlight
>   gleam and glitter.
> It holds such wondrous treasures for I
> who am content to sit and dream here."

"You remembered." Emily looked as thrilled as if he had just given her a fortune in gems. Then she blushed and added in a confiding tone, "I realize I ought to rework parts of it. I do not precisely care for the way 'dream here' rhymes with 'glitter.' Twitter or flitter would be better, don't you think?"

"Well," Simon began carefully, "it is hard to say."

"Not that it signifies at the moment," she told him cheerfully. "I am working on a major project and it will be some time before I get back to *Verses on a Summer Day Beside a Pond*."

"A major project?" Somehow the conversation was beginning to get away from him, Simon realized.

"Yes, I am calling it *The Mysterious Lady*. It is to be a

long epic poem of adventure and the darker passions in the manner of Byron." She glanced up at him shyly. "You are the only one besides the members of the literary society whom I have told about it thus far, my lord."

"I am honored," Simon drawled. "Adventure and dark passions, eh?"

"Oh, yes. It is all about a young woman with hair the color of a wild sunset who goes in search of her lover who has disappeared. They were to be married, you see. But her family disapproved of him and forbade them to see each other. He was obliged to take his leave. But before he left he gave her a ring and assured her he would be back to carry her off and marry her in spite of her family."

"But something went wrong with the plan?"

"Yes. He has not returned and the heroine knows he is in trouble and needs her desperately."

"How does she know that?" Simon inquired.

"She and the hero are so close, so united by their pure and noble passion for each other that they are capable of communicating on a higher plane. She just *knows* he is in trouble. She leaves home and hearth to search for him."

"A rather risky business. Perhaps he simply used her parents' disapproval as an excuse to abandon her. Perhaps he had gotten tired of her and being kicked out by her family was a neat way to extricate himself from the embarrassment of an entanglement he did not want." As soon as he had said the words, Simon wanted to kick himself. The appalled expression on Emily's face was enough to touch what small bit of conscience he had left.

"Oh, no," Emily breathed. "It was not like that at all."

"Of course it wasn't," Simon said, forcing a grim smile. "I was merely teasing you. You must forgive me. How could I know the story behind your poem? You are the one writing it."

"Precisely. And I promise you it will have a happy ending. I prefer happy endings, you see."

"Tell me something, Miss Faringdon. If someone gave you ten thousand pounds today, what would you do with it?"

The otherworldly excitement vanished as if by magic. Behind the lenses of her spectacles, Emily's dreamy gaze turned abruptly shrewd at his sudden question. Razor sharp intelligence glittered like green fire in those elfin eyes. "I would buy several shares of stock in a new canal venture I have recently learned about, perhaps buy some bank stock, and then put some money into the four percents. I would be careful with the latter, however. The tiresome war against Napoléon will soon be over and the values of the funds might well drop. One must be ready to move swiftly when one is dealing with government money."

"Excellent," he muttered under his breath. "I just wanted to make certain I had the right female. For a moment there I had begun to wonder."

Emily blinked. "I beg your pardon?"

"Never mind. A private joke." Simon smiled down at her. "Your financial advice makes very good sense, Miss Faringdon. Your strategy and mine are very much the same."

"Oh. Do you gamble on 'Change?"

"Among other things. I have a wide variety of financial interests." He brought the horses to a halt and tied the reins to two nearby trees. Then he took Emily's arm and guided her over to a large boulder beside the pond.

He watched her sit down and gracefully adjust the heavy skirts of her habit. For a moment he was distracted by the movement of her hands as she dealt with the thick folds. Then he brought himself up short. *Time to get back to the purpose at hand,* Simon thought.

"You cannot imagine what this means to me," he announced as he sat down beside her and studied the pond. "I have often pictured this place in my mind. And when I did, I always pictured you beside me. After I read your poem I knew you appreciated this spot as much as I do."

She looked around, frowning intently at the grassy banks and shallow, pebble-lined pond. "Do you think I got it right, my lord? Are you sure you recognized this exact spot from the description in my verses?"

Simon followed her gaze, remembering all the times he

had come here in his lonely youth, seeking refuge from his cold tyrant of a father and peace from the endless demands of his weak-spirited, constantly ailing mother. "Yes, Miss Faringdon. I would have known this place anywhere."

"It is so beautiful. I come here quite often to be alone and to think about my epic, *The Mysterious Lady.* Now that I know you were once accustomed to sit and meditate here, the place will have even more meaning for me."

"You flatter me."

"I merely speak the truth. It is odd, is it not?" She turned to him, her brows knitting together in an earnest expression. "But I have felt very close to you from the moment I read your first letter. Do you not find it the most amazing stroke of fate that we discovered each other through the post?"

"A most amazing stroke." Simon thought about how many weeks he had spent researching the best approach to take with Miss Emily Faringdon. A letter written to her on the pretext of having heard mention of her interest in poetry had finally seemed the quickest, easiest way to get a foot back in the door of St. Clair Hall.

"I knew from your first letter that you were someone very special, my lord."

"It was I who was struck by the impression that I was corresponding with a very special female." Gallantly, Simon picked up her hand and kissed it.

She smiled mistily. "I had dreamed so long of a relationship such as ours," she confessed.

He slanted her an assessing glance. Easier and easier. The woman was already half in love with him. Once again Simon slammed the door on that niggling sense of guilt that played in some distant corner of his mind. "Tell me, Miss Faringdon, just how do you view our relationship?"

She blushed, but her eyes were gleaming with enthusiasm. "A very pure sort of relationship, my lord. A relationship formed on a higher plane, if you know what I mean."

"A higher plane?"

"Yes. The way I see it, ours is quite clearly an *intellectual* connection. It is a noble thing of the mind, a relationship that takes place in the metaphysical realm. It is a friendship based on shared sensibilities and mutual understanding. One might say we have a spiritual communion, my lord. A union untainted by baser thoughts and considerations. Our passions are of the highest order."

"Hell and damnation," Simon said.

"My lord?"

She looked up at him with such inquiring innocence, he wanted to shake her. She could not be that naive, in spite of her poetry. She was, after all, twenty-four years old and there was that matter of the Unfortunate Incident Gillingham had mentioned.

"I fear you have sadly overestimated my noble virtues, Miss Faringdon," he said bluntly. "I did not come down here to Hampshire to foster a shadowy metaphysical connection with you."

The glow went out of her eyes in an instant. "I beg your pardon, my lord?"

Simon gritted his teeth and retrieved her hand. "I came down here with a far more mundane goal, Miss Faringdon."

"What would that be, sir?"

"I am here to ask your father for your hand in marriage."

The reaction was not at all what he had expected from a spinster with a clouded past who should have been thrilled to hear an earl was going to speak to her father on the subject of marriage.

"Bloody hell," Emily squeaked.

Simon lost his patience with the strange female sitting beside him. "That tears it," he announced. "I think what is needed here, Miss Faringdon, is a means of cutting through all that romantical claptrap about love on a higher plane that you have been feeding yourself all these months."

"My lord, what are you talking about?"

"Why, the darker passions, of course, Miss Faringdon." He reached out and jerked her into his arms. "I am suddenly consumed with curiosity to see if you really do enjoy them."

Chapter 3

Emily was stunned to find herself locked in an unbreakable embrace. It had been five years since a man had held her in this intimate fashion. And that it should be Simon, of all people, who was holding her this way now was almost beyond comprehension. Simon was her companion of the metaphysical realm, her noble, high-minded, sensitive friend, her intellectual soul mate.

Only in the darkest hours of the night and in her most secret dreams had she allowed herself to fantasize about him as a flesh and blood lover.

"Oh, Simon," she breathed, gazing up at him with a sense of wonder and longing that was so fierce it made her tremble in his arms.

He did not answer. His golden eyes were glittering with an intensity that in any other man would have been alarming. There seemed to be more annoyed impatience than sweet affection in his gaze, however. But perhaps that was just her imagination.

Without a word he removed her spectacles and bonnet and set them on the rock beside his hat. Then his mouth came slowly and deliberately down on hers and Emily forgot everything else except the hard, commanding heat of his kiss.

It was all she had ever dreamed his kiss would be during those still, dark hours in the middle of the night when she had allowed herself to dream hopeless dreams.

In truth, it was more than she had dreamed. She could never have fully imagined the feel of his mouth on hers because she had never experienced anything quite like it. This was nothing like those kisses she had received five years ago. The sensation of Simon's arms around her and the overwhelming intimacy of his mouth effectively shattered the fragile romantic illusions of a lifetime and taught her the true meaning of passion in one searing moment.

Simon's hand, which had been curved around her waist, began to slide up along her side toward her breast. Emily sensed dimly that she should call a halt at once but it seemed beyond her power to do so. This was S. A. Traherne, the man she had put on a pedestal, the man she had loved from afar with a pure and noble passion . . . the man of her dreams.

Now, in a blinding moment of sensual clarity, Emily realized that Simon reciprocated her love. The wonder of it was overpowering.

Simon's fingers continued upward over the bodice of the riding habit until the small, soft weight of Emily's breast was resting on the edge of his hand. Emily heard him groan as his thumb gently traced the outline of one soft curve. Her nipple was suddenly, achingly, taut under the heavy wool. Emily shivered and Simon's palm closed possessively over her breast.

"Come here, elf," Simon murmured in a rough, husky voice as he eased her across his thighs. He trapped her close to his chest with one bent knee and two iron-hard arms. The strength in him should have frightened Emily, but it did not. This was her dragon and she knew he would keep her safe.

Her fingers splayed across his chest, her nails digging urgently into the fabric of his coat. He smelled good, she thought. A combination of leather and horse and masculine heat. The scent of him was curiously intoxicating and she found herself burrowing closer into his warmth.

"Part your lips for me," Simon urged softly.

Emily obeyed instinctively. Without any warning, his tongue slid boldly into her mouth. The shock of it made Emily gasp and pull back. She was suddenly aware of the heavy bulge of his manhood under her thigh. She knew she was turning a bright pink.

"My God, Emily."

For a moment the world seemed to halt. She could barely breathe, let alone respond.

"Emily, open your eyes and look at me."

Dreamily, Emily lifted her lashes and looked up into Simon's harshly carved face. He was so close that she could see him without the aid of her spectacles. She was fascinated by the glittering heat that had washed away the coldness in his eyes. Fire lit the beautiful golden gaze now, a wild flame of masculine desire held under rigid control.

"Dragon," she whispered softly, touching his hard cheek with gentle fingers. "My very own golden-eyed dragon."

He narrowed his eyes as he stared down at her. "Dragons have a dangerous reputation around fair maidens."

She smiled softly up at him. " 'Tis no use breathing fire and smoke in an attempt to frighten me, my lord. I know I am quite safe with you."

"What makes you so certain of that?"

"I know you very well. I have read and reread every letter you have ever sent to me. Still, I must admit, I cannot quite believe this is happening."

"Nor can I." He shifted position abruptly, sliding her off his lap. He raked a hand through his dark hair. "Good God. I must have lost my wits."

"I know what you mean. I feel certain this is what the poets refer to as a wild, sweet excess of emotion. It is rather exciting, is it not?" Emily straightened, feeling a little shy and shaky, but otherwise wonderful.

"Exciting is one word for it. I can think of a few others."

"Such as?"

"Stupid."

Emily frowned at the sardonic tone. "Is something wrong, my lord?" She groped for her spectacles because he had moved too far away to enable her to see clearly the expression in his eyes.

"Here." Impatiently he thrust the spectacles into her hands and she put them on.

Emily saw at once that Simon was scowling fiercely. "There is something wrong. What is it, my lord?"

He gave her a derisive, sidelong glance. "You ask me that? After what almost happened a moment ago?"

Emily tilted her head to one side, studying him. "You kissed me. It was wonderful. The most wonderful experience of my life. Why should anything be wrong?"

"Damn it, woman, another five minutes and we would have been . . . Hell. Never mind."

"Another five minutes and we would have been *cast adrift upon love's transcendent, golden shore,* perhaps?"

"Good God. This is no time for poetic euphemisms." Simon glared at the quiet waters of the pond. He started to say something else and then his lips twitched. An instant later a wicked grin came and went on his hard mouth. *"Cast adrift upon love's transcendent, golden shore?* From whose works did you glean that line?' "

"I invented it myself," Emily told him, not without some pride. " 'Tis a line from the epic poem I told you I am currently working on, *The Mysterious Lady.* I am still searching for the proper rhyme for 'shore.' "

"Have you tried 'bore'?"

She grinned. "Now you are teasing me. Tell me the truth, sir. What do you think of the line?"

He glanced back at her over his shoulder, golden eyes gleaming with what should have been passion but which Emily was very much afraid was amusement. "It is most apt, Miss Faringdon. Come here."

She went willingly back into his embrace but this time he merely kissed her lightly on the forehead and then on the tip of her nose before setting her a short distance away from him again. "Now, pay attention, Miss Faringdon, for I have something extremely important to say to you."

"Yes, my lord?"

"Henceforth, whenever we are threatened with being cast adrift upon love's transcendent, golden shore, I want you to slap my face. Do you understand?"

She stared at him in shock. "I shall not do any such thing."

"Yes, you will, if you have any common sense at all."

"I am certain you would not go beyond the limits of what is proper, my lord."

"I have already gone beyond them," he said through gritted teeth, his amusement fading rapidly.

"The thing is, my lord," she said with a small, considering frown, "I am not at all certain we can rely upon my common sense in this sort of situation. I have been assured that in such matters, I do not have a great deal. Therefore, we must depend upon your sense of honor and propriety. Do not worry, my lord, I am certain you will know exactly how to go on."

"What in God's name do you mean, you don't have any common sense in this sort of thing?"

"Oh, nothing—nothing, really," she said hastily, not wanting to have to explain about the Unfortunate Incident until it was absolutely necessary. After all, once Simon became aware of what had happened when she was nineteen, he would be obliged to cease all this wonderful talk of love. "It is just that my family feels I have been rather badly affected by my love of romantic literature," she explained weakly. It was true as far as it went.

"And have you?" His golden eyes were unreadable.

Emily blushed and looked at his perfectly tied cravat, which did not seem to have been in the least disturbed by the recent excess of passion. "You should know the answer to that, my lord. You know me better than anyone else knows me."

"Because of your letters?" He caught her chin gently on the edge of his fist and forced her to meet his eyes. "Do you know, you may be right. I have the distinct impression that you are a sadly misunderstood young woman. But it is a mistake for you to assume that you know as much about me as I do about you."

"I do not think for one moment that my belief is a mistake, my lord." She looked up at him very earnestly. "Through our letters you and I have developed the most perfect intellectual and spiritual companionship of the mind. I am quite certain that our communication, which takes place on the highest of planes, has led us to a true comprehension of each other's—"

"Enough," he interrupted curtly. "Miss Faringdon, it is always a mistake to assume you can trust a man completely when it comes to matters of passion."

She smiled serenely, knowing he was wrong. "I do not think so, my lord. Not in your case. I would trust you with my heart and my life."

"Damn." Simon shook his head slowly and released her chin. "Your family appears to have the right of it. No common sense in this sort of thing at all. You do not mind the risks involved in the game of love, I take it?"

She shrugged lightly. "I come from a long line of gamesters, my lord. It is in the blood."

"And how often have you taken this particular sort of risk?" he inquired with sudden, silky menace.

Emily looked out over the small pond, choosing her words carefully. She knew honor required her to be honest, but she could not bear to ruin this idyll by telling him the whole story. "I have never before been in love. Not really. I know that now. Once, a long time ago, I thought I was, but I was proven wrong. Since then there has been no one else with whom I have wanted to take such a risk."

"Interesting."

Uneasily she turned her head to find him watching her with his cold, assessing eyes. "My lord?"

He said something under his breath and got to his feet. "Pay me no heed. I am obviously not thinking very clearly at the moment. A direct result of sailing too close to a transcendent, golden shore, I imagine. Come. I will ride with you until you are within sight of St. Clair Hall."

"Have I said something wrong, my lord?"

"Not at all. I believe everything is going to go very smoothly between us from now on. I simply needed to acquire certain information before proceeding further and I have done so."

"I see. Very wise." Emily relaxed and smiled up at him, not caring if her heart was in her eyes. She knew very well there was no future for them, but there was the present and she was determined to enjoy it as long as possible. "In your most recent letter you said you were very affected by my verses about urns and broken hearts."

His mouth curved faintly as he took her arm and led her back to the waiting horses. "Indeed I was, Miss Faringdon."

"Well, I am glad you are interested in them," she said cheerfully. "Mr. Pound, the bookseller and publisher, was not. I got another nasty rejection from him in the morning post."

"Mr. Pound obviously has even less taste than the critics of the *Edinburgh Review*."

Emily laughed in delight. "Very true." She paused once more, her expression sobering as a shaft of guilt assailed her. She really ought to give him a small warning about the doomed nature of his affections. "My lord?"

"Yes, Miss Faringdon?" Simon was busy untying the dappled gray mare.

"Did you mean it when you said you were here to . . . to speak to my father about asking for my hand in marriage?"

"Yes, Miss Faringdon. I meant every word." He hoisted her lightly up into the saddle.

She touched his hand as it slid away from her waist. Tears began to well up in her eyes. "It is quite impossible, as you will soon see. But I want you to know that I will be forever grateful for this moment. I shall hold the memory of it close to my heart for the rest of my life."

"What the devil?" Simon scowled up at her.

Emily could not bear to stay near him any longer. He was bound to inquire about the tears. Applying her ankles gently to her mare's flanks, she turned and cantered away from him toward the road to St. Clair Hall.

The chilly breeze whipped away the drops of moisture that trickled down her cheeks.

Simon managed to contain his brooding curiosity until Lady Gillingham, graciously vague as always, had risen from the table to leave the gentlemen to their after-dinner port.

As soon as the lady had departed, the gentlemen promptly relaxed. They leaned back in their chairs, thrust their legs out beneath the table, and picked up their glasses. Lord Gillingham lit a cigar.

Simon prepared himself to do what unconscionable gentlemen had done since time immemorial: discuss a lady over a bottle of port. He waited for an opening and it came quickly. Gillingham was in a talkative mood, having already consumed a fair amount of claret at dinner.

"Enjoy your visit with the lit'ry society?" Gillingham inquired as he squinted through the blue haze of his cigar smoke.

"I found it interesting." Simon turned the cut crystal glass in his hand, watching the light play on the facets. "It's obvious the rage for the new romantic poetry has spread beyond London. At least among the ladies."

"Don't know what will come of it," Gillingham said with a grim shake of his head. "All that romantical nonsense is bound to have a very bad effect on females."

"Surely not on the good ladies of Little Dippington?"

"Well, p'raps no real harm done to the older ones like the Inglebright sisters and the others, but t'ain't at all healthy for young ladies."

"Such as Miss Faringdon?" Simon inquired gently.

"Damn poetical nonsense was the ruination of that poor gel. Pity. But, then, never had much chance anyway, not growing up in that nest of wastrels and gamesters. Just a matter o' time 'fore she got into trouble after her mother died."

"Her mother died about six years ago, I understand?"

"Lovely woman. Beautiful, o' course. All the Flighty

Faringdons is dashed good-looking, male and female alike. 'Cept for Miss Emily. That red hair and those freckles ain't the thing, y'know. Then there's the spectacles. Might have been able to cover up some of the defects long enough to get her through a Season but the poor gel never had a chance."

"Because of her mother's death?"

"Followed by the Unfortunate Incident," Gillingham explained sadly.

"Just how bad was the Unfortunate Incident?" Simon asked carefully. It was time to get all the sordid details, he thought.

"Bad enough, according to her father. Poor chit."

"It happened five years ago?" Simon probed.

"About that, I believe. Miss Faringdon was nineteen at the time. She'd lost her mama a year or so before. That damn father o' hers and those rakehell brothers were always gone, leavin' her alone in that big house. Can't pry a Faringdon away from the gaming hells for long, y'know. In any event, Miss Faringdon was more or less left to her own devices with only the servants for company. Lonely, no doubt. No one to advise her. Poor thing was ripe for disaster."

Simon reached for the bottle of port and topped off his host's glass. "And it struck?"

"Disaster? It struck right enough. In the form of a young rake, naturally. Always the way, ain't it?"

"Yes." Simon sipped his own port and wondered why he suddenly felt like halting the conversation then and there. He could guess how the tale was going to end now and already he did not look forward to hearing any more. But he had long ago learned that information of any kind was a vital commodity, especially when one was plotting vengeance. "This young man. Is he still in the neighborhood?"

"Ashbrook? Hell and damnation, no. Never saw him again after the Incident. Heard he came into his title a couple years ago. He's a baron now. And a poet. Hang around London drawing rooms long enough and y'er bound to run into him and his admirers. You've probably caught a glimpse of him at some crush. All the rage just now."

Simon's fingers tightened of their own accord around his glass. Carefully he loosened them, not wanting to crack the fragile crystal.

At the mention of Lord Ashbrook's name he had a sudden, clear recollection of five pairs of accusing eyes turned on him that afternoon when he had casually mentioned the poet's latest epic. The extent of his *faux pas* earlier in the day made him wince.

"So it was Ashbrook who ruined Em . . . I mean, Miss Faringdon?"

"Talked her into running off with him. Very sad."

"An elopement?"

"Poor Miss Faringdon believed she was eloping. But personally I doubt Ashbrook ever had any intention o' marrying her. Faringdon caught up with 'em the next day and word has it Ashbrook did not hang around to confront the outraged father. But by then the damage was done, o' course. The pair had spent the night together at an inn, Faringdon told me privately."

"I see."

"Damn sad. Emily's a sweet little thing. No one around here talks about the Incident. Don't like to see the gel hurt. 'Preciate it if you'd keep quiet about it, sir."

"Of course." Simon had a sudden image of Emily's face as she had tried to explain that it was quite impossible for him to ask for her hand in marriage. She was obviously as convinced as everyone else that she was socially ruined. The most she could hope for in the way of romance these days was a pure, noble, high-minded connection maintained through the post. No wonder she had been dismayed to see him turn up in person.

Simon recalled that he had encountered Ashbrook once or twice in a couple of London ballrooms. The man put a great deal of effort into projecting an image of smoldering sensuality and jaded, cynical tastes. The ladies who clustered around him obviously found him fascinating. It was no secret that they saw him as the epitome of the new romantic style made popular by Byron.

"Why didn't Faringdon insist Ashbrook marry his daughter?" Simon asked.

"Probably tried. Ashbrook obviously refused. Can't exactly force a man, y'know. Matter of honor and all that. And t'weren't like Faringdon was important in the social world. No real position, of course. Broderick Faringdon has some distant family connection to an impoverished baron up in Northumberland, but that's all."

"So Faringdon let the matter drop?"

"Afraid so. Our little Miss Faringdon lacked the looks and, at that time, fortune enough to engage Ashbrook's interest for a permanent commitment. I fear the young man was merely toying with her affections and the lady paid the price of her indiscretion, as young ladies frequently must."

Simon studied his port. "I am surprised that neither Broderick Faringdon nor one of twins attempted to call Ashbrook out."

"Faringdons take their risks at the gaming tables, not with their necks."

"I see."

"A pity, all in all," Gillingham concluded, reaching for the port. "Thank God for the ladies of the local literary society."

Simon looked up. "Why do you say that?"

"A dull but thoroughly respectable lot, the bunch of 'em. They banded together and took Miss Faringdon into their group. Made it clear they were not going to cut her even if she was ruined in the eyes of the world. If you ask me, there's not a one of the lit'ry society ladies who don't secretly envy the gel. She brought a little excitement into their humdrum lives."

Simon thought that was a surprisingly perceptive comment on the part of his host. He wondered if Gillingham knew that Emily was repaying her benefactresses by ensuring them all comfortable pensions for their old age. "So Miss Faringdon has never married because of the scandal. Do you know, I find it difficult to believe that someone around here was not prepared to overlook it long enough to ask for her hand. She's an intriguing little thing."

"Well, there's always Prendergast," Gillingham said thoughtfully.

Simon frowned. "Who is Prendergast?"

"Country gentry. Owns a fair amount o' land in the area. His wife died a year ago and he's made it clear he's willing to overlook the Incident in Miss Faringdon's past. Ain't precisely a young girl's dream, but Miss Faringdon ain't precisely a young girl anymore. And it ain't as if she's got a lot of choice."

Several hours later Simon gave up his attempt to get to sleep. He pushed back the heavy covers, got out of bed, and dressed in his breeches, boots, and a shirt. Then he picked up his greatcoat and let himself out into the hall.

The restlessness had been gnawing at him since he had retired. Perhaps a walk would help.

The house was chilled and dark. Simon thought about lighting a candle and decided against it. He had always been able to see quite well at night.

He went silently down the carpeted stairs and then along the hall that led to the kitchens. A moment later he stepped out into the clear, frosty night.

It was easy enough to find his way through the moonlit woods to St. Clair Hall. It had been years since he had walked this land at night but he had not forgotten the way.

Ten minutes later Simon strode up the long, elegant drive of the hall, his boots crunching on the icy ground. He paused at the foot of the elegant staircase, turned, and went through the gardens to the side of the house. He was startled to see lights still blazing in the library window.

His stomach clenched. The lights had been shining just as brilliantly on that night twenty-three years ago when he had burst into the library to find his father sprawled facedown on the desk in a pool of blood.

Simon knew now what had drawn him to the library window tonight. He had come here to see if his father's ghost still hovered near the mahogany desk.

Some distant part of Simon's mind half expected to see

the pistol still clutched in the earl's dead hand, still expected to see blood and torn flesh and gray matter spattered on the wall behind the chair. He had lived with the grisly image for years.

But instead of the ghost of a man who had lost everything and taken the coward's way out, leaving a twelve-year-old son to cope as best he could, Simon saw Emily.

She was perched on the edge of the big chair, looking very small and ethereal as she bent industriously over the huge mahogany desk. In the candlelight her red hair gleamed as richly as Lap Seng's coat did in sunlight.

She was wearing a little white lace cap and a prim, ruffle-necked dressing gown. Her feet, which were tucked back under the chair, were encased in soft satin slippers. She was scratching busily away with a quill in a leather-bound volume.

It occurred to Simon that a romantic creature like Emily was bound to keep a journal. If so, he was no doubt figuring heavily in this night's entry.

Or perhaps she was composing new stanzas for *The Mysterious Lady*.

He watched for a few more minutes, telling himself he should leave. But he did not turn around and start back through the woods toward the Gillinghams until Emily finally put down her quill. He watched as she reached up to put out the lamps. Then she picked up a candle to light her way upstairs and let herself out of the room.

The library went dark.

Simon realized he was still standing there, staring into the deeply shadowed room. Eventually he forced himself to turn and walk back toward the Gillinghams'.

He realized he had not seen what he had come to see. The ghost of his father, which should have occupied the library, had been banished by the redheaded, green-eyed Titania who had been sitting at the desk.

Emily floated through the week that followed as though she were on a cloud. Never had her rhymes come so easily.

She was inspired by everything she saw or touched, especially Simon. And she was seeing a great deal of the earl.

She knew this particular cloud on which she soared would soon be ripped to shreds and she would fall to earth with a sickening thud. But she was determined to enjoy the ride for as long as possible. She was absorbing sufficient transcendent experience to last a lifetime.

Emily was in love and her lover, it seemed, arranged to be everywhere she was during the week.

She encountered Simon at the Hathersages' card party on Saturday night. He partnered her at whist and they won. Naturally. How could such a team have lost? Emily had pointed out later.

He attended the Sewards' musicale on Monday afternoon. Emily exchanged a secret, laughing glance with him when the youngest Seward daughter lost her place in the Mozart divertimento. Together they clapped so strongly at the finish that the flushed girl offered an encore.

Simon was in the village when Emily went shopping. He made a point of stopping to chat with her.

He seemed to be riding on the road that led to St. Clair Hall every time Emily went out on horseback.

Toward the end of the week, Simon materialized at the vicarage garden gate just as Emily was saying farewell to Mrs. Ludlow, the vicar's wife. He was riding the chestnut stallion he called Lap Seng. He greeted Mrs. Ludlow with due courtesy, dismounted, and stayed talking for quite some time to both women.

Eventually he bid the ladies good day and vaulted back into the saddle, where he sat for a moment smiling down at Emily.

"I trust you will promise me a dance tomorrow night at the Gillinghams' ball, Miss Faringdon," he said as he tightened the stallion's reins.

"Oh, yes, of course," Emily said breathlessly. It would be the first time they had danced together, she thought as she watched him canter off down the lane. She could hardly contain her excitement.

"My, my," the vicar's wife murmured with a knowing

look. "Blade is certainly showing a marked interest in you, young lady."

Emily blushed, horribly aware of what Mrs. Ludlow must have been thinking. The vicar's wife was a kindly person. She was no doubt feeling sorry for Emily because everyone knew that sooner or later Blade would learn about the Incident and that would be the end of Emily's courtship.

"The earl has been very kind in his attentions," Emily said weakly. She was surprised by Mrs. Ludlow's next remark.

"His family lived around here at one time," Mrs. Ludlow said thoughtfully. "More than twenty years ago, I believe."

Emily, who had been expecting a gentle warning against leading the earl to think his attentions had a future, blinked in surprise. "So Miss Inglebright said."

"The boy and his mother left after the father died. Very sad situation, that was." Mrs. Ludlow looked as if she were about to say more but abruptly changed her mind. She shook her head quite firmly. "Never mind, dear. It was all over and done years ago and certainly does not signify now. Well, Emily, you must be certain to wear your best gown tomorrow night, eh?"

Emily smiled, wondering if the lecture and warning would come now. "I intend to," she said with just the smallest touch of defiance.

"Good, good. Young people should enjoy themselves when they can. Off with you, now, and I am certain the poor of Little Dippington will be most thankful for the clothes you brought by this afternoon."

So there was to be no warning. Emily heaved a sigh of relief as she walked back toward where she had tied her mare. Still, it was puzzling. No one seemed to feel she should be restrained from flirting with the earl. Nor, apparently, had anyone felt obliged to warn Blade about the Unfortunate Incident.

Emily began to wonder if the good folk of Little Dippington were actually hoping the romance would have a happy ending. But sooner or later someone would feel bound to say something to him.

When Simon showed up for the next meeting of the Thursday Afternoon Literary Society, Emily was finally forced to admit that matters were getting to the awkward stage. She knew in her heart of hearts she simply could not allow Simon to court her so openly when it was all so hopeless.

Guilt began nibbling at her. She knew she could not let this go on much longer. Scandal always emerged, sooner or later. If no one else was going to say what must be said, then she would have to deal with the awful task herself.

She dreaded the moment of truth more than she had ever dreaded anything in her life. But she reminded herself that she had known from the start that the love she felt for the Earl of Blade had been doomed. It was time to end the romantic masquerade.

Chapter 4

Emily came to the end of the Scottish reel, aware that she was laughing too gaily and feeling much too flushed. Her mood was one of unnatural cheerfulness and she knew the cause. She was fortifying herself for the task that lay ahead.

Her conscience would no longer allow her to put off telling Simon about the scandal.

This evening as she had dressed for the Gillinghams' party she had vowed to herself she would do what had to be done without further delay. As much as she loved the fantasy in which she was living, Emily knew she could no longer abide waiting for the ax to fall. She had to get the matter over and done. The longer things went on like this, the more she was going to feel sorry for herself when Simon eventually discovered the truth and walked away in disgust.

She had deliberately chosen to wear her very best gown, which had been made for her by the village seamstress. Tonight was the first time she had worn the pale green muslin trimmed with yellow ribbons and several rows of deep flounces. Her quizzing glass dangled discreetly on a ribbon attached to her gown.

The quizzing glass was a nuisance, but Emily refused to wear her spectacles tonight.

The deep neckline of the high-waisted dress had been designed to reveal a magnificent bosom. When Emily had ordered it she had somehow hoped it would magnify her less than impressive curves. When she had dressed earlier tonight, however, she had fretted that all it succeeded in doing was calling attention to the smallness of her own shape.

"Not a bit o' it," her maid, Lizzie, had insisted as she admired her mistress with delighted eyes. "It makes you look all airy and delicate like. As if you could fly away in the moonlight or somethin'."

Emily hoped she was right. She did not feel particularly light and airy tonight. There was a ball of lead in her stomach that seemed to be growing larger by the minute.

The Gillinghams' small ballroom was filled to the brim with the local gentry turned out in their finest. Lord and Lady Gillingham had a reputation for being kind enough to invite their less fashionable neighbors in once or twice a year. Simon's presence in their household appeared to have been an excuse for such an event. Champagne and a buffet of sweets and savories had been set out.

Simon had made himself and Emily the focal point of attention earlier when he had danced the first dance with her. Without her spectacles and lost in a romantic haze, Emily was able to ignore the many stares and curious looks she knew she and the earl had received. Simon, as usual, had not appeared to notice them either but that was because he never condescended to notice such things.

Emily could not imagine anything making a dent in Simon's calm self-confidence. That sense of inner strength and sureness that was so much a part of him could be a bit daunting at times, but it was certainly impressive.

Emily raised her quizzing glass for a few seconds and surreptitiously scanned the crowd until she spotted Simon talking to the vicar. Blade was, she decided, quite definitely the most glorious man in the room tonight. Of course, she was slightly biased. But there was no denying the fact that in his austere black and white evening attire Simon was dangerously attractive in a room that was overcrowded with brightly colored jackets and waistcoats.

"Good evening, Miss Faringdon. May I get you a glass of lemonade?"

Emily stifled a groan at the unwelcome sound of Elias Prendergast's voice. She lowered her quizzing glass, not needing any assistance in seeing the familiar fat, florid, heavily bewhiskered face.

Nor did she need her spectacles or the glass to see that the portly Mr. Prendergast had strapped himself into his corsets for the occasion. She could hear them creak when he moved.

"No, thank you," Emily murmured, thinking that what she really needed was a glass of champagne. She opened her fan and began fanning herself industriously as Prendergast leaned closer. The man smelled as if he had not bothered to bathe for the party. Prendergast was of the old school and had a strong distrust of the new fashion for frequent use of soap and water. He much preferred to utilize a quantity of perfume instead.

"Been meanin' to call on you now that I'm out of mourning, Miss Faringdon," Prendergast began with an air of importance. "Feel there is somethin' we should discuss."

Emily smiled politely. "I am persuaded that would not be at all correct, sir. Surely you will want to wait until my father is in residence."

"That's just it, damme," Prendergast said with obvious annoyance. "Yer father don't spend much time here in the country. Unpredictable in his comings and goings, ain't he?"

"He is very busy with his affairs in town. Lovely party, is it not?" Emily waved her fan in a graceful arc that took in the entire brightly lit room. "But, then, Lady Gillingham is always a gracious hostess."

Prendergast's bushy brows drew together in a scowl. He cleared his throat. Emily's heart fell. She had an awful premonition of what was coming next.

"Miss Faringdon, my dear, I feel that I am by way of being something of an advisor to you since your parent is so often absent," Prendergast said in ominous tones. "And it has come to my attention that we have a visitor in the neighborhood who has been seeing rather a lot of you lately."

54 *AMANDA QUICK*

"You shock me, sir. I had no idea you made it your business to pay heed to local gossip. I vow it must be very tiresome keeping up with it."

Prendergast snorted and glowered intimidatingly. It was well known that when she had been alive, Mrs. Prendergast had been a little mouse of a creature who would never have dreamed of making such a snippy remark.

"Now, see here, young lady. I am only too well aware of how a woman's head can be turned by the sort of romantical attention that Blade is lavishing upon you, Miss Faringdon, if you don't mind my saying so."

"But I do, sir. Mind your saying so, that is." Emily's smile grew bright and sharp as anger began to ignite within her. Prendergast was well on his way to spoiling what little time she had left with Simon.

Prendergast's heavy face congealed into a thunderous expression that Emily could see quite clearly without her glass.

"I speak only out of the deepest concern for your reputation, Miss Faringdon."

"Everyone knows my reputation is already beyond repair, sir. Pray do not concern yourself with it."

"Now, now, you must not be so hard on yourself," Prendergast admonished. "It's true enough that there is a nasty bit of scandal in your past. But you were young and foolish and made a mistake. These things happen to young gels. I, being a man of the world and not without some experience in schooling high-spirited females, am prepared to overlook the Incident."

"How very kind of you, sir."

"Well, yes, 'tis, rather. Blade, naturally, won't be able to do so. Got his family name and title to think of, y'know."

Emily's fingers clenched on the fan. "Pray, do not trouble yourself with any further advice, sir."

Prendergast drew himself up to his full height. He loomed over Emily, his corsets groaning. "Miss Faringdon, you once allowed your excessive passions to run way with you and in doing so brought social ruin upon yourself.

Surely you have not forgotten the lessons learned on that unhappy occasion?"

"I assure you, I have forgotten nothing," Emily said through her teeth. "But you are beginning to annoy me, sir."

"Miss Faringdon, you misunderstand me. My intentions are quite honorable. I only wish to assist you by providing you with a respectable outlet for your rather high-spirited tendencies." He caught hold of her hand and crushed it between his damp, beefy palms.

"Please give me back my hand, sir." Emily tried unsuccessfully to withdraw her fingers from his sweaty grip.

Prendergast ignored her efforts, his fingers tightening painfully. He leaned closer until his bad breath and thick perfume nearly overpowered his victim. Then he lowered his voice to confidential tones.

"Miss Faringdon, I fully comprehend how difficult it must be for a woman of your high passions to be forced to be subjected to the depressing strictures of society. I feel certain that you would be far happier married. Within the sanctity of the marriage bed you would be able to give free rein to those impulses which you are now obliged to keep under control."

"Sir, if you do not let go of me this instant, I vow I will be forced to do something drastic."

But Prendergast was very intent on his mission now. "You need a man who can accommodate your excesses of emotion, my dear. I assure you I am that man. Furthermore, I intend to call upon your father at the earliest opportunity to tell him of my intentions."

"No," Emily gasped, horrified at the very thought.

"To that end," Prendergast continued as if he had not heard the alarm in her voice, "I have written him a letter informing him of the danger you are presently facing and assuring him that I will look after you until he returns to protect you from Blade's attentions."

"Attend to your own business, sir. I do not wish to be protected from his attentions."

"He is merely toying with your affections, my dear. Just as that other rake did five years ago."

Emily finally lost her temper. She folded her fan with a snap and brought it down quite sharply on the back of Prendergast's hand. The blow contained such stinging force that the sticks snapped.

"*Yeow.*" Prendergast released her fingers abruptly, rubbing the back of his hand. The color in his plump cheeks was high. "Ah, Miss Faringdon, you are, indeed, a creature of great passions. I cannot wait until we are wed. I assure you I will manage you very well, my dear. Very well, indeed."

"Best not hold your breath waiting for that momentous occasion," Simon advised in his cold, dark drawl.

Emily jumped and whirled around to find that the earl had materialized at her elbow. She smiled brilliantly up at the dragon. He was satisfyingly large and ferocious, she thought, and he had lots of strong, white teeth. Furthermore, they were his own, which was more than could be said about Elias Prendergast's.

"Hello, my lord," Emily said happily. "I trust you are enjoying yourself?"

"Very much. I thought you might need this." He handed her a glass of champagne.

"How very perceptive of you, sir." Emily's fingers closed gratefully around the glass.

"Miss Faringdon prefers lemonade," Prendergast announced.

"You are wrong." Emily took a swallow. "At the moment Miss Faringdon has a strong preference for champagne."

Prendergast glowered at her unrepentant features. "We will discuss this matter further at a more convenient time, Miss Faringdon."

"What matter? My preference for champagne? I assure you, there is nothing to discuss."

"I was referring to other, more pressing concerns," Prendergast hissed. He inclined his head in a jerky motion. "If you will excuse me, I must speak to a friend." He took himself off with a great dignity that was somewhat marred by the sound of his creaking corsets.

Emily stifled a small sigh. As obnoxious as Prendergast was, he was also right in one respect. She could not continue to lead Simon on any longer. She took another swallow of champagne and looked up at the earl. She was standing close enough to him to see that he was watching her with a familiar mocking amusement in his gleaming eyes.

"It would seem I have competition for your hand," Simon murmured.

Emily shook her head quickly, her curls bouncing. "Pay no heed to Mr. Prendergast. He has been something of a nuisance ever since his poor wife finally faded away. Simon, I must speak to you."

"You have my full attention."

"No, not here. Not now." She glanced furtively around, squinting to see if there was anyone standing too close. "Simon, I must speak to you in private."

"That sounds promising."

"I fear it is not a joking matter, my lord. Indeed, it is most serious. Please, when can I see you? This has gone on long enough and there are . . ." Emily broke off, raised her quizzing glass for another quick glance around, and then added in a very low, unhappy voice, "There are things you must be told."

"Ah."

"I have been very remiss in not informing you of these particular matters earlier in our relationship. It was quite cowardly of me, but I suppose I assumed someone else would perform the task for me."

"You alarm me, my dear. I feel like a character in a Minerva Press novel. I believe I am beginning to tremble with the Uneasy Dread of the Unknown."

"My lord, you know very well that nothing could make you tremble with dread," Emily said crossly. "I vow this is difficult enough as it is. Please do not mock me."

"I would not dream of it. Very well, if I am not allowed to tremble with dread, I shall muster my courage and meet you for this terrifying pronouncement. How about your library at, say, one o'clock this morning? You will be safely home by then and your servants should be in bed."

Emily dropped her quizzing glass in shock. "My library? You mean to come to St. Clair Hall? Tonight?"

"Can you arrange to be in the library alone at that time?"

"Well, yes. Of course I can. I frequently work in the library after the servants have gone to bed." She frowned, thinking about the practical problems involved. "I shall have to unbolt the front door for you."

"No need." He sipped his own champagne and watched the couples who were promenading between dances. "Just be sure you are in the library at one. I will come to you there."

Emily raised her quizzing glass and searched his face. As usual, she could tell almost nothing about what he was thinking from his expression. She found it perfectly amazing that he could disguise his sensitive, passionate nature so completely behind that facade of cool detachment.

"Very well, my lord. One o'clock."

Emily had to admit that, even though the evening was destined to end in heartbreak, the mysterious manner in which Simon was setting up their final clandestine meeting was wonderfully intriguing. But, then, nothing was ever ordinary around the Earl of Blade. She would remember his brief courtship all of her life and those haunting memories would inspire her writing and her dreams for years to come.

A few minutes before one that morning, Emily sat down at the mahogany desk and stared fixedly at the brandy decanter. She had put her spectacles back on but she was ready to whip them off and stuff them into the top desk drawer as soon as Simon arrived.

The brandy decanter looked very inviting.

The decanter was full and Emily was cold with nerves and anticipation. For the past half hour she had been deliberating about whether to pour herself a fortifying glass.

The hands on the face of the tall clock near the fireplace

were moving so slowly that Emily was beginning to wonder if they had stopped altogether. A couple of candles glowed nearby but that was the only illumination in the room. The fire had been laid for morning but she dared not light it. One of the staff would notice tomorrow that she had been up late again and they would all worry that she was working too hard. As a result the room was growing quite chilly.

With a start, Emily felt the gooseflesh on her arms as a sudden draft of chilled air rushed into the room behind her. She shivered in her frilled dressing gown and wondered if a window had blown open. She started to rise from her chair.

In that same instant she sensed another presence in the room.

Emily leapt to her feet, her lips parting in a scream, as she grabbed the letter opener that was laying on the desk.

But the scream was never uttered. A large masculine hand clamped quite firmly over her mouth and Emily was pulled quickly back against a hard male body.

She went limp with relief as she realized who held her.

"I would feel a great deal more welcome if you would put down that letter opener," Simon said, lowering his hand from her mouth. He extinguished the candle he held in his other hand.

"Simon. Bloody hell." Emily tossed aside the letter opener and spun around to glare up at him through her spectacles. "You gave me a terrible fright. Where did you come from? How on earth did you sneak up on me like that? I have been watching the door for an age."

Simon unfastened his greatcoat and stepped aside. He nodded casually toward a section of bookshelving that was slowly, silently sliding back into place against the wall. Emily saw the dark entrance that yawned in the stone behind the bookcase and her eyes widened in amazed delight.

"A secret passageway. Simon, this is wonderful." She darted around him and scurried toward the rapidly disappearing passageway. All thoughts of the long-planned confession vanished in the face of the promise of high adventure.

"Contain your enthusiasm, Miss Faringdon." Simon

reached out and caught her arm, drawing her to a halt. "The bookcase will close on you. It is far too heavy for you to open by hand. One must use the hidden lever."

"What hidden lever? Where is it? Oh, this is so thrilling. Just like something out of one of those bloodcurdling Minerva Press novels you spoke of earlier this evening. I can hardly believe it. To think I have lived here nearly all my life and never knew about this secret."

"Calm yourself." Obviously amused by her irrepressible excitement, Simon glanced around the room until he spotted the brandy decanter. He tossed the heavy greatcoat down over a chair. "There are two levers," he explained as he crossed to the small table where the brandy stood.

"Two?"

"One in the passageway behind the wall and one hidden inside the bookcase itself." He poured two glasses of brandy as he spoke. "The man who built St. Clair Hall believed in maintaining emergency escape routes."

"But how did you know about the secret passageway?" Emily watched with regret as the bookcase sealed itself against the wall once more.

"Have you not reasoned that out yet? You astonish me. I know about the passageway because I used to live here."

That captured her full attention. Emily swung around quickly and saw that he was leaning against the desk with languid ease, sipping his brandy. She realized he had changed out of his evening clothes. He was dressed very casually in breeches, boots, and a linen shirt. He was not even wearing a cravat. He looked like a man relaxing in the comfort of his own home.

His own home.

Wordlessly Simon offered her the second glass of brandy. *Just as if he were the host and I the visitor,* Emily thought suddenly.

"St. Clair Hall was your family's country home?" Emily took the brandy glass in both hands, searching his face. "What an amazing coincidence."

"Yet another one for you to note in your journal." He swallowed a mouthful of brandy.

Emily chewed on her lower lip, uncertain of his mood. "You must have been a very young boy when you left."

"Twelve."

"Why did you not mention that the hall had once been your home?"

He shrugged. "It did not seem particularly important."

Emily took a sip of the brandy, frowning again. She had the distinct impression she was missing something here, but for the life of her she could not think what it was. Her romantic imagination took hold once more.

"It is obvious this strange coincidence is just one more haunting element in our doomed relationship, my lord," Emily finally announced.

Simon gave her a sharp glance. "Doomed, did you say? I confess I am not as well schooled in the elements of romantic literature as yourself. Perhaps you will explain?"

Emily took another sip of brandy and began pacing the room. Her soft slippers made no sound on the carpet. "I must tell you, my lord, that there can be no happy ending for us. And it is all my fault."

He watched her through narrowed, hooded eyes. "Why is that?"

Emily clutched the brandy glass so fiercely that her knuckles went white. She could not meet Simon's eyes as she turned at the end of the room and started pacing back toward the desk. *Best to say it quickly and get it over and done,* she decided.

"My lord, I must confess I have misled you most shamefully. I have flirted outrageously with you. I have led you on in a shocking fashion and allowed you to believe that I would welcome an offer of marriage from you."

There was a short, charged silence from the vicinity of the desk. Then Simon asked coldly, "Are you trying to tell me you would not welcome such an offer?"

"Oh, no, my lord. It is not that at all." She threw him an anguished glance, spun around on her heel, and strode bravely back toward the opposite end of the room. "I assure you I would be deeply honored by such an offer. *Deeply* honored. But I cannot in good conscience allow you to make one."

"How do you intend to stop me?"

"By telling you the truth about myself. A truth that I fully expected someone else to have told you long before now." Emily frowned for an instant. "Indeed, I cannot imagine why someone has not mentioned the Unfortunate Incident to you before this but since the good people of Little Dippington have seen fit to keep their mouths shut, I must confess all."

"The confession must be an interesting one, indeed, if it must be made in secret at this hour of the night."

The sound of crystal clinking gently on crystal came from the brandy table. Emily risked a quick sidelong glance and saw that the earl had poured himself another brandy. It struck her that she could do with another one herself.

"My lord, I shall try to make this as brief as possible so that you may get on about your affairs." Emily took a deep breath and steeled herself. "The horrid truth is that you cannot possibly ask for my hand in marriage for the simple reason that I am a ruined woman."

"Ruined for what? You look in fine fettle to me. Healthy as a horse."

Emily squeezed her eyes shut and came to a halt facing the bookshelves at the far end of the room. "You mistake my meaning, my lord," she said quietly. "I am trying to tell you that I am socially ruined. To be blunt, there is a great scandal in my past."

"A scandal?"

"A scandal involving a man. The scandal is of such proportions that I have been assured by my family that no decent man, especially a man with a duty to a noble title such as yours, could possibly wish to marry me."

There, Emily thought bleakly. *It is done.* She waited for the storm that must surely come. The Earl of Blade would not appreciate the fact that she had allowed him to make a cake of himself for more than a sennight.

"Are we by any chance discussing that bit of nonsense

that occurred when you were nineteen?" Simon asked
blandly.

Emily was thrown into instant confusion. "You have
heard about the Incident, my lord?"

"Rest assured, my dear, I always try to fortify myself
with as much information as possible before I set out on a
project. It is an old habit of mine. One I picked up during
my years in the East."

She turned to stare at him, not understanding how he
could be taking this so lightly. "My lord, it was not a trifling
matter. It was an elopement. Or rather, it was supposed to
be an elopement. I fear I foolishly surrendered to an excess
of romantic passion and paid the price."

"This grows more interesting by the moment."

"Bloody hell, Blade, this is not a joke. Do you not understand? *I ran off with a man.* My father caught up with us
but it was . . ." she cleared her throat with a small cough,
"it was too late."

"Too late?" The earl cocked a brow, not looking in the
least alarmed.

"We were obliged to spend the night on the road," Emily
mumbled. She averted her gaze from Simon's gleaming eyes.
"My father did not find me until the next morning."

"I see. Tell me something, Emily. Why is it I have the
distinct impression you do not entirely regret the Incident?"

Emily resumed her pacing. "I assure you, I do now. But
I confess that at the time, it was the most exciting thing that
had ever happened to me." She sighed forlornly. "But my
father soon explained that it was the *only* exciting thing that
would ever happen to me because after that no decent man
would have me. He brought me home and said I must
devote my life to my studies of the stock exchange and investments."

"Do you enjoy those studies?"

"Oh, yes, at times. There is a certain fascination to it all,
you know." She waved a hand vaguely. "But that is neither
here nor there." She drew a breath. "My lord, I appreciate
that in light of this information you must, of course, abandon your intention of asking for my hand in marriage."

"I rarely abandon any of my intentions, Emily. I have a reputation for following through to the finish. Just ask anyone in London."

"Well, you can hardly mean to do so in this matter," she shot back. "Men of your position do not marry women who have been ruined. Now, then, my lord, I have made my confession and if you have not taken a complete disgust to me, I would like to say something else."

"I assure you, Emily, I am not about to leave now. I am fascinated to hear whatever else you have to say."

"Very well, then, you may be wondering why I wore my dressing gown to this clandestine meeting."

"I assumed it was because you are freezing and your wrapper is no doubt considerably warmer than that very charming gown you had on earlier this evening. This room was always cold."

Emily groaned. She wondered for the first time if the Earl of Blade was just a trifle dense on some matters. She kept her eyes focused on the bookcase as she forced herself to continue. "I wore my dressing gown because I am about to offer you an illicit connection of a romantic nature."

"I fear I do not understand, my dear. We already have a legitimate connection of a romantic nature."

She whirled around, glowering in exasperation. "I thought you a man of the world, sir. Pray, pay attention. As there is no possibility of a marriage between us and as I have fallen quite hopelessly in love with you, I have come up with the notion of offering you a . . . a liaison."

"A liaison?" He gazed at her quizzically.

"I am offering you an affair, you blockhead." Emily sucked in a horrified breath as she realized what she had just said. She closed her eyes in mortification. Her face flamed. "My lord, forgive me. I did not mean to call you a blockhead. I fear my nerves are quite overset and I must own that I have something of a temper. Occasionally it gets the better of me."

"You are obviously a woman of strong passions, just as Prendergast observed."

"And you are obviously a man who appears to be

amused at the oddest things." She put down her brandy glass. Clearly she'd had more than enough to drink. She shoved her hands into the pockets of her dressing gown. "Well?" she demanded testily. "What about my offer?"

The earl straightened slowly and set aside his empty glass. He crossed the room to where she stood, his strong hands closing warmly around her shoulders. "Emily, my dear, please be assured that I am deeply honored by your charming offer."

Her heart sank. "But?"

"But I think that, as you are a creature of excessive passion and possessed of a spirited romantic temperament, it would be best if you allowed me to guide you in this matter."

"Why?" she asked baldly. "Do you think you can be cold-blooded about this sort of thing the way you try to be about everything else?"

"Those who know me will tell you I can and usually am quite cold-blooded about everything. Be warned, Emily."

"Fustian. It is just an attitude you affect. It is no use trying to tell me you are cold-blooded because I know the truth. Do not forget I have learned a great deal about you from your letters, my lord. Our thoughts have met and mingled on a higher plane. We have looked deeply into each other's souls."

"Believe what you wish, my dear. Nevertheless, you will allow that, if nothing else, I am older than you and have seen far more of the world."

"No doubt. I have been stuck in Little Dippington all of my life."

"Then you will grant me the advantage of wider experience and allow me to make the decisions regarding the course of our future relationship."

"I will?"

"Yes, Emily," he said quite gently. "You will." He bent his head and kissed the tip of her nose. "I am convinced it would be best if you wait until your wedding night before you surrender completely to another bout of excessive romantic passion."

"Then I shall wait forever, my lord," she snapped, "because I certainly do not intend to wed Elias Prendergast and he is about the only one who is likely to offer for me."

"No, my dear, he is not. I am going to offer for you. Just as soon as your father returns to Little Dippington."

Emily looked up at him in blank incomprehension. "You are going to offer for me? But, my lord, I just finished explaining that I am a ruined woman."

"I think," Simon said coolly, "that we will not discuss the Unfortunate Incident in your past again."

"We will not?"

"You begin to understand." He brushed his mouth lightly across hers and then drew back, smiling faintly.

She caught one of his big hands in her two small fists. "Simon, do you mean it? You intend to go through with making an offer for me regardless of the great scandal in my past?"

"Oh, yes, Emily. I fully intend to ask your father for your hand."

She could hardly believe it. Joyous excitement threatened to swamp her. "And you do not wish to begin an illicit romantic liaison tonight instead?"

"It is, naturally, difficult to resist a woman of such warm passions as yourself, Emily, but I intend to wait until our wedding night to consummate our union."

"Oh."

Simon laughed softly at the rueful disappointment in her eyes. He brought one of her hands to his lips and kissed her wrist, his eyes never leaving hers. "Which is not to say, my sweet, that we cannot avail ourselves of a taste or two of forbidden fruit."

She glowed up at him and wrapped her arms around his neck. "Does that mean you are going to kiss me?"

"Among other things." He lowered his head, his dragon's eyes the color of molten gold. His mouth was warm on the curve of her throat.

"Oh, *Simon.*"

"I like it when you say my name in just that manner. I

like it very much. Almost as much as the way you shiver when I touch you."

He gripped her firmly around her waist and lifted her up off the floor. She looked down at him with a sense of wonder, her hands braced on his shoulders as he carried her over to the mahogany desk.

Simon seated her on the edge of the desk and then very deliberately began to unfasten Emily's chintz wrapper. His eyes held hers in thrall as he slowly parted the edges of the garment to reveal the embroidered, high-necked muslin nightdress underneath.

Emily felt herself going pink from head to toe. No doubt he could see the way her nipples were thrusting against the soft fabric. She reminded herself she was a ruined woman and he would be expecting some level of sophistication about this sort of thing from her.

She cleared her throat. "My lord, is this what you call kissing?" she said in what she hoped was a suitably blasé fashion.

"No, this is what I call tasting forbidden fruit." He smiled down into her eyes and bent his head to cover her mouth with his own. His hand went to her breast.

Emily stiffened with shock and then moaned softly. Her arms tightened around his neck. Simon's thumb moved over her nipple, causing it to form a tight bud of desire. His mouth slid druggingly across hers. The heat of his body as he leaned close kept away the chill of the room.

Lost in the wonder and excitement of Simon's kiss, Emily barely noticed when his hands went to her legs. He pushed the hem of the nightdress up to her thighs and then he gripped her knees very firmly. Slowly, gently, he forced her legs widely apart and then, in a shockingly intimate move, stepped boldly between them.

Emily's eyes flew open. "My lord . . . Simon, I . . ."

"Hush, my sweeting." He did not lift his mouth from hers as he spoke. His fingers slid along the insides of her thighs in seemingly random patterns. "You are very soft. Like warm silk."

Instinctively she tried to close her legs and found his

hard, muscled thighs in the way. She could feel the rough texture of his breeches against her bare skin, the sensation sending an alarmed thrill through her body.

"Close your eyes and do not think about what I am doing," Simon ordered softly.

His hands moved closer to Emily's most secret places. She closed her eyes, suddenly short of breath.

"Kiss me, Emily." Simon's voice was husky and coaxing.

Emily realized with a flare of guilty alarm that her entire attention had been fixed on the movement of his hands. She was obviously supposed to be paying more attention to returning his kiss.

Anxious not to disappoint him, she caught his face between her palms and urgently ground her mouth against his until their teeth clinked.

"Much better, my sweet," Simon murmured encouragingly. "But you must relax a little. Open your mouth for me."

With a shudder, Emily did so. Simon's tongue immediately thrust deep inside and at the same time his fingers found the flowing warmth between her legs.

Emily froze. She tried to speak and could not. She tried to take a deep breath and could not. She tried to think of how a sophisticated, ruined woman would react to such an intimacy and could not. The whole thing was simply too overwhelming. Her senses were reeling.

Simon did not seem to expect anything from her but the small shivers that were making her tremble from head to foot. His mouth stayed locked on hers as his fingers stroked her with a shockingly gentle intimacy.

Emily began to forget about the strangeness of the whole thing as a tide of heat and tension rose in her lower body. Her fingers clenched violently into the fabric of Simon's linen shirt.

"Simon," she finally managed, tearing her mouth free from his for an instant and staring up at him with huge, questioning eyes.

"Hold on to me very tightly, elf," he advised softly. "I

promise you, all will be well. Remember what the poets say. One must open oneself to the world of sensual experience if one is to know the truth concerning the nature of the metaphysical world. Open yourself, Emily. Give yourself over to me."

Not knowing what else to do, feeling utterly at sea in a wave of stunning, unfamiliar emotions, Emily obeyed. She closed her eyes and clung to Simon as though her life depended on it.

His fingers were damp now and moved with slick ease over the delicate petals that shielded her secrets. And then those gentle, probing fingers seemed to find a very special place. Emily arched her back helplessly as the sense of urgency within her threatened to explode. She was in desperate need of something but she did not know what that something was. She finally decided it was Simon's touch. Instinctively she widened her legs even farther, silently pleading for more of the astounding sensations.

"Yes." Simon kissed her throat and his hand moved on her. "Yes, my sweet. Now, Emily. Show me what a passionate creature you really are." One finger slid gently just inside her damp sheath.

Emily gasped. She opened her mouth on a keening cry of excitement as her whole body convulsed. Simon's mouth swooped down over hers, muffling the soft, feminine scream of release.

Emily felt herself hovering on what could only be described as a truly metaphysical plane for several seconds and then she slowly collapsed in a soft heap against Simon's chest.

"Bloody hell," she muttered in a dazed voice against his shoulder.

Simon made a small, choked sound that might have been a laugh or a groan. It was impossible to tell. "Ah, Emily. You are indeed a creature of great passions." He slowly withdrew his hands from between her legs and gently rearranged her clothing.

Emily lifted her head from his shoulder. She still felt dazed and she seemed to have difficulty focusing on his face.

Then she realized that at some point he had removed her spectacles.

"Oh, Simon."

"Oh, Emily." He kissed the tip of her nose and handed her the spectacles with courtly grace.

When she got them on, she saw that he was smiling his faint, unreadable smile. But his eyes were hooded and glowing with yellow fire. Never had he looked more dangerous or more compellingly attractive. Then Emily glanced down and saw the distinct bulge in his tight breeches. "Simon?"

Some of the fire dimmed in his eyes as his gaze followed hers with rueful awareness. "Do not worry, Emily. I will be quite all right. But to avoid surrendering any further to the delightful temptation you are offering tonight, I believe I had best be on my way. The long walk home in the cold night air will take care of my current problem." He stepped away from her and picked up the greatcoat.

"I will see you soon?" She wished desperately that he need not leave.

"If I recall correctly, I and the other members of the literary society have accepted an invitation to tea here at St. Clair Hall tomorrow afternoon. I am looking forward to it."

Emily smiled her most dazzling smile and jumped down off the desk. She staggered and had to grasp the edge to steady herself. Her eyes filled with laughter as she suddenly realized she was feeling extraordinarily good, although the dampness between her thighs was disconcerting.

"Yes, that's right. Tea tomorrow. My lord, if you are not inclined to taste any more forbidden fruit tonight, would you please do me a very great favor?"

He eyed her with watchful amusement as he shrugged into the caped coat. "And what would that favor be?"

"Would you show me how to open the entrance to the secret passageway?"

The earl grinned wryly. "It is obvious that learning the secret of the hidden passage is every bit as exciting a thought for you as surrendering to a night of illicit passion."

Emily was afraid she had offended him. She patted his hand placatingly. "It is just that I am very fond of things like secret passages, my lord. And I would dearly love to use this one in my poem, *The Mysterious Lady*. I vow it would suit the story perfectly."

"Who am I to stand in the way of your literary muse?" Simon took her hand and led her over to the bookcase.

Chapter 5

Emily frowned intently over the letter from her father's man of affairs, Mr. Davenport.

> My Dear Miss Faringdon:
>   This is to advise you that I have followed your instructions to sell the South Sea Annuities and the India Bonds. You will be pleased to know that the final price of both was most satisfactory.
>   Kindly let me know your decision on the mining investments you mentioned in your last letter.
>   Yr Humble Servant,
>   B. Davenport.

Emily smiled with satisfaction and jotted down a note to tell Davenport to go ahead with the investment in the Northumberland mining project. When she was finished she reached up and pulled the bell rope that hung beside her desk. Duckett, the butler, appeared almost at once.

"Oh, there you are, Duckett." Emily grinned cheerfully. "Please advise the staff that the South Sea annuities and India bonds have come to fruition. Your investments real-

ized a handsome profit and were sold on Monday. The draft
is in the bank."

Duckett's dour features lit up with gratitude and pleasure. "Staff will be most delighted, Miss Faringdon. Most
delighted, indeed. Please accept our most earnest appreciation. You cannot know what a great relief it is to contemplate a financially secure retirement." He hesitated briefly.
"Circumstances being what they are."

Emily wrinkled her nose. "We have known each other
for many years, Duckett. We can be honest with each other.
I know perfectly well that if the household staff relies upon
my father's remembering to set aside something for their
pensions, you will all starve in your old age."

"A rather dramatic statement, but quite probably true."
Duckett permitted himself the briefest of smiles. "In any
event, we are exceedingly grateful for your investment advice and services, Miss Faringdon."

"I am the one who is exceedingly grateful, Duckett,"
Emily said very seriously. "You all take excellent care of me.
I do not know what I would do without you. It would be
very lonely around here, that is for certain."

"Thank you, Miss Faringdon," the butler said gently.
"We do try."

She smiled. "And succeed very ably. Oh, Duckett, one
more thing before you leave."

"Yes, miss?"

Emily paused, searching for just the right words. She
was loath to offend. "Does Mrs. Hickinbotham have any,
uh, questions concerning this afternoon's arrangements?"

Duckett's eyes softened. "Not at all, Miss Faringdon. I
assure you that in the course of her previous employment,
Mrs. Hickinbotham had a great deal of experience serving
tea to guests."

Emily was immediately embarrassed to have called the
housekeeper's qualifications into question. "Yes, of course. I
expect I am just the tiniest bit anxious. We do so little entertaining here at St. Clair Hall. And we have never had an earl
to tea before."

"I believe Mrs. Hickinbotham once mentioned she had

supervised preparations for tea for a marquess a few years back."

"Wonderful." Emily felt humbled and relieved. "Thank you, Duckett."

"You are most welcome, Miss Faringdon. I assure you all will go quite smoothly this afternoon."

"I am certain you are right. Just one more thing. Will you ask Mrs. Hickinbotham to see if we have any of the Lap Seng tea left? If so I would like her to serve it rather than the Congou blend."

"The Lap Seng? I will inquire."

"Thank you. It is for the earl, you see. For some reason he has named his horse Lap Seng, so I assume he has a strong preference for that particular type of Souchong tea."

"His horse?" Duckett looked slightly startled but recovered himself instantly. "I see. I will speak to Mrs. Hickinbotham at once, Miss Faringdon." The butler let himself quietly out of the library.

Emily watched the door close, thinking that one of these days she must remember to ask Simon just why he had named the chestnut stallion Lap Seng. There were so many things to ask him, she thought, so many fascinating topics waiting to be discussed. It was going to be quite wonderful being married to a man with whom she could share an intellectual connection, one with whom she could communicate on a higher, transcendental plane, a man of refined sensibilities.

Of course, their communication on the more mundane physical plane was going to be quite exciting, also. Emily felt herself growing quite warm, even though there was no fire on the hearth.

She stared dreamily out the window for a moment. Never in her life had she experienced anything quite like that shattering sense of release she had experienced last night here in the library. It had given her a whole new insight into certain poetical passages written by her favorite authors.

It had also given her a whole new understanding of the phrase *an excess of passion.*

A small tingle of pure, unadulterated happiness went through her like a jolt from one of the electricity machines people used for scientific experiments. The whole thing was incredible. It was almost too much to comprehend.

She was not accustomed to good luck in anything except financial matters.

"Bloody hell," Emily whispered aloud. Then she promptly scowled. She really must stop cursing in such an unladylike fashion. She would be a countess soon and she was quite certain countesses did not curse.

She hoped Simon's high and noble standards would not oblige him to insist on a long engagement. Year-long engagements were not unusual among the *ton.* There were generally a great many details to be resolved, the sort of details that all came under the vague heading of "settlements." Emily did not think she could bear to wait a year.

Reluctantly Emily turned her attention back to the letters, journals, and notes piled high on her desk. The last thing she felt like doing this morning was work on her investments. But at the rate the Faringdon men went through money, constant attention to finances was essential. Her mother had often explained to Emily that someone had to look after Papa and the twins. Indeed, Mrs. Faringdon had impressed that notion on Emily one last time from her deathbed.

Unenthusiastically Emily pulled the latest issue of *The Gentleman's Magazine* toward her and opened it to the monthly summary of stock exchange prices. She scanned the daily fluctuation in prices on canal bonds, India bonds, bank stock, and the funds, making a few quick notes to herself before turning the page.

Then she ran her fingertip down the summary of recent prices paid for wheat, rye, oats, and beans in the inland counties and compared them to the prices paid in the maritime counties. Again she picked up her quill and jotted down a comment or two. Next she checked the average prices of flour, sugar, hay, and straw for the preceding month, looking for trends.

When she was finished noting recent prices on commodities, Emily turned to the monthly meteorological table. This she gave only a cursory glance. It was still winter and the daily temperatures and rainfall amounts were not as important to her calculations now as they would be in the spring and summer. In a couple of months she would begin watching them closely in an attempt to anticipate the harvests.

When she had finished gleaning what she could from *The Gentleman's Magazine,* she turned to her correspondence. Sir Alfred Chumley had news of a new coal mining enterprise and a certain Mrs. Middleton had written to inquire about Emily's interest in a ship that would be leaving soon for the West Indies. It was expected to return with a sizable profit, just as the last one had.

Mrs. Hickinbotham found the Lap Seng.

Emily watched anxiously as Simon took his first sip of the exotic, smoky brew. When he smiled at her over the rim of the cup and gave her a knowing look, she wanted to hug Mrs. Hickinbotham. The housekeeper's eyes sparkled but her expression remained appropriately restrained as she curtsied and left the members of the literary society to their discussions.

Emily had changed her mind three times about which dress to wear before Lizzie finally talked her into the ruff-necked, flounced muslin. The gown was a pale yellow with tiny little white stripes and Lizzie claimed it set off the color of Emily's hair. Emily was not at all certain it was a good idea to set off red hair but Lizzie overrode her mistress's concerns.

The ladies of the literary society had arrived with an air of great expectation. They were growing accustomed to having an earl in their midst these days and his attentions to Emily had not gone unnoticed. The good ladies were all secretly thrilled by the high-minded romance blossoming in their midst and they now greeted Simon with friendly cordiality.

As usual, once seated among them, he looked like a dark, golden-eyed beast surrounded by a bunch of lively, chirping birds. Simon did not appear to mind the contrast. But, then, it was blazingly clear to Emily that the earl was quite unflappable.

The whole event, including refreshments and conversation, went off with such effortless ease that Emily began to suspect she had a heretofore undiscovered talent for entertaining. She really must do more of it, she decided as the discussion became quite lively.

"And how is your poem coming along, Emily?" Miss Bracegirdle asked after they had concluded a spirited debate of the merits of Samuel Coleridge's lectures on Shakespeare. No one present had actually attended the lectures but reports had been widely circulated and the general conclusion was that they were not of the high caliber expected from Coleridge.

"I am working on expanding the verses to include a new adventure," Emily announced. She glanced at Simon and a slight flush warmed her cheeks. "I have a marvelous idea for a scene in a secret passageway."

"How exciting." Miss Ostly, who enjoyed Minerva Press novels more than most, was clearly entranced. "And perhaps a ghost? I dearly love a ghost."

Emily's brows rose above the frames of her spectacles as she considered the addition of a ghost to *The Mysterious Lady*. "Ghosts are always an excellent thing in a tale of adventure and romance. But it is difficult to find things to rhyme with ghost. One always ends up with toast or boast."

"Or roast," Simon offered.

Miss Hornsby, who had earlier accepted a glass of sherry instead of tea, giggled. Lavinia Inglebright shot her a quelling frown. She opened her mouth to suggest another possible rhyme but was interrupted by the sound of carriage wheels and horses' hooves in the drive. She looked at Emily in surprise. "I do believe you have visitors."

Emily went very still, her glance flying to Simon's unperturbed face. She almost never had visitors and everyone in the drawing room knew it. "My father and brothers, no doubt." So Elias Prendergast's letter had reached London and had had the expected result. "I was not expecting them." *Not now. Not so soon.*

But Simon, who obviously knew precisely what she was thinking, merely smiled his inscrutable smile and sipped his smoky Lap Seng.

There was the stamp of booted feet in the hall, the drone of impatient masculine voices, and a moment later the drawing room door was thrown open.

The three magnificent Faringdon men strode into the room like three gilded whirlwinds. Tall, handsome, and dressed to the nines in the latest riding clothes, they all looked dashingly disheveled from their journey. The twins, Devlin and Charles, quickly scanned the group for a pretty female face and, upon finding none to their liking, glowered at Simon.

Broderick Faringdon, Emily's father, was losing some of his hair and what he had left was turning from gold to silver, but he still managed to maintain the same stylish appearance as his sons. His hawklike nose and blue eyes together with his air of raffish dissipation still made him very attractive to women.

"Good afternoon, ladies. Blade."

As the ladies murmured a rush of polite greetings, Broderick Faringdon inclined his head brusquely at Simon.

Emily felt the sudden chill in the room. Something was very wrong. Her instincts told her there was more going on here than a disgruntled father dealing with an unapproved suitor. Her eyes flew to Simon.

But the dragon merely acknowledged her father's greeting with a mocking inclination of his head and went back to sipping his Lap Seng.

"Papa." Emily jumped to her feet. "You sent no word ahead. We did not know to expect you."

"I sent no word because I knew I'd be here before the post. Got a new stallion that can beat anything on four feet. Come and give your papa a proper greeting, miss."

Dutifully, Emily went toward him and gave him the requisite peck on the cheek. Then she stepped back, eyes narrowing. Now that the first shock was over, she was annoyed at having her tea party interrupted. "Really, Papa, I do think you could have given me some warning."

"This is my home, girl. Why should I announce myself like a visitor?"

Behind Emily the covey of literary society ladies were quickly getting to their feet, preparing to leave.

"Really must be off," Priscilla Inglebright said. "Thank you so much for having us in this afternoon, Emily."

"Yes, a lovely treat," Miss Bracegirdle said stoutly as she picked up her reticule.

The farewells came fast and furious after that. Emily stood at the door with a determined smile on her face while she fumed inwardly. Her father and brothers had ruined everything. Only Simon was delaying his departure.

Out in the hall wraps were hastily donned and bonnets were quickly tied. In a moment all of the ladies were being handed up into the carriage Emily had ordered to take them to their respective residences.

A cold, dangerous silence descended on the drawing room.

Bloody hell, thought Emily. She whirled to confront her father. "Well, Papa, to what do I owe the honor of this rushed visit?"

"Ask Blade. I expect he knows the answer to that." Broderick Faringdon glowered at Simon, who was calmly finishing his tea. "What the devil do you think you're about, sir?"

Simon's brows rose slightly. "I should think that was obvious, Faringdon. I was invited to tea and I am enjoying a very fine cup of Lap Seng."

"Don't try to fob me off with that tea nonsense. You're up to something, Blade."

Simon smiled his coldest smile and put down his empty cup. Something that might have been satisfaction or triumph blazed in his eyes. "In that case, I will call on you tomorrow at three to discuss it."

"The hell you will," Faringdon snarled.

Emily was startled by the ugly red flush in her father's

face. Devlin and Charles were staring at her as if she had brought disgrace and ruin to herself a second time.

"Yes. I most certainly will." Simon rose to his feet with lethal grace, taller than even the tall Faringdon men. "Until tomorrow, Faringdon." He walked over to Emily, took her hand, and kissed it. His eyes gleamed at her. "Thank you for tea, Miss Faringdon. I enjoyed myself very much. But, then, I always do in your presence."

"Goodbye, my lord. Thank you for attending our salon this afternoon." Emily suddenly wanted to grab the tails of his beautifully cut blue coat and hold him fast there in the drawing room. She did not want to face her father and brothers alone. But there was nothing she could do.

A moment later Simon had collected his curly-brimmed beaver hat and York tan gloves from Duckett and sauntered out the front door to where the Gillinghams' curricle waited. There was a clatter of hooves and wheels and he was gone.

Emily clasped her hands in front of her and glared at her father and brothers. "I hope you are all satisfied. You have quite ruined my tea. We were having a wonderful time until you burst in here without so much as a by-your-leave."

"I told you, this is my home, girl. Don't need to ask permission to walk into my own drawing room. Devil take it, Emily, what's going on here?" Broderick Faringdon faced his daughter, his hands on his hips. "I had a letter from Prendergast telling me you were being courted by the Earl of Blade, for God's sake."

"I am. I should think you would be pleased and proud, Papa."

"Proud?" Devlin poured himself a glass of claret from a bottle that had been set out for Simon. He shot a pitying look at his sister. "Have you lost your wits, Em? You know what will happen when Blade finds out about the Incident. What made you lead him on in the first place? You know how it's going to end."

Charles shook his head. "How could you let things come to such a pass, Em? Bound to be an embarrassing scene now. All the old mud will be dredged up and you're going to feel like a prize fool."

"He already knows about the scandal," Emily shouted, her hands clenching into small fists. "He already knows and he does not care. Do you hear me? He does not care a fig about it."

There was an acute silence. And then, with a weary air, the senior Faringdon helped himself to a glass of claret.

"So that's his game," Broderick said quietly. "Knew he was hatching some vicious scheme. Man's bloody damn dangerous. Everyone in London knows it. I wish to God he'd stayed out there in the East Indies. Why in hell did he have to come back?"

"What scheme?" Emily demanded. "What are you talking about, Papa? The man is going to ask for my hand in marriage. He knows I am socially ruined but he loves me anyway."

"Emily, my dear. You are so bloody naive." Broderick threw himself down onto the sofa and gulped his claret. "Men like Blade do not marry women such as yourself. Why should they? With his title and the fortune he has made for himself in the East Indies, Blade can have his pick of the pretty little virgins that come up in the marriage mart every Season. Why should he take soiled goods?"

Emily flushed, fighting back the old humiliation. "He does not seem to care about such things, Papa."

"Every man cares about such things," Charles told her with brotherly ruthlessness.

"Is that so?" Emily flashed furiously. "Then why do you go to such lengths to seduce every poor, wretched female you can find and turn them into *soiled goods*?"

"Here, now," Devlin snapped. "Charles and I are gentlemen. We don't go about seducing innocent young women of quality."

"Just the innocent young women of the lower classes? The ones who have no choice? I suppose you think their inferior social status makes it all right?"

"Enough!" Broderick Faringdon roared. "We stray from the subject. Emily, I will be blunt. You have gotten all of us into a very serious situation and I am only just now beginning to suspect what it will cost us."

"Why will it cost us anything?" she shouted back. "I am going to be married. What is wrong with that?"

The glass in her father's hand hit the table with a loud crack. "Damn, girl, don't you see what's up here? Blade don't intend to marry you. Not for a moment."

"Then why is he going to offer for me?"

Broderick Faringdon went quiet for a moment. He was a man who had grown very adept at reading the intentions of his opponents in high-stakes games. "What he'll no doubt offer is a trade."

"Damn. You're right, Father." Charles poured himself more claret.

"Hell and damnation. Of course. Should have seen it coming," Devlin muttered.

Emily stared at her father. "A trade? Papa, what on earth are you talking about?"

Broderick shook his head. "Don't you get it yet, girl? Blade don't want to marry you. What he intends to do is threaten to run off with you unless I give him what he wants." He cast a brooding eye around the elegant drawing room. "And I think I know what he will demand in exchange for doing us the great favor of getting out of our lives."

Devlin looked at him sharply. "What does he want, Father?"

"St. Clair Hall." Broderick swallowed the remainder of the claret in his glass in one gulp. "Bloody bastard hates me. He's waited twenty-three years to get his vengeance and now he's finally found a way to do it."

Emily felt dazed. She sank stiffly down onto a brocade chair, her eyes never leaving her father. "I think you had better explain, Papa. Now."

Broderick surveyed his three offspring for a long moment and then sighed heavily. "Wish your mama was still with us. She always used to handle this kind of unpleasantness. Had a way about her. I could leave it all up to her."

Devlin glanced at Charles and then looked directly at his

father. "Charles and I understand part of this. We know Blade is trying to use Emily somehow. But what is this about St. Clair Hall? Why would he want it in exchange for not running off with Em? Man's rich as Croesus. He could buy a dozen houses as fine as this one."

Emily clenched her fingers tightly together. "He said this was his home at one time," she said slowly. "He lived here as a boy."

Broderick wore a hunted expression. "He told you that?"

"Oh, yes, Papa. We are very close." Emily narrowed her eyes defiantly behind the lenses of her spectacles.

"How close?" Devlin demanded abruptly. "Intimately close? For God's sake, has that bastard already seduced you, Em? Is that why he thinks you'll run off with him?"

"The earl has been a perfect gentleman." Emily informed him proudly.

"Well, at least we can be grateful the man's got some shreds of a conscience left," Broderick observed wearily. "Doubt they'll do me much good, though."

"Papa," Emily said sharply, "You will explain all of this and you will do so now."

The elder Faringdon nodded glumly. "You will have to know all of it sooner or later. Blade has made certain of that, the damn bloody bastard. The long and the short of it is, I did not purchase St. Clair Hall after a particularly good run of luck, as I once told you. I won it and the bulk of the Traherne fortune directly from Blade's father in a card game twenty-three years ago. The earl paid his debt like the gentleman he was."

"And?" Emily scowled at him. "I know there is more to this, Papa."

"And then the fool came back here and put a bullet through his head."

Emily closed her eyes in horror. "Dear God in heaven."

Charles spoke up. "I fail to see the problem. It was a debt of honor and the man paid. The fact that he committed suicide later is no concern of ours."

Emily shuddered. "How can you be so callous? Don't you realize what must have happened?"

Broderick swore heavily. "There's not much more to the tale. The young boy and his mother vacated the house and went to live somewhere in the north. The mother never made another appearance in Society as far as I know. She died several years back, I understand."

"What about Blade?" Devlin asked. "What happened to him?"

"Some relative—an aunt, I believe—eventually scraped together enough blunt to buy him a commission. Probably did it to get rid of him. Blade went to the Peninsular Wars for a couple of years. Then he sold out and headed for the East Indies."

"Because he had no fortune of his own," Emily put in fiercely. "You had stolen his inheritance, stripped him of his rightful lands and property. After his father killed himself, Simon and his mother were thrown out of their home, penniless. They became dependent on the charity of relatives. How Blade must have hated that. He is so proud. How could you have done such a thing, Papa?"

Broderick shot her a fulminating glance. "I won everything in a fair game and don't you ever forget that, Missy. That's the way of the world. A man's got no business playing if he can't afford to pay."

"*Papa.*"

"In any event, Blade's done all right for himself. Word in the clubs is he lived like a pasha out there on some island. Did some favors for the East India Company and they rewarded him with a slice of the tea trade. He's got a fair-sized fortune of his own now. God knows, he don't need anything from us."

"But he feels you owe him St. Clair Hall?" Devlin asked.

Broderick nodded. "Vengeful bastard. I've only seen him a couple of times over the years. He looked me up before he left for the wars and again just before he sailed to the East. Both times all he said was that someday I would pay for what I had done to him and his family. He swore my family would suffer as much as his had. He also vowed to get St. Clair Hall back. I thought it was all bluster."

"And now he thinks he's found a way to force you to give him the house," Charles said, glowering at his sister. "But if he's so rich, why don't he just offer to buy it back?"

"Expect it's the principle of the thing. He thinks I owe it to him. I told you, he wants vengeance. And he probably knows I would not sell it, even if he made a decent offer."

"Why not?" Charles demanded impatiently. "We're hardly ever in residence, anyway. Except for Emily, of course."

Broderick looked around again, savoring the furnishings of the beautiful room. "This is the finest home any Faringdon has ever owned, by God. Finer than anything my father ever acquired or my grandfather or the baron himself, the stingy bastard. I've done better than any of 'em. First Faringdon to ever amount to something. And this house proves it."

Devlin shot a narrow glance at Emily's white face. "This could get very nasty, indeed. Blade ain't the type to bluff. Emily, you surely ain't been so stupid as to lose your heart to Blade?"

" 'Course she has," Charles muttered. "Look at her. Thinks that son of a bitch really wants to marry her. And that's what he'll tell her when he invites her to run off with him. She'll believe him, just like she believed Ashbrook. Christ, what a mess. We'll have to lock her up."

"Do not be idiotic," Emily said. "I could escape from any room in this house." She drew herself up proudly, rage pouring through her veins like red fire. "But you will see. Blade is going to ask for my hand and I am going to marry him."

"He don't want you, girl. Not for his wife. Ain't that clear enough?" Charles shook his head in exasperation. "He ain't going to offer for you tomorrow at three. He's going to blackmail Father, instead."

"He bloody hell will make a respectable offer," Emily retorted, her voice high and tight with tension. "I know him, damn you."

Broderick sighed heavily. "No, Emily, you do not know him. No one knows Blade. You have not heard the talk in the clubs. The man is cloaked in mystery. Bloody powerful, too. They say even men like Canonbury and Peppington are under his thumb. All anyone is certain of is that he is both very rich and very dangerous."

"Do not tell her such things, Father," Devlin muttered. "You will only make him sound more intriguing to her. You know her romantic imagination."

"Listen to me, Emily, you're a sensible girl when it comes to managing finances," Broderick said in cajoling tones. "I expect you to be sensible about this matter, too. This is not some damn romantic novel. This is real. Your future is at stake. Blade's game is an old one, although I'll grant you 'tis not one usually played by men of his rank. The usual routine is for some impoverished scoundrel to offer to drop his suit for the daughter of the house in exchange for a large sum of money."

"The only difference here," Charles said, "is that Blade ain't impoverished."

"I am convinced you are wrong," Emily said through her teeth. "The earl's offer will be a valid one and I am going to accept it, even if you do not give your permission, Papa. You cannot stop me."

Broderick massaged his temples. "Remember that disaster five years ago, m'dear. You cannot be wanting to go through that humiliation and heartbreak again. You pined for days."

"It is not the same," Emily cried. "The earl will marry me."

"It is the same, damn it all," Broderick shot back. "And Blade will never marry you. But by the time you figure that out, we'll all be—" He broke off abruptly.

"You'll all be what, Papa?" But a sudden realization had just struck Emily. When it came to financial matters, she was rarely blinded by romance. Her eyes widened in comprehension. "Ah, I think I am beginning to perceive the full extent of the earl's threat. He is very clever, is he not?"

"Now, Em, don't go worrying your head about the details here," Charles said quickly. "Let Father handle this." He traded a worried glance with Devlin, who was frowning darkly.

"It is not just the threat to my reputation that worries you, is it?" Emily said slowly. "After all, you've already suffered that trial once before. No, the real risk is that Blade might indeed take me away for some time. Months, perhaps. Even a year or two. And once deprived of my financial skills, all three of you would lose St. Clair Hall and everything else soon enough at the tables."

"Damme, Emily, that ain't it at all. It's you I'm worried about, girl. You're my only daughter. D'you think I want to see you ruined for a second time?" Broderick glared at her.

Emily crossed her arms under her breasts and nodded in satisfaction. "Very clever, indeed. I'll wager that without me to repair your fortunes periodically on 'Change, you three would not be able to keep this house, or your expensive bloodstock, or much else for more than a year, at most."

"That ain't true," Charles snapped. "It's you we're concerned about. Your reputation and happiness are what's important here."

"Thank you," Emily said dryly. "So kind of you."

"Now, see here, Em—" Devlin began furiously.

"Do you know," Emily mused thoughtfully, "the most interesting question here is how the earl came to understand just how crucial I am to your financial status, Papa."

"Damn good question," Broderick muttered as he poured himself another glass of claret. "Which ain't to say your brother ain't right," he added quickly. "I am concerned about you, girl. Very concerned."

"So are we," Charles assured her. "The money ain't got anything to do with it."

"I am relieved to hear that," Emily murmured. "So nice to know one's family cares about one." She got up and walked out of the room.

Behind her Broderick Faringdon poured himself the remainder of the claret. He and his sons sank into a gloomy silence.

• • •

Emily went straight to her sanctuary, the library. There she sat behind the big mahogany desk and stared unseeingly out into the gardens. For a long while she did not move. Then she opened a drawer and removed the beautiful box that contained the carefully bound stack of Simon's letters.

It was time to step out of the romantic haze in which she had been living for the past several days. Her father had been right about one thing: Her whole future was at stake. It was time to do some serious thinking about the problem that confronted her.

It was time, in fact, to apply the same razor sharp intelligence she normally brought to bear on financial matters to the situation in which she now found herself. Emily opened the first letter in the bundle. She had read it countless times and could have quoted it from memory.

My Dear Miss Faringdon:
    I take the liberty of introducing myself through the post because it has come to my attention that you and I have some intellectual interests in common. I have heard that you have an interest in certain poems that were recently published by a bookseller named Pound. Mr. Pound was kind enough to give me your direction . . .

After an hour of rereading the letters and rethinking everything that had been said between herself and Simon during the past few days, Emily forced herself to confront certain inescapable conclusions.

The first conclusion was that her family was right. Simon had established a relationship with her for the sole purpose of using her to extract vengeance against her father. The entire chain of events she had been attributing to a benevolent fate now exhibited a terrible, implacable logic.

But Emily had reached a second conclusion after rereading Simon's letters. The man who had written those sensitive, intelligent notes could not be the kind of monster her father claimed he was.

The third inescapable conclusion was that she was still in love with the mysterious, golden-eyed dragon of the East.

She came from a long line of gamblers, Emily reminded herself. It was time she took a risk for the sake of her own future happiness.

Pulling a piece of foolscap toward her, she picked up her quill and penned a short note.

My Dear Sir:
   I must see you immediately. Please do me the courtesy of meeting me in secret at that spot where we first discussed the difficulty of finding a rhyme for *glitter*. Please exercise discretion and caution and *tell no one*. Much is at stake.
                    Yrs, A Friend.

Emily frowned over the note as she folded it and rang the bell to summon a footman. She hoped the wording was vague enough not to give anything away in the event the message was intercepted. One had to be very careful when one arranged clandestine meetings.

Simon was waiting for her at the pond. Emily heaved an enormous sigh of relief when she saw the chestnut stallion loosely tethered to an elm.

The dragon came toward her through the trees, his golden eyes unwavering. Emily steeled herself.

"As you can see, I received your note, Miss Faringdon." The earl reached up to help her dismount.

"Thank you, my lord." Emily deliberately kept her voice formal and totally devoid of emotion. The heat of his hands warmed her through the fabric of her habit. She stepped back from Simon as soon as her feet touched the ground. Briskly she turned to walk toward the stream. "I will not take up much of your time. It is getting late."

"Yes, it is." He followed her, his black Hessians making

no noise on the soft carpet of old leaves that blanketed the ground.

Emily sat down primly on the boulder where Simon had first kissed her and risked a quick glance up at him from under the brim of her chip straw bonnet. He did not smile. He simply braced himself with one booted foot on the boulder, rested his elbow on his knee, and waited.

This man is good at waiting, Emily realized. He had waited twenty-three years for vengeance.

"I have been speaking with my father and brothers. Several things have become clear," Emily began slowly.

"Have they indeed?"

She looked toward the stream. "I want you to understand, my lord, that I fully comprehend your reasons for this rather bizarre course of vengeance you have embarked upon. In your shoes, I would most likely have tried something just as drastic. We are not unalike in some ways."

"Your father has been quite talkative, I see."

"He has explained about what happened all those years ago. How my family acquired St. Clair Hall. And about the terrible tragedy of your father's death. You have a right to pursue revenge."

"You are very understanding, my dear."

She wondered if he was mocking her. It was impossible to tell from his cool tone. Emily drew a breath and kept going. She was committed now. "I realize that you have no real intention of extending a legitimate offer for my hand. You plan to threaten to run off with me and keep me tucked away as your mistress for a few months or so unless my father hands over St. Clair Hall. You will not doubt keep me dangling emotionally during that time by promising marriage."

"Only for a few months?"

Emily nodded. "Just long enough to ensure that my family comes to some financial disaster that is severe enough to force them to give up the great house. Without me to guide their investments and restrain their excesses the way Mama used to do, that should not take long. Especially if you arrange for them to be lured into particularly deep play at the tables. Once you have St. Clair back you no doubt intend to send me home to my family in disgrace."

"How very Machiavellian of me."

"It is quite a brilliant plan, actually." Emily felt obliged to give credit where it was due.

"Thank you," Simon said softly. "But I assume it will all come to naught now that you have discovered my scheme?"

"Oh, no, you can still make it work. All you need is my cooperation. And you know well enough you have that, my lord."

"You are telling me that you are willing to run off and live for a time as my mistress?" He picked up a small twig and toyed with it.

Emily folded her hands together. "Yes. If that were my only option. You know my feelings for you are very deep, my lord. I would, however, prefer to marry you. I would like to live with you for the rest of my life, not just for a few months or a year."

"I see."

"I know marriage was not your initial intent but I would like you to consider certain aspects of this matter that may not have occurred to you."

Simon did not respond to that for several seconds. And then the twig snapped in his fingers. "What aspects?"

She did not look at him. "I realize I am not precisely what a man of your position would wish for in a wife. I have no looks or position to speak of and you cannot have any affection for any Faringdon at the moment. And then, of course, there is the Unfortunate Incident in my past. But I feel I can make up for my deficiencies in several ways."

"Miss Faringdon, you never cease to amaze me. I cannot wait to hear the rest of this."

"I am very serious, my lord. First, I would like to point out that if you marry me, you will have achieved your goal of vengeance just as surely as if you had merely run off with me. You will have made my family financially dependent on you. They would only have access to my investment skills by applying to you for permission to consult me. Would that not be a suitable sort of revenge?"

"An interesting notion."

"You can keep all the Faringdons dangling on your financial puppet strings forever."

Simon looked thoughtful. "That is true."

Emily bit her lip anxiously. "Please consider something else, my lord. I think you will find that I will make you an excellent wife. I understand you, you see. I feel I know you very well through your letters. We have a great deal in common intellectually. We will have a certain conversational rapport that most couples never achieve."

"In short, you will not bore me over dinner, is that it?"

"I am certain we shall find much of mutual interest to discuss through the years. Surely that sort of companionship would be very rewarding to a man of your intellectual nature?"

"You are proposing that our relationship continue on the higher plane that characterized it in the beginning? You foresee our union as an intellectual association of two like-minded people?"

"Yes, precisely," Emily said, gaining enthusiasm as she saw he was paying close attention. "My lord, I fully comprehend now that you are not in love with me. Knowing that, I also realize you will not welcome any excesses of romantic passion on my part and I assure you I will not press for any from you."

"Miss Faringdon, you shock me."

"And you mock me," she retorted, stung.

"Not at all. I merely wonder what led you to conclude that I would not welcome any excesses of passion from you."

She looked down at her clasped hands, her face burning. "A detailed analysis of last night's events in the library, my lord."

"What about last night?"

She stifled a small sigh. "I thought at the time that you refused my offer of an illicit affair because you were being quite noble and gallant. I assumed you halted your lovemaking because you could not bring yourself to take advantage of a woman you cared about, even if she already had a sordid past."

"In other words, you assumed I was behaving like the gentleman I claim to be?"

She nodded quickly. "Yes. I realize now that you rejected my quite shameless offer because you are not in love with me."

"I see."

"And as you were not planning to actually marry me and were very unlikely to be forced into running off with me because my father is certain to give in to your demands, there was no real need to pretend to a passion you did not feel. Actually, under the circumstances you did behave like a gentleman." She frowned thoughtfully. "That is to say, as a gentleman plotting revenge might behave. I believe you are innately noble and generous, Blade."

"Now you flatter me."

"My lord, let me finish this business. I will summarize the advantages involved in marrying me. You will have achieved your goal of having a most excellent revenge against my family. You will be acquiring a wife with whom you can communicate on a higher plane. You will have a guarantee that I will not pester you with my ungoverned romantic passions. And there is one more thing."

"I am already overwhelmed by my good fortune, but pray continue."

Emily lifted her chin to face him. She was counting on this last item to carry the day for her. "Why, it is obvious, my lord. You will have full advantage of my financial abilities."

Simon's eyes glittered briefly. "That is certainly an interesting notion."

"My lord, consider," Emily said earnestly. "I know you are very wealthy but I would bid you remember that even the greatest fortune is subject to disaster. A few bad decisions in one's investments, a few reckless nights in the gaming hells, a bad spell in the funds, and all can soon lie in ruins."

"But with you around I will be assured of being able to

recoup any losses I might sustain in the years ahead, is that it?"

Emily's hopes soared. She sensed she had finally driven home the bargain. "Yes, that is it exactly, my lord. Think of it as something like marrying an heiress. My talents on 'Change and related financial matters will constitute a sort of economic security for you, just as they have for my family in recent years."

"In other words, my dear, you are telling me that marrying you would be a particularly shrewd investment on my part?"

Emily relaxed for the first time since her tea party had been ruined. She smiled brilliantly. "Precisely, my lord. Marrying me will no doubt be the best investment you have ever made." She paused as honesty got the better of her. Her smile faded. "There is, of course, the Unfortunate Incident to be considered. I realize that it is a great strike against me. But perhaps if I stay in the country and do not attempt to enter Society, no one will notice?"

"Miss Faringdon, I assure you, the Unfortunate Incident is the least of my concerns."

"You believe we can successfully keep the scandal hidden?" she asked eagerly.

"I can safely promise you, Miss Faringdon, that if we wed, the scandal will cease to exist."

Chapter 6

"Marry her. Damnation, man, you cannot be serious. What devil's game are you playing now?" Broderick Faringdon, barricaded behind the massive mahogany desk in the library, glared at his visitor in open-mouthed astonishment. "We both know a man with a title like yours ain't about to marry a chit with a past."

"I believe I should warn you to be extremely careful about the manner in which you speak of my fiancée. The fact that you are Emily's father would not stop me from calling you out. In fact, it would give me great pleasure." Simon walked over to the brandy decanter and poured himself a glass of the amber liquid.

He knew the simple, overly familiar act would further infuriate an already confused and angry Broderick Faringdon.

"Calling me out? *Calling me out?* Damn it, Blade, I cannot believe I am hearing this. It makes no sense. Tell me what is going on here, blast you. I know what you originally intended. You planned to blackmail me into giving you St. Clair Hall on the threat of making my daughter your mistress."

"Whatever gave you that notion? My intentions are quite honorable, I assure you."

"The devil they are. I've heard about you, sir. You're known for being a deep one. There's something strange going on here. Why should you want to marry my daughter?"

Simon studied the view outside the window as he sipped the brandy. "My reasons are no concern of yours. Let us just say that I am convinced she and I will do very well together."

"If you think to hurt her somehow, you'll pay for it. I swear it."

"I am relieved to hear you have some fatherly feelings for her. But do not fret. I do not intend to beat her." Simon glanced over his shoulder in the direction of the bookcase. "Not unless she causes me an excessive amount of trouble, that is," he added, raising his voice just slightly.

"Do you think I'll give you St. Clair Hall as her dowry? Is that your game?" Broderick demanded. "If so, you can think again."

"Oh, you will give me St. Clair Hall, Faringdon. I intend to take both your daughter and the house."

"The hell you will. How do you propose to make me turn my house as well as my daughter over to you?"

"Because I am going to dangle the possibility of seeing Emily once in a while in front of you as a lure. We both know that as long as you perceive any chance at all of communicating with her, you will do whatever I say. On the other hand, if I forbid contact altogether, which as her husband I can do, you and I are well aware of what your fate will be. St. Clair Hall will be on the market within three months. Six on the outside."

"I can maintain this place on my own. I kept it all going while she was growing up," Broderick snarled.

"Yes, you did. I found that fact quite amazing, initially. The first thing I did when I got back to London was look into just how you had managed to keep things going until Emily's remarkable talents began to emerge. As it happens, my man of affairs knows yours. Davenport explained everything to him one evening over several glasses of claret."

"How dare you pry into my private affairs."

"The answer was simple," Simon continued, swirling the brandy in his glass. "It took you several years to gamble your way through my father's fortune, thanks to your wife's efforts at restraint. Also, your sons were still quite young at that time and had not yet joined you in your irresponsible ways."

"Your father lost his inheritance in a fair game, damn you. It was not his fortune after I won it. *It was mine.*"

"I am not at all certain it was a fair game."

Broderick turned livid. "Are you accusing me of cheating, sir?"

"Calm yourself, Faringdon. I am not accusing you. I can prove nothing after all these years. I merely admit I have a few questions. My father was an excellent player, from all accounts, and he had never gambled to excess before. One does wonder."

"Damn you."

Simon smiled slightly at the note of impotent rage in Broderick's voice. "Even the Blade fortune could not hold out forever. But just as you were facing disaster again, your next stroke of luck came through. That bit of luck was the death of Emily's aunt on her mother's side, was it not? The woman conveniently died, leaving Emily a large sum of money. But the aunt made the mistake of making you the poor girl's trustee. You went through Emily's inheritance by the time she was sixteen. And then things got a bit desperate for a while, didn't they?"

"You make it sound as if I frittered away my daughter's inheritance, you bastard."

"So you did."

"I spent it on her and this house, which is her home," Faringdon rasped.

"And on your London life, your excellent bloodstock, expensive clothes, and the gaming debts you were piling up. As I said, the money was gone before your daughter was even out of the schoolroom. I doubt if you could have scraped together enough to give her a Season even if you had been inclined to try. Which you were not, of course, because by then she was starting to show her remarkable talents. Davenport told my man about those, too, and how you capitalized on them."

"There was no point giving her a Season. She's not the sort to attract much notice on the marriage mart."

"And you certainly did not want to assist her chances of contracting a good marriage by giving her a decent dowry, did you?"

"Damn you, her mother died the next year. We were in mourning. No possibility of a Season. Then she went and ran off with that bastard, Ashbrook. Impossible to bring her out after that." Faringdon beetled his brows and gave his nemesis a shrewd look. "She was ruined, sir. Do I make myself clear? Utterly ruined."

"That is a matter of opinion." Simon put down the empty brandy glass. "Now, then. I shall want you and your sons to vacate St. Clair Hall by the wedding day. I think we shall set the date for the first week of April."

Broderick gasped. "That's less than six weeks away."

"I see no need to delay matters. We have settled the financial end of things. And I do not believe Emily is inclined toward a long, formal engagement. I will want to spend my honeymoon here at St. Clair, so you and your sons will definitely have to be gone by then. Your staff can stay. Emily seems quite fond of them and they appear to be well trained."

"There is the matter of settlements," Broderick said desperately.

Simon smiled grimly. "There will be no settlements as such. You must rely on me to look after your daughter."

"I do not believe this is happening." Broderick looked rather like a fish that had just been pulled out of the water. He was gasping for air and his face was blotched with unnatural color. "You cannot want to marry her. Not after that scandal of five years ago. Think of your title, man."

Simon's mouth hardened. "I warned you not to say any more on that score, Faringdon. I meant it. Now, I believe that seals the bargain."

"No, by God, it does not. I will speak to Emily. She is a

smart little thing, even if she is inclined to indulge foolish romantic fantasies. I will convince her that you are up to no good."

"You are welcome to try, of course, but I doubt you will have any luck changing her mind," Simon said confidently. "Face it. Your only hope of ever seeing Emily again is to agree to what I want."

"Damme, this is a diabolical piece of business. She is my only daughter. I will make her see reason."

"You must suit yourself on that score. Why don't we ask Emily if she's likely to come around to your way of thinking?" Simon strode over to the bookcase, found the hidden lever in the bottom of the cabinet, and pressed it.

The bookcase slid soundlessly away from the wall and Emily, who had obviously had her ear pressed against the wood on the other side, spilled into a colorful heap at Simon's booted feet.

"Bloody hell," Emily muttered.

"Good God, what is this?" Broderick stared in astonishment, first at the opening in the wall and then at his daughter.

Emily sat up, attempting to douse the candle she had been carrying, straighten her skirts, and adjust her spectacles all at the same time. She peered up at Simon, who towered over her. "How did you know I was back there, my lord?"

"You must attribute my uncanny knowledge to the fact that we obviously do communicate on a higher plane, my dear. In the metaphysical realm such things as mental communication are no doubt everyday occurrences. We shall have to accustom ourselves to the experience."

"Oh, of course." Emily smiled in delight.

Simon reached down, helped her up, and set her lightly on her feet. He smiled down into her brilliant eyes and wondered if he should add that her presence on the other side of the bookcase had been a safe enough guess on his part. He knew her well enough by now to know she would have been unable to resist the opportunity to eavesdrop. Especially not when there was a secret passageway conveniently available in which to do so.

Emily sighed philosophically as she brushed at the dust on her peach-colored muslin gown. "So much for my dignity. But at least the business is completed, is it not?" She looked up at him quite hopefully. "We are engaged to be married?"

"We are, indeed, my dear," Simon assured her. "I have many faults, as you will no doubt discover soon enough, but I am not stupid. I could not possibly pass up the chance of making the best investment of my life."

On a dreary, damp morning two weeks later Simon sat in the library of his Grosvenor Square townhouse reading the letter from Emily that had arrived at breakfast. It contained, as usual, a lively report on the discussions at the latest meeting of the literary society, discussions which seemed to have been devoted entirely to Byron again. There was also a long paragraph describing the new verses being added to *The Mysterious Lady* and a few desultory remarks about the weather.

When he finished reading, Simon was vaguely aware of an odd flicker of disappointment. It was obvious Emily had fought valiantly to resist the temptation to put anything into her note that might be interpreted as an excess of passion.

Simon gently refolded the letter and sat gazing into the fire. After a moment's contemplation, he reached out to pick up the beautifully enameled Chinese teapot that sat on a nearby table. He poured the Lap Seng into a gossamer thin cup decorated with a green and gold dragon. As he started to lift the cup, he paused, studying the figure of the mythical beast.

Emily had called him a dragon. And her eyes had been full of wonder and passion and sweet, feminine adoration when she said it.

Simon glanced around the room in which he sat. When she saw his townhouse she would undoubtedly term it a suitable lair for a dragon.

The entire house was done in the rich, exotic shades he had grown to appreciate while living in the East: Chinese red, dark green, midnight black, and glowing gold.

The lush library was filled with reminders of the strange lands he had traveled. The richly hued Oriental carpet was a suitable backdrop for the black lacquered cabinets with their fabulous motifs. The heavily carved teak settee and armchairs were covered with red velvet and trimmed with gold tassels.

The desk was a massive thing, intricately inlaid and worked by master craftsmen. He'd had it made in Canton. Incense urns from India filled the room with a fragrance that had been blended in Bombay to his exact specifications. Huge golden silk brocade pillows large enough to double as beds were arranged near the hearth.

And everywhere there were dragons, beautifully sculpted images of ferocious mythical creatures from the folklore of the Far East. The dragons were green, black, red, and gold and each was encrusted with a fortune in gems. Wherever one happened to look in the library one saw fantastic beasts with emerald and ruby eyes, golden scales, onyx claws, and topaz-studded tails.

Simon had a hunch the creatures would appeal to Emily.

He inhaled the smoky-scented tea as he leaned his head back against the crimson cushion of his chair and thought about his forthcoming marriage. He did not know quite when he had decided to marry Emily Faringdon. He'd certainly had no such intention when he'd laid his initial plans several months past. But life, he had learned over the years, had a way of reshaping a man's intentions.

He was mentally composing a reply to Emily's letter when his singularly ugly butler announced Lady Araminta Merryweather. Simon got to his feet as a vivacious woman in her late forties swept into the room amid a cloud of expensive scent.

Lady Merryweather was, as usual, dressed in the first style of fashion. Today she was wearing a pale blue merino wool gown cut with long, tight sleeves and a delicate flounce. Her height, which was unusual for a woman, gave her a regal air. Her hat was a charming little confection perched rakishly atop her graying curls. Her eyes were the same yellow gold as Simon's. Her handsome, patrician features were flushed from the cold.

"Simon. I have only just got back to town and discovered the news of your engagement. To a Faringdon, no less. I came around at once, of course. I can scarcely believe it. Absolutely astonishing. And never a hint. You must tell me all about it, dear boy."

"Hello, Aunt Araminta." Simon kissed the back of her hand and invited her to seat herself in front of the fire. "I appreciate your coming here this morning. As it happens, I was going to call on you tomorrow."

"I could not have waited until tomorrow," Araminta assured him. "Now, then, I want to know precisely what is going on here. How on earth did you come to get yourself engaged to the Faringdon girl?"

Simon smiled faintly. "I am not precisely certain of just how it happened myself. Miss Faringdon is a most unusual creature."

Araminta's eyes grew speculative. "But you are far too clever to have gotten caught up in any woman's toils."

"Am I?"

"Of course you are. Simon, do not play games with me. I know you are up to something. You are always plotting. I vow you are the most devious creature I have ever met and there is not a soul in town who does not agree with me. But surely you can trust me."

Simon smiled faintly. "You are the only person in the whole of England whom I completely trust, Araminta. You know that."

"Then you know I would never breathe a word of your plans. Have you developed some monstrous scheme that will bring down the entire bunch of Flighty, Feckless Faringdons?"

"There have been some modifications in the original scheme," Simon admitted. "But I will be getting St. Clair Hall back."

Araminta arched her elegantly thin brows. "Will you, indeed? How did you arrange that?"

"The house will be my wife's dowry."

"Oh, my. I know you have been obsessed with that house since the day your father died, but was it worth shackling yourself to a Faringdon in order to get it?"

"Emily Faringdon is not an ordinary Faringdon. Soon, she will not be a Faringdon at all. She will be my wife."

"Do not tell me this is a love match," Araminta exclaimed.

"More of a business investment. Or so I am told."

"A *business* investment. This is too much, by half. Simon, what on earth are you about?"

"I am thirty-five years old." Simon studied the flames on the hearth. "And the last of my line. You have been telling me for some time that I should do my duty and set up my nursery."

"Granted. But you are the Earl of Blade and you have accrued a sizable fortune during the past years. You could have your choice on the marriage mart. Why choose Miss Faringdon, of all people?"

Simon's brow tilted. "I believe it was the other way around. She chose me."

"Dear heaven, I do not believe I am hearing this. I assume she has the Faringdon looks, at least? Tall and fair?"

"No. She is rather short, has bright red hair and freckles, a nose that tilts upward, and she is almost never without a pair of spectacles. She looks rather like an intelligent elf and she has a habit of saying 'bloody hell' when she is overset."

"Good heavens." Lady Merryweather was genuinely appalled. "Simon, what have you done?"

"Actually, I think she will become something of a sensation when you take her out into Society, Aunt Araminta."

"You want me to introduce her?" Araminta looked horrified at first and then rather intrigued by the challenge. "You want me to turn an elf into a social triumph?"

"I cannot think of anyone more suited to the task. It will be a delicate business, I fear. Emily will definitely need some guidance, as she has never been out in Society, but I would not have her spirits depressed or dampened by too many rules and strictures. You, I think, are quite capable of appreciating her unusual qualities and finding ways to set them off to their best advantage."

"Simon, I am not certain there is a best way to set off a short, redheaded elf who says things such as 'bloody hell' when she is overset."

"Nonsense. You will find a way. I have complete confidence in you."

"Well, I shall certainly do my best. Lord knows, it is the least I can do for you after all you have done for me, Simon. I would still be stuck in that moldering pile of stones in Northumberland if you had not rescued me from genteel poverty a few years ago."

"You owe me nothing, Araminta," Simon said. "It is I who shall be forever grateful to you for helping me take care of Mother and for selling the last of your jewels to buy me a commission."

Araminta grinned. "Giving you a start in life was the best investment I could have made. The jewels and clothes I am able to buy now are worth a great deal more than the paltry few I had back in those days."

Simon shrugged. "You deserve them. Now, then, as to the matter of introducing my wife to Society. As I said, I shall leave the project largely in your hands. But I will undertake to quash the one potential problem that looms on the horizon."

Araminta eyed him cautiously. "What is the nature of this potential problem, Simon?"

"My fiancée is a rather impetuous sort and there apparently was a rather Unfortunate Incident a few years back."

"An Incident?" Araminta demanded in distinctly ominous tones. "Just how bad was this Incident?"

"As Emily explains it, she was temporarily overcome with an excess of romantic passion and ran off with a young man."

Araminta leaned her head back against the cushion and closed her eyes in horror. "Dear God." She promptly opened her eyes and shot her nephew a shrewd glance. "How bad was it? Did her father stop the pair before they got to the border?"

"There is every indication that the man involved had no real intention of making it to Gretna Green. In any event, Emily ended up spending the night with him at an inn. Faringdon caught up with her the next day and brought her home."

"The next day? He did not find her until the following day?" Araminta was clearly beyond shock now. She leaned forward, her eyes fierce. "Simon, you cannot be serious about any of this. It is all some sort of bizarre joke you are playing on your poor aunt. Confess."

"It is no joke, Aunt Araminta. I am about to marry a lady with a past. But you need not fret. I shall see to it that her past effectively ceases to exist."

"Good God, Simon. How?"

He shrugged without any concern. "My title and fortune will prove a most effective stain remover. We both know that. And I will personally blot up any small leftover drips that may appear."

"Dear heaven. You are enjoying this, aren't you?" Araminta gazed at him in sudden comprehension. "You are having yourself another great adventure."

"Emily has a way of adding spice to one's life, as you will no doubt soon learn."

"Simon, I am going to be blunt. The chit may be an original and I know you are attracted to the unusual. But you must think of what you are doing. We both know you simply cannot marry a young female who is not a virgin, no matter how charming she is. It is one thing for a woman to have discreet affairs after she is married, quite another for her to have been involved in a scandal with a man before marriage. You are the Earl of Blade. You must think of your name and position."

Simon took his gaze off the fire and gave his aunt an amused, quizzical glance. "You misunderstand, Aunt Araminta," he said gently. "There is no question about my wife's innocence. She is, I assure you, as pure as snow."

"But you just said there was a great scandal in her past. You said she ran off with some young man and spent the night with him."

"I do not know yet precisely what happened that night," Simon mused. "But I am quite satisfied that Emily did not share a bed with the young man."

"How can you be so certain?" Araminta retorted, and then her brows climbed. "Unless you have already been to bed with her yourself?"

"No, I have not, more's the pity. I assure you, I am certainly looking forward to my wedding night. I am persuaded it will be a most interesting experience."

"Then how can you be sure she is innocent?" Araminta asked, exasperated.

Simon smiled to himself. "It is rather difficult to explain. I can only say that Emily and I have established a unique form of communication that takes place on a higher plane."

"A higher plane?"

"I refer to the metaphysical world. Your problem is that you do not read very much modern poetry, Aunt Araminta. Let me assure you that certain things are very clear on the transcendental level where two like minds may meet in an excess of pure, intellectual emotion."

Lady Merryweather stared at him speechlessly. "Since when have you concerned yourself with higher planes and pure intellectual emotion? I have known you long enough to realize you are up to some dark business here, Blade. I can feel it."

"Can you really? How fascinating. Perhaps you have access to a higher plane of knowledge yourself, Aunt Araminta."

Lord Richard Ashbrook did not normally frequent the same clubs Simon favored. It was necessary, therefore, to seek out the dashing young poet at one of the smaller clubs in St. James that catered to the dandy set.

Simon eventually located his quarry in a card room.

Ashbrook was playing with the sort of devil-may-care reck-
lessness that was quite the height of fashion.

Simon could see at a glance that the poet was obviously
every maiden's dream, assuming said maiden did not mind
the weakness about the eyes and chin. Ashbrook was indis-
putably handsome in a Byronic manner: black hair, brooding dark eyes, and a jaded, somewhat petulant tilt to his
mouth.

Simon waited quietly in a winged chair, amusing himself
with a bottle of hock and a newspaper until his quarry left
the tables around midnight. Ashbrook joined a companion
and together they strode toward the door of the club mutter-
ing something about going to look for more interesting action in the hells.

Simon got up and followed slowly, delaying his move
until Ashbrook had summoned a carriage and leapt into the
cab. When the poet's companion made to follow, Simon
stepped forward and tapped his shoulder. The man who
turned in annoyance to confront him was older and far more
dissipated-looking than Ashbrook. He was also quite drunk.
Simon recognized him as a gamester named Crofton who
frequented the hells.

"What's this? Who are you?" Crofton demanded in a
surly, slurred voice, his once handsome face twisted in irritation.

"I require a word with Ashbrook. I fear you will have to
wait for another carriage." Simon gave Crofton a small
push, just enough to send him staggering backward.

"Damn you," Crofton snarled as he tried to catch his
balance.

"Grosvenor Square," Simon said to the coachman as he
stepped up into the carriage and slammed the door.

Inside the darkened carriage Ashbrook lounged in the
shadows and scowled. "What the devil is this all about?
You're Blade, aren't you?"

"Yes. I am Blade." Simon sat down as the carriage lum-
bered forward through the crowded street.

"What have you done with Crofton? He and I had plans
for this evening."

"This will not take long. You can return to pick up your friend after you have set me down at my townhouse. In the meantime you and I must come to an understanding about a small matter."

"What the deuce are you talking about? What understanding?" Looking almost overcome with ennui, Ashbrook removed a small snuffbox from his pocket and took a pinch.

"You may congratulate me, Ashbrook. In case you have not yet heard, I am about to be married."

Ashbrook's gaze sharpened warily. "I heard."

"Ah, then you must also have heard that the young lady I am going to marry is not unknown to you."

"Emily Faringdon." Ashbrook turned his head to stare out the window of the cab.

"Yes. Emily Faringdon. It would appear that you and my fiancée shared a small adventure some years back."

Ashbrook's head came around swiftly. "She told you about that?"

"Emily is a very honest young woman," Simon said gently. "I do not think she would know how to lie if she tried. I am also well aware that nothing of a, shall we say, *intimate* nature occurred between the two of you that night."

Ashbrook groaned and turned his gaze back to the darkened streets. "It was a fiasco from the start."

"Emily can be unpredictable."

"No offense, sir, but Emily Faringdon is not only unpredictable, she is dangerous. I suppose she told you everything?"

"Everything," Simon echoed softly.

"I had a sore head for three days from the blow she gave me with that damn chamber pot."

"Did you, indeed? Emily is quite strong for her size."

"Nearly caught my death of cold from spending the night on a pallet in the hall. That bastard of an innkeeper said he did not have a spare room. Personally I think his wife told him to say that. God knows why she felt so protective of Miss Faringdon. She'd never even seen the chit before that night."

"Many people find themselves feeling protective toward Miss Faringdon. She has any number of friends. But from now on it will be my privilege to protect her and you may be assured that I will do so."

Ashbrook slid him a quick glance. "Are you trying to say something, Blade?"

"I merely wish to tell you that should the subject of your adventure with Miss Faringdon ever come up in conversation, you will make it very clear that there never was any adventure."

"You want me to pretend it never happened?"

"Precisely."

"But it did happen. I assure you, I have no intention of discussing it, but you can hardly pretend it did not occur."

"You would be amazed at what can be made to vanish when one has power, fortune, and title. And a little cooperation from certain parties."

Ashbrook stared. "You think you can make the scandal just disappear?"

"Oh, yes. I can make it disappear."

Ashbrook hesitated, looking momentarily uneasy. Then he smiled insolently and took another pinch of snuff. "What do you expect me to say if someone raises the question?"

"If anyone is so impertinent as to inquire into the matter, you will inform him that you were nowhere near Little Dippington at the time and you know nothing about any scandal. You will say you were up in Cumberland worshiping in the footsteps of Coleridge, Wordsworth, and the other Lake poets."

"Must I?" Ashbrook drawled. "Such a dreary, dull lot."

"Yes, I fear you must."

Ashbrook watched him in silence for a few taut seconds, clearly attempting to take Simon's measure. "They say you are a mysterious sort, Blade. Full of dark schemes that others do not discover until too late. You must be up to something. What game are you playing with the Faringdon girl?"

"My plans do not concern you, Ashbrook."

"Why should I bother to assist you by lying about what happened five years ago?"

"If you do not, I will do what one of the Faringdons should have done five years ago. I will call you out."

Ashbrook straightened with a jerk. "The devil you will."

"If you check with the crowd that practices at Manton's gallery, you will find that I am accounted an excellent shot. Now, I will bid you good night, Ashbrook. It has been a most informative evening." Simon used his stick to tap on the roof of the carriage. The vehicle came to a halt.

Ashbrook leaned forward as Simon opened the door. His dark eyes were suddenly intent. "You did not know, did you? Until I told you about the chamber pot and sleeping in the hall, you did not know that nothing had happened between me and Emily that night. It was all a bluff."

Simon smiled fleetingly as he stepped down onto the street. "You are wrong, Ashbrook. I knew from the beginning that nothing of a serious nature had transpired. My fiancée has a taste for adventure but she is far from stupid. I simply was not aware of all the particulars of the incident. Be grateful for that chamber pot, by the way."

"Why?"

"It is the only reason I am letting you live now."

Ashbrook leaned back against the cushions again and reached for his snuffbox. His eyes glittered angrily in the shadows as he looked at Blade. "Damnation. What they say about you is true. You are a cold-blooded bastard. Do you know? I believe I pity little Emily."

Ten days later Simon was again sitting down in his dragon-infested library to enjoy a letter from Emily when he was again interrupted by his butler informing him of unexpected visitors.

"Two gentlemen by the name of Faringdon to see you, my lord. Are you at home?" Greaves announced forebodingly. His naturally ferocious features were accented with a variety of old scars including an interesting knife slash that had once laid open most of his jaw. Simon had been the only one on hand to sew the wound closed and he had done his best. He was the first to admit, however, that while his stitches were functional, they had lacked artistry.

Simon reluctantly refolded the letter. "Show them in, Greaves. I have been expecting them."

A moment later Charles and Devlin Faringdon strode into the room, looking as stern and determined as it was possible for two such handsome men to appear.

"Ah, my future brothers-in-law. To what do I owe the honor of this visit?" He motioned the two young men to chairs across from his own.

"We have decided it is imperative to speak to you personally, sir," Devlin announced. "We are fully aware you are playing some devilish game with this nonsense of an engagement to Emily. We thought you would show your cards before you went through with the wedding."

"But now you appear determined to actually marry her," Charles concluded darkly.

"I most certainly am determined to go through with it." Simon rested his elbows on the crimson velvet arms of his chair and steepled his fingers. He regarded the two Faringdons through hooded eyes. "I would not dream of doing anything so ungentlemanly as crying off. So if that is your concern, you may rest assured that this wedding will go through as scheduled."

"Now, see here," Devlin said, "Charles and I are men of the world. You ain't fooling us, Blade. You're up to something and we know it. We've thought this thing through and we've decided there's only one reason why you would want to marry Emily."

"And that reason is . . . ?" Simon inquired softly.

Charles held his chin at a challenging angle. "You have decided she can make you a second fortune on 'Change. This way you get it all, don't you? St. Clair Hall, your revenge on Father, and the promise of a second fortune from the stock exchange."

"You are planning to use our sister in a most unprincipled fashion," Devlin announced. "And she, poor chit, is so foolish and so romantically inclined, she does not have a hint of your true intentions."

Simon considered that briefly. "What makes you think I am not marrying your sister simply because I have become quite fond of her and have decided she will make me an excellent wife?"

"It won't fadge, Blade," Devlin snapped. "You ain't in love with her. Only the promise of having her make you a second fortune could make you overlook the scandal in her past."

"Damn right. We ain't fools, y'know. You could do a lot better for yourself than marry a silly young female who's gone and ruined herself," Charles added with a man-to-man air. "Not to put too fine a point on it, our poor Emily is soiled goods."

Simon got languidly to his feet and took two steps over to where Charles was sitting. He reached down, took a fistful of Charles' immaculately tied cravat, and hauled the younger man bodily to his feet. Charles' eyes widened.

"What the devil . . . ?"

The remainder of his comment was lost as Simon pivoted swiftly in the graceful movements of the ancient fighting art he had learned in the East. He knew his unorthodox, potentially lethal method would have astounded the young bloods who practiced boxing at Gentleman Jackson's academy. They would have been even more perplexed by the elaborate techniques for establishing mental discipline and control that the monks had taught along with the physical skills.

Charles went spinning wildly toward the fireplace. The young Faringdon fetched up against the mantel, cracking his chin on the black marble. With a stunned look in his handsome eyes, Charles collapsed slowly to the carpet.

"Good God, sir." Devlin shot to his feet and took a step toward his brother. "What have you done to him?"

Simon caught Devlin in midstride and sent him flying ignominiously after his brother. Devlin hit the wall, doubled over with a muffled cry, and then sprawled on the carpet beside Charles.

The two brothers, dazed and furious, glared at Simon as they struggled to recover themselves.

"What was that for, you bloody bastard?" Devlin hissed as he wavered to his feet.

"That was for insulting your sister, of course. What did you think it was for?" Simon absently checked his cravat. It was still perfectly tied. "It was also, I believe, for failing to call Ashbrook out five years ago as you ought to have done."

"Emily wouldn't let us," Charles growled, rubbing his chin as he staggered over to a chair and sat down heavily. "Said the whole thing was as much her fault as his. Told us Ashbrook was going to be a great poet someday and we shouldn't deprive the world of a great talent."

"Emily should have had nothing to say about it." Simon surveyed the two handsome young cubs with a look of disgust. "It was your duty to take care of the matter."

"Father said the whole thing should be hushed up as much as possible. Calling out Ashbrook would have caused an even bigger scandal," Devlin muttered.

"As it happens, Emily took care of her own honor that night. But, then, Emily has always had to fend for herself, hasn't she?"

Devlin looked at Simon, scowling. "What are you talking about? She spent the night with him, for God's sake. She lost her honor."

"No, she did not. She hit Ashbrook over the head with a chamber pot and he wound up sleeping in the hall."

"Well, we know that's what actually happened," Charles said impatiently. "Emily explained it all the next morning. But the damage to her reputation was done, right enough. Father said so."

"As of now," Simon said coldly, "the Incident never occurred. And I will personally destroy anyone, *anyone at all,* who says it did. Do I make myself clear, gentlemen?"

The twins gaped open-mouthed at him and then exchanged bemused glances with each other.

"You cannot make the great blot on her reputation simply vanish, sir," Charles finally ventured carefully.

"Watch me," said Simon.

Chapter 7

"That will be all, Higson. You may go now." Simon heard the uncharacteristic impatience in his own voice as he dismissed his valet. He frowned. The fact that this was his wedding night should not have affected his ironclad self-control in any way.

"If that will be all, then, sir, may I take the liberty of congratulating you on your marriage?" Higson, a short, stocky, powerfully built man who looked a little like a bulldog and who had remained in the earl's employ for the past ten years because he had many of the valuable attributes of one, paused at the door. He showed no sign of having taken offense at Simon's abrupt tone. In fact there was a distinct twinkle of amusement in his pale eyes. A man who had once fought pirates side by side with his employer could occasionally take liberties.

"Thank you, Higson," Simon said curtly.

"Sir." Higson inclined his head and let himself out into the hall.

Simon's gaze went instantly to the door that connected his bedchamber to Emily's.

Something in him tightened. There had been no sounds

of activity from the other room for the past several minutes. His wife was obviously in bed waiting for him.

His wife. Simon stared at the connecting door, remembering how Emily had looked earlier that day as she had entered the crowded village church. She had walked rather cautiously down the aisle, owing to her stout refusal to wear her spectacles. But the slight hesitancy in her steps, together with the shy excitement in her green eyes, had given her the aura of a fairy princess venturing into a strange new world. Her white gown with its silver ribbon trim had enhanced the effect. Simon had been astonished to find himself feeling at once very protective and extremely possessive.

The entire town had turned out in all its country finery. There was no doubt that Little Dippington had put its seal of approval on the alliance. Among the members of the literary society there was not a single dry eye.

His unexpected fascination with his new bride had caused him to virtually ignore the presence of Broderick Faringdon and Emily's two brothers. All three had watched the proceedings with satisfyingly gloomy expressions, looking as though Emily were about to be transported to Australia rather than become a wealthy countess.

Of course, Simon reminded himself as he walked toward the connecting door, for all intents and purposes, Emily was now as lost to the Faringdons as if she had been transported across the sea. After tonight she would belong completely to her husband. She would no longer be a Faringdon. Simon was determined that none of the remaining Faringdons ever forgot that.

Hand on the doorknob, Simon glanced around the master bedchamber that had once been occupied by his father. A fierce sense of elation swept over him. St. Clair Hall and everything in it was once again in the hands of a Traherne.

"Rest assured I will not lose it the way you did, Father," Simon vowed to the ghost who hovered in the back of his mind.

Twenty-three years was a long time to wait, but it had been worth it. And the revenge was just beginning. Watching the Faringdons slide inevitably down into financial disaster was going to be as satisfying as taking St. Clair Hall back today had been.

Simon opened the door and stepped into the darkened bedchamber that adjoined his.

"Emily? Why did you not have your maid leave a candle burning? Are you feeling shy, my dear?" Simon moved farther into the room, letting his eyes adjust to the shadows. "There's no need. You and I have established communication on a higher plane, remember?"

He halted at the foot of the canopied bed and frowned as he realized there was no redheaded elf under the covers. "Emily?"

Then he saw the note neatly folded and left on the pillow. A flicker of alarm went through him. Simon strode around the side of the bed and snatched up the piece of paper. He carried it back to the open doorway to read it by the light that filtered in from his bedchamber.

> My Dearest Simon:
>
> If you have found this note it is because you have felt obliged to carry out the conjugal duties of a husband. How very like you to abide by the dictates of honor and responsibility even when your personal inclinations are otherwise! But I promise you it is entirely unnecessary.
>
> Please be assured that I have no intention of burdening you with my excessive passions tonight or any other night until such time as you are able to feel a spark of true emotion and affection for me. I am fully prepared to wait as long as necessary, even if it takes years.
>
> Your Loving Wife.

"Hell and damnation." Simon crumpled the note in his hand. Then a rueful smile edged his mouth, replacing the flare of irritation. Well, he had known that his wedding night had been virtually guaranteed to be out of the ordinary. Elves were an unpredictable lot.

He wondered where one would go to hide and remembered that this particular elf would undoubtedly be unable to resist scribbling in her journal tonight of all nights.

Simon went out into the darkened hall and headed toward the staircase. The house was very still and quiet tonight. Other than himself and Emily, there were only the servants around and they had long since retired.

Simon had refused to allow his new in-laws to spend so much as a single night under his roof. The three Faringdon men had been told they would have to find other accommodations immediately after the wedding ceremony. Simon did not particularly care where they spent the evening. He was under the impression they had all left for London, however, and that suited him. The sooner they returned to the gaming hells, the sooner they would slide into disaster.

Simon reached the bottom step and saw a bar of light shining under the closed door of the library. He grinned fleetingly and strode across the marble-tiled hall. Tracking down an elusive wife was not so very difficult.

Simon opened the door of the library and walked into the room. Emily, seated behind the big desk, was writing furiously in a bound volume. She glanced up as she heard the door open. She was wearing her prim little chintz dressing gown and her hair was tucked into a frilly white cap. Her eyes widened behind the lenses of her spectacles as she stared at him.

"Simon."

"Good evening, my dear. Don't you think this a rather odd place to spend your wedding night?" Simon closed the door and walked over to the cold hearth. He went down on one knee to light the fire that had been laid there. "Not nearly as comfortable as your bedchamber."

"Simon, what are you doing here?" Emily jumped to her feet. "Did you get my note?"

"Oh, yes, I got your note." Simon rose and took the crumpled paper out of his pocket. He tossed it into the flames he had just ignited. Then he turned his head and smiled at Emily over his shoulder. "Very thoughtful of you, my sweet, to consider my delicate sensibilities in this matter."

Emily blushed and looked down at the top of the desk. "It is only that I do not wish to burden you with my excessive passions, my lord."

Simon rested one arm along the mantel and contemplated his wife. He had himself a bride who had convinced herself she was in danger of intimidating her husband with passion. Only Emily could have come up with such a twist on a wedding night. "I would have you know, my dear, that I do not consider your passions a burden. I look forward to carrying out my responsibilities as a husband."

"That is very kind of you but it is quite obvious that you would merely be doing your duty tonight if you were to make love to me and I could not bear that."

"I see. And you felt you could not explain that to me in person? You had to leave a written message?"

"I thought it would be easier if I simply left that note informing you that I do not expect anything of you." She clasped her hands in front of her and stared down at them. "It is a little awkward to talk about that sort of thing in person, my lord, if you see what I mean."

"Surely not for us," Simon said gently. "As you have pointed out, our communication takes place on a higher plane. You and I are free to discuss matters that other couples can only allude to in the vaguest of terms."

"Do you really think so, Simon?" She raised her eyes to meet his.

Simon saw the anxiety and hope in her gaze and he smiled to conceal a surge of cool complacency. The lady was about to fall into his palm like a ripe peach. "Yes, Emily, I am certain of it." He went over to the brandy table and picked up the decanter. "I thought you were certain of it, too. You were, after all, the one who explained it to me."

"Well, I had hoped it was true," Emily said candidly. "But after I realized exactly why you were marrying me, I could not be altogether certain that you were experiencing the same sense of pure, metaphysical communion as I am. At least, not at the moment."

"But you have hopes that I will come to experience it?"

"Oh, yes, Simon. I am pinning all my hopes on such an

event. That is precisely why I talked you into marrying me. But in the meantime, I do not want you to feel obligated in any way to perform the duties of a husband. It is bad enough that I coerced you into this venture."

Simon coughed once as a mouthful of brandy went down the wrong way. "I assure you I did not feel coerced into marriage, Emily. I rarely do anything I do not wish to do."

"I can well believe that, my lord, but in this instance, you must allow I produced some rather forceful arguments in favor of an alliance between us. I would not have it on my conscience that I also demanded that you perform your husbandly duties in bed on top of everything else. You have already given me so much simply by giving me your name. It would be unjust and incredibly greedy of me to expect any more of you."

"Very thoughtful, my dear." Simon regarded her with solemn consideration. She looked so tragically determined to take the noble course and resist her own sweet passion. Meanwhile just the sight of her aroused him as no other woman had in years. It was all he could do to control a sudden, savage impulse to pull Emily down onto the carpet and make her his right then and there.

A shudder of raw desire went through him. The realization that his unshakable self-control might be threatened startled Simon. He had never lost that sense of control around a woman.

"Simon? Is something wrong?"

He shook his head and carefully put down the half-empty brandy glass. *Damnation.* He was the one in charge here. He was the one who had made the decision to marry, whatever Emily might think. He had decided on his course of vengeance. It was a vengeance that would bring down an entire family. Bedding Emily tonight was simply the next step in the process. Broderick Faringdon must be gnashing his teeth at this very moment. Faringdon was, after all, a man and a father. He would understand that by morning his daughter would belong completely to the enemy in a way that only a woman can belong to a man. She would be lost to the Faringdons forever.

But first the elf had to be coaxed into surrendering to her own charming passion, Simon reminded himself.

"No, my dear," he said thoughtfully. "I was simply reflecting on one very salient fact that you appear to be overlooking."

"What is that?"

"You say we are capable of a rare metaphysical form of communication."

"I believe that with all my heart, Simon. I would never have pushed for marriage otherwise. I swear it."

He nodded. "And you would wish this unique communication between us to be deepened and enhanced, is that not correct?"

"Oh, yes, my lord." Her eyes shone like jewels. "I wish that with all my heart. It is my ultimate goal and I am prepared to work very hard to achieve it."

"A worthy objective and I assure you I share your goal."

"Simon, you cannot know how happy it makes me to hear you say that."

"Now, then. I have given this problem some thought. It seems to me you would do well to consider that one method of, shall we say, enhancing our unusual metaphysical relationship, would be to extend it into the physical realm as swiftly as possible."

Emily stared at him. "Extend it into the physical realm, my lord?"

"Precisely. It seems logical, does it not, that the physical and the metaphysical must be closely connected?"

"Well . . ."

"What happens on one plane must surely affect what happens on another. Don't you agree?"

Emily frowned in concentration. "You think that the events on the metaphysical level may be shadows of what happens on the physical plane? It is a fascinating notion. And you are quite right, my lord. There is a certain logic to it."

"With that theory in mind, I propose that you consider the merits of allowing me to perform my husbandly duties tonight."

"Oh, but, Simon, I could not possibly—"

He held up a palm to silence her. "Not for your sake, but for mine."

"Your sake?" She looked stunned by the concept.

"Precisely. If I am right, then the end result can only be in both our best interests. Our powers of transcendental communication will be vastly increased. I am just as eager to strengthen our metaphysical union as you are, Emily."

Emily's beautiful eyes filled with a heart-wrenching expression of deep feminine longing. Her hands were clasped so tightly that her knuckles had gone white. Her soft mouth trembled. "Simon, do you really believe that would be the result?"

Simon decided no woman had ever looked at him with such honest need. His whole body reacted to it with violent force. Desire swirled in his veins like a potent drug. Memories of the night he had brought her to her first shivering climax burned in his brain. *She was his and soon all that feminine heat and passion would belong irrevocably to him.*

"Yes, Emily, I believe that would be the result." Simon realized his voice was growing husky, his words thickening. "I assure you I have no objections to such an experiment, my dear. Shall we try it and see what happens?"

"Oh, *Simon.*" Emily flew around the edge of the desk and hurled herself into his arms. "My lord, you are so generous, so noble. I cannot believe I have been so lucky as to marry you."

Simon smiled into the red curls that peeked out from under the lacy white cap. Anticipation made him throb with desire. "It is I who am the lucky one, Emily."

"No, no, I am the fortunate one. I probably do not deserve a wonderful husband such as you, not after the way I ruined myself five years ago, but I have got you and I am so very grateful. It must be destiny."

"Very likely." He kissed her brow and gently removed her cap and spectacles. Her hair tumbled like fire around her shoulders. Then he kissed her eyelids. Her lashes fluttered like small butterflies.

"Simon?" She looked up at him, clutching at the lapels of his black brocade dressing gown.

"Hush, love. We've done enough talking for tonight. The time has come for us to learn to communicate in other ways." His mouth closed over her parted lips and he heard the soft little moan that caught in her throat.

Simon groaned softly as he let his tongue slide into the warmth of Emily's mouth. The hunger in him was so strong now that he could not think clearly. He vaguely realized that he ought to take his bride by the hand and lead her upstairs, but somehow her bedchamber seemed much too far away. He wanted her now. He had never wanted a woman with such intensity. He was on fire with his need.

And she wanted him. He could feel it. The sweet desire Emily was experiencing was causing her to tremble in Simon's arms. She was shaking with it and the knowledge that she was weak with longing for him made him feel incredibly powerful.

He unfastened her wrapper and slipped it off her shoulders. Emily made no demur as the garment pooled at her feet. Simon looked down and saw the small, dark circles of her erect nipples pushing against the fine muslin of the nightdress.

"You want me," he whispered against her throat.

"More than anything else in the world. I love you, Simon." She wound her arms around his neck and shyly kissed his jaw. "I shall be a good wife to you, I swear it."

"Yes, you will, elf. You most definitely will."

He eased her down onto the carpet in front of the fire. She went willingly, clinging to him and burying her flushed face against his dressing gown. Simon could hear the small catch in her breath as she shivered again.

"Are you cold?" he asked, stretching out beside her.

"No." She looked up at him quickly and then veiled her eyes behind her lashes. "No, the fire is quite warm. I am not cold, but I seem to be somewhat nervous, for some reason."

He smiled and slid his hand up under the hem of her nightdress. Then he bent his head and kissed the base of her

throat. "It is a very understandable reaction, under the circumstances."

"Do you think so?" Her gaze was anxious.

"It is just that you are not accustomed to this type of
communication on the physical plane."

"Are you?"

Simon was jolted by the question and even more startled
by his response. "No," he heard himself say thickly. It had
never been like this before in his life. The need had never
been so raw and uncontrollable. "No, this is new to me, my
sweet."

Her answering smile was tremulous. "Then we shall explore this strange realm together, voyagers on a mysterious
journey."

"Indeed we shall," he vowed.

His fingers shook slightly as he undid the ties of the
nightdress and slowly tugged it free of her body. He drew a
deep breath as he propped himself on one elbow and stared
down at the treasure he had uncovered. He was awed by the
graceful, womanly curve of her small breasts, fascinated by
the sensual flare of her hips, mesmerized by the sleek shape
of her legs.

"Emily, you are lovely." He reached out to trace the
rosy circle that crowned one creamy breast. Then he caught
the nipple between thumb and forefinger and rolled it gently
back and forth. It felt ripe and full, like a luscious berry
about to burst. Unable to resist, Simon bent his head and
captured the small fruit between his teeth.

Emily gasped aloud and arched herself against his
mouth. Her fingers clenched wildly in his hair. *"Simon."*

He was aware of the tension singing through her and he
gloried in it. His own body was clamoring in frantic response. His hand crept down over her hip, seeking the tight,
red curls between her legs. When he found the hot, flowing
honey he thought he would go mad. The raging hunger was
consuming him now. His entire body was on fire.

"Simon, I feel so strange."

Dazed, he raised his head and saw the new, languid sensuality in her face. Catching hold of her hand, he guided it

beneath his dressing gown. "I know, love. So do I. Touch me, Emily." He shrugged out of his dressing gown. *"Touch me."* He pushed her palm firmly against his engorged manhood.

Emily's eyes widened in shock and wonder. "Simon, are you all right?"

"No, but you will soon put me right." He kissed her lips reassuringly but he did not allow her to pull her hand away. "That feels so good, my sweet. Ah, yes, curl your fingers around me. Hold me." He moved himself slowly between her fingers, torturing himself until he thought he would go up in flames.

When she stopped trying to withdraw her fingers and instead seemed to grow intrigued by his body's response, Simon released his grip on her hand. Then he touched the silken skin of her thighs, tracing a random pattern that ended at the plump petals that guarded her secrets. Slowly he eased one finger inside the small, tight opening. At the same time he found the little nubbin of sensitive feminine flesh with his thumb.

Emily cried out and her hand tightened convulsively around his shaft. Simon sucked in his breath as his control cracked and fractured without further warning. It was then he realized he could not wait another minute. Her effect on him was too powerful. He would not humiliate himself by climaxing in her fingers, spewing his seed over her soft belly.

"Emily, 'tis time. God help me, I cannot wait." He rolled on top of her, reaching down to spread her thighs wide apart. He guided his shaft to her small, humid hearth.

"Simon?"

"Do you trust me, little one?"

"Oh, yes, Simon. I trust you completely." She looked up at him through her lashes, her arms wound around his back.

"I vow I will always protect you, Emily. Remember that. Whatever else happens, know that I will always take care of you."

"Yes, Simon."

Simon gazed down at her for a few seconds thinking he had never seen anything so wonderful as the sight of Emily hovering on the brink of her own passion. The tip of her tongue ran across the fullness of her lower lip. There was a lovely flush on her cheeks. Her body felt firm and resilient and amazingly erotic. He must be careful with her, he reminded himself. She was a virgin and he did not want to hurt her.

But his need to bury himself within Emily's warmth was overwhelming his senses. He parted her with his fingers, stretching her slightly before he pushed himself slowly into her. Then he was fighting to control the surging forces of his own body. Sweat broke out on his brow and dampened his chest.

"Simon?" Emily sounded confused. There was a different sort of tension gripping her body now, one based on trepidation rather than sensual anticipation.

"This first time may not be easy for you," he managed. "You are so small and tight."

"I am not sure I like this part, Simon."

He groaned. "Try to relax. Trust me, little one. Hold on to me and give yourself over to me."

"Do you really believe this will enhance our communication on a higher plane?" she asked with a touch of desperation.

"Yes. God, *yes.*" He could not hold back any longer. With a sharp, strong, thrusting movement, he surged deeply into her. Simultaneously he locked her close and his mouth covered hers, drinking the small gasp of astonishment from her lips. He felt her nails dig into his back.

"Bloody hell, Simon." Emily's eyes were squeezed shut. She was breathing rapidly and her whole body was trembling.

Simon willed himself to hold still for a moment, drawing in great gulps of air while he waited for Emily to adjust herself to the invasion. She did not move. It was obvious she was afraid to do so.

"Emily. Emily, my sweet, look at me," Simon pleaded. He was at the ragged edge of his control. "Did I hurt you?"

Her lashes fluttered and lifted. All traces of sensuality

were gone from her gemlike eyes. They had been replaced
with a brave, determined look. "Is it over?"

Simon swore softly. She was so small and slender and
soft. He felt big and heavy and awkward and he could not
seem to stop shuddering as he struggled to hold himself in
check.

"No," he muttered. "It is not quite over."

"That is . . ." she licked her lips, "unfortunate."

"Damnation, Emily. I have not managed this well. I am
sorry. I should have gone more slowly."

"That might have helped," she agreed breathlessly. "But
you must not blame yourself, my dearest Simon." She
stroked his back experimentally. "This sort of communication apparently takes a bit of practice."

Simon choked back an exclamation that might have been
either a laugh or a groan. He was not sure which. His senses
were straining like a team of blooded stallions under the
reins.

"Yes. Practice," Simon said. "We shall practice a great
deal, you and I." Cautiously, exerting every ounce of will-
power he could still summon, he began to move within her.
He eased himself almost all the way out of her tight passage
and then he forged slowly back into her.

Simon felt Emily wriggle hesitantly beneath him, trying
to accommodate herself to the strangeness of having a man
inside her. The small, delicious movement was too much. It
sent him over the edge.

"Emily, no, love. Hold still . . ."

It was too late. With a harsh, muffled shout, he was
pumping himself into her, crushing her into the carpet,
holding her as though he would never let her go. The heat
from the dancing flames on the hearth seemed to combine
with the warmth of Emily herself. Simon surrendered to the
overpowering climax, lost in a woman's body as he had
never been lost before.

For an endless moment he hovered in midair and then,
with a low groan, he collapsed on top of Emily. For a long
time he lay there, his body slick with perspiration, every
muscle relaxed. He was vaguely aware he had never felt so

utterly replete and satisfied in his life. Slowly he caught his breath and opened his eyes.

Emily was smiling tentatively up at him, her gaze full of curiosity and questioning wonder. "Well?" she demanded when she saw his lashes lift.

Simon stared down at her, feeling extremely dull-witted. "Well, what?"

"Did it work, do you think?"

Simon realized he had lost the thread of the conversation. He tried to concentrate. "Did what work?"

"Our experiment in enhancing metaphysical communication. Do you feel any closer to me now on the transcendental plane, Simon?"

"Good God." He blinked and slowly rolled to the side, wrapping her against his bare chest. For a few seconds he stared at the high ceiling, trying to clear his mind.

"Simon?" She shyly touched the hair on his chest.

"Hell and damnation, yes," he growled, thinking that metaphysical communication was the last thing he wanted to contemplate at the moment.

"I am glad," she said simply, putting her head down on his shoulder.

Simon looked at her red curls glowing in the reflected heat of the fire. *Like polished copper,* he thought. Then reality hit him full force. "This is our wedding night."

"Yes."

"Our wedding night and I just bedded you on the floor of the library. The *library,* for God's sake."

"I prefer to think that you just *made love* to me on the floor of the library," Emily said, yawning hugely.

"I must have taken leave of my senses." Simon sat up abruptly, running his fingers through his hair. "We should be upstairs in your bed. Or my bed."

"Do not fret, Simon. It does not particularly matter to me where we spent our wedding night." Emily smiled sleepily. "I can leave the details out of my journal, if you like."

"Good God. By all means leave the details out of your damn journal." He got to his feet and hastily donned his dressing gown. Then he reached down, tugged Emily to her feet, and dropped the muslin nightdress over her head. He saw that it was stained with the results of their lovemaking and the evidence of her virginity and he realized she must have been lying on the garment when he had taken her. He quickly tucked her into her chintz wrapper. A vague flicker of guilt washed over him.

"Emily, are you all right?"

She wrinkled her nose. "I feel sticky. And a bit sore. But otherwise I am fine. What about you? Are you feeling all right, Simon?"

"Yes, I am quite all right," he told her gruffly. He swung her up into his arms and started toward the door.

But he was not all right. He was feeling very strange and he did not like the sensation. *He had completely lost his self-control with this woman.*

That had never happened to him before. He should have been in command of the situation from start to finish. He ought to have handled the whole business with far more finesse. Instead he had been swept up into the vortex of a passion that had swamped his control.

Simon acknowledged grimly that his redheaded elf of a wife had been the one in command tonight, whether she knew it or not. She had led him a pretty dance from the moment he had found the note on her pillow. Simon wondered if she had any inkling of just how much power she had wielded this evening. Women were never slow to comprehend their own power and a Faringdon female would be quicker than most to take advantage.

But she was no longer a Faringdon, Simon reminded himself. She was his now.

"Simon"—Emily peered uncertainly up at him as he carried her toward the staircase—"are you angry?"

"No, Emily," he told her as he started up the red-carpeted steps. "I am not angry."

"You have a rather odd expression on your face." She smiled serenely. "I expect it is the aftereffects of our efforts to communicate on both the physical and the metaphysical plane simultaneously. Very fatiguing, is it not?"

"Bloody damn fatiguing," Simon said.

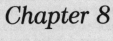

Chapter 8

Emily hurried expectantly downstairs to breakfast the next morning only to realize immediately that her lovely new morning dress of blossom pink had been wasted. Simon was not waiting to compliment her on the pleated neck frill or the embroidery on the skirt which the village seamstress had worked on so industriously. She was informed he had gone out riding quite early.

Deflated, Emily sat down and morosely watched a footman pour her coffee. Last night when Simon had carried her upstairs to bed and then gone to his own room she had been deeply disappointed. But she had told herself that was the way things were done in the fashionable world. Everyone knew couples rarely slept together for the entire night. Marriages of convenience led to relationships in which people demanded a great deal of privacy.

But even though she knew she was guilty of coercing Simon into a marriage of convenience, at least on his part, Emily had been certain that her relationship with him would be vastly different. Especially after what had happened last night.

Emily felt a small, transcendent thrill course through her again as the memories returned. She blushed now just thinking about how she had felt lying naked in Simon's arms in front of the fire. Her nerves tingled as she remembered the strange, mesmerizing glitter in her husband's golden eyes as he had crushed her into the carpet. It had been shocking yet oddly exciting to realize he had actually entered her, had become a part of her.

The experience was totally unlike anything she had ever imagined. Her senses had literally reeled beneath the onslaught. True, she had not experienced the thrilling sense of release that Simon had given her the first time he had caressed her intimately, but what had happened last night was far more profound. They had been joined into a single being for a time.

Simon had been quite right, Emily reflected as she sipped her coffee. Such a physical union was bound to enhance their union on the transcendental plane. It was inconceivable that anything so stunning, so powerful and overwhelming, could fail to affect events in the metaphysical world. There had to be a connection between the two realms.

Trust Simon to understand that and to nobly insist upon carrying out his husbandly duties in the name of metaphysical experimentation. He was obviously determined to make this marriage work. And Emily just knew that sooner or later he would come to love her as deeply as she loved him.

It was inevitable, especially now that their communication was being enhanced on the physical as well as the metaphysical level.

Still, accustomed as she was to eating breakfast alone, today the silence in the morning room seemed unexpectedly gloomy. She had no desire to linger. She was thinking wistfully that it would have been nice if Simon had invited her to ride with him when Duckett entered the room. His dour face was set in grave, disapproving lines.

"Your pardon, madam," Duckett said austerely, "but your father has sent a lad around to the kitchens with a message. It seems your presence is requested in the south garden."

Emily looked up, astonished. "My father? But he left for

London with Devlin and Charles directly after the wedding."

Duckett looked more bleak than ever, if such a thing was possible. "Apparently not, madam. I fear he is presently in the south garden."

"How odd. Why does he not come to the house?"

Duckett cleared his throat and said with a hint of satisfaction, "I believe his lordship, the earl, has forbidden your father to enter the house without his lordship's express permission, madam. I understand the arrangement was made yesterday after the services."

Emily's eyes widened in astonishment. She knew there was no love lost between her father and her husband. But a bargain had been struck that day when she had eavesdropped on the two men as they negotiated her future in the library. Simon had implied that if her father met his demands, Broderick Faringdon could continue to communicate with Emily. She was certain that was what had been agreed upon.

"There has been some misunderstanding," Emily told the butler.

Duckett chose to ignore that indisputable fact. "As to that, I could not say, madam. Shall I send someone to tell Mr. Faringdon that you are not available?"

"Good heavens, no, Duckett." Emily jumped to her feet. "I am quite available, as you can plainly see. Actually, I am glad to hear my father is still in the vicinity. I did not have an opportunity to bid him or my brothers a proper farewell yesterday. I was so very busy. I did not even realize my family had left for London until Blade mentioned it. And by then it was too late."

"Yes, madam." Duckett inclined his head. "I'll send Lizzie upstairs to fetch you a wrap. It is rather chilly outside today."

"Never mind, Duckett." Emily looked out at the bright April sunshine that was pouring through the morning room window. "I won't be needing anything. 'Tis going to be a pleasant day."

"As you wish, madam." Duckett cleared his throat. "I

realize it is not my place to say anything further on the subject, madam, but . . ."

"Yes, Duckett? What is it?"

"I was just wondering if madam has considered the, er, wisdom of meeting Mr. Faringdon in the south garden."

Emily laughed. "Good lord, Duckett, I am going to meet my father, not a paramour or a murderer."

"Of course, madam." Duckett's expression implied he questioned the assumption. "It simply occurred to me that perhaps his lordship might have certain notions concerning the propriety of the situation."

"Oh, for pity's sake, Duckett. You are not making any sense at all. We are talking about my father." Emily went around the table. She smiled reassuringly at Duckett as she went past him through the door. "Do not concern yourself with whatever Blade might have to say on the subject. He and I share a unique form of communication, you know. We understand each other very well."

"I see." Duckett looked unconvinced.

Emily paid no further attention to the butler's obvious qualms. Duckett had no way of knowing what had transpired between herself and Simon last night. Therefore he could not begin to comprehend the nature of the greatly enhanced metaphysical relationship Emily now shared with her husband.

Emily determined to clear up the misunderstanding at once. Simon would certainly never have barred her father from seeing her after the wedding. There was no need. The threat had been merely a negotiating tool that Simon had employed in an effort to exact justice.

The day was, indeed, turning out to be sunny, but there was a decided nip in the air. Emily had lived all her life in the country and she knew the signs. A storm was moving in. There would be rain tonight.

She glanced around the south garden with satisfaction as she made her way to the far end. Daffodils and early roses were starting to bloom in showy profusion and the air was filled with the heady perfume of flowers. A small, ornate fountain topped by a cherub with a watering pot formed the focal point of the garden. There was a tall hedge behind the fountain.

Broderick Faringdon was waiting behind the hedge. He emerged with a furtive expression, glancing quickly to the left and right.

"Papa." Emily smiled at her handsome father and hastened forward. "I am so glad you came back to say goodbye. I was very sorry to have missed making my farewells to you and the twins yesterday. There was so much going on and so many people around. It was a lovely wedding, was it not? Everyone in the vicinity was there and they all seemed so happy for me."

"Aye, Blade kept you busy enough, didn't he?" Broderick agreed darkly. "Ran you right off your feet, he did. Kept you dancing and drinking and visiting so that you wouldn't even notice when he sent your family away from you. Here I am, forced to creep around like a thief in the night just to say farewell to my one and only daughter."

Emily tilted her head to one side. "He sent you away? What on earth are you talking about, Papa?"

Broderick shook his head with an air of bitter sadness. "My poor, innocent girl. You still have no notion of what you've got yourself into, do you?"

"Pray, do not worry about me, Papa. I know what I am doing and I am quite content with my marriage."

Broderick gave her a sharp glance. "Are you? I wonder how long you will be content. I expect the damage is done, in any event, eh? Blade ain't likely to miss a trick."

"What damage? Papa, I wish you would explain yourself."

Broderick eyed her speculatively, a spark of hope in his gaze. "I don't suppose there's any hope that Blade left you alone last night, is there? Any chance of an annulment?"

Emily's face flamed. "Good grief, Papa. What a thing to say."

"Here, now. This is no time for maidenly blushes. This is business." Broderick looked even more hopeful. "Just tell me the truth, girl. Are you still untouched? Because if you are, it's not too late. We can see about having the whole thing overturned."

"Really, Papa." Emily's embarrassment turned to irritation. She drew herself up proudly. "I am not about to seek an annulment. I am a very happily married woman."

"Damn. Then there's no hope."

"No hope for what? What are you trying to say?"

Broderick sighed dramatically. "This is the end, my dearest child. Say farewell to your loving papa, for you will never see him again."

"Do not be ridiculous. Of course we shall see each other again. Simon and I will be going to London after our honeymoon. I shall have ample opportunity to visit with you and the twins. I shall very likely see more of you there than I did here at St. Clair Hall. After all, the three of you only came to visit when you were having a streak of bad luck at the tables."

"No, Emily. You still do not realize what a monster you have married. Blade is determined that you never have anything to do with your family again."

"You misunderstand him, Papa," Emily said quickly. "It was true he insisted on having St. Clair Hall turned over to him and used the threat of keeping me from you to enforce his demand. But he has achieved his goal. Justice has been done."

Broderick sank down wearily on the edge of the fountain. "You do not know him, Emily. Regaining the house was only the beginning. He will not rest until he has destroyed every last Faringdon."

"Papa, if you are worried about finances," Emily began slowly, "you need not be. I am quite certain that Blade will be content with his revenge now. He may not approve of me covering excessive extravagances on your part, but he will certainly have no objection to me continuing to manage your business affairs."

"Ah, my innocent lamb. You simply do not yet comprehend the nature of the beast you have been tricked into marrying. I, too, had hopes he would allow us to continue as before. T'was the only reason I agreed to his offer. But yesterday after he had you safely leg-shackled, he told me he did not intend to let you attend to any more Faringdon business matters."

Emily frowned. "I heard nothing about such a decision. I do not believe you understood him correctly, Papa. As I said, he will no doubt be somewhat restrictive regarding your financial excesses, but he would not cut you off completely."

"What a silly, naive little goose you are, my dear child." Broderick shook his head and then rose to his feet and held open his arms. "This may be the last time I shall ever see your sweet face again. Come and kiss your papa farewell. Remember me and your brothers with kindness, Emily. We truly cared for you."

Emily began to grow alarmed. "Papa, I do wish you would stop talking such nonsense."

"Goodbye, my dear. I wish you a happy life but I fear you are as doomed as the rest of your clan."

"You have it all wrong, Papa." Emily stepped uneasily back into her father's embrace. "I would never agree to be parted forever from my family. You know that. And Simon would never insist upon such a thing."

Broderick hugged her tightly as if he truly did not expect to see her again. Then he released her to look down at her with narrowed eyes. "Emily, if you truly mean not to abandon us—"

"Of course, I will not abandon you," she assured him impulsively. "I love you and the twins, Papa. You know that."

"If you mean that, if you intend to do your duty by us, then we must make some practical arrangements," Broderick said swiftly. "We must devise a way for you to continue to manage affairs and send instructions to Davenport. Now, I've been giving this some thought and I believe the easiest way to handle the problem is to arrange for regular, secret meetings."

"Secret meetings?"

"Precisely. Listen closely. Either I or one of the twins will find a way to contact you twice a month. You can relay instructions to Davenport on those occasions. We shall have to be extremely discreet, of course, but I think that can be managed, especially when you're in town. Much more opportunity there, what with the parks and the theaters and the pleasure gardens."

"But, Papa—"

"Don't fret, Emily. It will all work out," Broderick said cheerfully. "Blade's bound to lose interest in you quite soon. He's done the necessary and you ain't exactly his type, after all, are you? He just sees you as a means to an end."

"What end?" she demanded.

"Why, totally destroying us Faringdons, of course. But we'll deal with him. You'll soon find yourself on your own a great deal of the time and that will suit our plans perfectly, eh? Things will be just like they were before he showed up."

Emily opened her mouth to tell her father that her relationship with Simon was far more profound, far more blissfully transcendent than what he apparently imagined. But before she could explain, she was interrupted by Blade himself.

She stared in astonishment as Simon sauntered casually out from behind the tall hedge. Then she brightened. "Excellent, you are returned, my lord. Now, perhaps we can clear up this misunderstanding."

Simon ignored her, his eyes glittering coldly as he studied her father. "I had a hunch you'd show up sooner or later, Faringdon. Come to bid your daughter a fond farewell, have you?"

The earl looked very large and intimidating in his riding clothes. His shoulders were broad and powerful under his close-fitting jacket and his breeches emphasized the sleek muscularity of his body. He slapped his riding crop idly against the top of his gleaming black boots as he eyed Emily's father with disdain.

Broderick Faringdon swung around in alarm, his expression first startled and then angry. "Now, see here, Blade. A man's got a right to say goodbye to his one and only daughter. You certainly did not give me a chance to do so yesterday."

Simon smiled thinly. "I did not want you hanging around any longer than absolutely necessary. But today my sources inform me you spent the night at a nearby inn rather than on the road to town. I was not particularly surprised a few minutes ago when my new butler told me Emily had received a message to go to the south garden. But I am afraid I really cannot allow this sort of clandestine meeting, Faringdon."

Emily laughed with relief. "That is just what I was telling him, Simon. I knew you did not mean to bar him from the house. There is no need to arrange this sort of meeting when we can have a nice visit in the drawing room. But Papa seems to be under the impression you do not want him to ever see me again."

Both men looked at her with as much amazement as if the cherub on the fountain had just spoken.

Simon gazed at her coldly. "It will probably not be possible to avoid your father altogether, especially when we are in town. But you are never, under any circumstances, to meet with him or the twins alone. On those rare occasions when we do find ourselves obliged to see your family, I shall always accompany you. Do you understand that, Emily?"

"But, Simon . . ." She stared at him, taken aback by the implacable tone of his voice. "Surely, you go too far. There is no harm in my visiting with my own family."

"Damn right," Broderick said quickly, swinging back to confront the earl. "Damn it, we're her *family*, man."

"Not any longer. Emily has a new family now," Simon said. "And you may rest assured that as her husband, I will look after her and protect her from those who would take advantage of her."

"Damn and blast, Blade," Faringdon sputtered. "You cannot keep the girl a prisoner."

"No?" Simon slapped the riding crop against his boot again. He looked almost amused.

Emily did not like the atmosphere between the two men. It frightened her. She put her hand on her father's coat sleeve. "Papa, please do not argue with Simon today. This is my honeymoon. I am certain everything will work out. Perhaps it would be best if you left for London now."

"An excellent notion, Faringdon." Simon braced one boot on the edge of the fountain and ran the riding crop through his fingers. He managed to imbue the small, casual gesture with threatening implications. "Best take your leave. The gaming tables of London are waiting for you, are they not? It will be amusing to see how long you can hold on to your memberships in the St. James clubs."

"Damn you." Broderick looked stricken. "Are you threatening to have me thrown out of the clubs?"

"Not at all." Simon flicked a tiny speck of dirt off his breeches. "I could do so, of course. But there is no need to take such extreme measures. You will get yourself thrown out soon enough and so will your sons, when you are no longer able to pay your debts of honor. And when your luck has run out in the respectable clubs, you will be forced into the gaming hells, where your luck will run out even faster, won't it?"

"My God, man," Faringdon breathed, turning pale.

Emily was truly horrified now. It finally dawned on her that the antagonism between Simon and her father was much deeper than she had initially realized. "Simon?" she whispered hesitantly.

"Go back to the house, Emily. I will talk to you later."

"Simon, I would speak with you now."

"Do that, Emily." Broderick crammed his beaver hat more firmly on his head, his blue eyes bright with rage and frustration. "Reason with this monster you have married, if you can. But do not count on being able to soften him toward your family. He hates us all, even the twins, who never did him any harm. And if he hates them, he must also despise you. After all, you're just one more Faringdon."

"Papa, you do not understand."

"One more Faringdon," Broderick repeated savagely. "Consider that well, Emily, when he comes to you in the middle of the night and demands his rights as your husband. Contemplate it as you lay there with him rutting away on you like a stallion covering a mare."

Emily gasped in genuine shock. Her hand flew to her mouth, her eyes widening behind the lenses of her spectacles. No man had ever talked that way in her presence, not even the twins when they teased her.

"Get out of here, Faringdon," Simon said in a dangerously soft voice. He took his booted foot down from the edge of the pool. *"Now."*

"I wish you joy in the marriage bed, my dearest daughter," Broderick said sarcastically. He turned on his heel and left.

Emily wanted to call out to her father but she seemed to have lost her voice. She just stood there staring mutely after him and then Simon moved. He came to stand directly in front of her, blocking her view of her father's retreating back. His eyes were terrifyingly emotionless.

"Oh, Simon, he does not understand," Emily said softly.

"I would not be too certain of that." Simon took her arm and guided her back toward the house. "I believe he is finally beginning to understand very well, indeed."

"But he does not realize that our relationship is entirely different from what he imagines." She slanted a beseeching glance up at her husband's impassive profile. Silently she urged him to agree with her. "He is concerned for me because he does not know about our special form of union. He has not studied metaphysical matters."

"That I can well believe. The only thing your father has ever studied is a hand of cards. Emily, I think I should make it very clear to you that I meant what I said a few minutes ago. You are not ever to be alone with your father or your brothers. I am to be with you whenever you see them and those occasions will be kept to the minimum. Nor are you to send any further instructions to Davenport concerning their financial arrangements."

"Simon, I know you wanted revenge against my father, but surely you are satisfied with having regained St. Clair Hall. I know you threatened my father that you would not let him have access to me but surely you did not mean to carry out that threat. Not if you got the house."

"What makes you think I should be satisfied with having

the house back? Your father sold off all the family lands.
Nothing can replace the properties that were lost. And
nothing can make up for the fact that my father put a bullet
through his brain because of what your father did to him.
Nothing can make up for the fact that my mother went into
a decline and died because of your father's actions. Nothing
can make up for the fact that your father destroyed my
family."

Emily was stunned by the depth of rage and bitterness in
Simon's voice. He had never before revealed such intense
emotion. For the first time she began to realize Simon's feelings toward her family went far beyond a simple demand for
justice.

"I understand and I am truly sorry," Emily said quickly.
"You must know that. But it all happened a long time ago.
It concerns our parents, not us. It was the work of an earlier
generation. Now that you have St. Clair Hall back, you
must let go of the past. It will only continue to torment you
if you do not. Simon, you must look to the future."

"Really? And what, precisely, do you propose I contemplate when I gaze upon the future?" Simon asked dryly.

Emily took a deep breath. "Well, there is the matter of
our relationship, my lord," she suggested tentatively. "As
you pointed out last night, it has been considerably enhanced and deepened now by our physical union. We share
something very special. Surely you will want to let go of the
sadness of the past and concentrate instead on the joys of
our greatly expanded methods of communication."

He looked down at her, brows arched in icy amusement.
"Are you suggesting that I forgo the remainder of my vengeance against your family in favor of the joys of the marriage bed?"

Emily was increasingly uncertain of Simon's odd mood.
A deep foreboding swept over her as she peered up at him
through her spectacles. He looked very dangerous suddenly;
a dragon had invaded the south garden, a dragon looking
for prey.

"Last night," Emily said slowly, "you said that for us
the pleasures of the marriage bed would be unique. You told

me they would be connected to the pure and noble passions of the metaphysical realm. That our union took place on the transcendental plane as well as on the physical plane. Surely that sort of relationship is very special and should be nurtured and cherished, my lord?"

Anger crackled in Simon's golden eyes. "For God's sake, Emily, even you cannot be that naive. What took place between us last night had nothing whatsoever to do with any damn transcendental plane. It was a matter of simple lust."

"Simon, you cannot mean that. You yourself explained about the connection between the physical and the metaphysical realms." She blushed but did not lower her gaze. She knew she was fighting for something very important now. "Our passions are transcendent in nature. Remember how you described the way our lovemaking in the physical world was bound to enhance our communication in the metaphysical realm?"

"Emily, you are an intelligent woman in many respects. . . ."

She smiled tremulously. "Why, thank you, Simon."

"But at times you talk like a complete twit. I went through all that nonsense about the mystical connection between the physical and the metaphysical realms purely to ease your maidenly fears of the marriage bed. Perfectly normal fears, I might add, given your lack of experience."

"I was not afraid of your lovemaking, my lord. And I am not without some experience, if you will recall."

"Of course you were anxious," he snapped. "It was very obvious. Unanxious brides do not leave notes for their bridegrooms. They are waiting in bed where they are supposed to be. And as for your much-vaunted experience, my dear, it is a joke. You are hardly a woman of the world. If you had really had any notion of relations between men and women, you would have been waiting for me in your bed last night, not scribbling in your journal."

"But, Simon, I explained I was concerned for you. I did not want you to feel obligated in any way to perform your duties."

Simon slashed the riding crop through the air and severed the blooms from two daffodils. "Hell and damnation, woman. You were anxious about the unknown and in your anxiety you invented all that ridiculous, high-minded nonsense about not wanting to impose on me. The plain truth, Emily, is that you needed to be reassured and I told you what you wanted to hear."

She bit her lip. "So you lied to me about wanting to enhance our unique metaphysical communication?"

"Emily, I did what I had to do in order to calm your bridal fears. We got the business over and done in a reasonable fashion and there is now no chance of an annulment."

"That is all you cared about? Making certain there would be no grounds for an annulment this morning?" she asked softly. "You did not feel that last night we were both cast adrift on love's transcendent golden shore?"

"*Bloody hell.* For God's sake, woman, will you cease prattling on about romance and metaphysics? I have had enough of your romantical nonsense. This is a marriage, not a verse from an epic poem. It is time you faced reality. You are no longer a Faringdon. You are now my wife. We shall manage to deal comfortably with each other if you keep that fact uppermost in your mind at all times."

"I am hardly likely to forget it, Simon."

"See that you don't," he said, his golden eyes blazing. "Emily, it is time you understood that I require one thing above all else from you."

"You require my love?" A spark of foolish hope still burned within her, Emily realized with chagrin.

"No, Emily," Simon said brutally. "What I require from you—what I will have from you at all costs—is your complete and unwavering loyalty. You are now the Countess of Blade. You are a Traherne. You are no longer a Faringdon. Is that entirely clear?"

The last, tiny flicker of hope died. "You make yourself very clear, my lord."

Emily turned away from the man she loved with all her heart and walked alone toward the big house. She resisted the urge to glance back over her shoulder as she slipped through the door. Tears burned in her eyes as she hurried upstairs to her bedchamber.

She would have to leave, of course. Her dreams and hopes had all been shattered. She could not possibly stay here as Simon's wife. To do so would make a mockery of all her pure and noble passions.

It would be utterly unbearable to look at Simon every day and know that he felt nothing important for her. Even more unthinkable to have him come to her at night and, as her father had so crudely stated, rut on her like a stallion covering a mare.

The tears spilled through her lashes at that last thought. She had to get away immediately. Emily rushed into her bedchamber and began choosing the items of clothing she would take with her when she fled St. Clair Hall.

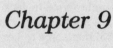

Chapter 9

Simon glanced again at the tall clock in the library as he paced back and forth in front of it. It was nearly six and Emily had still not come downstairs to join him for a glass of sherry before dinner.

He was beginning to realize that he had probably crushed her completely that morning. She was such a romantical little creature, completely addicted to happy endings.

Simon rarely lost his temper. He prided himself on controlling it as well as he controlled his other passions. But something had snapped inside when he had arrived home from his morning ride to discover that his new bride was already meeting Broderick Faringdon in a secretive fashion.

That news, coming as it did on top of the mixed emotions Simon had about his wedding night, had been more than enough to light the flames of rage.

Simon examined the golden sherry in his glass and recalled how Broderick Faringdon had boldly tried to talk Emily into secretly continuing to manage his business affairs.

The bastard. Did he really believe he could get away with such tricks? Simon wondered. Of course, he did. Far-

ingdons were a sneaky, conniving lot who would try anything they thought they could get away with undetected.
But their financial genius of a daughter belonged to him now
and Simon knew how to protect what was his.

He had enjoyed informing Faringdon at the wedding
that he had no intention of allowing Emily to continue making investments for her father and brothers. It had been
extremely satisfying to see the expression on his old enemy's
face when he had yanked back the lure he had dangled in
front of Faringdon for the past few weeks.

Typical of Broderick Faringdon to come nosing around
the very next day after losing his valuable daughter to see
what could be salvaged from the disaster.

Simon sighed. And typical of Emily not to have realized
that her new husband intended to make his vengeance complete.

*She'd actually had the nerve to tell him he should let go
of the past and work on forging a pure, romantic, transcendental union with her.*

The unfortunate part, Simon realized ruefully, was that
she genuinely believed all that nonsense about love on a
higher plane. She had badly needed a dose of reality and he
had finally lost his temper and administered it.

Still, it had been unkind of him to demolish her sweet,
romantical notions in such a heartless fashion. On the other
hand, he assured himself now, there had not been much
choice. After seeing Faringdon with her, Simon had been
forced to make Emily's situation crystal clear to her.

She was no longer a Faringdon. She was his wife now and
she had to know what that meant. It had precious little to
do with the romantic wonders of the metaphysical plane. It
had everything to do with giving her complete and unswerv-
ing loyalty to her husband. Simon saw no reason he should
not be able to command the same degree of loyalty from
Emily as he did from every member of his staff.

He glanced irritably at the clock again. Then he pulled
the velvet bell rope.

Duckett appeared almost instantly, his expression graver
than usual. "Yes, my lord?"

"Send someone upstairs to see what is detaining Lady Blade."

"Immediately, my lord." Duckett retreated and closed the library door.

Simon watched the clock as time ticked slowly past. He wondered if Emily was going to be one of those annoying females who collapsed in tears and took to their beds with their vinaigrette whenever a man showed them the edge of his temper. If so, she would soon learn he did not intend to allow such excessive displays of feminine sensibilities.

The library door opened. Duckett stood there looking as though he were about to announce a death in the family.

"Well, Duckett?"

"Sir, I regret to report that madam is not here."

Simon scowled and glanced out the window. "Is she fooling about in the gardens at this hour?"

"No, my lord." Duckett coughed tentatively. "My lord, this is rather difficult to explain. Apparently madam ordered the carriage this afternoon after you left to visit Lord Gillingham. I am told she went to see the Inglebright sisters. She sent Robby back with the carriage saying she would walk home but she has yet to return."

"Good God. What does she think she's doing discussing that silly romantic poetry with her friends today? This is her honeymoon."

"Yes, my lord."

Simon swore. "Send someone around to Rose Cottage and fetch her ladyship home."

Duckett coughed behind his hand again. "Sir, I fear there is more. Robby says that madam wore a carriage gown and took two rather large items of luggage with her."

Simon went cold. "What the devil are you trying to say, Duckett?"

"I believe, sir, that you may wish to interview her maid, Lizzie," Duckett said bluntly.

"Why would I want to do that?"

"The girl is crying in her room and she apparently has a note she has been requested to give directly to you."

Simon did not need any special mental powers to guess

that he was about to discover his bride of barely twenty-four hours had run off. "Get the maid in here at once, Duckett. And send around to the stables for Lap Seng. I shall want to leave within fifteen minutes."

"Yes, my lord. May I say, sir, that staff is extremely worried about madam's safety." The unspoken accusation hung in the air. It was obvious the new master of St. Clair Hall was being blamed for bruising madam's delicate sensibilities and causing her to run off.

"Thank you, Duckett. I shall inform her of that fact at the earliest opportunity."

Madam, Simon thought grimly as Duckett closed the door, *had better prepare herself to have more than her delicate sensibilities bruised when her husband catches up with her.*

How dare she leave like this? She belonged to him now. It was she who had made the marriage bargain. She could bloody well abide by it.

Emily stood in the middle of the tiny inn bedchamber, her pitiful collection of belongings at her feet, and nearly broke into tears all over again. She was exhausted, she was hungry, and she had never felt so lost and alone in her life.

Now she was going to be obliged to spend the night in this dingy little chamber that looked as if it had not been properly cleaned or aired in years. She was certain she could smell the acrid scent of masculine body odor emanating from the yellowed bed linens.

Emily had never traveled by stage before. She had been amazed at the discomfort involved. She had been squashed between a massively built gentleman who had snored the entire trip and a pimply-faced youth who had kept leering at her. Twice she had been forced to use her reticule to push his hand off her knee.

The only consolation was in knowing she would be in London the next day. Her father and brothers would no doubt be surprised to see her but Emily was certain they would welcome her with open arms. She was not looking forward to being told she had made a fool of herself, of course, but there was no help for it. She should have listened to her family rather than her foolish, romantic heart.

Emily leaned down and hoisted one of the heavy bags onto the bed. First things first. She was exceedingly hungry and she knew she must keep up her strength. Emily set about preparing herself for dinner in the inn's public dining room.

A few minutes later she went hesitantly downstairs, fully aware that ladies never traveled alone unless they were extremely poor. She was inviting trouble by appearing in the dining room without an escort or a maid. But there was no help for it. She could not bear to stay another minute in the wretched little bedchamber. Perhaps she would be invited to join another party of travelers, one that included ladies. She was, after all, a countess now.

The first person Emily saw when she glanced into the dining room was exactly what she was looking for, an attractive, well-dressed young woman of obviously good background. Emily heaved a sigh of relief. She would introduce herself, explain she was also alone, and ask to share the young lady's table. Everything would be fine.

The young woman was sitting alone by the fire in the small, uncrowded dining room. Emily approached cautiously and saw with a shock that the lady had a suspicious redness about the eyes which indicated a recent spate of crying. Her elegantly gloved hands were clenched tightly in the lap of her expensive traveling gown. Obviously there was more than one heartbroken female in the vicinity tonight.

"I beg your pardon, miss," Emily said hesitantly. "I see you are all alone and I wondered if perhaps you would care to share a table. My name is Emily Faringdon . . ." she paused and then added scrupulously, "Traherne." She did not feel it was necessary to inform the woman of her recently acquired title. She had only been a countess for a mere day and the truth was Emily did not feel like one at all.

The pretty young blonde, who could not have been much above nineteen, looked up with a start. Then a relief as great as Emily's own shone in her damp hazel eyes.

"Please join me, Miss Faringdon-Traherne," she begged. "I would be ever so grateful." She looked frantically about the empty dining room and then added in a very low voice, "My name is Celeste Hamilton."

"I am pleased to make your acquaintance, Miss Hamilton. Are you traveling to London?" Emily sat down across from her new friend.

"London? Dear God, no," Celeste burst out in a heartfelt wail. She began crying and quickly reached into her reticule for an already crumpled hankie. "I only wish that were the case. Oh, Miss Faringdon-Traherne, I am so miserable. I have made a terrible mistake. I fear I am bound for Gretna Green."

Emily was amazed. "You are running away to be married?"

"Yes." Celeste sniffed into the hankie.

"But you are all alone, Miss Hamilton. I do not understand. Where is your husband-to-be?"

"Seeing to the carriage and horses. There was an accident and a wheel came off. He will be back any minute. To tell you the truth, I was very glad when the accident occurred. I had begun to realize I had made a grave error in judgment. I saw the accident as a way to escape the situation."

Emily frowned. "But it did not work out that way?"

Celeste blew her nose daintily into the hankie and shook her head. "Nevil says we will continue on as soon as the wheel is fixed but we will not reach the border until tomorrow. I will be forced to marry him, come what may, as my reputation will be in ruins. What can I do? I realize now that I really do not love him." She sighed deeply. "To be perfectly truthful, I do not even like him very much anymore. He is not the man I thought him to be. But I will be tied to him for the rest of my life. And my parents will be so hurt. Oh, Miss Faringdon-Traherne, I would rather die than face what lies ahead of me."

"My dear Miss Hamilton. You have my deepest sympathy." Emily reached across the table and patted Celeste's hand. "I know exactly what you are going through. I understand everything, including the great tragedy of marrying the wrong man. But there is no need to worry. You are fated to be more fortunate than I."

Celeste looked at her with a distraught expression. "What do you mean?"

Emily smiled reassuringly. "Is it not obvious? I am here. You shall stay with me tonight and in the morning we shall travel on to London together. Your parents will no doubt be quite angry with you but your reputation will survive intact because it will be common knowledge that you had a woman companion with you overnight." She leaned forward and added conspiratorially, "I am actually a countess, you know. The Countess of Blade, which might be extremely useful under the circumstances. I shall be able to lend all sorts of countenance to this situation."

Celeste gazed at her with startled wonder in her eyes. "It was rumored he had married. You are truly the Countess of Blade?"

Emily nodded gloomily. "I was married only yesterday but the damage has been done."

"Dear heaven. I have never been introduced to Blade but I have heard my father speak of your husband. Blade is reputed to be very mysterious. I distinctly recall Papa telling Mama once that the earl was an extremely dangerous man to cross." Celeste confided softly, "Blade spent years in the East Indies and picked up strange notions, they say."

"Who says that?"

"The young ladies on the marriage mart, of course. They are all quite terrified of him. Especially Lucinda Canonbury, Lord Canonbury's granddaughter. She actually had the vapors once when Blade walked into a ballroom where she happened to be in the crowd. Fainted dead away, I am told. I suppose she thought he might ask her to dance."

Emily wrinkled her nose. "How silly. Blade would never dance with a female who was prone to the vapors."

"Lucinda Canonbury is not the only one who fears him," Celeste said. "Several young ladies have been known to admit that they were terrified Blade would make an offer for them and that their parents would be unable to refuse it.

Apparently Blade can be extremely intimidating. There will be great relief all around on the marriage mart when it is confirmed he is safely wed."

"Hah! Any relief expressed will be no more than sour grapes," Emily declared stoutly, not stopping to wonder why she felt obliged to defend the earl. "I'll wager all the young ladies were quite fascinated with him and will be secretly disappointed to hear he has married. In any event, please do not call me Lady Blade. I do not really feel like a countess. Call me Emily."

"But if you were married yesterday, where is your husband? Attending to the horses? Good grief, Lady Blade—I mean, Emily—you must be on your honeymoon."

"No," Emily said sadly. "My honeymoon is over. One night of transcendent bliss that ended at dawn." She hesitated and then added honestly, "Well, one night of *near*-transcendent bliss. I must admit the whole event was not quite what I had hoped it would be. But that is neither here nor there now."

"But why only one night?"

Emily thought swiftly. She realized abruptly she could not bear to humiliate Simon by telling Celeste the truth about him. "I fear a tragic twist of fate has parted us."

"Good heavens," Celeste whispered, suitably impressed. "How perfectly awful for you."

"Yes, it is, rather. But my misfortune shall be your salvation," Emily announced briskly, rallying instinctively to take charge of the situation. "You shall have a respectable female companion from now until you are safely back in the bosom of your family and all will be well with your reputation."

Celeste's lovely face started to brighten and then immediately crumpled again. "But there is Nevil to consider. You do not know him, Emily. Indeed, I did not know him, either, as it turns out. He is quite nasty and he has become most insistent on this marriage. I confess I must admit Father was right. Nevil was all along planning to marry me for the sake of my inheritance. And I trusted him."

Emily's heart ached with sympathy. "I know just how you must be feeling. But you must not worry about Nevil."

"You do not comprehend. He is quite strong and possessed of a terrible temper. I had no notion until the accident occurred just how vicious he could be. I am afraid of him, Emily. He will drag me away with him when he returns and you will not be able to stop him."

Emily shot a quick glance toward the door. "I have it. We shall both go straight upstairs to my room and lock ourselves in for the night. Perhaps I can persuade the innkeeper's wife to send up some food. Come, we must hurry before Nevil returns."

Emily got to her feet and went quickly toward the door. After a start of surprise, Celeste jumped up and hurried after her. Emily paused in the hall long enough to beg the innkeeper's wife for a cold collation and then both young women scurried upstairs to safety.

The food arrived a few minutes later. It was not particularly exciting fare, consisting as it did of two slices of game pie and some bread and cheese. Nevertheless, Emily and her new friend attacked it with healthy appetites.

The dreaded Nevil arrived shortly after the spartan meal had been consumed. A furious pounding on the locked door was the first indication that the man did not intend to be thwarted.

"Celeste, I know you are in there! What the devil is going on here? Come out at once," the man roared through the door.

"Go away, Nevil. I told you I no longer wish to marry you," Celeste called back. "You are not the man I thought you were."

"You damn well are going to marry me, you little bitch. I have bloody well not gone through all this trouble for naught. In any event, it is much too late to change your mind, you silly creature. You must marry me or you'll be ruined and well you know it. Come out of there immediately." Nevil began kicking the door with his booted foot.

"Dear God." Celeste stared at the shuddering door in abject horror.

"If you do not come out this minute, I shall have the innkeeper up here with his keys," Nevil vowed. The door trembled again under the onslaught of his boot. "Open up now, damn you, you stupid bitch."

Emily realized the door might not hold. She leapt into action. "Help me move this under the doorknob," she urged Celeste as she began dragging a heavy chair across the room.

Celeste grabbed for the chair as the pounding continued. She was nearly in tears again. Nevil hurled several threats about what he intended to do to her as soon as he was her husband and there was a great deal more shouting and kicking.

"Pay no attention to him," Emily said, panting, as she shoved the chair into position. She started to push a heavy chest next to the chair.

"He is going to break down the door." Celeste gasped, pale with terror.

"I do not think he can manage that." But Emily eyed the door uneasily. It did not look all that stout, even with the chair and chest in front of it. "Perhaps we should push something else in front of it," she whispered to Celeste.

"There is nothing else except the bed."

"Damn you, you bitch," Nevil yelled. "I shall take a horsewhip to you when I have you out of there. Do you hear me, you stupid little chit? A horsewhip, by God. We'll see how long you defy me after I've given you a taste of the lash."

And then a new voice cracked down the hall: dark, intimidating and totally in command. "What the bloody hell is going on here?"

Emily, who had grabbed a poker just in case the door gave way, swung around to stare at the locked door with a startled gasp. "It's Simon."

"Simon?" Celeste looked at her, confused and terrified. "Who is Simon?"

"My husband." Emily smiled in exultant relief. "Do not worry, he will take care of everything."

"But you said you had been tragically parted from him," Celeste reminded her.

"That's another matter entirely." Emily dismissed this problem with a wave of the poker. "The important thing at the moment is that he will take care of Nevil for you."

"He will?" Celeste looked extremely uncertain. "Why should he bother to do that?"

"Blade has a very noble and gallant nature," Emily assured her.

Nevil's voice rose out in the hall. "See here, this is none of your business, my good man," Nevil informed Simon in a very loud and aggrieved tone. "My fiancée has locked herself up in this room with some other female. I am not leaving until I have Celeste out of there."

"The other female in there with her, according to the innkeeper, is my wife," Simon said icily. "Get away from that door or I shall break your damn neck."

"Who the hell do you think you are to order me about?" Nevil squawked. "I will not tolerate any interference. I'm on my way to the border and I'll thank you to . . . What the hell?"

Emily brightened as she heard the startled squeak with which Nevil ended his question. It was followed by a yell and a loud crashing noise. Emily put down the poker and turned proudly to Celeste. "I told you Simon would take care of Nevil."

"Emily?" Simon's voice sounded astonishingly calm on the other side of the door. "Are you in there?"

"Yes, Simon, I am in here." Emily hurried toward the door.

"Open up at once. I have had enough of this nonsense."

"One moment, Simon," Emily called back, dragging the chair away from the door.

Celeste cringed. "He does not sound very pleased to have found you after being tragically parted from you."

"Details. In any event, if I do not open the door, you can be certain he will find a way to break it down in a much more efficient fashion than your Nevil did."

"Oh, Emily, you poor thing. He sounds a perfect beast."

"A dragon, actually." Emily was panting again with the exertion of moving the chair and the chest. She finally managed to clear them away from in front of the door.

Then she hastily unlatched the locks and a few seconds later yanked open the door with a triumphant smile. Simon stood there in a damp greatcoat, riding breeches, and mud-spattered boots. His expression was calm and totally controlled except for the banked flames in his golden eyes.

"Well, Emily?"

Emily did not hesitate. She hurled herself straight into his arms. "Simon, you saved us. I told Celeste you would."

Simon hesitated, clearly taken by surprise at his welcome. Then his arms went around her, squeezing her so tightly she could not breathe. Emily was swamped in the multiple capes of the heavy greatcoat for a minute or two. When she finally struggled free of them to glance down the corridor, she saw a young man lying crumpled and ominously still on the floor.

"Oh, excellent work, Simon." She looked up at her husband with glowing approval. "You certainly took care of that wretched man. Is he dead?"

Simon cocked a brow at her expectant expression. "You are a bloodthirsty little thing, are you not? Strange. I had not realized. No, he is not dead. But I do not think he will be kicking in any more doors for a while."

A new voice sounded from the top of the stairs. "Sir, sir, what is all this fuss about?" The innkeeper hurried forward, wringing his hands. "I run a respectable establishment. I cannot allow fighting in the halls. The other guests will be most annoyed by the noise."

Simon gave the small man a lethal look. "In respectable establishments young ladies of quality do not find themselves obliged to barricade their doors."

The innkeeper glanced nervously at Emily and then at Celeste, who was peeking out of the bedchamber. "Well, yer lordship, as to that, neither of these young ladies was traveling with a companion or a maid and I naturally had to assume they were not genuinely of the quality, if you take my meanin'."

Simon's glance grew even more dangerous. "You obviously made some very stupid assumptions. This lady is my wife and the lady with her is a friend. They had arranged to rendezvous here and wait for me. I was temporarily delayed by the weather. You may have noticed there is a severe storm going on outside."

"Yes, yer lordship," the innkeeper agreed immediately. "Coming down in buckets, it is."

Simon smiled thinly. "I expected my wife and her friend to be safe and comfortable here while I took care of other matters."

The beleaguered innkeeper looked more harried than ever. His anxious, darting glance went from Emily, who was smiling at him with a very superior sort of smile, to the silent, still Nevil. "I beg your pardon, sir. I did not properly understand the situation. Obviously there has been a mistake."

"Obviously." Simon nodded curtly toward the man on the floor. "I suggest you remove him at once."

"Yes, yer lordship, I shall see to it immediately." The innkeeper turned away to bellow down the stairs for his servant. "Owen, come up here and lend me a hand, boy. Hurry."

Simon glanced over Emily's head into the bedchamber where Celeste was hovering. His gaze narrowed thoughtfully. Then he looked down at Emily again. "Now, suppose you and your *friend* come downstairs at once and explain precisely what is going on here, madam?"

"Of course, Simon." Emily beamed. "It is really very simple."

"Somehow, I find that difficult to believe. Pray, do not keep me waiting long." Simon turned toward the stairs, the greatcoat swinging around him like an elegant cape.

"Yes, Simon. We will be right down," Emily called after him.

But he was already on the stairs and did not bother to acknowledge her obedience. Emily stepped back into the room and found Celeste gazing at her with huge eyes. The hankie in her hand was crushed into a mangled lump.

"What on earth is wrong now?" Emily asked.

"I fear your husband is quite angry," Celeste said weakly. "Perhaps he will blame me for getting you into this situation."

"For pity's sake, Celeste. Simon is not about to blame you. He is a very just and honorable man. We shall soon have it all sorted out. I think it would be best if we do as he instructed, however. Are you ready to go downstairs?"

"Yes. I suppose there is no help for it." Celeste dabbed at her eyes with the hankie. "I wish Mama were here."

"Well, she is not, so we shall have to muddle through on our own. You may leave all the explanations to me. I am very good at that sort of thing." Emily straightened her spectacles, shook out her skirts, and led the way toward the stairs.

Simon was waiting for them in a private parlor. He had removed his greatcoat and hat and was sitting in front of the fire, a mug of ale in his hand. He rose with grave politeness as Emily and Celeste entered.

Emily rushed to properly introduce Celeste, who looked more nervous than ever. There was a deliberate pause before Simon responded to the introduction.

"Northcote's daughter?" he finally murmured, his gaze hooded.

Celeste nodded mutely. Emily started to ask why she had given her last name as Hamilton, but Simon was speaking again.

"You were running off to Gretna Green?" he asked Celeste. "I imagine your father will have a few words to say about that."

Celeste looked down at the floor. "Yes, my lord. He probably will."

Emily frowned at Simon as she hugged Celeste reassuringly. "Do not worry, Celeste. Blade will talk to your father and all will be well."

"Will I, indeed?" Simon took a swallow of ale and eyed his wife over the rim of the mug. "Just what do you suggest I say to the marquess?"

Emily blinked. "Marquess?"

"Your new friend is the eldest daughter of the Marquess of Northcote."

"Oh." Emily considered that. "I believe I have heard of him."

"No doubt," Simon said dryly. "He is one of the richest and most powerful men in London." He glanced at Celeste. "And I presume he will be close on the heels of his fleeing daughter."

Celeste burst into tears once more. "Papa will never forgive me."

"Of course he will," Emily said bracingly. "I told you, Blade will explain everything."

"I have no particular interest in explaining anything to Northcote at the moment," Simon said. "As it happens, I am expecting a few explanations myself, madam."

Emily chewed on her lower lip. "Did you get my note?"

"Yes, madam, I got your note. We will discuss it later in private, however."

"Oh. Yes, of course." Emily was not certain she cared for the sound of that but before she could say anything further there was a commotion out in the hall. A few seconds later the door of the small parlor was thrown open to reveal a patrician-featured man in his mid-forties and an elegant, dark-haired woman dressed in an extremely fashionable traveling gown.

"Mama." Celeste broke into tears all over again and ran toward the dark-haired woman, who hugged her close. "Mama, I am so very sorry."

"My dearest daughter, I have been frantic with worry. Are you all right?"

"Quite all right, Mama, thanks to Lady Blade." Celeste pulled free of her mother's arms and smiled tearfully at Emily. "She saved me from a terrible fate, Mama. I owe her more than I can say."

The Marchioness of Northcote looked uncertainly at Emily. There was a certain watchfulness in her gaze. "I regret we have not yet been properly introduced, Lady Blade," she said somewhat stiffly. "But I have a feeling I am forever in your debt."

"Do not be ridiculous, Lady Northcote," Emily said cheerfully. "You are not at all in my debt."

Relief flickered in the marchioness's eyes. She glanced at her daughter again and then back at Emily. "All is well, then?"

"Quite well, madam." Emily chuckled softly. "Celeste has had an adventure, but there was no harm done and Blade took care of Nevil for you."

The Marquess of Northcote glanced sharply at his daughter and then he looked at Simon. He spoke for the first time, his eyes even more cautious and watchful than those of his wife. "Blade."

Simon inclined his head in a rather casual acknowledgment of the greeting. "Northcote."

"It would appear my wife is correct. We are apparently in your debt, sir."

"Not mine," Simon said coolly. "It was my wife who befriended your daughter and kept her out of that young rogue's clutches until I arrived."

"I see." Northcote closed the door and came farther into the room. "Would you mind explaining just what transpired here?"

Simon shrugged. "Why not? I was warned I would be stuck with the explanations."

"Are they that complicated?" Northcote gave him a searching glance.

"Not at all." Simon's expression was one of cold satisfaction. "I suggest you and your lady sit down, however, and order some ale. This may take a little time."

Northcote nodded, looking grimly resigned. "Peppington, Canonbury, and now me. You finally have us all where you want us, don't you, Blade?" he asked softly.

"Yes," Simon murmured. "You were the last. I shall consider you a wedding present from my bride."

Chapter 10

"I must say, Simon, you handled that brilliantly." Emily sat down in the chair near the fire and watched her husband as he locked the door of the bedchamber he had booked for the night.

Earlier he had taken one brief look at the room assigned to Emily and his mouth had tightened grimly. He'd ordered that a new chamber be prepared at once. The innkeeper had hastily retrieved Emily's possessions and moved them into the larger, more comfortable room.

"The thing is, Simon, you made it all sound so perfectly normal and matter of fact. Quite as if we had simply encountered Celeste on our honeymoon trip and had taken her under our wing."

The Marquess and Marchioness of Northcote had left for town a few minutes ago in their fast, comfortable traveling coach. If all went well they would have Celeste safely abed in her own bedchamber by early morning. It had been agreed that the simplest approach to the whole matter was to arrive home at dawn with their daughter as if they were all returning from a ball. No one would be the wiser.

"I am glad you approve of the way I dealt with the matter. I confess I am not as accustomed to inventing romantic tales on the spur of the moment as you are." Simon crossed the room and dropped languidly into the chair across from Emily. He stretched his booted feet out in front of the fire and regarded his runaway wife with a hooded gaze.

"Well, you certainly did a magnificent job," Emily assured him happily. "You even managed to figure out quite quickly what I had already told Celeste so that our stories meshed rather nicely."

"You dropped several useful hints, my dear." Simon's brows climbed. "Parted tragically on the morning after our wedding, were we? It was extremely fortunate for you that Lady Celeste did not inquire into the exact nature of the tragedy that had separated us."

"You have a point." Emily considered that closely for a moment. "I wonder if her mother will inquire."

"I doubt it. I do not think there will be any further questions from that direction. Northcote will accept my version of the story about being delayed with the carriage and sending you on ahead to get you out of the storm. He and his wife were far more concerned with their daughter's plight than with yours."

"Poor Celeste. At least she was saved from having to wed the wrong man." Emily brightened. "It was a marvelous rescue, Simon. Quite what I would have expected of you."

"You flatter me." Simon propped his elbows on the arms of the chair, laced his fingers under his chin, and fixed his wife with an unwavering gaze. "And now I think the time has come for you to make a few explanations of your own."

"Explanations?"

"I warn you, I do not wish to hear any of that nonsense you wrote in your note about broken hearts and broken urns. I have already read that particular poem, if you will recall. It was not one of your better efforts."

Emily's elation over the successful culmination of her adventure with Celeste faded rapidly under the implacable expression in Simon's eyes. She lowered her gaze to her hands, which were folded in her lap. "You once called that poem very affecting."

"Somehow it left a different impression this time around. Perhaps it was the circumstances under which I read it. Your maid was sobbing into one of my best linen handkerchiefs at the time. Duckett was hovering about like a mourner at a funeral. Mrs. Hickinbotham was ranting and raving about how I would undoubtedly find you shot dead on the road by a highwayman. Or worse."

Emily was momentarily diverted. "What could have been worse than being shot by a highwayman?"

"I believe Mrs. Hickinbotham had visions of you suffering a fate worse than death," Simon explained blandly.

Emily gave her husband a quick, accusing glance. "Some might say I already suffered that last night, my lord."

Simon surprised her with a faint smile. "Was it really that bad, Emily?"

She heaved a sigh. "Well, no, actually. As I told Celeste, it was a night of *near*-transcendent bliss."

"Good God," Simon muttered.

"I have been thinking about it a great deal and I have decided it was not entirely your fault that the experience was not what it should have been, my lord. After all, you did tell me you had never done that sort of thing before."

"Did I say that?"

"Yes, you did. So I imagine part of our problem was that we were both a bit inexperienced at creating transcendental unions and such. Bound to be a few problems in the early stages." She gave him a hopeful look. "Do you not agree, my lord?"

"It is very generous of you not to blame me entirely for failing to transport you to a higher plane, my dear."

Emily frowned, detecting sarcasm. "Yes, well, perhaps the problems with the physical portion of our union were not all your fault, but that does not excuse you for what happened later. You were most unkind and I left you that note with the lines from my poem about urns and such because I thought it rather apt."

"Apt? You get yourself embroiled in a potentially dangerous situation, we are miles from home on a wet and exceedingly unpleasant night, we are obliged to put up in a shabby little inn with bad food and worse beds, and all because you chose to indulge yourself in a fit of the sulks. Madam, let me tell you I did not find romantical references to broken hearts and broken urns at all apt."

"My heart *was* broken," Emily declared passionately. "You broke it this morning when you told me that last night had meant nothing to you."

"I did not say that, Emily."

"Yes, you did. You told me that what I took to be a transcendent union of like souls was nothing more than mere lust." All the resentment welled up inside her once again. "What's more, you were perfectly horrid to me simply because I had gone out into the gardens to say farewell to my father. I know he has his faults, but he is my father and you have no right to forbid me to see him or the twins."

"I did not forbid you to see them, Emily. I merely said you would not see them on your own."

"I cannot allow you to restrict me like that."

"You are my wife," Simon reminded her, his voice growing dangerously soft. "I have every right to restrict you in any way I feel is appropriate. The actions I have taken are for your own good."

"Rubbish." Emily flared. "They are to prevent me from continuing to manage my family's financial affairs. It is another element in your revenge plot and that is all there is to it."

"Your father has taken advantage of your business talents for years."

"What does that signify? You married me for those same talents. You only want to use me, too."

"You were the one who begged me to marry you," Simon said through set teeth. "Or have you forgotten so soon how you bargained with me that day by the stream? You have gotten what you wanted, Emily. You are now my countess. You must abide by the terms of our agreement."

Emily's fingers twisted together as she looked at her husband in defiant anguish. "I did not realize you meant to cut my family off completely from me."

"It is only the financial connections I am severing completely."

"But you allowed my father to think you would not cut him off entirely," she reminded him.

Simon smiled coldly. "Yes, I did dangle that lure for a while. It made everything so much easier, you see."

"You are taking your vengeance too far, my lord."

"You, my sweet, know nothing about vengeance."

"And you do?"

"Oh, yes," Simon said softly. "I have spent twenty-three years dreaming of it. Now, I have had enough of this topic. My notion of revenge need no longer concern you. You are my wife and you will henceforth conduct yourself in a manner befitting your title as Countess of Blade. Is that quite clear, Emily?"

Emily's heart sank. "What if I do not wish to be your countess any longer?"

"That is most unfortunate because it is too late to change your mind. You surrendered to your romantic impulses and excessive passions, my dear, and now you must pay for the experience."

"But, Simon, we shall both be so grossly unhappy if we continue as we are. Surely you must see that."

"Nonsense," Simon said heartlessly. "There is no reason this marriage should not work very well. If I had not reached that conclusion several weeks ago, I would not have gone through with it. You will make me a suitable countess once you have settled down to the business. In any event, there is no going back. An annulment is out of the question and I will certainly not allow you to contemplate a divorce. I know you treasure your scandalous past, but a divorce would be too much even for you to handle. And I, of course, have my title to consider."

"Yes, of course." Emily studied her clenched hands, aware of a guilty sense of relief. A divorce was naturally out of the question. She was bound to Simon for the rest of her life.

The rest of her life. Emily's mood began to lighten. Much could change in a lifetime, she told herself with renewed optimism, including a man's attitude toward his wife.

Simon's gaze grew even more stern. "Now, listen well, Emily, because I do not wish to find myself forced to chase after a runaway wife again. There will be no more haring off for parts unknown whenever you happen to feel unsatisfied with your lot in life. There will be no more miserable little poems left behind with your maid. I am prepared to grant you a fair amount of freedom but you will obey the few rules I do impose, the principal one being that you are not to see any member of your family unless I am present. Do I make myself clear?"

Emily eyed him through lowered lashes. "Very clear, my lord. It all sounds perfectly horrid. Not at all what I had envisioned marriage to you would be like."

Simon's mouth curved faintly. "You must look on the bright side, my dear. You are a creature of excessive passions. Now you are free to indulge those passions. Concentrate on that end of things and the rest will fall nicely into place."

That was too much. Emily was incensed by the condescending words. "Elias Prendergast once offered me the same opportunity. I was not interested then and I am not interested now. I can restrain my excessive passions until such time as they can be indulged with someone who is capable of a truly noble, spiritual, and metaphysical connection."

All signs of complacency vanished from Simon's expression in the blink of an eye. The dragon's golden gaze was suddenly ablaze. "I am well aware that married women of the *ton* frequently conduct affairs, but you will not even contemplate a liaison with another man. Understand me well, Emily. I do not share what is mine and as of last night *you are most definitely mine.*"

Emily eyed him uneasily. "Celeste said you had picked up strange notions living in the East."

"If it is any consolation, I have always been inclined to guard what is mine. Living in the East only served to teach me various ways of doing so more thoroughly and efficiently."

Emily believed him. She was not particularly alarmed, however, as she certainly could not envision making love with any other man except Simon. "You need not fret, my lord. I was not so overly impressed with what we did last night that I would immediately seek out the experience with anyone else."

The dangerous fire in Simon's eyes faded. It was replaced with a distinctly annoyed expression. "I promise you that you will enjoy it more next time."

Emily chewed thoughtfully on her lower lip and narrowed her eyes mutinously. "Since we are on the subject, my lord, I may as well tell you that I am not interested in trying it a second time."

Simon looked away from her. He reached out, seized the poker, and began stoking the flames on the hearth with stabbing motions. "As I said, you will soon feel differently about the matter."

Emily gathered her courage. "No, my lord. I do not think so."

Simon glanced at her over his shoulder. "What do you mean by that?"

"Simply that I do not wish to have you make love to me again," Emily said bravely. She was determined on her course of action now. She knew what she had to do. "That is, not unless certain conditions are met."

"Emily," Simon began ominously, "I realize you are in something of a state because of your recent adventures, but I warn you, I will not tolerate—"

She held up a palm to silence him. "Pray, allow me to finish, my lord. I do not want you to make love to me again until we have truly established a pure and transcendent relationship, the sort of relationship I believed us to have when I asked you to marry me. You are not to trick me into lovemaking again, Simon, do you understand?"

"I did not trick you into lovemaking," he said through his teeth. "I explained to you that I merely eased your normal, maidenly wedding night anxieties. Some would say I behaved like a very thoughtful and concerned husband."

"Rubbish. You tricked me. And you will not do so again. That is final."

Simon's eyes gleamed dangerously, reflecting the flames on the hearth. And then he appeared to relax slightly, like a hunter who is content to lie in wait before pouncing on his quarry. "Very well, madam."

Emily was nonplussed by his ready acceptance of her mandate. "You agree you will not force yourself on me?"

Simon shrugged. "I have no particular interest in forcing myself on an unwilling wife." He put down the poker and sat back. His fingers drummed briefly on the arm of the chair. There was a lengthy silence and then his mouth curved coldly once more.

Emily did not like the looks of that smile. "What are you thinking, my lord?"

"Merely that I am content to wait until you come to me, Emily. In fact, I believe it will be infinitely preferable that way." He nodded, as if confirming some private conclusion. "Yes. Much better."

Emily hesitated, wondering if she had overlooked some glaring hole in her clever plan. Simon's acceptance of it was much too quick. "What if I do not come to you, my lord?"

"You will. And very soon." Simon got to his feet and poured two glasses of sherry from the decanter on the table. "I do not believe I shall have long to wait, you being a creature of excessive passions, and all. You are intelligent enough to know very well that while last night might not have lived up to your romantic expectations, there is more to be discovered on the physical plane. Surely you have not forgotten your experience that night I sat you down on the library desk, parted your thighs, and introduced you to your own passionate nature?"

Emily blushed and looked away. "No," she admitted quietly. "I have not forgotten."

"Imagine how it would have felt to go through that same rush of sensations with me buried deep inside you," Simon said deliberately. "Think about how much more truly *tran-*

scendent the experience would have been. How very meta-physical. How stimulating to all your sensibilities. How damn exciting. Because, my dear, that is what it will be like the next time we make love. You have my personal guarantee on the matter."

Emily was suddenly feeling much too warm and she knew it had nothing to do with the heat from the fireplace. "You are trying to trick me again. Simon, I do not want to discuss this. I have made my decision and I insist you honor it."

"By all means, madam." He began to pry off his boots. "Not another word on the subject until you come to me and ask me very nicely to show you what you are missing and how much you have left to experience."

"Do not hold your breath waiting for that event, my lord," she shot back.

Simon started to unfasten his shirt. He smiled with a hunter's anticipation. "My sweet, rest assured you will not merely ask for it next time, you will beg me to bed you."

"Never," she vowed, driven to rashness by Simon's cool, masculine certainty.

"A woman of excessive passions should be very careful about making such sweeping statements."

"I will make any sort of statement I wish. Simon, what are you doing?" Emily's eyes widened in shock as he stripped off the linen shirt and slung it carelessly over the back of the chair.

"Getting ready for bed. I have had a very hard day, my sweet, as you well know." He started to unfasten his breeches.

"But I have just told you, I will not make love with you."

He nodded. "I heard you. I intend simply to go to bed and sleep as best I can on that lumpy-looking mattress. In the morning I shall hire a post chaise to take us home as soon as possible. I have no wish to spend any extra time here at this depressing inn."

"You are going to sleep on the bed?" Emily looked

around, fully appreciating her surroundings for the first time. "Simon, there is only one bed."

"It is big enough for both of us." He started to step out of the breeches. Firelight gleamed on the sleek contours of his back and buttocks.

Emily stared, utterly fascinated, at the sight of her husband's lean, hard body. He stood with his back to the fire as he undressed but in the shadows she could see that he was half aroused. His manhood jutted boldly from its thicket of crisp, black hair. She remembered touching that broad staff last night, remembered the instant response of his flesh. She remembered, too, the way he had used that part of himself to forge a path into the very core of her being.

"Is anything the matter, Emily?" Apparently oblivious to her longing gaze, Simon strolled across the room to the bed and pulled back the covers. He got in and folded his arms behind his head on the pillow. "Well?"

Emily touched the tip of her tongue to her dry lips. "No. No, there is nothing the matter." She yanked her spectacles off and put them on the table. It was better not to be able to see too clearly at the moment. She jumped to her feet and began pulling a footstool into position in front of the hard wooden chair.

"What are you doing?" Simon asked, sounding curious.

"It is not obvious? I am preparing myself a place to sleep tonight." She stalked over to the bed, grabbed a blanket, and stalked back to the chair. Then she sat down, propped her feet on the stool, and arranged the blanket over herself.

"That chair is going to be very uncomfortable by morning. And when the fire dies, this bedchamber will get exceedingly cold," Simon warned.

"I do not expect to be comfortable, my lord. I expect to suffer. I shall consider it a punishment for my crimes of bad judgment and worse luck." Emily blew out the candle and settled down to ponder her wretched fate.

Half an hour later, Simon, who had been kept awake by a series of small, restless, miserable little noises from the vicinity of the chair, lay gazing up at the ceiling. The fire was now a mere pile of glowing coals but there was just enough light to reveal Emily's small form huddled under the blanket. She was no doubt freezing and Simon told himself he had no wish to have her get sick. An ailing wife would be a genuine nuisance.

He contemplated the best way to get Emily into the warmth of the bed. He was well aware it was only her pride keeping her in the chair. But pride was a very powerful thing, as he knew from personal experience. Sometimes it was all one had.

There was no need for Emily to suffer unduly tonight, Simon decided. Her feminine pride was due for a major blow soon enough. It would come when she was forced to finally admit defeat in this small war she had instigated.

He regretted having to set her up for the humiliation she would face when she finally surrendered. But there was no help for it. She would have to learn the hard way that he intended to be master in his own home and in his own bed.

In any event, it was Emily who had drawn the battle lines when she had made that rash vow not to grant him his rights in bed. Apparently there was still enough Faringdon in her to lead her to believe she could manipulate him, Simon reflected grimly. He would soon eradicate that element in her nature. They would both be happier and more content once Emily had accepted her new role in life.

In the meantime Simon decided he had no wish to listen to any more squirming about in the chair. He opened his mouth to order Emily over to the bed. But he was interrupted before he could speak.

"Simon?" Emily's voice was a soft, tentative thread of sound in the darkness. "Are you asleep?"

"No."

"I was just wondering about something."

Simon smiled to himself in satisfaction. Even better, of course, if she made the first move tonight. Would she ask straight out to join him in the bed or try the more subtle tactic of telling him she was cold and needed to get under the covers? he wondered. Either way he would make it easy for her.

"What were you wondering about, Emily?"

"Did you really cause Lucinda Canonbury to have a fit of the vapors when you entered a ballroom?"

"What the devil are you talking about?" Simon glowered at the figure in the chair.

"Celeste says that's what happened in London. She says all the young ladies on the marriage mart, including Lucinda Canonbury, were quite terrified of you and of the possibility that you would make an offer of marriage."

"I never noticed any of the silly chits having the vapors when I walked into a ballroom," Simon muttered. He had been informed, of course, that the Canonbury girl had fainted, but he had not actually noticed at the time. The ballroom had been quite crowded.

Emily giggled in the darkness. "I told Celeste it was all a lot of fustian. I am quite certain all the young ladies on the marriage mart were completely enthralled by you and you probably piqued them terribly by failing to even notice them."

It occurred to Simon that Emily still apparently had no real inkling of the reputation he enjoyed in town. As usual, she had romanticized the situation.

"You are quite right," he said evenly. "It is all a lot of nonsense." A thought struck him. He toyed with it for a moment and then made his decision. "Emily, would you like to go to London?"

"Oh, yes. Very much. But do you think I ought to do so? Papa always said I must not go into town too frequently lest someone mention the scandal in my past. I would not want to embarrass you, Simon."

"There is no longer a scandal in your past, Emily."

"There isn't?" She sounded confused.

"No. I have informed the few people, including Lord and Lady Gillingham and Prendergast, who know something of your little adventure five years ago that it is never again to be mentioned. That goes for you, as well. As far as you are concerned, Emily, there was no scandal."

"But, Simon—"

"We will not discuss it. There is nothing to discuss. And if anyone attempts to discuss it, you are to tell me immediately. Do you understand?"

"Yes, but, Simon, I really think—"

He softened briefly. "I know you cling to the memory of the Unfortunate Incident as one of your life's more thrilling moments, but I believe I can provide you with even more exciting moments to remember."

"Well, I thought so, too," she said candidly. "That is why I asked you to marry me. But now I am not so certain. I seem to have made a large mistake."

"Your only mistake, my dear, is in thinking you can manage me the way you manage your business affairs. I am not so easily controlled, madam."

"What a ghastly thing to say."

"It is the truth. But we shall soon remedy the problem. You will come to me and apologize very prettily for setting yourself against me. Then you will plead with me to take you back into my bed and that will be the end of it."

"Bloody hell, it will."

"I believe we were discussing a trip to London."

"We were discussing your insufferable arrogance," she retorted.

"We shall leave for town as soon as practicable."

"Why?" Emily demanded. "Why must we suddenly rush off to London?"

"Because," Simon said, thinking of the profound gratitude of the Marquess and Marchioness of Northcote, "I believe this would be a most opportune time for you to enter Society." Northcote, like Peppington and Canonbury, was now vulnerable at last. The marquess could be useful and Simon fully intended to use him and his lady to introduce Emily into Society.

Emily was silent for a long moment. "Do you really think so, Simon?"

He smiled again to himself. "Yes." He pushed back the covers and stood up. "Now, I find I am getting quite cold and uncomfortable. I must insist you come to bed and bring that blanket with you."

Emily sat up in alarm as he moved toward her, clutching at the blanket. She peered warily up at him in the shadows. "I have told you, I will not allow you to make love to me, Simon."

He reached down and scooped her out of the chair. "You may relax, my dear. This is a matter of practical comfort and health. I gave you my word I would not force myself on you." He stood her on her feet and began methodically and efficiently stripping off her clothing.

"Hah! Do you think I will beg you to make love to me once you get me into your bed?" she challenged as she batted ineffectually at his hands. "Do you believe I am so weak-willed?"

"You are not weak-willed, my sweet." Simon dropped the carriage gown over the chair, leaving Emily in only a thin muslin shift. "You are high-spirited, passionate, and impulsive. It is not at all the same thing."

Emily stopped slapping at his hands and looked up at him, squinting to see his face more clearly. "Do you really think so, Simon?"

He grinned briefly as he picked her up and carried her over to the bed. "I am quite certain of it, my dear. And even though you are presently annoyed with me, I know you would not wish me to freeze to death tonight. As we cannot both use the blanket unless we share the bed, we have no choice. You must join me."

Emily sighed in resignation and slithered quickly under the sheet. She lay rigidly on the far right edge of the bed, staring up at the ceiling as Simon got in beside her. "Very well. For the sake of our health, I will agree to share the bed. But you are not to make love to me, Simon."

"Do not concern yourself, Emily. I shall not pounce upon you in your sleep. I am content to wait until you come to me."

"That will not happen until I am convinced that what you feel for me is akin to what I felt for you until you broke my heart last night," she vowed.

"We shall see, madam wife. In the meantime, I suggest you get some sleep. You have had a very busy day."

"It was all rather exciting," she admitted, yawning. "I must say, it was very romantic of you to come after me the way you did. I feel there is hope for us, Simon."

His jaw set. "Because I followed you? Do not pin too many romantical hopes on that fact. I came after you because you belong to me and I keep what is mine. Do not ever forget that again, Emily."

There was silence from the other side of the bed. Simon waited for some acknowledgment of his stern admonition. When none was forthcoming he turned on his side and looked at Emily.

She had fallen fast asleep.

Simon watched her in the shadows for a moment and then he carefully gathered her close. Without waking, Emily snuggled against him as if she had slept in his arms for years.

A few minutes later, Simon, too, fell asleep.

Chapter 11

Simon looked up from the papers on his desk at the sound of loud commotion out in the hall. Apparently his aunt and Emily had returned from their shopping expedition. Curious about the results of the foray to Oxford Street, Simon stood up and crossed the lair full of jeweled dragons. He opened the library door and smiled in amusement at the sight that greeted him.

The two footmen were hastening to fetch a vast quantity of parcels from the carriage that stood at the bottom of the steps. Emily, dressed in one of the pastel morning gowns she had brought with her from the country, was dashing about giving orders in an excited voice. Her red curls were partially concealed under a flower-trimmed straw bonnet and she had her spectacles perched slightly askew on her nose.

Lady Araminta Merryweather stood aside to watch the scene, obviously as amused as Simon.

"Please take it all straight upstairs," Emily said, inspecting each package as it came out of the carriage. "Tell Lizzie she is to unpack everything immediately. I shall come up at once and just make certain all is in order. Oh, do be careful with that, Harry. It's the most beautiful parasol you have ever seen. It's got little green and gold dragons all over it."

"Aye, ma'am," Harry said, giving his mistress a broken-toothed grin that had been known to make grown men flee in terror. "No need to sass. I'll look after it as if it were something I'd snaffled for meself."

There were a few other things broken and missing on the beefy ex-pirate besides some teeth. The list included a broken nose that had never healed properly and a missing left hand that had been replaced by a vicious-looking hook. Due to the footman's unpredictable effect on visitors, Greaves did not allow him to serve at the dinner table on the rare occasions when Blade entertained at home. But when the butler, on Simon's orders, had cautiously assigned Harry to serve the new lady of the house, Emily had been completely unperturbed by the hook. Harry had been won over instantly.

"Thank you, Harry. That is very kind of you." Emily gave the footman a brilliant, grateful smile.

Simon watched Harry blush and stammer like a schoolboy and wondered fleetingly if Emily understood that *snaffled* was thieves' cant for *stolen*.

Emily turned a delighted face toward Lady Merryweather. "I have had an absolutely thrilling morning, Araminta. How can I ever thank you?"

"It was my pleasure, Emily." Araminta stood back as an especially large box was brought into the hall.

"Gracious, do have a care, George," Emily instructed the other footman as he carted a parcel up the steps and through the door. She hurried over to check anxiously on the condition of the box. "It came from Madam Claude's and it is the cleverest little hat in the world." She caught sight of Simon lounging in the doorway and her eyes brightened. "Wait until you see it, my lord. The hat is *a la militaire,* and I have ordered a beautiful riding habit to accompany it. It will have epaulets and frogging and all sorts of military details and it will be positively dashing."

"I look forward to seeing you in it," Simon said gravely.

George, the footman, a hatchet-faced individual who had led a boisterous life on the rough docks of the Far East, headed for the stairs cradling the precious hatbox as if it were a baby.

Emily spotted yet another parcel being unloaded and scurried forward to supervise. "These are my new half boots," she told Simon over her shoulder. "I also bought several pairs of slippers and pumps. It was a fearful expense but your aunt said I must have a different pair for every gown."

Simon folded his arms across his chest and cocked a brow at his fashionable aunt. "Lady Merryweather would know."

Araminta gave him a serene smile.

"I also got several fans and four new reticules," Emily called back over her shoulder as she flew up the stairs. "I shall be down in a few minutes."

She vanished at the turn on the landing, the pale skirts of her gown sailing out behind her.

Araminta gave Simon a laughing look as he ushered her into the library. "She is charming, Simon. Utterly charming. And she will be quite an original when she is properly dressed. She still needs to be reminded to take off her spectacles when she is in public, and those red curls need taming with a pair of shears, but I can already predict the end result will be quite spectacular."

"I leave it all in your hands, Aunt. But see that she is not allowed to put any of those foul concoctions made of mercury water, lead, or sulfer on her face in an effort to cover up the freckles."

"You need not worry. I am a great believer in homemade cosmetics made from herbal ingredients. I take it you like the freckles?"

"Yes," said Simon. "I do."

Araminta chuckled. "I should have guessed that when you finally chose a wife, you would pick something quite out of the ordinary. I still cannot believe she is a Faringdon."

"She is not a Faringdon. Not any longer." Simon closed the door very firmly and crossed to his desk.

Araminta gave him a sharp glance as she sat down on one of the ornate black lacquer chairs and stripped off her gloves. "She seems to think she is not yet entirely your wife, either. Where does that leave her?"

"She said something about not being my wife?" Simon asked sharply.

"Not precisely. Just something to the effect that she does not feel in total harmony with you yet. I believe there was some vague comment about the two of you existing on different celestial planes at the moment or some such nonsense. What on earth is going on, Simon?"

Simon relaxed. "Nothing that need concern you. Emily often expresses herself in rather odd ways. She is very fond of romantic literature."

"I have noticed. I heard a great deal about an epic called *The Mysterious Lady* which she is apparently working on. Have you read it?"

"I am told it is not yet ready to be read," Simon said dryly.

"She is quite amazing, you know. She already knows the names of everyone on your staff and they obviously adore her. Perhaps you should caution her against becoming too familiar with this band of cutthroats and rogues you brought back with you from the East."

Simon was unconcerned. "Everyone on my staff understands that he would answer directly to me if he so much as looked at her in an improper fashion. In any event, none of them is about to harm a single hair on her head. She has already started to discuss several investment schemes for them with my butler. They are all quite fascinated by the notion of making so much money legally."

"Good heavens. Investments? For staff?"

"Yes, I know. It is quite a novel thought, is it not?"

Araminta shook her head in wonder. "As I said, a complete original. Wait until you see the gowns she had ordered, Simon."

"She appears to favor modestly cut gowns and soft, pale shades," Simon said, reflecting with approval on Emily's country wardrobe.

"Not any longer." Araminta grinned. "Henceforth she might as well be wearing your livery when she goes out in public, Simon. Everything we ordered today is to be made up in what she calls dragon colors."

Simon looked at his aunt. "Dragon colors?"

"Gold, green, black, and red, for the most part." Araminta glanced around the exotically decorated library. "I cannot imagine where she got the notion for such unusual hues. And all the motifs for embroidery, trim, and jewelry design are going to appear quite familiar."

"Dragons?"

"For the most part. Emily has decided upon her own personal style and she apparently plans to immerse herself in it." Araminta gave Simon a speculative glance. "As I said, she might as well be wearing your livery or flying a flag that proclaims her your personal property. You do realize, of course, that everyone will be bound to notice?"

Simon smiled with satisfaction. "I see no problem in that. Araminta, can you have her ready for her first ball by Friday?"

Araminta straightened alertly in her chair. "I believe so. Have you begun receiving invitations already?"

Wordlessly Simon handed her the card that had arrived that morning. He watched the startled look appear in his aunt's eyes when she read it.

"The Marquess and Marchioness of Northcote's ball," Araminta breathed in awed tones. "Simon, this is wonderful. What a coup for us. It is the perfect place to introduce Emily to the *ton*. Once it is known she has been entertained by Lady Northcote, all doors will be open to her."

"It should serve its purpose," Simon agreed laconically.

"It certainly will serve to launch Emily properly. But, Simon, how did this come about? You and Northcote are hardly friends. Not after what happened all those years ago. Why would his wife undertake to introduce your wife to Society?"

"Through a rather odd circumstance, their daughter and Emily have become fast friends. In addition, the marquess and his lady find themselves grateful to Emily."

"Grateful? Simon, what is going on here?"

"I am merely arranging for my wife to make a comfortable entrance into Society. If Northcote had not made things convenient, I would have found another means of accomplishing the same end."

"Really?" Araminta gave him an assessing glance. "Who would you have used if Lady Northcote had not come forward?"

Simon considered briefly and shrugged. "Peppington or Canonbury, no doubt. I am certain either one could have persuaded their ladies to be cooperative."

"Two more old enemies." Araminta stared at him. "Good lord, Simon. I begin to perceive what is happening here. I have heard rumors about your present connection with Peppington and Canonbury. They are both dangling on your strings, I am told. There are rumors that each is facing financial disaster. What is the real story?"

"I doubt you would be interested, Araminta. A dull business involving some mining investments, a canal, and some bad judgment on the part of Canonbury and Peppington."

"Ah, Simon," Araminta said, slowly shaking her head, "people are right when they call you mysterious and dangerous. Three of the most important men in London are in your pocket. You have them all, now, don't you? Northcote, Canonbury, Peppington, and Faringdon. You are playing cat and mouse with each of them."

"It is a game I learned well in the East."

Araminta shuddered delicately. "I vow, I am very glad I am on your good side, Simon. You make my blood run cold at times. But I do not think your lady elf understands that she is only a pawn in your grand scheme. She is still talking in terms of creating a pure and noble metaphysical connection with her new husband."

Simon scowled. "Emily is a very intelligent female but her thinking is frequently clouded by romantical nonsense. She will soon learn her proper role as a wife."

Emily plunged into the glamour, excitement, and sophistication of her first major town ball with zest. The glittering chandeliers, the crush of people dressed in the first stare of fashion, the dancing, and the witty conversation all left her breathless and enthralled. It seemed to her that everyone in the *haute ton* must have been invited to the marchioness's grand event.

Dressed in an emerald green silk gown cut far lower than anything she had ever worn before in her life, Emily felt marvelously fashionable. She had green satin slippers embroidered with little gold dragons to match her gown and she was wearing a delightful little gold dragon in her newly styled hair. The dragon's eyes were tiny rubies. Two matching dragons dangled from her ears.

Lady Merryweather's hairdresser had pulled Emily's red curls back into an artful cascade that fell from the crown of her head to the nape of her neck. There were several artfully arranged tendrils curling down the sides of her cheeks. The whole was finished off with an elegant fan featuring a spectacular hand-painted dragon that dangled on a gold cord from her wrist, and a quizzing glass. Lady Merryweather had refused to even contemplate the notion of wearing spectacles to a formal ball.

Simon had been waiting in the hall when Emily descended the stairs on her way out for the evening. He had examined his wife from head to toe and looked extremely satisfied with what he saw.

"Will you be joining us later, Simon?" Araminta had inquired as she was handed up into the carriage.

"I am going to my club for an hour or so but I will find you both later and escort you home." He looked at Emily as he helped her into the vehicle. "Enjoy yourself, elf. You are definitely a diamond of the first water tonight. And definitely the most unusual creature Society will have seen in an age. You will set the polite world agog."

Emily glowed. "Thank you, Simon."

His mouth quirked as he closed the carriage door. "See that you do not get into any trouble."

Emily sat back in the carriage seat as they set off. "I do not know why he feels obliged to say things like that all the time. What sort of trouble could I possibly get into at Northcote's ball?"

Araminta smiled. "Sometimes I get the impression Blade does not always know quite what to expect from you, Emily. I think that is a good thing, on the whole. He needs to be rattled about a bit now and then."

"Nothing rattles Simon," Emily said with pride. "He is the coolest man I have ever met."

"Yes," Araminta said, looking out the window at the crowded street. "He does have that reputation. Some say it goes beyond cool all the way to cold-blooded. Some people are actually afraid of him."

"They must be people who do not know him well," Emily said confidently.

"Oh? And you do know him well?"

"Yes, indeed. As I have told you, we communicate on a higher plane." Emily frowned thoughtfully. "Sometimes. Perhaps people are a bit put off by his unusual staff. They are somewhat forbidding in appearance, although extremely pleasant and most interesting. I wonder where Simon obtained them."

Araminta smiled slightly. "You do realize what it was Simon did for the East India Company, don't you, Emily?"

"It is my understanding that he assisted them in some business matters and the company was suitably grateful."

"Grateful, indeed. His function was to discourage the pirates who are a constant threat to the company's ships. Simon used a most unusual approach to the problem."

Emily laughed softly. "Let me hazard a guess. Did he by any chance recruit ex-pirates to deal with the practicing pirates?"

"That is exactly what he did."

"Brilliant notion," Emily said with satisfaction. "And a few of them returned to England with him as his servants."

"If you can call them that," Araminta said dryly.

Celeste and her mother were all that was charming and welcoming. They introduced Emily to everyone and people lined up to meet her. Araminta explained during a brief lull in the introductions that it was because Society was fascinated to learn just what sort of exotic female the mysterious Earl of Blade had married. Emily had giggled behind her fan at the notion of being thought exotic.

Emily's exuberant mood lasted right up until the moment when she raised her quizzing glass for a quick look around and happened to spot Richard Ashbrook coming toward her. She froze for an instant as old memories rose to confront her.

He was *Lord* Ashbrook now, she thought as she quickly allowed the glass to drop to her waist on its velvet cord. Ashbrook had become a baron since she had last seen him five years ago.

He had always been quite handsome but now he was the perfect picture of the romantic poet, with his artistically tousled dark curls, intense, brooding gaze, and elegant figure. She noted that during the past few years he had achieved just the precise curl of lip that implied the appropriate mixture of jaded ennui mixed with cynicism. Emily did not find the look particularly attractive. But, then, she suddenly realized, she did not find Ashbrook very interesting at all any longer.

Next to the dragon who had entered her life, Ashbrook was nothing more than a somewhat amusing pet dog. Emily wondered what she had ever seen in him.

" 'Tis Ashbrook," Celeste whispered excitedly. "Mama said she had invited him but I was afraid he would not come. He has the entrée into any drawing room or ballroom in town and it is very difficult to entice him. He claims soirees and balls bore him."

Emily was about to reply but Ashbrook was suddenly in front of her, mouth twisted into an ironic smile, dark eyes veiled beneath half-lowered lids. His snowy white cravat was tied in a sculptured knot.

"Hello, Emily," Ashbrook said softly.

"Richard." Emily gave him her hand and wondered again why she'd once found him irresistible. After knowing a dragon, Ashbrook seemed quite tame.

"It has been a long time." Ashbrook bent his dark head gallantly over her wrist.

"Emily, you did not tell me you knew the baron," Celeste said.

"Lady Blade and I are old friends," Ashbrook said smoothly without taking his eyes off Emily. "Is that not so, Emily?"

"Acquaintances," Emily amended tartly. "Now, if you will excuse me, Richard—"

"Surely you will not be so cruel as to dismiss me without giving me the honor of a dance. Lady Northcote has allowed one waltz this evening, I am told, and I believe this is it."

"But, I—"

It was too late. Ashbrook was already leading her out onto the dance floor. His arm went boldly around her waist and Emily was swept up into the delightfully scandalous music of the waltz. It was a dance perfectly suited to a woman of excessive passions. Emily just wished Simon were her partner.

"You have changed, Emily."

"Not that much, Richard. Honestly, you make it sound as if I had turned into a different sort of creature altogether."

"Yes," he mused. "You have truly metamorphosed into *a being of ethereal light and radiant beams, a creature who dwells on other planes,* it seems."

"Richard, are you quoting yourself, by any chance?"

"A line or two from *The Hero of Marliana.* Have you read it?"

"No," Emily said crisply, "I have not."

Ashbrook nodded understandingly. "Too painful for you, I imagine. Do you ever think of us, Emily?"

"Rarely."

He smiled whimsically. "I think of you often, my dear. And of what I lost forever five years ago."

"I lost something, too," Emily reminded him.

"Your heart?"

"My reputation."

Ashbrook looked briefly irritated. "The incident apparently did not affect your marriage prospects. You have done very well for yourself, Emily. An earl, no less. And a very exotic and rather dangerous one, at that."

"Blade is not dangerous," she said impatiently. "I cannot imagine where everyone has gotten that impression of him."

"You, I take it, do not go in fear of your husband?"

"Of course not. I would never have married him if I had been afraid of him," she retorted.

"Why did you marry him, Emily?"

"We are twin souls who communicate on a higher plane," she explained. "We share a mystical, transcendental union."

"You and I once shared that sort of communication," Ashbrook reminded her in a meaningful tone.

"Hah! Not bloody likely. I was much younger then and did not know the true meaning or nature of a metaphysical union."

"And that is what you enjoy with your husband? Forgive me, but I find it difficult to believe Blade is capable of such refined sensibilities."

"Well, we are working on it," Emily mumbled. "It takes a while to develop perfect transcendent communication, you know."

"With us, it was instantaneous, as I recall. At least on my part."

"Is that so, my lord?" Emily lifted her chin proudly. "Then why did you presume to attack me that night at the inn, pray tell?"

Ashbrook came to an abrupt halt on the dance floor, took her wrist, and pulled her out through the open windows into the garden. There he turned and faced her.

"I did not attack you," he said brusquely. "I came to you that night because you had led me to believe our hearts were already forever joined in a nonphysical connection. I thought you were already one with me in the metaphysical realm and wished to be one with me in the physical realm, also. If we had spent the night together you would have learned the truth of a true, transcendent union."

Emily's brows drew together in a quelling frown as she recalled her wedding night. "I have heard the theory that what happens on one plane affects what happens on the other plane, Richard. I may as well tell you, I have serious doubts about the validity of that philosophy."

"Perhaps your grasp of metaphysical science is not as fully developed as it could be," Ashbrook said. "Tell me, Emily, do you still dabble in poetry?"

She hesitated. "As it happens, I am working on an epic poem at the moment."

Ashbrook was amused. "Going to give me some competition, eh?"

Emily felt herself grow pink with embarrassment. Whatever else he might be, Ashbrook was a published poet and she had never published so much as a single verse. "Hardly," she muttered.

"What are you calling this epic?"

"The Mysterious Lady."

"It sounds promising," Ashbrook allowed thoughtfully.

Emily looked up quickly, raising her quizzing glass to see his expression. "Do you really believe so?"

"Definitely." Ashbrook paused with a deliberate air. "Excellent title. Quite suited to the sort of people who buy that kind of thing. Do you know, Emily, I might be able to take a look at your work and see if it does, indeed, appear promising. If so, I would be happy to introduce you to my publisher, Whittenstall."

"Richard!" Emily was stunned by the generous offer. "Do you mean it?"

"But, of course." Ashbrook smiled with a negligent confidence. "A word from me would certainly help to get Whittenstall's attention, I believe."

"Richard, it would be so very kind of you. I cannot believe this is happening. I shall have to get back to work on *The Mysterious Lady* immediately. I have been thinking of adding a ghost and a secret passageway to the story. What do you think?"

"Ghosts and secret passageways are always very popular. I have used them myself on occasion."

"I have not as yet allowed anyone else to read *The Mysterious Lady*. It needs some work before you see it." Emily reminded herself of all the changes, additions, and corrections she wanted to make on the poem. "But I shall start at once. Richard, this is so exciting. I cannot tell you how much your offer means to me. To undertake to introduce me to your own publisher. It is beyond anything."

"It seems little enough to do for an old friend."

"I do not know how to thank you, Richard."

He lifted one shoulder in a casual shrug. "There is no need to thank me. But if you feel the necessity, you may do so by joining a small literary salon I attend on Thursday afternoons."

Emily was thrilled. "A real London literary salon? I would so enjoy that. I have missed my Thursday afternoon meetings of the literary society of Little Dippington." A pang of uneasiness assailed her. "But do you think your literary friends will want me there? They are probably much more widely read than I am and ever so much more sophisticated. I shall probably appear very rustic to them."

"Not at all," Ashbrook murmured. "I assure you Lady Turnbull and my other friends will welcome you. They will no doubt find you quite . . . charming."

Emily sighed happily. "It is almost too much to contemplate. My first important ball, an introduction to a literary salon, and an opportunity to have a real publisher look at my writing. Town life is certainly a great deal more exciting than life in the country."

"Yes," Ashbrook said. "It certainly is. And as a married woman," he added softly, "you will find you have a great deal more freedom here in London than you ever did as a spinster buried in Hampshire. The only rule in town, my dear, is to be discreet."

"Yes, yes, of course." Emily was totally unconcerned with the problem of discretion simply because she was not planning any indiscretions, least of all with this man who had once so casually ruined her. No woman who was married to a man like Blade could possibly be interested in a shallow creature such as Ashbrook.

Emily frowned thoughtfully. "Richard, do you really believe my title is a good one? I am not averse to altering it if you think it would make my work more interesting to a publisher."

"We shall discuss it after I have had occasion to read your poem," Ashbrook said, gazing over her head into the brilliantly lit ballroom. "And now, speaking of discretion, I believe we should return to the ball."

"You are quite right. Celeste will wonder what has happened to me."

Emily turned cheerfully to walk back through the open windows, her mind churning with ideas for *The Mysterious Lady.* She raised her glass for a quick glance around the room and nearly collided with her husband, who materialized like a large boulder out of nowhere.

"Oh, hello, my lord." She smiled up at him. "I was hoping you would arrive soon. It is all so exciting, is it not? I am having the most wonderful time. I was just speaking to . . ." She paused, glanced from side to side with her quizzing glass, and realized Ashbrook had not followed her back into the ballroom. "Never mind. Goodness, you look spectacular, Simon."

Blade, dressed in his elegantly severe evening clothes, gazed thoughtfully over her head into the garden for a few seconds. Then he looked down at Emily.

"I am glad to hear you are enjoying yourself, my dear. Will you honor me with this waltz?"

"Another waltz is to be played? I was under the impression Lady Northcote had only authorized one waltz tonight."

"I prevailed upon her to sanction another so that I could dance it with you." Simon led her out onto the floor.

"Simon, how wonderful of you," Emily breathed, thoroughly enchanted by the gesture.

"I was rather pleased with the notion myself." He swept her into the gracious pattern of the dance. "And Lady Northcote was, shall we say, cooperative."

All thoughts of *The Mysterious Lady* and her plans to join Ashbrook's literary circle flew out of Emily's head. She was dancing the waltz with her beloved dragon. Nothing could be more perfect.

Simon glided coolly around the room, aware that the eyes of the *ton* were upon him and his new bride. By tomorrow morning Emily would be the talk of the town. He and Emily made a compelling contrast on the dance floor and Simon knew it. The fact suited him.

What did not suit him was the flash of searing jealousy he had experienced when he had witnessed Emily returning from the garden with Ashbrook directly behind her.

Chapter 12

"I adore your house, Simon," Emily declared as she waltzed alone around the red, gold, green, and black library. As she whirled past each of the jeweled dragons, she reached out to affectionately pat the savage heads. The dark green skirts of her gown floated around her slippered feet.

The ball had ended an hour ago and it had taken almost that long to collect their carriage and get home through the crowded streets but Emily could not seem to stop dancing. She felt giddy and effervescent and transcendently alive. She hummed the strains of the waltz she had danced earlier with Simon. "And I especially adore this room," she continued with a definite little nod. "It is quite perfect, exactly how I had imagined it would be. Exotic and luscious and full of strange and mysterious objects." She patted a black and gold dragon as she waltzed past the fireplace.

"I am not surprised. I had a feeling you would like it." Simon poured two glasses of brandy and held one out to her.

"That only shows how well attuned we are." She took the glass from his hand as she danced past. "You see, Simon? I keep telling you that we communicate—"

"On a higher plane," he finished for her. "Yes, my dear. I have heard you comment on that fact often enough." He raised his glass in a small salute. "To you, madam wife. You were a great success tonight."

"Thanks to Lady Merryweather." Emily giggled and waltzed away toward the far end of the room. "And Lady Northcote. She was so kind. She and Celeste introduced me to absolutely everyone and I danced nearly every dance, Simon. Two of them waltzes."

"Araminta told me the first one was with Ashbrook."

Emily shot him a quick, sidelong glance as she flitted past one of the huge satin pillows. She wondered if Simon knew that it was Ashbrook she had run away with five years ago. And if he did know, would he be jealous? she asked herself. Not bloody likely. Simon was much too self-controlled and sure of himself to be jealous. Besides, he knew he had her heart.

"Yes. Ashbrook invited me out on the floor for the first waltz. Simon, I think I should tell you something about him."

"What would that be?" Simon watched her intently over the rim of his glass.

Emily came to a halt in front of a delicate Chinese painting featuring plump horses and strangely clad warriors. She studied it closely through her spectacles. "Richard was the man I thought I loved five years ago—the one I ran off with."

"But you did not run off with anyone five years ago," Simon stated quietly. "I thought I explained to you that for all intents and purposes, there is no Unfortunate Incident in your past."

Emily swung around in surprise. "But, Simon . . . Oh, I see," she said, suddenly understanding and appreciating what he was doing. "This is part of your scheme to introduce me successfully to Society, is it not? We shall deal boldly with the problem of the scandal. We shall simply deny it ever happened."

"Precisely."

"A brilliant approach." She scowled thoughtfully. "But what if Richard says something about it?"

"I do not think he will do that."

Emily nodded, considering the matter. "You are probably right. I imagine it would be embarrassing for him."

Simon's mouth kicked up wryly at the corner and his golden eyes gleamed. "Somewhat more than a little embarrassing, I think. Rather dangerous, in fact."

"Yes, he has his own reputation to consider."

"Among other things."

Emily nodded again and resumed waltzing. She slid Simon another speculative glance. "I do not suppose you are jealous of Lord Ashbrook, by any chance, are you?"

"Because of the nonexistent Unfortunate Incident or because he waltzed with you tonight?"

"Either one," Emily said eagerly. Her heart leapt at the possibility.

"Should I be jealous?" Simon's voice was utterly emotionless.

"No, not for a single second," Emily assured him grandly. "I made a very foolish mistake five years ago. The truth is, I realized almost immediately after we left Little Dippington that I did not really want to marry Richard. It was all very exciting dashing off to the border like that and Richard kept quoting the most beautiful poetry. But I was soon obliged to face the fact that I did not love him. I could not possibly have married him."

"And the waltz tonight? Did you discover any new feelings toward him when he took you in his arms?"

"No." Emily tilted her head, thinking about her reactions. "No, not at all. It was rather like meeting an old acquaintance whom one has not seen for some time."

She decided then and there that she did not want to tell Simon about Ashbrook's generous offer to take a look at her manuscript. Not yet, at any rate. After all, nothing was certain. Ashbrook might declare *The Mysterious Lady* completely unpublishable. It would be humiliating enough just having Ashbrook know it was unsuitable.

"I see. Like meeting an old acquaintance."

"Yes. Precisely." Emily hummed a few more measures of the waltz. "Do you know, Simon, it is very strange, but I do not seem to be able to calm myself tonight. I am still very excited."

"You should be exhausted." Simon leaned back against his black lacquered desk. He had already taken off his jacket and unknotted his cravat. The length of white silk hung loose around his throat.

"I know, but I am not the least bit tired." Emily took a sip of brandy. Her gaze fell on the nearest of the large, tasseled pillows. "Simon, tell me, did you get these pillows from some Turkish harem?"

"No. I had them made up here in London, as it happens." He sipped his brandy. "Do you fancy them?"

"They are marvelous." Emily put down her glass and threw herself full length onto the nearest gold satin pillow. She lounged back in what she thought was the sort of languid, sensuous position that a harem lady might adopt. "How do I look? Could I pass for a sultry Eastern courtesan?"

Simon's eyes moved slowly from the tip of her dragon-embroidered emerald satin slipper to the cascade of red curls at the top of her head. "Perhaps," he finally allowed.

"You look unconvinced. Maybe the spectacles mar the effect." She took them off and set them on the nearest lacquered table. Then she leaned back on the pillow again and essayed a killing glance from beneath her lashes. Simon was a large, dark blur across the room. "Is that any better?"

"A bit more authentic-looking, I believe."

Emily stretched out on her side. The skirts of her gown edged up the length of her leg, revealing her stockings. She pursed her lips and tried for a harem lady's pout. "There. How is that?"

"Emily, are you by any chance flirting with me?" Simon asked softly.

"Well, as to that . . ." It helped not to be able to see his expression clearly. Emily felt the warmth rising in her cheeks as she considered the question carefully. "Yes, I believe I am." She held her breath, waiting for his response.

"You are in a rather strange mood tonight, are you not?"

"I am happy, Simon," she said, waving one hand to encompass the whole world. "I feel as if I am floating. I have had the most exciting, most wonderful evening of my whole life."

"And now you want to conclude it by having me make love to you?"

Emily sighed and flopped onto her back, her arms stretched high above her head. She contemplated the blurry ceiling. "I told you, Simon, I am a creature of excessive passions. Perhaps my sensibilities have been overstimulated by all the excitement tonight."

"A possibility."

"Simon?"

"Yes, Emily?"

She drew a deep breath. "You told me that the last time we made love I did not quite get the hang of it."

"I told you that you needed practice, as I recall," he murmured.

She rolled back onto her side and propped herself on her elbow. "Yes. Practice. I believe I should like very much to practice tonight."

There was a faint pause. Then Simon's voice came, low, dark, and silky with sensual menace. "I also told you something else, Emily."

Emily sat up on the pillow, drawing her knees up under her chin so that her skirts foamed around her toes. She groped for the brandy glass. When she found it she took a large swallow and put the glass carefully back down on the table. Then she wrapped her arms around her updrawn knees.

"You told me I would have to beg you to make love to me," Emily finally said, hugging her knees very tightly.

"I will settle for being asked very nicely. The point is, my dear, I do not wish there to be any accusations in the morning. You are not going to be able to say I tricked you."

"I will not say that, Simon." She waited in an agony of anticipation mixed with uncertainty. "Simon?"

"Yes, Emily?"

"Will you please make love to me?"

A strange stillness settled on the dark, exotic room.

There was a faint clink and Emily knew Simon had just set his brandy glass down on the desk. She watched him come toward her. She was unable to see his expression without her spectacles but her whole body was tingling with awareness. She could sense the heavy, enveloping aura of his masculinity and knew that could only be because they really did communicate on a higher plane.

Simon halted at the edge of the huge satin pillow, the most powerful dragon in a room full of the creatures. Without a word he lowered himself down beside Emily and took her into his arms.

Slowly, deliberately, he pushed her back down onto the gold brocade. Leaning over her, he looked down into her face. He was so close now that Emily could see the molten gold in his eyes.

"Are you sure this is what you want?" Simon stroked the delicate line of her jaw with his thumb.

"Yes," she whispered, almost unable to get the single word out because of the tightness in her throat. The odd breathless feeling was sweeping through her again, as it always did when Simon took her in his arms. "Please, Simon."

"Very well, Emily." He bent his head and dropped a heated kiss on the top of her breast, which was exposed by the low neckline of her ball gown. "Just remember in the morning that this was all your idea."

"Yes, Simon." She wrapped her arms slowly around his neck. Then she smiled tremulously. "It was not nearly so bad as you probably thought it would be, you know."

"What was not so bad?" He slid the puffy little sleeve of the gown slowly down over her shoulder.

"Begging you to make love to me." Her smile turned into an exuberant little laugh. "It was not so bad at all."

"I am glad." Simon eased the bodice of the gown lower and one apple-shaped breast was freed. He circled the nipple with his forefinger. "Perhaps you will ask me again sometime."

"I expect I will," Emily said complacently. "If it turns

out to be as transcendent an experience as you have promised."

Simon gave a husky laugh that turned into a groan. "I can see that I shall have to do it properly this time."

Emily shivered as she felt his finger trace another circle around the tip of her breast. She stirred restlessly, her legs sliding over the brocaded satin. Simon's mouth came down over hers and at the same time he pinned her thighs with one of his own.

Emily parted her lips and Simon's tongue slipped into the warmth of her mouth. She could taste the brandy he had been drinking. At the same time the scent of him filled her head. She tightened her arms around his neck and instinctively tried to arch her hips against his.

"No," Simon whispered, breaking the contact with her mouth. "This time we will do things very slowly." He unfastened the bodice of the gown and pushed the gossamer fabric to her waist.

Emily had her eyes closed now but she could feel the heat of his gaze on her breasts. It burned her, branded her, heated her blood. The big pillow on which she reclined was like a great, fluffy, golden cloud. She was sinking deeper and deeper into it as Simon let more of his weight come down on her.

"You have beautiful skin, Emily. Soft and delicate and made to be touched." Simon trailed a string of small, damp kisses down her throat and over her breast. His teeth closed gently over her nipple and his hand slipped beneath the lowered bodice of the gown.

Emily sucked in her breath. She twisted beneath his hand, already aching for a more intimate touch. "Simon?"

"No, not yet. I told you, this time I am not going to rush things. This time I will stay in control of myself and you will go wild, elf."

He tugged the emerald ballgown and the thin petticoat she wore under it off over her head. Then he reached down and deftly untied her garters. His hand slid intimately along the curves of her legs as he slipped the stockings off.

Emily turned her flaming face into his pleated white

shirt, clutching at him. Simon laughed softly and cupped her buttocks, squeezing gently.

Emily was aware of the feel of the gold satin under her back and hips. It was a wonderfully pagan sensation. "Do I look like a harem lady now?"

Simon smiled slowly and combed his fingers through the triangle of red hair at the top of her thighs. "A very rare and unusual harem lady," he agreed. "You would bring a very high price, indeed, if you were to go on the auction block."

She looked up at him through her lashes, feeling deliciously wanton. "Would you sell me?"

"Never," he vowed, voice darkening abruptly. His fingers tightened possessively in the red curls. Then he drew back slightly.

Emily's eyes flew open as he pulled away. "Is something wrong?"

"Nothing at all, my sweet. I am just going to get a bit more comfortable." Simon tugged off his shirt and the dangling cravat. Then his hands went to the fastening of his breeches. In a moment he was gloriously naked. The firelight gleamed on the muscular contours of his shoulders and thighs, revealing his full arousal.

"Pashas generally take their clothes off when they make love to one of the members of their harem," Simon said as he came back down beside Emily.

Emily giggled as she felt herself being pushed back down onto the pillow. "I must warn you, my lord, I will not tolerate any other residents in this particular harem. Only myself."

"So I am to have a harem of one?"

"I fear that is the case. I do not intend to share you with any other female." She smiled wickedly. "Nor do I think you will need any other."

"You intend to keep me quite busy, then?" He slid his palm warmly along her thigh and looked down at her with a gaze that brought a flush to her throat and breasts.

"Very busy," Emily promised huskily. She curled her fingers in the hair on his chest, loving the crisp texture as well as the sense of strength in the powerful muscles beneath his skin. "Simon, you are so beautiful," she said in wonder.

"No, elf, you are the beautiful one. Your breasts are perfectly suited to my hand." He cupped one briefly, grazing his thumb over the nipple until she shuddered. "Your mouth fits mine perfectly." He kissed her deeply, thoroughly, druggingly until she wriggled in his grasp. "And the insides of your thighs are softer and warmer than anything I have ever known." He eased his hand between her legs.

Emily gasped as she felt Simon's fingertips touch her with scalding intimacy. She clutched at his strong shoulders and strained against him. A deep, aching sense of need was blossoming swiftly within her. Her whole body began to yearn for the explosive release she had once before experienced at Simon's hands.

"Not yet," Simon muttered. He caught hold of her fluttering hands, stretched her arms out over her head, and pinned her wrists. Then he leaned over her and kissed her eyelids. "I vow this time you will not drive me mad. This time I will be the one in control and you will learn to enjoy this business of making love."

"I do enjoy it, Simon. Honestly, I do." Emily lifted her hips, seeking his warmth. She was truly aching for him now.

"It will get even better," he promised. Still holding her wrists above her head, he reached down and spread her thighs widely apart, settling himself between her legs.

Emily tightened her legs instinctively and struggled to free her hands so that she could wrap her arms around his neck and hold him close.

Simon looked down at her and smiled slowly. "I am going to release your wrists now, but you must not move."

"Do not be silly. I cannot stay still," Emily said, panting.

"Then I shall give you something to aid you." Simon scooped up his cravat from where it lay on the carpet. He looped the large length of white silk around the clawed foot of the heavy settee which was just behind Emily's head. Then he placed the ends of the cravat in Emily's outstretched fingers.

"You must hold on very tightly," Simon told her as her fingers clenched instinctively in the silk.

Bewildered, but anxious to get on with things, Emily obediently grasped a section of the starched, white silk in each hand. "Now what?" she demanded impatiently.

"Now you must tug very hard on my cravat whenever the urge to move becomes overwhelming. Do not concern yourself. You will not pull the settee over. It is very heavy and the cravat is made of very strong silk."

Arms stretched above her head, Emily glared up at her husband. "Bloody hell, Simon, I do not want to play with your cravat."

"Do as you are told," he instructed with a deep chuckle. "You are a harem lady, remember? Harem ladies always do what they are told."

"But, Simon . . . *Oh.*" Emily moaned and her fingers tightened obediently around the strip of silk as she felt Simon's tongue in the very center of her soft, curved stomach.

"Remember, just pull very hard on the cravat when you cannot stand it any longer." Simon eased himself lower, his hands closing firmly around Emily's hips. He held her still as he kissed the inside of her thigh.

"Simon." Emily froze with shock.

"That's better. You are not moving at all now. You are stretched as taut as a bowstring. Beautifully arched and straining for my touch." His hand moved down the length of her and she shuddered. His mouth was on the inside of her thigh now.

"Simon."

"Tug harder on my cravat," he ordered softly. Then he kissed her again, even more intimately. "Harder, Emily."

The riot of sensation that threatened to swamp Emily was startling and confusing. She felt as though she were sinking below the surface of a warm sea. She could hardly even breath now, let alone try to think. She obeyed Simon's murmured commands blindly.

Emily seized the white silk in a fierce grip and tugged at

it with all her might. The twisting, tightening feeling in her lower body grew more intense.

"Pull harder, Emily. You must use all your strength now. Tug just as hard as you can." Simon's finger slid into her moist passage and he sucked gently on the small, erect nub of exquisitely sensitive feminine flesh.

"Bloody hell." Emily was in the center of a sensual storm. She responded to Simon's softly murmured orders, hauling violently on the handfuls of silk. The harder she pulled, the more she felt as if she were going to burst into flames at any second.

"Just a little harder, Emily. Pull just a little more. You are very wet now, very tight. Very ready. You are almost there. Just a little harder on the cravat, I think. Yes, that's it."

Emily gasped as she felt Simon's hard shaft probing at the entrance of her body. Clinging tightly to the ends of the cravat, she looked up through her lashes and saw him looming over her.

"Simon."

"Don't let go of the silk, Emily." He pushed into her very slowly. "You are very tight, elf. But this time there is no pain, is there?"

"No. No, oh, Simon, I do not think I can stand this," she gasped. Her fingers were crushing the white silk.

"No?" He started to ease himself back out of her.

"Simon, do not leave me." She was panicked at the thought that he was going to pull away just as she was hovering on the brink of this wondrous, transcendent experience.

"I have no intention of leaving you, elf. And you will never leave me, will you?" Simon eased himself slowly back into her.

"No, never. I would never leave you, Simon. *Oh. Bloody hell.*"

"Tighter on the cravat, Emily. Just a little bit tighter."

He was deep inside, stretching her, becoming a part of her. Emily could not stand it anymore. Her whole body convulsed.

"*Simon.*"

There was a distant ripping sound as the silk cravat tore in half. Emily's arms were suddenly free. She flung them around Simon, clinging to him as the incredible shivers of release raced through her from head to toe.

She heard Simon's hoarse, exultant shout of satisfaction and felt him pumping himself violently into her. Mindlessly Emily clutched at him as the waves of passion took them both under the surface of the warm sea.

A long while later, Emily felt Simon stir in her arms. She opened her eyes lazily, feeling much too languid to move.

"It would appear I am in the market for a new cravat," Simon observed as he rolled onto his side. He grinned as he picked up the severed strips of white silk that had once been an extremely stylish item of neckwear. He dangled the ends over Emily's nose. "You do not know your own strength, madam."

"Apparently not." She laughed and blew on one of the bits of white silk. It fluttered in the air. "Was it one of your favorite cravats, by any chance?"

"Definitely. I am quite shattered at the loss."

Emily giggled. She stretched, sat up, and folded her arms on his chest. She rested her chin on her arms. "I shall try to compensate you for it."

"It will take a great deal of effort on your part." Simon's teeth gleamed in a wicked smile.

"Do you know something, Simon? I think you would have made a very good pasha. There is something quite barbaric about you at times."

"I'm not at all barbaric." Simon wrapped his hand around the nape of her neck and pulled her close for a kiss. "In fact, in some ways, I am quite civilized. Even a bit dull."

"Never."

"You think not? Well, let me tell you this, my passionate wife. Just once, I would dearly like to make love to you in a bed rather than on the floor of the library. How is that for being staid and dull?"

"A bed?" Emily frowned. "How very normal and un-imaginative that sounds. I stand corrected. You may be a bit dull, after all, my lord. What a surprise. You certainly had me fooled."

"Vixen." He pushed her back down into the depths of the gold satin and kissed her soundly.

The kiss was intended as playful punishment, but it was quickly transformed into something much more potent. Emily gave herself up to it with joyous abandon before Simon finally broke it off to gaze down at her with eyes that were no longer amused. Instead, they were strangely watchful.

"Well, Emily? Was that more what you expected from lovemaking?" he asked quietly.

"Oh, yes, Simon. I truly felt cast adrift upon love's transcendent, golden shore that time." She smiled shyly, knowing her heart was probably reflected in her eyes. "It was wonderful—truly a metaphysical experience. Extraordinarily stimulating to the sensibilities. I cannot wait to do it again."

Simon groaned and then fell back, laughing. "I ought to have known a woman of excessive passions such as yourself would be utterly insatiable." He sat up and got to his feet, reaching for his shirt. "Come, wife. We are going to go upstairs and behave like a civilized married couple for once."

"What an excellent idea, my lord." Emily reached for her spectacles and adjusted them on her nose. "Just think. You have an entire drawer full of cravats upstairs in your bedchamber."

"Very true." Simon looked at his wife, who was wearing nothing except her spectacles, and grinned again. "Madam, I promise you that you will be positively amazed at the versatility of a well-made cravat."

It was nearly dawn but Simon was far from sleep. Emily's slender, warm body was snuggled closely against him and he could smell the scent of her mingled with the odors of their recent lovemaking. A length of white silk still dangled from her fingers, which lay across his chest.

He had handled matters much better this time around, Simon decided. He had held to his vow to make Emily come to him. She had done so, surrendering very sweetly, with a womanly grace that had charmed him. Even more important, he had been in control right up until the moment he allowed himself to take his own satisfaction.

His relationship with his new bride was now much more as it should be, Simon concluded, trying to be coolheaded and objective about the situation. Emily had learned that he could give her pleasure when he made love to her and she had also learned that he was quite capable of an unshakable self-control.

She had been obliged to acknowledge that his was the stronger will in this union. He had bided his time and it had been worth it. By waiting until she succumbed to her own inevitable curiosity and budding sense of passion, he had made his point. He would be in charge from now on and Emily would know that.

It was necessary for a wife to respect her husband's strength of will. Especially when that wife was an ex-Faringdon.

"Simon?" Emily's voice was languid.

"I thought you were asleep, elf."

"I was. But I just remembered something I meant to tell you earlier. I had a conversation with Lady Northcote this evening." Emily yawned.

Simon was instantly alert. "Did you, indeed? And what did you discuss?"

"Well, I was thanking her for inviting me to her ball and she assured me she could have done nothing less because of my having saved Celeste from Nevil. She also seemed to think she owed me the kindness because of something that had happened in the past between Northcote's father and yours."

"Is that what she said?"

"It was all very vague, but I naturally assured her that she was not to worry about it any longer."

Simon went still. "What, precisely, did you tell her, Emily?"

"Just that whatever obligation might have existed in the past had been more than amply repaid by her kindness in launching me into Society. She has been so nice to me, Simon. I could not bear to have her think she owed me anything. And I certainly do not want her friendship based on a feeling of obligation."

"So you told her the debt had been paid in full?"

"Yes. Precisely. And she was very relieved, I must say."

"Bloody hell," Simon muttered. "I'll wager she was. And that is nothing compared to how Northcote no doubt feels."

"Well, I certainly hope so. Such a nice couple."

So much for being in charge of the situation.

Ah, well, Simon consoled himself. Northcote had been the least of the four. It was Northcote's father, after all, not the present marquess, who had ignored the letter Simon had written twenty-three years ago.

And Simon was obliged to admit that Lady Northcote had done a fine job of launching Emily. Perhaps the Northcote debt had, indeed, been paid in full.

"Emily," he said as sternly as possible, "in future you will not make promises or commitments on my behalf without consulting me first. Is that plain?"

"Perfectly, Simon. But I knew in this case you would not mind in the least. It was all obviously some sort of old misunderstanding."

"You are wrong there, elf. Northcote and I understand each other very well."

Chapter 13

"Well, Blade?" the Marquess of Northcote asked quietly. "My wife tells me your wife feels that the old debt is repaid. Is that true?"

Simon slowly lowered his newspaper and regarded Northcote with a cool gaze. The familiar, subdued sounds of masculine conversation, rustling papers, and gently clinking bottles behind him indicated the club was busy this afternoon. But he and Northcote had this corner of the room to themselves.

"My wife enjoyed herself very much last night," Simon said without inflection. "Lady Merryweather assures me Emily is well launched in Society. Please convey my gratitude to your lady."

Northcote lowered himself into the chair beside Simon's and reached for the bottle of port that stood on the end table. He poured himself a glass. "I am not talking about our wives and you know it. I am asking if you now consider matters between us to have been evened out."

Simon shrugged. "It would appear so. A husband must honor his wife's promises and obligations and Emily appears to have taken it upon herself to let you off the hook." He went back to scanning the newspaper.

"Damn it, Blade, do not play any of your deep games with me. Just tell me straight out if you consider the old debt fulfilled."

"You have my word on it." Simon did not look up from his perusal of the latest dispatches from the Continent. But beside him he sensed Northcote relax.

"Thank you, Blade. You are known to be as hard as iron but your word is equally solid. My wife was in hysterics that night at the inn. She was convinced Celeste's future had been shattered by that damn fortune hunter."

"I assume you took care of the wretched Nevil?"

"He will not be returning to London at any time in the near future," Northcote confirmed, not without satisfaction.

"Then all is well." Simon turned the page.

There was silence from the other chair for a long moment as Northcote sipped his port. Then he said in a low voice, "You may not believe this, but I regret what happened all those years ago, Blade. I apologize for my father's behavior."

Simon lowered the paper and met Northcote's steady gaze. He let another beat of silence pass and then he nodded curtly, surprised by the apology. "Consider the matter settled."

Northcote stretched out his legs and studied his glass of port. "I was the last one, was I not? You eventually managed to trap all of us. Me, Canonbury, and Peppington. And of course, Faringdon. It was devilishly clever of you, Blade. I regret that my father did not live long enough to appreciate your brilliance."

"I share your regret," Simon said with mocking sincerity.

"It took you long enough to find a way of bringing pressure to bear on me. Finding my daughter that night at the inn was a stroke of luck for you."

"It was useful," Simon agreed, pouring himself a glass of port. "But sooner or later something would have turned up. It always does if one knows how to wait."

"And you are very good at waiting for an opportunity. I am well aware that I got off lightly. I am greatly relieved that all you wanted from me was my wife's social connections. If my father had still been alive, I imagine you would have demanded a much higher payment for what he did to you."

"Yes."

Northcote sighed. "If it is any consolation, he told me before he died two years ago to keep an eye on you. He said you would return one day and when you did, you would be dangerous. When are you going to make Canonbury and Peppington pay?"

"I prefer to keep them dangling for a while."

"Living with financial uncertainty is their true punishment, is it not?"

Simon sipped his port. "Revenge is best savored slowly, not gulped."

"Slow, steady torture." Northcote smiled grimly. "A very Eastern sort of vengeance, I believe. Again, I can only be grateful that your wife is impulsively generous."

"I shall keep a closer eye on her impulsive gestures in the future," Simon assured him dryly.

Northcote grinned. "Lady Blade has made a most delightful splash in the social world."

"So I am told."

"I must tell you, Blade, that both my wife and daughter are genuinely fond of your lady, in spite of the fact that she is married to you. How does she figure in your vengeance?"

"She is not involved," Simon said flatly.

"But she is a Faringdon," Northcote pointed out with a shrewd glance.

"Not any longer," Simon said.

"It has not escaped my notice that she belongs to you now and so does St. Clair Hall." Northcote hesitated. "My father, Canonbury, and Peppington all owed you because they turned their backs on your family after your father's death. But the Flighty, Feckless Faringdons owed you the most of all. It was a Faringdon who caused your father to take his own life. It was a Faringdon who took away your home and effectively destroyed your family. And in the end you will crush Broderick Faringdon and his clan, will you not?"

"It is a logical conclusion," Simon agreed in a neutral tone. "But my wife is no longer a member of that clan."

"Do you know, Blade, I am extremely grateful that my father's offense was a relatively minor one and that you consider the debt repaid," Northcote said with some humor. "I would not like to be a Faringdon at this moment."

Emily emerged from Asbury's Book Shop feeling extremely cheerful. Her maid Lizzie and the hatchet-faced footman named George were trailing behind her, their arms piled high with a collection of the latest romances and epic poetry which Emily had just finished selecting in the shop.

The little parade made its way to where the black and gold carriage waited near the curb. George was hurrying to open the door for his mistress when a familiar blond-haired Adonis jumped out of a nearby vehicle and rushed forward.

"Hello, Em. Fancy meeting you here."

"Devlin!" Emily smiled happily at her handsome brother. "How wonderful to see you. Where is Charles?"

Devlin cast an uneasy glance at the footman and maid and then took his sister's arm and led her a short distance away. He lowered his voice. "It is because of Charles that I have been waiting for an opportunity to speak to you, Em. Something terrible has happened."

"Dear God." Emily's eyes widened in sudden horror. It dawned on her that she had never seen Devlin looking so grim. "Is he hurt or ill? Dev, tell me, is he . . . is he dead?"

"Not yet," Devlin said roughly. "But he likely will be quite soon."

"He is ill, then. Good heavens, I must go to him at once. Quick, get into the carriage, Dev. Have you sent for a doc-. tor? What are the symptoms?" She made to turn away but halted as her brother grabbed her arm again.

"Wait, Em. It ain't like that. That is, Charles ain't exactly ill." Devlin scowled at the waiting maid, footman, and coachman. All three scowled back. Devlin lowered his voice another couple of notches. "You may as well know the full truth, Em. He's going to fight a duel in two days' time."

Emily raised her gloved hand to her mouth. "Bloody hell."

"It don't look good, Em. Charles and I have had some experience at Manton's gallery, of course, but God knows neither one of us is a crack shot." Devlin shook his head. "I am acting as one of his seconds. We are looking for another."

"I do not believe this." Emily was shaken. "Who challenged him?"

"Well, it was Charles who did the challenging," Devlin admitted. "Had to, you know. Matter of honor."

"Dear God. But who did he challenge?" Emily demanded.

"An out-and-outer named Grayley. The man's said to have fought two other duels and won them both. Wounded his opponents seriously on each occasion but they both lived, so there was no scandal. The thing is, Em, there ain't no guarantee Grayley won't kill Charles. They say it's just luck that the other two survived. The man's a cold-blooded marksman."

"I do not believe this," Emily whispered.

Devlin looked down at her. "Look, Em, I know you ain't supposed to socialize with your family now that you're married to Blade. But you're our sister, damn it. And I figured you'd want to say goodbye to Charles."

Emily straightened her shoulders. "I intend to do a great deal more than say goodbye to him. I intend to put a stop to this foolishness. Take me to him at once, Dev." She swung around and headed for the carriage.

"Dash it, Em, there ain't no way to stop the thing." Devlin hurried after her. "Matter of honor, as I said."

"Nonsense. It is a matter of idiocy." Emily climbed into the carriage, followed by Lizzie and her brother. She was aware that her maid and the ferocious-looking George were both eying Devlin with disapproval but she ignored them.

"Give the coachman the direction to your lodgings, Dev-lin," she said firmly.

Devlin raised the trapdoor in the carriage roof and quickly issued instructions. Then he dropped into the seat across from Emily and Lizzie. "Damn and blast. Hope I'm doing the right thing here."

"Of course you are." Emily frowned. "Where is Papa?"

"I went around to his lodgings first thing this morning but he ain't there. Place is locked up for the week, I was told. He's ruralizing with friends in the country. Had a bit of bad luck at the tables. No time to find him and bring him back." Devlin heaved a morose sigh. "Wouldn't do any good even if we did locate him."

Emily opened her mouth to ask another question but she saw the warning look in Devlin's eyes and paused. She realized her brother was silently cautioning her not to let Lizzie know what was happening. Emily sat back and waited with seething impatience for the carriage to reach the lodgings Charles and Devlin had taken.

The door opened as the vehicle drew to a halt. George looked more forbidding than ever. "Begging your pardon, ma'am, but are you sure this is where you want to be set down?"

Emily glanced over her shoulder. "Is this the correct address, Dev?"

"Yes." He grabbed his walking stick and jumped down behind her. Then he used the stick to rap once on the coachman's box. "You may wait for your mistress out here. She won't be long."

"Aye, sir." But the coachman looked as dubious as George.

Emily paid no attention to any of the forbidding looks she was receiving from her staff as she walked up the steps on her brother's arm.

A moment later she stepped into the rooms shared by the twins. Curiously, she glanced around at the comfortable, masculine surroundings. She had been aware that her brothers lived the life of carefree bachelors on the town but she had never actually seen their lodgings.

There was a pleasant view of the park from the bay window, two desks piled high with an assortment of papers, a liquor table, and two large, wing-backed leather chairs.

Charles Faringdon was sprawled in one of the chairs. He was steadily working his way through a bottle that sat on the table beside him. His blue eyes narrowed in astonishment when his sister and brother walked through the door.

"What the devil is she doing here, Dev?" Charles slammed his glass down onto the table.

"What a silly question, Charles." Emily sat down in the other wing-backed chair and peered anxiously at her attractive brother. "I had to come."

"Dev should never have brought you." Charles shot to his feet and began to pace restlessly around the small room. "This ain't your affair."

"I had to fetch her." Devlin crossed the room to pour himself a drink. He gulped it down in one swallow. "She's got a right to say goodbye to you."

"Damn it all, who says I'm going to cock up my toes day after tomorrow? It may be Grayley who does that." Charles glared first at his brother and then at Emily. "You shouldn't have come here, Em. I know you think you can talk me out of this, but there ain't no way you can do it."

"Why on earth did you challenge this Grayley to a duel?" Emily demanded softly. "Was it over a card game?"

"Not bloody likely," Devlin muttered, pouring himself another drink. He paused dramatically. "It was a woman."

Emily could not believe her ears. She pinned Charles with a stunned gaze. "You are proposing to fight a duel over a woman? What woman?"

"Her name must not be mentioned," Charles declared in solemn accents. "Suffice it to say she is as innocent and pure as a newborn lamb and she has been grossly insulted. I have no option but to demand satisfaction."

"Oh, dear," Emily murmured, sinking deeper into the chair. She forced herself to think. "Are you in love with this female?"

"I am. And if I survive the duel, I intend to ask for her hand in marriage."

"Won't do much good to ask," Devlin said from his position near the window. "Word is already getting about that our days are numbered. Everyone is saying Blade has cut the purse strings and you, me, and father will soon be in dun territory."

"Maryann will marry me even if I am done up. She loves me."

"Well, her mama and papa don't," Devlin said bluntly.

Charles shot his brother an angry look. "I will worry about that later. Emily ain't going to turn her back on her family forever, are you, Em? Father says you'll take care of those wretched business matters sooner or later. When all's said and done, you're still one of us. You're a Faringdon, by God."

"Your financial situation is the least of your concerns at the moment," Emily said quickly. "We must find a way to halt this duel. You simply cannot fight this Grayley person, Charles."

"No choice," Charles said with great finality. He reached for the bottle. "A lady's honor is involved, after all."

"But, Charles, you might very well be shot dead by this horrid man." Emily began to feel desperate as she realized how intent her brother was on this dangerous course of action. "In any event, dueling is illegal."

"Everyone knows that, Em," Devlin said irritably. "That don't matter. A gentleman's honor is above the law."

Emily looked from one brother to the other and her heart sank. "You intend to go through with this, don't you, Charles?"

"No choice."

"Stop saying that," Emily retorted. "You do have a choice. Surely you can apologize or something to this Grayley."

"Good God. Don't even suggest an apology." Charles looked genuinely shocked. "A gentleman has to do what's right where a lady's honor is involved."

"Bloody hell," Emily said in disgust. She got to her feet

and headed toward the door. "I can see there is no point talking to you about this."

"Emily, wait," Devlin said, coming after her. "Where are you going?"

"Home."

"Goodbye, Em," Charles said very quietly behind her.

She stopped and turned back toward him. "Charles, do not say that. Things will work out."

Charles gave her the reckless, charming Faringdon smile. "Yes, but just in case they do not, I want you to know I was always fond of you, little sister. And I hope you will be happy."

"Oh, Charles, thank you." Tears burned in Emily's eyes. She snatched off her spectacles and wiped the moisture away with the back of her gloved hand. Then she went across the room and kissed her brother lightly on the cheek. "All will be well. You will see."

She turned and hurried toward the door, her mind churning with the problem of what to do next. The answer was obvious, she thought as George handed her up into the carriage. The situation was quite desperate. She would go straight to Simon and ask for his help. He would surely understand.

Her dragon would handle everything.

As it turned out, Emily was forced to cool her heels for over an hour while she waited for Simon to return home. When Lizzie finally came upstairs to tell her that Blade was in the library, Emily leapt to her feet and practically flew down the stairs. Harry, the footman with the missing hand, jumped to open the door for her.

"Simon, thank heavens you are here," Emily exclaimed as she dashed into the room. "I must talk to you at once."

Simon eyed her with some amusement as he rose politely to his feet. "So I have been given to understand. Greaves said you had been inquiring after me every ten minutes or so for the past hour. Why don't you sit down, madam, catch your breath, and tell me what this is all about?"

"Thank you." Emily sank into the nearest chair, vastly relieved. "It is about Charles. A disaster has occurred, Simon."

The amused indulgence vanished from Simon's eyes. He sat down, leaned back in his chair, and drummed his fingers on the black lacquered surface of his desk. "We are speaking of Charles Faringdon?"

"Of course. What other Charles would I be discussing?"

"An interesting question, given the fact that I have told you quite plainly that you are not to see any of your family unless I am present."

Emily dismissed that with an impatient wave of her hand. "Oh, that is neither here nor there now. This is very serious, as you will understand once you have heard the whole story."

"I cannot wait."

"Yes, well, I encountered Devlin on the street outside Asbury's Book Shop and he took me straight to see Charles. He told me I might never see him alive again."

"Who? Charles?"

"Yes. Simon, the most terrible thing has occurred. Charles is planning to fight a duel with a man named Grayley. My brother will very likely be killed. At the very least, he will be badly wounded. Devlin says this Grayley has already fought two other duels and put bullets in both his opponents. You have got to stop it."

Simon studied her with a hooded gaze. "I told you that you were not to see your brothers alone."

"I know, Simon, but this is a matter of life and death. I realize you are not particularly fond of them, but surely you can see that you will have to put aside your personal feelings and do something about this disaster."

"Why?"

Emily stared at him, perplexed. "Why? Simon, Charles is my brother. And he knows almost nothing about fighting duels."

"I expect he will soon learn."

"Have you gone mad? This is not a joke. You have got to rescue him from this foolishness. He could be killed."

"I doubt it. Grayley will probably be content with wounding him. He's a good enough marksman to avoid killing your brother. No point in it. Killing his opponent would oblige Grayley to leave the country and he has no desire to do that."

Emily was speechless for a moment. When she finally got her voice back, it was faint. "Simon, please do not tease me like this. You must promise you will save Charles."

"You do not seem to have grasped a very essential point here, madam."

"What point is that?" Emily asked plaintively.

"I do not give a damn what happens to Charles or any other Faringdon. It sounds as if your brother is going to be the first of the clan to pave his own road to hell and I have no intention of getting in his way."

Emily's knuckles went white as she clutched the arms of her chair. "You cannot mean that."

"Every word, my dear. It ought to have been clear to you from the start that I have no interest in saving Faringdons. If it has not been made plain, then it can only mean you failed to pay attention."

"But, Simon, I was certain you would help me save him."

"Were you, my dear? Did you think, perhaps, that because you are now sleeping with me as a proper wife should that you can therefore manipulate me? Do you believe that I am so bemused by your charms in bed that I will allow you to control me outside of it? If so, you still have much to learn about your husband."

The chilling softness of the question and the accusation it carried swept over Emily like a cold wind. She rose unsteadily from the chair. "I was so certain you would help me," she said again, unable to believe the rejection.

"You have been looking after those rakehell brothers of yours long enough, Emily." Simon gave her an annoyed glance. "It is time they learned to take care of themselves."

"But they are my brothers."

"You owe them nothing." Simon got to his feet behind the desk, his gaze colder than ever. "Less than nothing. The

duel they should have fought ought to have taken place five
years ago. The fact that it did not gives me absolutely no
inclination to halt this one."

"I do not understand what you are talking about." Emily walked blindly toward the door. "And I do not care. I
cannot believe you will not help me save Charles. In fact, I
simply will not believe it. I was so very certain—"

"Emily." Blade's voice was a whiplash cracking across
the room full of dragons.

Emily paused, her hand on the doorknob. A flicker of
hope flared to life. "Yes, my lord?"

"I have told you before, but it would appear I must
repeat myself. It is high time you understood that you are
no longer a Faringdon. When you married me, you severed
all connection with your family. You belong to me now and
you will do as you are told."

Emily did not attempt to find a response to that appalling comment. She went out the door without a word.

She walked listlessly up the stairs to her bedchamber and
sat down in a chair near the window. Staring out into the
gardens, she gave herself over to self-pity and the accompa-
nying tears for several long moments.

When she had finished crying, she went over to the table
that held the pitcher of water, splashed some into the bowl,
and washed her face. Then she confronted herself in the
mirror.

Something had to be done at once.

Dry-eyed now, Emily sat down at her small escritoire
and picked up her quill. Idly she sharpened the nib with a
small knife as she considered possible solutions to the enormous problem that confronted her.

After a few moments, the obvious became clear. She
must find a way to make certain that Charles did not arrive
for his dawn appointment. She must apply herself to the
task of finding a plan to prevent that, just as she would
apply herself to the business of inventing a plot for a tale of
romance and adventure.

The ideas began to flow at once and Emily decided on a
particularly brilliant scheme within a very short time. She

began to feel much better as the outline of the whole thing took shape.

It seemed to Simon that the ticking of the library clock was much louder than usual. In fact, the silence in the room was growing oppressive. Now that he considered the matter, the entire house seemed unusually quiet.

It was odd how Emily's moods seemed to affect the staff these days. Hardened men who had once waded in blood up to their ankles now went around whistling or looking glum, depending on whether or not their mistress was smiling or dejected. It was ridiculous.

Simon got up from the desk and went to stand near the window. It was inevitable, he supposed, that sooner or later the elf would learn that his indulgence had definite limits. Emily had a disturbing tendency to go blithely through life applying her silly romantical notions to everything and everyone. She was a natural optimist, always looking for happy endings.

She also had a bad habit of believing she could cajole him into doing whatever she wished. That belief had evidently grown considerably stronger since last night's passionate session here in the library.

Simon's gaze flickered briefly toward the gold satin pillow where Emily had lain in his arms, her fingers desperately clutching handfuls of white silk. His body began to harden at the memory. He had never known such an exciting creature in his entire life as his bewitching green-eyed elf.

"My lord?"

Simon blinked away the image and regained control of himself. He turned his head to glance over his shoulder at his butler, who was standing in the doorway. "What is it, Greaves?"

"I am sorry to bother you, sir. I knocked, but you apparently did not hear me."

"I was lost in thought," Simon said impatiently. "What did you want?"

Greaves coughed discreetly, his scarred face looking more forbidding than usual. "I believe there is something you should know, sir. Lady Blade has, ah, delivered certain instructions to George, the footman."

"What instructions?" Simon walked back to his desk.

"She has asked George to find her a member of the criminal class who is skilled in the art of kidnapping."

Simon looked up swiftly, staring at his butler in stunned amazement. "Kidnapping! Are you certain?"

"Quite certain, sir. George was horrified, as you can imagine. He came straight to me and I have come directly to you. It seems my lady wishes to interview a successful villain who is in the market for temporary employment. Perhaps she is doing research for her epic poem, sir?"

"And perhaps she has decided to take certain matters into her own hands," Simon muttered. He sat down at his desk and reached for paper and pen. Quickly he dashed off a note.

Madam:
    I am interested in the employment you have specified. Let us meet on the Dark Walk at Vauxhall this evening at midnight. Carry a white fan. I shall find you and we shall discuss terms.
                              Yrs,
                              X.
P.S.: Use your husband's carriage and bring your maid with you.

Simon scanned the note, folded it carefully, and handed it to Greaves. "See that Lady Blade receives this in about an hour's time. And do not fret, Greaves. The situation is under control."

"Yes, my lord." Greaves looked somewhat relieved.

Simon waited until his butler had left the room before getting up to pour himself a glass of claret.

This was what came of overindulging females. Things had gone far enough. It was time Emily learned a very important lesson.

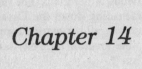

Chapter 14

The fireworks that lit up the sky above Vauxhall Gardens were a serious distraction, not only for Lizzie, but also for Emily. She had never seen such a display and in spite of her concerns she kept pausing to look up at each colorful flash. Cascades of light showered down from the heavens, the loud hissing explosions partially drowning out the crescendos of the energetic orchestra and the cheers of the crowds.

It was a thrilling spectacle and Emily would have been thoroughly captivated if she had not had far more important matters on her hands.

"Lord love us, ma'am, I never saw anything like this back in Little Dippington." Lizzie gazed in awe as another display of fire and light lit the night sky.

"Yes, I know, Lizzie. It is quite wonderful, but we must not linger. We must find the Dark Walk."

" 'Tis way off at the far end of the grounds, ma'am," Lizzie said promptly. "Very dark and narrow it is, too, not like the one we're on now. Surrounded by trees and bushes, it is. Young ladies have been known to be carried off the walk, straight into the woods and ravished."

Emily shot her maid a suspicious glance. "How would you know about the Dark Walk, Lizzie?"

"George the footman took me there the night you went to the Northcotes' ball," Lizzie confided with a cheerful grin. "Bought me ice cream, he did."

"I see." Emily clutched her shawl more tightly around her shoulders and tried to sound stern but she could not help feeling a bit envious of her maid. The thought of eating ice cream and promenading down the Dark Walk with Simon was enough to revive all her natural romantic impulses. "Then you will be able to show me how to find the walk."

"This way, ma'am."

Lizzie skipped off into the shadows. Emily followed, glancing around uneasily. The farther she and her maid got from the main promenades, the fewer lanterns were about to light their path. Giggles, small, feminine yelps, and masculine laughter drifted out from the woods that lined the paths.

Eventually Emily and Lizzie reached the narrow, tree-bordered Dark Walk. Here and there couples strolled, lost in a world of their own. One young man on the path ahead of Emily bent his head and said something into his girl's ear. She giggled, glanced back and forth along the path, and then followed her escort into the undergrowth. The couple promptly disappeared.

"Just like I told you, ma'am. Ravishers is hovering everywhere waitin' to prey on innocent young females," Lizzie whispered in an excited voice.

"Stay close to me, Lizzie. We don't want you being snatched. Where would I find another maid as skilled as you?"

"True enough, I suppose."

There was no one else in sight now. Emily looked about and saw only the night-shrouded woods. Involuntarily she moved closer to her maid.

"Do not forget to show your fan, ma'am," Lizzie said, sounding a bit more subdued now as they found themselves alone on the Dark Walk. "George particularly said you was to bring it. He said that's how this professional villain would recognize you."

"Oh, yes. The fan." Emily hastily unfurled the white fan

with the elegant dragon motif on it. She waved it about
industriously. "I do hope George knew what he was doing
when he hired this person from the criminal class."

"No offense, ma'am, but I hope *you* know what you're
doing. This is a strange business we're at here, if you don't
mind my sayin' so."

"Do not be impertinent, Lizzie." But the truth was, Emily was beginning to agree with her. The plan had seemed
perfect when she had drafted it in the safety of her own
bedchamber but now she admitted to herself she was having
a few qualms. She really did not know all that much about
dealing with professional villains. A sudden movement on
the path ahead startled her.

"Bloody hell." Emily bit back a small shriek when a
young urchin suddenly dashed out of the woods and came
to a halt directly in front of her. Lizzie gave a scream of
fright and clutched at Emily's arm.

"You be the lady with the white fan?" the lad demanded.

"Yes," Emily said, trying to calm her racing pulse.
"Who are you?"

"No matter. Yer to go straight into them bushes.
Alone." The boy looked meaningfully at Lizzie.

"What about me?" Lizzie asked fearfully.

"Yer to stay right there and wait for yer mistress to come
back," the boy told her brusquely. Then he whirled and
dashed off. In a few seconds he had vanished back into the
woods.

Lizzie looked plaintively at Emily. "I do not want to be
staying here all alone, ma'am."

"Calm yourself, Lizzie. You will be quite all right. Stay
right here in the center of the path."

"But, ma'am . . ."

"You must be brave, Lizzie." Emily patted her maid's
arm reassuringly and straightened her shoulders. She
wished there was someone around to reassure her.

It took courage to step off the walk into the shadowy
woods. The darkness thickened immediately as drooping
branches closed in around her. Emily held her fan in front
of her as if it were a talisman and peered sharply into the

heavy undergrowth. She could not help remembering what her maid had told her earlier about ravishers lurking in these woods.

When the deep, rasping, masculine voice came softly from behind a large tree on her right, Emily jumped several inches.

"You be the lady what's wantin' to hire herself a kidnapper?"

Emily swallowed, aware that her palms were suddenly damp. "That is correct. You, I assume, are the, uh, professional villain seeking employment?"

"Depends what exactly yer wants done."

"Nothing terribly difficult," Emily assured the rasping voice. "A little matter of kidnapping, as my footman no doubt told you. There is a gentleman whom I would like to have removed from town for a few days. I do not want him hurt, you understand, but merely held in a safe place for, oh, say five days. Can you do that?"

"It'll cost yer plenty."

Emily relaxed a bit. This was familiar territory. Apparently business deals in the criminal world were similar to those conducted in the *ton*. "I understand. I am prepared to pay a reasonable sum, naturally. But before you tell me your price, let me be clear that there really is no danger attached to this job. A very simple matter, really."

"Why five days?"

"I beg your pardon?" Emily frowned.

"Why d'ya want this gentry cove to disappear for five days?" the rasping voice repeated, sounding impatient.

"Not that it is any of your business," Emily said curtly, "but that is approximately how long I imagine it will take to clear up the problem here in town. When things are settled here, it will be safe for Charles—that is, for the gentry cove —to return to his lodgings."

"Yer just a female. How do you plan to fix matters here for the cove? Or do yer intend to hire me fer that part, too?"

"Oh, no, I shall not be needing your services to handle the main problem," Emily explained breezily. "My husband will be taking over soon. He will see to the details of settling the issue. When that is done, you may release my bro—er, the gentry cove."

There was a distinct pause from the other side of the tree. When the rasping voice spoke again, it sounded somewhat baffled. "Yer husband is going to settle things?"

"Of course."

"If that be so, why the devil ain't 'e 'ere tonight? Why ain't he arrangin' the snatch?"

Emily cleared her throat. "Well, as to that, he is a trifle annoyed with me at the moment. He does not completely approve of my efforts to save this particular gentry cove, you see. But he will soon come around. He just needs a little time to think about it."

"Damnation, lady. What makes yer think 'e'll change 'is mind?" the rasping voice demanded, sounding incensed. "Ye think ye got 'im on leading strings? Ye think 'e's so besotted with ye that all ye got to do is beckon 'im into bed with yer little finger and 'e'll do what 'ere you want 'em to do?"

Emily drew herself up proudly. "It has nothing to do with the way he feels about me. My husband is a just and honorable man and he will do the right thing. He just needs a little time to think about it first. And I do not happen to have a great deal of time."

"Mayhap 'e don't think savin' this gentry cove is the right thing," the voice snapped.

"Well, it is and he will soon see that for himself. The gentry cove is an innocent young man who happens to have gotten himself into deep water and will very likely get killed before he can swim out of it. My husband will not allow that to happen."

"Bloody 'ell," the voice muttered. "I 'ear different. I 'ear yer 'usband is a 'ard un. Not one to let 'imself be led about by a female. It's my guess 'e'll not only let this gentry cove take 'is chances, but 'e'll be out to teach you a sharp lesson, too."

"Nonsense," Emily said briskly. "You know nothing about my husband. He is a true gentleman. His thinking just gets a bit muddled at times, but I find that is true of most men. Now, then, let us get on with our bargain. What is your asking price?"

"A great deal more than yer wantin' to pay, I'll wager," the voice grated.

"How much?"

"What if I was to say the price for me services was a toss in the 'ay?" The voice was suddenly savage.

Emily froze, truly frightened for the first time that evening. She edged backward a step. "If you ever dare say such a thing to me again I shall tell my husband and he will break your damn bloody neck."

"Is that a fact?" the voice taunted roughly.

"Most definitely," Emily declared fiercely. "My husband protects his own. If you so much as touch me, I guarantee he will not rest until he tracks you down. I doubt if you would survive a day."

"Christ. Ye 'ave me shiverin' in me boots, lady," the voice drawled.

"As well you should be." Emily lifted her chin. "Be aware that if you are contemplating anything treacherous, you had better know that I left a letter at home in my bed-chamber. In it I told my husband precisely what I was going to do tonight. In the event I am harmed in any way, he will know to go to George, the man who hired you. From George he will learn your identity. You will not stand a chance of escaping his lordship's wrath. Do you understand me?"

"No," Simon said ruefully as he stepped out from behind the tree. "But I am beginning to believe that it is my fate to be forever unable to comprehend your strange fits and starts."

"Simon." Emily stared in astonishment at the tall, dark figure shrouded in a greatcoat. "What on earth are you doing here?"

"Damned if I know. I believe I had some vague notion of giving you a good scare and thereby teaching you a much-needed lesson. But that is surprisingly difficult to do when you insist on threatening me with myself."

"Oh, Simon, I knew you would help me save Charles."

Emily flung herself into his arms. "I knew you just needed a little time to think about the matter. You could not possibly allow my poor brother to fight a duel."

Simon crushed her against him for a moment. "I ought to beat you soundly and lock you in your room for a month for hatching this insane plot. You know that, don't you? Good God, woman, what do you mean by arranging to hire professional villains? Do you have any notion of what you were getting involved in? Kidnapping, of all things."

"I know you are annoyed with me, my lord," Emily said, her voice muffled by the thick wool of his coat. "But you must see time was of the essence. I knew you would come around eventually, but I had to do something about rescuing Charles immediately. I was merely trying to buy a little time for you to come to your senses and realize that you had to help me save my brother."

"And I suppose you now believe that is exactly what I will do?" Simon asked coolly.

Emily raised her head to look up into his shadowed face. "I do not believe you can let him risk death, Simon. Surely you do not hate him. He had nothing to do with what happened all those years ago. He was only a boy."

"The sins of the fathers . . ." Simon quoted softly.

"Nonsense. If that applies, then it applies to me, as well as Devlin and Charles. And you do not hold me responsible for what happened to your family twenty-three years ago, do you?"

Simon exhaled heavily and gave her a gentle push back toward the path. "We will discuss this later."

Emily glanced back over her shoulder as he followed her out of the woods. "What are we going to do now, Simon?"

"It appears there is nothing for it but to see what I can do about rescuing that scapegrace brother of yours. Obviously I will not have any peace otherwise."

"Thank you, Simon."

"It would be well for you to remember, elf, that this is the one and only favor I ever intend to do for a Faringdon."

"I understand," Emily said softly. "And I shall be forever grateful."

"I do not particularly want your gratitude," Simon told her.

"What do you want?"

"Assurance that you will never again get yourself into a scrape like this. You could have been robbed, raped, or killed tonight, Emily. Sending George to hire a villain was a monumentally stupid notion."

She tightened her grip on her shawl as they stepped back out onto the path. "Yes, my lord."

"Furthermore, in future, you are not to—" Simon broke off with an oath as Lizzie cried out at the sight of them and rushed toward her mistress.

"There you are, ma'am. Thank the sweet Lord. I was so worried. I was afraid you'd been carried off and ravished and I did not know what on earth I was going to tell his lordship when he asked about you and it would have been hard to keep him from knowing you was gone. Sooner or later he would have been bound to notice and—" Lizzie halted abruptly as she realized who it was standing next to Emily.

"You are quite right," Simon said coldly. "Sooner or later I would have been bound to notice if her ladyship had been carried off."

"Oh, sir." Lizzie gave a jerky little curtsy and stared at Simon in shock. " 'Tis you, sir."

"Very observant of you. And if you do not wish to find yourself on the street looking for a new position without benefit of references, you will endeavor to make certain that in future her ladyship never promenades along the Dark Walk alone again."

"Yes, sir." Lizzie looked terrified now.

Emily gave her husband a chiding look. "Simon, do stop frightening the poor girl. As for you, Lizzie, stop sniffling and collect yourself. All is well. His lordship was on to my scheme right from the start. Was that not brilliant of him?"

"Yes, ma'am." Lizzie cast an uncertain glance at Simon's forbidding face. "Brilliant."

"And now," Emily said cheerfully, "you will go straight home in the carriage, Lizzie. His lordship and I must be off.

We have business to attend to tonight. Do not wait up for me."

"A moment, if you please, madam," Simon drawled. "There seems to be some misunderstanding here. You will be going straight home with your maid."

"But, Simon, this was all my idea and I want to see it through to the end."

"You have involved me now and when I am involved in a plan, I prefer to be in charge. You are going home. I will walk you out of the gardens and put you into the carriage myself."

"But, Simon, you will need me with you."

"This is men's business."

"This is my brother we are talking about," she said desperately.

"You have turned the problem over to me to resolve."

Emily ignored him and plunged into a detailed explanation of why she simply had to accompany him while he set about rescuing Charles but she might as well have been talking to a brick wall. Simon was implacable and unswervable.

Several minutes later she found herself bundled into the carriage together with Lizzie. Simon closed the door and gave his coachman strict instructions to drive straight home. Then he swung around and walked off into the night without looking back.

"Bloody hell." Emily flounced on the seat, snapped her fan in annoyance, and then, with a small sigh, surrendered to the inevitable.

After a moment she smiled in relief. Everything would be all right now. The dragon was in charge.

Simon walked up the steps of the lodgings shared by the Faringdon twins with mixed emotions. He rapped on the door. It was opened almost at once by one of the twins, who stared at him in bemusement.

"I believe you are Devlin. Is that correct?" Simon asked laconically.

Devlin collected himself. "Yes, my lord. What the devil are you doing here, Blade?"

"An excellent question. One I am still asking myself, in fact. May I come in?"

"Well, yes, I suppose so." Devlin moved reluctantly back from the doorway.

"Thank you," Simon said dryly. He stepped into the room and tossed his hat, coat, and gloves to the manservant.

Charles Faringdon belatedly realized who had come calling and half rose from the chair near the fire.

"Blade. Why in God's name have you come at this hour?"

"Emily tells me you are to fight a duel with Grayley." Simon went to warm his hands in front of the fire.

Charles shot a scathing look at his twin. "I told you that you should never have brought her here today. Now she's gone and blathered the whole tale to *him.*"

"I had to give her a chance to say farewell to you," Devlin protested. "I had no choice."

"You should never have said a damn thing. This is a private matter." Charles slumped back in the chair.

"I agree that it would have been far more convenient all the way around if you had simply arranged to get yourself killed." Simon told him. "But as you have involved Emily, I have no choice but to become involved."

"This is none of your affair," Charles muttered, staring broodingly into the flames.

"Ah, but it is. You have alarmed Emily and upset her greatly. I cannot allow that; therefore, I must do something about the situation." Simon pinned Charles with a grim look. "Now, suppose you tell me the whole story so that I can decide what needs to be done."

"It's a matter of honor," Charles growled, slanting Simon a sidelong glance. "A woman's honor."

"Since when have you become overly concerned about protecting a woman's honor?"

There was a deathly silence before Charles said slowly, "Devlin and I have done some thinking since that day you knocked us about in your library."

"Have you, indeed?" Simon gazed into the flames.

"He is right, sir," Devlin said quietly. "We have discussed the matter at length. You were correct. We should have called Ashbrook out after he ran off with our sister."

Simon considered that. "Strictly speaking, it was your father's task."

"Yes, well, whatever. It did not feel right to do nothing about it at the time but father said—" Devlin broke off abruptly, shrugging.

"Father said the damage was done and there was no sense getting killed over the matter," Charles finished quietly. "And Emily agreed. She claimed it was all her fault in the first place."

"Which it probably was, knowing Emily," Devlin said, picking up his brandy. "But Charles and I have decided that was neither here nor there. The least we could have done was to have thrashed Ashbrook."

"Yes." Simon studied the golden flames. He was beginning to see the problem. Apparently he had only himself to blame for this mess. "So an opportunity has come along to allow at least one of you to redeem yourself in your own eyes and you grabbed it. Who is the lady?"

"I cannot tell you that, sir," Charles said stiffly.

"I understand your reluctance, but I am afraid I must insist. I never make a move until I have all the information it is possible to obtain. And I hardly see that telling me matters a great deal at this juncture. After all, Grayley apparently knows and that is the main problem."

"He's right, Charles," Devlin said morosely. "Tell him."

"Maryann Matthews," Charles said.

Simon nodded. "A pleasant enough chit. Family comes from Yorkshire, I believe."

"Exactly, sir. I intend to marry her," Charles said somewhat defiantly.

Simon shrugged. "That is your affair. How did the girl come to get herself insulted?"

Charles glowered. "She did nothing whatsoever objectionable. She is an innocent with charming manners and a sweet temper. Grayley simply walked up to me in my club last night and made a totally uncalled-for slur on her character."

Devlin looked at Simon. "Grayley said she was just another countrified lightskirt who had probably been to bed with every farmer in Yorkshire."

Simon raised his brows at that. "A bit extreme."

"It was a damn deliberate provocation," Charles announced, slamming his fist down on the arm of the chair.

"Yes, it was. Grayley is looking for fresh blood, apparently."

"What do you mean?" Devlin asked.

"Grayley is one of those rare individuals who actually enjoys the thrill of terrifying his opponent on the dueling field." Simon's mouth hardened. "He is a crack shot who derives a certain excitement from the whole process. He is always careful to choose victims he knows are not good marksmen. But his reputation has spread and he has difficulty these days finding anyone foolish enough to meet him. When he does manage to force a challenge, most men are wise enough to have their seconds convey abject apologies."

"I shall not send apologies," Charles vowed. "I would sooner die on the field of honor than allow Maryann's honor to be impugned."

Simon gave him a considering look. "I believe you actually mean that."

"Do not bother to try to talk me out of this meeting, sir. I have taken a vow."

"I see." Simon drummed his fingers thoughtfully on the mantel. "Very well, then, Devlin and I will act as your seconds. Come along, Dev."

Devlin looked at him. "Where are we going?"

"Why, to meet with Grayley, of course. There are all sorts of small details that must be worked out."

"But we already know when and where the meeting is to be held," Devlin said.

Simon shook his head, feeling a hundred years older than these young cubs. Broderick Faringdon had much to answer for, he reflected. "You have a great deal to learn and, unfortunately, it begins to look as though I shall have to be the one to instruct you."

Simon and Devlin sat in the darkened carriage and watched the front door of the club until it opened at last to reveal Grayley. His eyes on his quarry, Simon tapped the roof of the carriage with his walking stick. As instructed, the coachman drew the hired vehicle directly up in front of Grayley.

Grayley, a pinched-faced, thin-lipped man with restless, predatory eyes, bounded inside. He flung himself into the seat before he noticed that the carriage was already occupied.

"Good evening, Grayley." Simon tapped the roof once more and the coachman set the vehicle in motion.

"What the bloody hell is this all about?" Grayley demanded, scowling first at Devlin and then at Simon.

"Faringdon and I will be acting as Charles Faringdon's seconds," Simon said. "We came to settle a few minor points."

"You should be talking to my seconds, Barton and Evingly."

"I think you will take a personal interest in these details." Simon smiled without any humor. "And I do not believe you will want Barton and Evingly to know about them."

Grayley sneered. "You've come to offer apologies on Faringdon's behalf?"

"Of course not. I understand you grossly insulted the lady in question," Simon said. "You are the one who must offer apologies."

Grayley narrowed his eyes. "Now, why would I do that, pray tell?"

"Because if you do not," Simon explained gently, "then Faringdon, here, and I will be forced to put it about that your business investments will soon be taking a very serious downturn and you will not be able to meet your considerable financial obligations, let alone your gaming vowels."

Grayley went still. "Damn you, Blade, are you threatening me?"

"Yes, I believe I am. I understand you have invested rather heavily in a certain trading venture in which I am also involved."

"What of it? I stand to make a fortune."

"That will be highly unlikely if I decide the risk is not worth the candle and decide to sell off my shares tomorrow. Word will get around town by noon that the deal has gone bad. If I pull out, everyone else will want out at once. The market for the shares will disappear and you, along with the other investors, will lose everything you have put into the project."

Grayley stared at him. "Good God. You would ruin me and the others."

"Very likely."

"For the sake of a Faringdon?" Grayley asked in utter disbelief. "I heard you had no love for any of that clan."

"Which is why you felt it safe to challenge one of them, I understand. But there you have it. Fate takes odd twists now and again. Shall I convey your apologies to Charles Faringdon and explain that it was all a misunderstanding?"

Grayley was silent for a long moment. "Those who call you a cold-blooded bastard are right to do so, Blade."

Simon shrugged, glancing idly out the carriage. The hour was late but the street was filled with carriages carrying the elegant members of the *ton* to and fro on their endless round of parties. "Well, Grayley? Surely you can look for easier meat elsewhere?"

"Damn you, Blade."

"Come, man," Simon said softly. "You do not need to prove your marksmanship on the Faringdon boy. Find some other victim."

"You will go too far one of these days, Blade."

"Possibly."

Grayley's mouth thinned. He rapped on the roof to signal the coachman to halt. When the carriage stopped, he opened the door and climbed down. "Convey my apologies to your brother," he said curtly to Devlin. "There will be no dawn meeting."

Grayley stepped back and slammed the door. The carriage clattered off down the street. Devlin looked at Blade with something approaching hero worship in his eyes.

"I say, that was astounding. You actually got Grayley to cry off the entire affair. I have never heard of such a thing."

"I do not expect to find myself with a similar task at any time in the future," Simon said bluntly. "Is that quite clear?"

"Yes, sir. Very clear." Devlin was exuberant now. "Dashed clever of you, though. The man withdrew from the duel simply because you implied his investments would suffer."

Simon shook his head over such naïveté. "Faringdon, it is time you and your brother learned that real power is based on money and information. Armed with those two things, a man can accomplish a great deal more than he can with a dueling pistol or a deck of cards."

"And if a man lacks the blunt?" Devlin asked shrewdly.

"Then he must concentrate on obtaining the information. With a sufficient amount of that resource, he will soon find the other."

"I shall remember that," Devlin said quietly. He was silent for a moment and then his mood lightened once more. "By the bye, Charles and I have been wondering if you would show us that fascinating fighting technique you used on us that day in your library. Would it be too much to ask?"

"I suppose I could demonstrate it for you. The thing I do not entirely understand," Simon said reflectively, "is how I came to be in this situation in the first place."

Devlin grinned the charming Faringdon grin. "You mean rescuing Charles and showing us a trick or two about how to be going on in the world? I expect it is all Emily's fault."

"You are correct, of course. It is all her fault."

"She is the one person on the face of the earth who does

not think you are a cold-blooded devil, you know," Devlin
said.

"Emily's tendency toward the romantical is occasionally
awkward."

"I know," Devlin said, not without sympathy. "One always hates to disillusion her."

Chapter 15

Emily stopped pacing her bedchamber at the sound of carriage wheels on the street outside. She flew to the window when she realized the vehicle was coming to a halt in front of the townhouse. She pushed the heavy drapes aside just in time to see Simon alight. His caped greatcoat swung around his boots as he started up the steps. Hastily she shoved open the window and peered down.

"Simon," she called softly. "Are you all right? Is everything settled?"

Simon glanced up and said in a distinctly irritable voice, "For God's sake, woman, get back inside and close the window. Whatever will the neighbors think?" He went on up the steps.

Everything must have been settled in a reasonable fashion, Emily decided cheerfully as she yanked the window closed. Things could not be all that bad if Simon was worrying about the neighbors.

She was getting to understand his moods quite well, Emily told herself happily. She tapped her slippered foot on the carpet and waited for the sound of bootsteps in the upstairs hall. Her communication with her husband in the metaphysical realm was definitely growing stronger every day. A direct result, no doubt, of their improved communication on the physical plane.

She heard his step in the hall and hurried over to the connecting door. But just as she started to open it she heard Higson's voice and realized the loyal bulldog of a valet had waited up for his master.

Dismayed at the delay, Emily silently eased the door shut and resumed her pacing until she heard Higson being dismissed for the night.

She rushed straight back to the connecting door and threw it open.

Simon was sitting in the shadows near the window, a glass of brandy in his hand. He was wearing his black satin dressing gown. There was a single candle burning on the table near the bed. His dark hair was tousled and in the faint glow of the flame his face looked as if it had been carved from the side of a mountain. He glanced up as Emily came into the room, his golden eyes glinting strangely.

"Ah, my reckless, impulsive, troublesome little wife. I imagine you are bursting with curiosity."

"Oh, yes, Simon. I have been waiting in agony for the past few hours." Emily dropped into the chair across from his and studied him carefully. "Is all well?"

"The matter is settled, if that is what you mean," Simon said coolly. "There will be no duel." He took another swallow of brandy and contemplated the glass. "But I am not certain if all is well."

A fresh uneasiness gripped Emily as she sensed that his mood was growing odder by the moment. "What is wrong, my lord?"

"Wrong?" He turned the brandy glass between his palms and rested his head against the back of the chair. "That is difficult to explain, my dear."

She peered at him more closely through her spectacles. "Simon, you are not hurt, are you?" she demanded in some alarm.

"Not a drop of blood was shed."

"Thank God." Emily grinned suddenly. "No, it is you I have to thank for fixing the matter, not God, and I am well aware of it. I am very grateful to you for resolving the situation, Simon."

"Are you?" He took another sip of brandy.

Emily bit her lip. "You are in a rather strange mood, my lord."

"Now, I wonder why that should be," he mused. "It has been a perfectly normal evening, has it not? Nothing untoward or unusual has occurred. Just the routine sort of thing. I find my wife promenading the Dark Walk at Vauxhall at midnight seeking an appointment with a member of the criminal class. I let myself get talked into rescuing a damn Faringdon from his own foolishness. I am obliged to put a potentially profitable investment at risk in order to scare off one of the most vicious young bloods of the *ton.* And I come home to discover my lady wife hanging out the window, calling down to me like a hoyden."

Emily sighed. "Somehow my life's little adventures always sound much worse when you describe them."

"I have noticed that."

Emily brightened. "Still, I must tell you I thought your plot to lure me to Vauxhall was a wonderful notion. That was very clever of you, Simon. Do you know, it never even occurred to me to be suspicious when I got your note. Now I realize that a member of the criminal class would be highly unlikely to read and write."

"Your praise is heartwarming, I assure you. But looking back on the matter, I conclude that I must have been temporarily mad to concoct such a scheme."

"No, no, you wanted to teach me a lesson, did you not?"

"I had some vague notion of doing so, yes." Simon took another sip of brandy.

"And you came up with a truly brilliant scheme."

"Really? I did not notice you looking appropriately chastened. You stood there and bargained like a shopkeeper with a man you thought to be a cutthroat and when he attempted to frighten you by demanding your favors in exchange for his services, you promptly threatened him with your husband's wrath."

It dawned on Emily that Simon was genuinely furious.

"Now, Simon, I do not see why you are so angry with me. You are the one who arranged the meeting at Vauxhall."

"As I said, I must have been mad." He swirled the remaining brandy in his glass and downed it in a single swallow.

"Actually, I think it was the deeply romantic element in your nature that prompted you to construct such a wonderful plot," Emily decided. "It was just like an incident from a tale of romance and adventure and you knew I would respond to it. I expect that is because we are so attuned to each other on the higher plane."

"Christ, Emily, will you cease prattling on about metaphysics and higher planes? I swear by God that if I am not already mad, *I soon will be.*"

Without warning Simon surged to his feet and hurled the empty brandy glass into the fireplace with a swift, violent motion of his hand.

There was a sharp, nerve-jarring explosion of sound that echoed through the bedchamber. The glittering shards fell into the cold ashes.

Emily gasped and sat very still in her chair as the last of the glass cascaded down the stone wall of the fireplace. She stared at the hearth and then turned her head slowly to look at Simon.

The rigid expression on his face and the fierce glitter in his eyes told her instantly that he was far more shocked by his own loss of control than she was. After all, she knew him to be a man of deep passions. But he did not always accept the truth about himself.

"Damnation." Simon stood staring into the fireplace. A great silence descended.

Emily's hands tightened in her lap. "I did not mean to annoy you, my lord," she said quietly.

" 'Tis unnatural, do you realize that?" He swung around to confront her, his face demonic in the flickering candlelight. "Damn unnatural."

"What is, my lord?"

"The addlepated manner in which you persist in thinking of me as some sort of hero. Once and for all, madam

wife, I am not a character from an epic poem. I do not make
my decisions or carry out my actions for the sole purpose of
indulging your frivolous romantic whims and fancies. I am
not a creature of passion like yourself. Every move I make is
carefully calculated. Everything is done to achieve my own
ends. *Do you comprehend that?*"

Emily took a deep breath. "You are annoyed with me
because you were obliged to rescue my brother tonight."

"Annoyed with you, madam? That does not begin to
cover the present state of my temper. I let you manipulate
and cajole me into doing something I have sworn never to
do."

"You mean help a Faringdon?" She risked a glance up at
him through her lashes.

"Yes, goddamn it. Yes, that is exactly what I mean. I do
not know what came over me tonight."

"I do not think your actions so strange, my lord," Emily
said softly. "You acted like the noble, honorable man I
know you to be. In your heart you are aware that my brothers were not responsible for your father's losses twenty-three
years ago."

"They are Faringdons. They are in their father's image,
by God."

"No, my lord. My father would never have agreed to
fight a duel over a lady's honor. Charles and Devlin are not
like him. They have been raised by him and they have followed in his footsteps only because they have had no other
pattern to follow. But they are different, I swear it. And
somewhere deep inside you, you understand that or you
would not have helped Charles tonight."

"I do not want to hear another word about why I did
what I did, Emily. You can have no notion of why I acted as
I did. Even I am not entirely certain." Simon flexed one
hand into a fist and struck the mantel. "I vowed vengeance
against the entire Faringdon clan twenty-three years ago. I
swore to myself I would bring down the entire family."

"Then why did you marry one?" Emily demanded with
sudden fierceness.

Simon narrowed his eyes. "Because it amused me. Because it served the purpose of separating your father and brothers from the source of their income. Because you begged me to marry you and because I rather enjoyed having a Faringdon woman groveling at my feet."

That stung. "I did not grovel, my lord. I presented the entire matter to you in terms of a business arrangement, if you will recall."

He ignored that. "And last, but not least, because I find your excessive passions, as you term them, quite amusing in bed. There. Now you know why I married you. It was not because our souls meet and mingle over tea on a higher plane, damn it."

Emily shivered. The dragon was breathing fire tonight. It was the first time she had ever seen him in such a mood and there was no doubt but that it was extremely intimidating. "Please, Simon, do not say any more."

"Why not, pray tell? Because it will break your silly, romantic little heart?"

"Yes, my lord."

"By heaven, you need to face reality, you little goose." Simon swung around and began to pace the room. "Not that I seem to have been successful thus far in forcing you to do so."

That was too much. Emily leapt to her feet. "Bloody hell, Simon."

"Stop saying *bloody hell*," he ordered. "Such language does not suit the Countess of Blade."

"I do not care what befits the Countess of Blade," she shot back passionately. "You go too far when you tell me I must face reality. You do not know how much reality I have had to face all my life. You have no notion of how much reality my poor mother had to confront. Rest assured that there were times when I hated my father just as much as you must have hated yours."

Simon turned his head abruptly to glare at her. "What the devil are you talking about now? I never hated my father."

Emily looked at him. "How could you not have been furiously angry after what he did to you?"

"You must be mad. Why should I hate him, for God's sake?"

"Because he put a pistol to his head and killed himself, leaving you behind with the full responsibility for your mother. Because he took the quick way out of the disaster he had created and left you to face it. Because you were only twelve years old, far too young to be able to undo the great damage that had been done. Dear God, Simon, how could you not have hated him?"

Simon stood, feet braced, and stared at her as if she had suddenly turned into a hydra-headed monster. "You are raving."

Emily turned her back to him. "If it is any consolation, I was in much the same situation."

"In what way?"

"The money ran out the year I turned seventeen. But by then my father discovered I had a head for economy and financial matters. He was ecstatic. It was clear I was expected to be the family's salvation. And I did not mind studying investments and making the decisions. Indeed, it was enjoyable, in a way. But I could never forget for a moment that the reason I had to become an expert was because my father was an irresponsible spendthrift. I still remember how he made Mama cry." Emily dashed a tear away from the corner of her eye with the back of her hand.

"Pray, do not start sniveling, Emily."

She blew her nose on a hankie she found in the pocket of her loose wrapper. "She cried often, you know. But almost never around my father. She loved him, you see, in spite of his ways. She used to tell me it was no use blaming him for his excessive gaming. It was in the blood, she would say."

"Emily, your emotions are overset. You had better go to bed."

"Oh, do stop being so bloody condescending, my lord." Emily sniffed back the last of the tears and stuffed the hankie into her pocket. "When my mother and brothers realized I could keep the family afloat financially, they told me it was my duty to do so. I shall never forget that on her deathbed my mother took my hand and told me I must look after my father and brothers. Without me they would all soon find themselves under the hatches, she said, and poor Papa could not live without plenty of money."

"I really do not wish to hear any more of this nonsense, Emily."

"It is not nonsense. It is reality. The reality you told me I never face. Well, you may rest assured I have faced it all my life, my lord. And I bloody hell do not like it. But it will not go away, so I shall continue to confront it when I must."

"Including the reality of our marriage?" he drawled in a dangerous voice.

"Our marriage is a different matter altogether. It is a pure and noble union of souls, even if you do not yet see it that way."

"No, Emily, it is not pure and noble. It is damn real. Just as real as your father's profligate ways and my vengeance. Perhaps it is time I made you confront that fact."

She frowned at the strange tone in his last words. "What are you talking about, my lord?"

"I am talking about teaching you to face the truth about why I married you. I am no hero, Emily."

"Yes, my lord, you are. You simply resist seeing yourself in that light. Probably because you fear it will make you appear weak to yourself or to others."

"Good God, woman, you are incredible. I know of no other female who can concoct such fancies," Simon said between his teeth. "You really do need a lesson." There was a deliberate pause and then he spoke again, his voice lower and harsher than ever. "Come here, Emily."

She did not move. Her own emotions were in a turmoil.

"Come here to me now, madam. I am in no mood to humor any of your romantic notions tonight."

She turned very slowly to confront him. She was suddenly, deeply wary. "What do you want of me, my lord?"

His hard mouth curved in a cold, taunting smile. "What do you think I want, wife? I told you the reasons I married you."

"So you did, my lord. I believe you said it amused you to marry me. And it suited your notions of vengeance."

"There was another reason, if you will recall. You are as yet rather unschooled in the delights of the boudoir, but you are learning fast. And you show such enthusiasm for the task, my dear. I would like you to demonstrate a bit of that enthusiasm now, if you please. Come here and apply yourself to your wifely duties."

The iciness of the command was alarming. There was no warmth or passion in Simon's face, only a savagely controlled fury.

"You are truly enraged with me because I prevailed upon you to rescue Charles," Emily whispered. "I did not realize it would make you so angry, my lord. Such fury can only stem from the fact that you think you have shown great weakness in obliging me. Please, Simon, do not view your rescue of Charles in such a light, I beg you."

"As much as I enjoy having you beg occasionally, you may do so some other time, madam. Right now, I want to bed you."

Simon stripped off his dressing gown and stalked across the bedchamber to the massive, four-poster bed. He was completely naked and the candlelight flickered on his skin, emphasizing the smoothly sculpted muscles of his back, his flat, taut stomach, and his hard buttocks. The soft light also revealed his aroused manhood.

Even as Emily watched uneasily out of the corner of her eye, his shaft swelled and hardened further. She clutched the lapels of her wrapper in one hand and looked away.

"You see the effect you have on me?" Simon asked as he slid into the bed. "You should be pleased, madam. It is a form of power, is it not, to be able to make a man react so instantly to your charms?"

"Not everyone thinks in terms of power and manipulation, my lord."

"You are wrong, Emily. Just as you are wrong about so many other things. Come here."

Emily hesitated and then very slowly she obeyed. She approached the bed with great caution, still clutching her wrapper tightly. She realized suddenly that she was dealing with a wounded dragon tonight. They were old wounds, true enough, but they had been freshly opened. The pain could cause even a man of Simon's nobility and character to slash at any hand that came within reach.

But she also knew that the dragon needed warmth and love tonight. He needed her. And while he might scorch her a bit with a few stray flames, he would not really hurt her.

Simon would never hurt her, never in a million years. She remembered the promise he had made to her on their wedding night: *I vow I will always protect you, Emily. Whatever else happens, know that I will always take care of you.*

Emily let the wrapper slide to the floor as she came to a halt beside the bed. She saw Simon's eyes go to the outline of her hips revealed through the fine lawn of her gown. That heated gaze traveled slowly, deliberately upward to where her nipples were pushing against the delicate fabric.

Emily felt exposed. She was accustomed to seeing controlled passion in Simon's expression but not this laconic, taunting look. She quickly got into bed and pulled the covers up to her chin. She waited nervously for him to touch her. She was certain that once he did, all would be well.

Simon made no move. He folded his arms behind his head and studied her with mocking amusement. "Well, madam? How do you expect to ensnare me with your excessive passions from under that pile of blankets?"

Emily blinked. "You are waiting for me to . . . to do something?"

"I am waiting for you to show me what you have learned thus far as a wife."

"Oh." Emily absorbed the implications. *He wanted her to make love to him.* The notion intrigued her greatly. She could explore him to her heart's content if she were in charge of the lovemaking. She could indulge herself, learn the feel of him, show him how much she loved him.

Emily turned on her side to face Simon. Tentatively she put out a hand and touched his shoulder. He did not move. She edged closer under the covers and kissed his bare chest. The scent of him stirred her senses.

Emily twisted her fingers gently in the crisp hair. She moved still closer and kissed one flat, masculine nipple. Simon drew a deep breath.

"You appear to learn quickly, madam wife," he muttered.

Emily paid no attention to the cutting edge of his tongue. "I love to touch you, Simon. You are so hard and sleek and strong. Like one of your beautiful, jeweled dragons come to life."

"You are not afraid I will rend you to pieces?"

She smiled faintly, bent her head, and touched the tip of her tongue to his chest. "You would not do that."

"You are very confident of your power, are you not? Perhaps a little too confident."

"It is not a matter of power, Simon. It is a matter of love."

Growing bolder now, she began to stroke him slowly, lingeringly. She felt the tension in the muscles of his thighs and realized with surprise that he was having to exert enormous control over himself.

"Relax, my lord." She squeezed the taut muscles slowly. "You are far too tense. I expect it is a result of all your efforts on behalf of my brother."

"You think me tense?"

"Very. Here, I will see if I can help you grow calm." Emily threw off the last of the covers and knelt beside Simon. Ignoring the blatantly thrust shaft of his manhood, she began to gently, firmly squeeze and stroke the long muscles of his thighs.

"What the devil are you doing?" Simon demanded, eyeing her through slitted lids.

"I have seen my father do this to his horses after a long, bruising ride. He says it helps keep them from stiffening up." Emily kept up the rhythmic squeezing and stroking. Slowly she worked her way from upper thigh to ankle, kneading the muscles of Simon's left leg.

When she was finished, she leaned across and began to work on the right leg. The gossamer folds of her nightdress fluttered over Simon's upthrust manhood. A spasm went through his whole body.

"Hell and damnation," Simon muttered.

"Are you all right, my lord?" Emily paused in her ministrations to glance at him.

"I believe I am still a bit tense in places."

Emily smiled reassuringly. "We shall soon have you soothed and quieted, my lord." She continued down his right leg and then patted him gently. "Turn over, please."

He hesitated, glowering at her. His eyes were fierce and hot with arousal now. "Turn over?"

"So that I can work on the muscles of your back. Have you not noticed how stiff one's shoulders get when one's nerves are overset?"

"Emily, I assure you, I am not suffering from the vapors." Nevertheless, Simon reluctantly turned onto his stomach. He grimaced and reached down to adjust himself.

Emily started to work on his broad shoulders, found the position awkward because she could not bring proper pressure to bear, and shifted closer. When the new position did not work, either, she hitched up the skirts of her nightdress, boldly put one leg over Simon's hips, and knelt astride him.

"Stop squirming about," Simon growled into the pillow.

"Yes, my lord." Emily inhaled suddenly as she leaned forward and began kneading the muscles of his upper back. This was certainly stimulating to a passionate creature such as herself, she realized. She could feel Simon's hard thighs between her knees and the sensation was rather like being on the back of a blooded stallion. *Or a dragon.*

"Emily, are you giggling?"

"No, my lord." She worked more intensely, rubbing, stroking, probing, and prodding. Some minutes passed and there was no sound from the depths of the pillow. "Do you feel any calmer now, my lord?" Emily finally asked.

"No."

Emily was dismayed. "Are you quite certain?"

"Quite certain. You may dismount now."

"I beg your pardon?"

"You heard me." Simon stirred and started to turn over.

Emily quickly scrambled off his back and again knelt amid the bedclothes.

"Simon?"

He lay back against the pillows and reached for her. "Come here, elf," he muttered, pulling her astride him once more. He pushed the hem of the nightdress up over her thighs. "If you want to ride me, then you must do it properly."

"Simon." Emily gasped sharply as he reached down and guided the broad tip of his throbbing manhood to the damp place between her thighs.

He grasped her hips and held her still while he surged upward, pushing through the natural resistance at the entrance of her body and on into the damp, clinging passage. He filled her completely in one long thrust. Emily stifled a small, startled exclamation and splayed her fingers across his chest.

"Now you will ride me, madam." His fingers tightened on her thighs. *"Hard."*

Eyes closed, her breath coming in soft gasps of excitement, Emily obeyed his command and quickly adjusted to the pace and rhythm Simon established.

"Yes. Faster. Harder." Simon's voice was hoarse now. His hands tightened on her. "Damn, that feels good, elf. So damn good. Show me how much you want me. Tell me you belong to me. *Tell me.*"

"I want you, Simon. I have waited all my life for you. There could never be anyone else." The words were torn from Emily in small, gasping cries. She was shivering with her own need, slick with desire. Her nails were digging into Simon's chest, leaving small, fierce marks on his skin.

"That's it, sweetheart," he muttered. "Give yourself to me."

"I love you," Emily whispered. "I love you with all my heart." And then the delicious excitement overwhelmed her. She went rigid and at the same time felt Simon surge deep into her one last time.

"Emily. Oh, God, Emily." Simon's words were thick with passion and release. He pulled Emily down across his chest and his arms went fiercely around her. He crushed her to him as he let himself flow endlessly into her.

Emily's last coherent thought was that she had mastered the fine art of dragon riding. She looked forward to trying it again in the near future.

Chapter 16

The library clock tolled eleven. Simon lounged in his chair and watched Emily. He had been engaged in the task for the past twenty minutes, possessing himself in patience while time ticked past and the rain poured down outside.

Studying Emily was not an unpleasant occupation. She appeared extremely fetching this morning in a green-and-gold-striped gown trimmed with flounces. There were several beautifully worked dragons embroidered around the hem. Her gleaming curls were drawn back in an artfully arranged style that gave the effect of a shower of flames cascading down her nape.

She was sitting on the opposite side of the black lacquered library desk, her head bent anxiously over a list of names. It was clear she was agonizing over the task to which she had been set, that of selecting those who were to receive cards for her first soiree.

"There is no need to work yourself up into a state over this matter," Simon finally said gruffly. "Just put a checkmark beside the name of everyone you wish to invite. My secretary will do the rest."

Emily looked up sharply, her green eyes narrowed behind the lenses of her spectacles. "It is not as simple as

selecting investments, you know. I must make weighty decisions here. I do not want to offend anyone. It will reflect
directly on you, Simon."

Simon sighed and fell back into a brooding silence. He
was feeling restless and uneasy and, he suspected, guilty.

Guilt was a new and disturbing emotion for him and he
did not care for it. There was no room for it in his clearly
focused life. He did not even begin to understand it. Until
now his world had consisted of simple, straightforward con-
cepts such as vengeance, justice, honor, and duty.

Simon's gaze slid to the sweet curve of Emily's breasts as
he realized that passion had now been added to that list.

There was no doubt about it. He was in a strange and
unpalatable mood.

He had been in this odd state since awakening early this
morning, memories of the night still seething in his brain.
One moment he would be contemplating his own weakness
in going to the rescue of the Faringdon twin. The next he
would find himself growing hard with desire as he recalled
Emily's sweet, generous passion.

He could still feel her gentle hands on his shoulders and
the warmth of her thighs as she sat boldly astride him,
charming and bewitching him until he thought he would go
mad trying to hold on to his self-control.

But most of all, Simon found himself recalling her disturbing words: *There were times when I hated my father just
as much as you must have hated yours.*

"The thing is, Simon," Emily explained with an intense
frown of concentration, "your secretary has prepared a very
long list of names from which to choose. I do not know
many of these people and I do not want to make any mis-
takes. Your aunt has explained to me how crucial it is to
have all the right people at my first soiree."

"You may rest assured there are no wrong people on
that list," Simon growled. "My secretary knows better than
to include any inappropriate names. Furthermore, there is
absolutely no risk involved in offending people by failing to
invite them. It merely emphasizes and reinforces your power
as a hostess."

She looked at him wonderingly. "I had not thought of it like that. But I do not wish to hurt anyone's feelings, my lord."

The way I must have hurt yours last night? Simon wondered silently. "If it makes you feel better, send a card to everyone on the list."

Emily's eyes widened in astonishment. "But we could not possibly fit everyone inside this house."

"You've been to enough balls and parties by now to realize that they're not considered a success unless the place is crammed full. The carriages must be lined up and down the street for blocks. The guests must be stacked like cordwood in the drawing room. With any luck one or two ladies will faint from lack of air. Everyone must pronounce the event a dreadful squeeze and a great crush. Invite them all, Emily."

She chewed on her lower lip. "I do not know, Simon. It sounds most uncomfortable. It would be much easier to converse and serve refreshments if we have a small crowd."

"To hell with intelligent conversation and proper service, my dear. This is not the time or place for them. The point of this whole thing, as my aunt will no doubt explain to you, is to see that you make a proper debut as a hostess. To do that people must talk about the party afterward. In order to get people to talk, it must be an extremely large and noisy event. Invite everyone on the list, Emily."

"What about Canonbury, Peppington, Adley, and Renton? I do not really know any of them and I—"

"Most especially Canonbury and Peppington," Simon said softly. "We will make very certain they both receive invitations."

Emily lowered the sheet of paper and looked at him, her head tipped thoughtfully to one side. "If you say so, Simon." Then she frowned again in sudden concern. "What if nobody responds to the cards we send out?"

Simon stifled a thin smile of satisfaction. "Believe me, my dear, they will all accept." He leaned across the desk and impatiently snapped the list from her fingers. "I will see that my secretary gets this and sends out the cards. Now, then, Emily, I want to talk to you."

"Yes, my lord?" She waited with an air of alert expectation.

"Damn. Must you always look at me that way, elf? I vow that you are going to turn me into a Bedlamite with that unholy combination of naïveté and mischief. You almost make me forget that just yesterday you were busy trying to employ a cutthroat."

"I am sorry, my lord," Emily said, not appearing the least bit repentant. "Are you planning to lecture me again on that matter?"

"No." Simon stood up and walked over to the window, turning his back on her. He studied the drenched garden behind the townhouse while he collected his thoughts. "I have a difficult task before me, Emily."

"What is that, my lord?"

"I wish to apologize to you," he said softly.

There was a small pause before Emily said carefully, "Whatever for?"

"For my unchivalrous behavior last night," Simon muttered. "I did not treat you well, elf. I behaved in a most ill-mannered and ungentlemanly fashion."

"You mean all that business about ordering me into your bed? Rubbish. Pray do not regard it, my lord," Emily said lightly. "I had an excellent time once I got there."

Simon shook his head in awe. "You are amazing, Emily."

"Well, 'tis not as if you were unkind or cruel, Simon. You were simply in a temper and you had every reason to be irritable, considering you had just been obliged to forgo a twenty-three-year-old vow of vengeance. If I had been truly alarmed, I would have escaped to my own room and locked the door. You did not frighten me in the least."

"Apparently not." He was silent for a long moment. "There is something else for which I must apologize."

"Now you are beginning to alarm me, Blade," she said, laughter in her voice. "What was your other grave sin?"

"I underestimated you, my dear. You come across as so naive and optimistic, so determined to see the bright side of everyone and everything, so damn certain that I am some

sort of hero when I know perfectly well I am not, that I did
not credit you with a proper comprehension of your family
situation. I should have known that anyone as shrewd with
investments and money as you are could not be entirely
blind to human nature. Did you really hate your father at
times in the past?"

"Yes." Emily's voice no longer held a light note.

"You were correct when you said I must have hated
mine for leaving me to pick up the pieces after he put that
damn bullet through his head." Simon clenched his hand
slowly and then forced himself to relax each finger. "I did
not even realize just how much I hated him until you
pointed it out last night."

"It seems a perfectly natural reaction to me, my lord,"
Emily said gently. "We were, both of us, given adult responsibilities at a very young age and expected to perform as
adults. We were obliged to look after the welfare of others at
a time when, by rights, someone should have been concerned about our welfare."

"Yes. I had not thought of it that way." Simon gazed out
into the gray mist. "It was raining that night when I found
him. He had come back from London two hours earlier. I
heard my mother asking him what was wrong. He would
not speak to her. He went into the library and announced he
was not to be disturbed under any conditions. Mama went
upstairs and cried. After a while we all heard the shot."

"Dear God, Simon."

"I reached the library first and opened the door. He was
lying facedown across the desk. The gun had fallen from his
hand. There was blood everywhere. And I saw that he had
left a note. For me. *Damn his soul to hell.* He did not say
goodbye or explain why he had to kill himself or tell me
how in God's name I was supposed to handle the mess he
had created. He just left a damn note telling me to take care
of my mother."

"Simon. My dear Simon."

He did not hear her rise from the chair, but Emily was
suddenly there behind him, her arms going around his
waist. She hugged him with a fierce protectiveness, as if she

could somehow banish forever the sight of his father's brains spattered on the wall behind the desk.

For a long while Simon did not move. He simply allowed Emily to hold him. He could feel her warmth and softness and he realized that this was akin to what he experienced when he made love to her, but slightly different. It was not passion he was feeling, but another kind of closeness, one he had never known before with any woman.

After a while it dawned on Simon that he was feeling calmer, more at peace with himself. The restlessness that had awakened him that morning was gone.

There was silence in the library until Greaves knocked on the door to announce the arrival of Simon's secretary.

Emily entered the park at a brisk trot, followed by her groom. The mare she was riding was a beautiful gray with fine, sensitive ears, delicate nostrils, and spectacular conformation. The horse had been a gift from Simon, who had surprised her with it two days earlier after their conversation in the library. Emily and her maid had promptly decided that the very new, very dashing riding habit *à la militaire* complimented the animal perfectly.

"Ah, there you are, Emily," Lady Merryweather said as she approached on a sleek bay. "You look spectacular in that black habit." She examined the red and gold trim on collar and cuffs with a critical eye. "I confess I had a few doubts when we ordered it, but I am very pleased to see how it sets off your fair skin and red hair. Quite dramatic."

Emily grinned. "Thank you, Araminta."

"You really should have removed the spectacles, however," Araminta admonished. "They do nothing for the habit."

"Araminta, I cannot ride a horse without being able to see what I am doing or where I am going."

"There must be some way to manage. We must work on the problem." Araminta drew her horse up alongside Emily's and the two started along the path, their grooms following at a discreet distance.

"Simon does not seem to mind my spectacles," Emily pointed out.

"Simon has a rather odd sense of humor. He finds your various eccentricities extremely amusing. And I must admit that they do not seem to be hurting your social success. The *ton* is quite taken with you these days. Your poor husband had a difficult time obtaining even one dance with you last night at Lady Crestwood's ball."

Emily blushed. "He could have had as many dances as he wished and well he knows it."

"Yes, I suppose that is true," Araminta acknowledged with a knowing glance. "I am certain he is well aware that you would trample over an entire mountain of your poor, faithful admirers to get to him if he but crooked his finger at you from the far side of a dance floor. Everyone else in Society is certainly aware of that fact."

"Really, Araminta, you make me sound like a hound who bounds straight to her master's side whenever she is called."

"Well, you do tend to make your preference for your husband quite clear. That is not particularly fashionable, my dear. And, to be perfectly frank, I am not altogether certain it is wise. You do not want Blade to begin to take you for granted."

"Blade takes nothing for granted," Emily stated. "He has a true understanding of everything he chooses to acquire and a full comprehension of the cost of whatever he does."

Araminta chuckled. "I can see it is hopeless to lecture you on the advantages of not giving away your true feelings to your husband. Now, then, my dear, you must tell me how the plans are going for your first soiree. Did you send out the cards?"

"Yesterday. I invited everyone on the list Simon's secretary prepared, Araminta. I trust I did the right thing. It is going to be a terrible crush."

"Just what you want. Trust me, my dear. You must be certain that the house is so crowded it takes people half an hour just to get in the door."

Emily grimaced. "That is what Simon said, but I still think it sounds uncomfortable."

"It is not a question of comfort, it is a matter of cementing your position as a hostess among the *haute monde*."

"Yes, I know. I must not embarrass Simon in any way," Emily said earnestly. "Believe me, Araminta, I am well aware of how important this soiree is to my husband. As Blade's wife it is my duty to make the affair a great success. The social world will be watching to see what sort of hostess the Earl of Blade has married and I am determined that Simon not be humiliated in any way."

Araminta frowned. "I do not think you quite understand, Emily. This is your debut as a hostess. It is *your* soiree."

"And everything I do will reflect on Simon," Emily concluded firmly. "The soiree must be perfect in every detail. I have spent hours on the plans already. Very exhausting, if you must know the truth."

Araminta gave up and nodded to a lady being driven toward them in a brown landau. "Smile," she commanded Emily in a low voice. "That is Lady Peppington. I shall introduce you."

Emily smiled cheerfully at the elegantly dressed middle-aged woman as Araminta made the introductions. Lady Peppington inclined her head in a frozen nod and then looked away. The landau went briskly on down the path.

Emily was seized with panic. "Bloody hell."

Araminta raised her brows. "What on earth is the matter now, Emily?"

"You said that was Lady Peppington," Emily hissed.

"What of it?"

"She's on my guest list and 'tis obvious she does not particularly like me. What if she will not attend my soiree? Simon will be furious. He distinctly told me he wanted the Canonburys and the Peppingtons to come. Araminta, what shall I do?"

"Absolutely nothing. You may be certain the Canonburys and the Peppingtons will come to your affair, along with everyone else who gets an invitation."

Emily shot her companion a speculative glance. "How can you and Simon be so positive of that?"

"Simon has not told you about Canonbury and Peppington, has he?"

Emily remembered the grimness in her husband's expression when he had informed her that Canonbury and Peppington would attend the soiree. "Araminta, is there something I should know about these people?"

"It is not my place to tell you," Araminta said, looking thoughtful, "but I believe I shall. It is in your own best interests to know what you are getting into here and I do not think Simon will rush to inform you. He is strongly inclined to keep his secrets to himself."

"Araminta, do not beat about the bush. What is it, for heaven's sake?"

"Northcote's father, Canonbury, and Peppington were all close friends and business partners of Simon's father."

"Yes?"

"Simon was only twelve at the time his father shot himself, but he knew, because he had heard his parent discuss it, that Northcote, Canonbury, and Peppington had all invested together with Simon's father in a South Seas trading company venture. The night he shot himself, the earl left Simon a note telling him, among other things, that after paying his gambling debts, the only financial resources left for his son and wife would be whatever was realized from the trade venture."

"Oh, dear," Emily said, beginning to grasp what was coming.

"Simon sat down and, at the tender age of twelve, wrote to all three men asking them to advance his mother some money on the basis of the profit expected on his father's shares."

"And they refused?"

"They did not even bother to respond. Instead, they took advantage of a clause in the trading company contract to sell Blade's shares to another investor. Simon and his mother were cut out of the partnership completely. They did not get a penny."

"Bloody hell."

"There was nothing illegal about what Northcote, Canonbury, and Peppington did, you understand. Simply a matter of business."

"But Simon and his mother were effectively cut off from their last source of income."

"Yes. Simon will never forgive or forget."

Emily frowned. "I am surprised he did not seek vengeance on all of them along with my father."

"Oh, he did, Emily." Araminta nodded at another acquaintance. "He most certainly did. A very subtle vengeance. He has ensured that each man is somehow at his mercy. As of six months ago he already held Canonbury and Peppington under his paw. You, my dear, apparently did something that handed him Northcote on a silver platter."

Emily's lips parted in shock as she recalled the rescue of Celeste and the cool wariness between Simon and the marquess that had been evident later. "Bloody hell. But the present marquess is the son of the man who wronged Simon and his mother, not the one who sold Blade's shares." Her voice trailed off as she recalled her husband's rigid code.

"Precisely," Araminta murmured. "Simon has lived in the East for a long time. In his eyes the sins of the fathers fall upon the children and indeed the entire family."

"No wonder Simon acted so strangely when I informed him that I had told Lady Northcote all obligations between our two families were settled."

"Yes. I imagine it came as something of a shock to Blade." Araminta's mouth quirked in amusement. "Word has it, however, that he did, indeed, honor your commitment to forgive the old debt."

"My father once said something about Simon having Canonbury and Peppington under his control. At the time I did not understand. I merely thought he meant Simon was a powerful man."

"Which he is. He got that way by ensuring that he always knows the deepest, darkest secrets of those with whom he deals. The information gives him power. And he does not hesitate to wield it."

"Just as he knew that I was my father's weak point," Emily said half under her breath. "My husband is an extremely clever man, is he not?"

"He is also a very dangerous one. You appear to be the only person in the whole of London who does not go in fear of him. That is no doubt one of the reasons the *ton* finds you so fascinating, my dear. You blithely dance where angels fear to tread. Are you quite certain you could not ride that horse without the aid of your spectacles, Emily?"

"I should run straight off the path and into the trees," Emily assured her. She pushed the offending spectacles more firmly onto her nose. "Come along, Araminta. I see Celeste up ahead and I cannot wait to show her my new mare."

"A moment, if you please, Emily. It is not like you to change the subject so quickly. What are you planning? I can tell you are up to something."

"Nothing significant, Araminta. I believe I shall invite Lady Canonbury and Mrs. Peppington to tea as soon as possible, however. Will you join us?"

"Good lord." Araminta stared after Emily. "I most certainly shall. The experience should prove interesting."

The salon held in Lady Turnbull's drawing room the following afternoon was not at all what Emily had expected. She had been exceedingly anxious ever since receiving the invitation because she knew she would be meeting and mingling with some of London's most sophisticated literary intellectuals.

She had spent hours choosing the right gown and the right hairstyle. In the end she had opted for the serene, classical look, on the assumption that a crowd of people interested in romantic poetry and other intellectual matters would favor the style.

She had arrived at Lady Turnbull's in a severe, high-waisted, modestly cut gown of fine, gold muslin, trimmed with black dragons. She'd had Lizzie do her hair *à l'antique*.

Emily had discovered immediately upon being shown

into Lady Turnbull's drawing room, however, that all the
other ladies were wearing gowns cut with fashionably low
décolletage and had frivolous little hats perched rakishly on
their heads.

Two or three of the women tittered as Lady Turnbull
came forward to greet Emily. As she took her seat, Emily
was painfully aware of the curiosity and amusement of those
around her. It was as if she had been hired to entertain them
with her eccentric ways, she thought in annoyance.

She began to wonder if she had made a serious mistake
in accepting the invitation to join the group. At that moment Ashbrook flicked shut an elegant enameled snuffbox
and straightened away from the mantel against which he
had been leaning with negligent grace. He came forward to
kiss Emily's hand, thereby bestowing instant cachet upon
her. Emily smiled back gratefully.

Emily was further disappointed, however, when the conversation turned straight to the latest gossip, rather than the
latest romantic literature. She listened impatiently to the
latest *on dit* and wondered how soon she could leave. It was
obvious she was not mingling with a group of clever intellectuals, after all. It was true everyone in the room had a marvelously fashionable air of ennui and every word spoken was
laden with world-weary cynicism, but there was no interest
here in literary matters. Across the room Ashbrook caught
her eye and winked conspiratorially.

"By the bye," a gentleman who was introduced as
Crofton drawled, "I have recently had the pleasure of playing cards with your father, Lady Blade."

That caught Emily's full attention. She glanced at him in
surprise. She was wearing her spectacles, so she could see
Crofton's cruel and dissipated face quite clearly. She
guessed he had once been a handsome man, with his bold,
saturnine features. But now he appeared jaded and thoroughly debauched. Emily had not liked Crofton from the
moment she had been introduced to him.

"Have you, indeed?" She took a noncommittal sip of her
tea.

"Yes, as a matter of fact. Quite a neck-or-nothing game-ster, your father."

"Yes." Emily prayed for a change of topic.

"His spirits seem a bit depressed of late," Crofton observed. "One would think he would be bursting with enthusiasm over your excellent marriage."

"You know how fathers are," Emily said, feeling desperate. "I was his only daughter."

"You were, I gather, extremely important to him," Crofton murmured. "One might even say vital to his well-being."

Emily looked at Ashbrook, smiling hopefully. "Have you read Mrs. Fordyce's latest effort, my lord?"

"Mrs. Fordyce is a silly frump of a woman, sadly lacking in intelligence and talent." Ashbrook volunteered the sweeping pronouncement with an air of complete boredom.

Emily bit her lip. "I rather enjoyed her new novel. Very strange and interesting."

The small group laughed indulgently at this display of rustic taste and went back to a discussion of Byron's latest antics. Emily risked a glance at the clock and wished it were time to leave. She listened to the prattle going on around her and decided that the literary society of Little Dippington accomplished far more in its Thursday afternoon meetings than this elegant salon ever would. As she always did when she was bored or unhappy, she mentally went to work on new stanzas for *The Mysterious Lady.*

A ghost was indeed called for, she decided. The poem needed more melodrama. Perhaps she could have the heroine encounter a phantasm in an abandoned castle. She must remember to tell Ashbrook she intended to add a ghost. She had brought the manuscript with her in her reticule this afternoon but she wondered if she should turn it over to him so soon. It might be better to wait until she had added the ghost.

Conversation in the drawing room drifted into a new channel.

"If we are speaking of likely investments," one foppish gentleman said portentiously, "I don't mind telling you about a new venture I am looking into at the moment. Canal shares for a project to be built in Hampshire."

Emily reluctantly let her attention snap back to the present. She raised quizzical eyes toward the gentleman who had just spoken. "Would that be the Kingsley Canal project, sir?"

The gentleman's glance swung immediately toward her. "Why, yes, it would. My man of affairs brought it to my attention recently."

"I should have nothing to do with that venture, if I were you, sir," Emily said. "I know something about the previous financial ventures arranged by the gentlemen behind the Kingsley Canal project and it is a record of failure and loss."

The man gave Emily his full attention. "Is that a fact, Lady Blade? I am most interested in hearing more about the project, as I am on the brink of putting quite a large sum into it."

"If you want to invest in canals," Emily said, "I would suggest that you first investigate coal mining areas. Or look into the potteries. I have found that wherever one finds a product that needs an economical path to market, one finds a need for canals. But one must consider the people behind the venture as carefully as the venture itself."

At that casual pronouncement, all male eyes in the room were on Emily, the women soon taking their cues from the men. Emily blinked owlishly under the unexpected scrutiny. She had continued her investment work here in town. After all, the ladies of the Little Dippington literary society still depended on her. But Emily had not expected to find herself discussing such topics today. She had come here to talk of higher matters.

"I say," one of the men began, instantly casting aside his carefully cultivated attitude of ennui, "Do you favor any particular projects?"

"Well," Emily said slowly, "I have several correspondents in the midland counties and two of them have recently written to me concerning a new canal project. I confess I have not been paying a great deal of attention to financial matters lately but I am rather intrigued by this arrange-

ment. I have had successful situations with this group of
investors in the past."

All pretense of a literary discussion was dropped as Emily became the focus of everyone's attention. She found herself inundated with questions and demands for more
information on investment projects. It was all familiar territory, if unexciting, and, anxious to make a pleasant impression, she concentrated on her answers.

An hour and a half went by before she chanced to glance
at the clock. She gave a start when she saw the time.

"I do hope you will forgive me," she said to her hostess
as she sprang to her feet and gathered up her reticule. "I
must be off. Thank you so much for inviting me."

"We shall look forward to having you attend our little
group next week," Lady Turnbull said, with a quick, assessing glance at the fascinated expressions on the gentlemen's
faces. "Perhaps you can give us more information on investments and such."

"Yes, do come back next week," one of the gentlemen
urged.

"I would very much appreciate hearing your opinions on
the corn harvest this summer," another said.

"Thank you," Emily said, edging quickly toward the
door. Mentally she made a note to be otherwise engaged
next week, if possible. "If you will excuse me . . ."

"I shall see you out to your carriage," Ashbrook said
with grave gallantry.

Emily looked at him in surprise. "Oh. Thank you."

Outside on the steps she waited in tense silence for him
to ask if she had brought along her manuscript. She could
not bear to thrust it upon him unless he requested it.

"I am glad you came today," Ashbrook said softly as
Blade's black and gold carriage approached. "I hoped you
would. Now I find I cannot wait until we meet again. Will
you be attending the Olmstead affair tomorrow night?"

"I believe so, yes." Emily clutched the reticule and wondered if she should casually mention the manuscript. Perhaps something charmingly offhand about Whittenstall,

Ashbrook's publisher, would do the trick. She frantically searched her brain for something suitable.

"Did you find time to work on your epic poem?" Ashbrook asked as he watched the carriage pull up in front of the steps.

Emily breathed a sigh of relief. He had not forgotten, after all. "Yes, yes, I did. I just happen to have it with me."

"Do you?" Ashbrook smiled deliberately. "Shall I have a look at it, then, to see if it might be suitable for publication?"

"Oh, Richard, that is so kind of you. I was afraid you had forgotten and I did not want to impose." Emily yanked open the reticule and hauled out the precious manuscript. "I have definitely decided to add a ghost," she said as she handed it to him with trembling fingers. "You might bear that in mind as you read."

"Certainly." Ashbrook took the manuscript and smiled suavely. "In the meantime, will you promise to save a dance for me tomorrow night?"

"Yes, of course," Emily said happily as Harry handed her up into the coach. "Thank you, Richard. And please, I beg you, be perfectly honest in your opinions of my work."

The door of the carriage slammed shut and Emily was whisked off before Ashbrook could reply.

A few minutes later the carriage came to a halt in front of the Blade townhouse. Emily alighted eagerly and headed immediately upstairs to her bedchamber.

She was going past the closed door of the old, unused nursery when a loud thump, followed by a distinct groan, brought her to an immediate halt.

"What on earth?" Opening the door and peering inside, Emily was startled to see Simon and the twins stripped to the waist. Charles was just picking himself up off the carpet. Simon was standing over him, feet braced, and Devlin was watching with an expression of deep concentration.

"You do not punch with your fist," Simon said sternly. "You let the man come straight at you and then you turn slightly to the right. He will instinctively follow you and in doing so, put himself off balance. Balance is everything. Do you understand?"

"I believe so." Charles rubbed his bare shoulder. "Let me try it again."

"What is going on here?" Emily asked, fascinated.

The three men swung around to face her, their faces reflecting a united sense of masculine outrage.

"Emily!" Charles yelped.

With horrified expressions, the twins leapt for their shirts, which were hanging on nearby chairs.

"Damnation, Emily," Simon said furiously. "This is no place for a female. Take yourself off at once. And close the door behind you."

"Are you practicing some odd form of boxing, Simon? Is it something you learned in the East? I would love to observe. Perhaps I could even take a few lessons." Emily looked at him hopefully.

"You will leave this room immediately, madam. And you will close the door behind you," Simon thundered.

Emily cast a quick glance at her brothers' scowling faces and found them equally implacable. "Oh, very well. But I must say, you three are certainly a bunch of extremely poor-spirited killjoys."

Emily retreated back into the hall and closed the door behind her.

Chapter 17

"Do tell me what you were doing in the nursery with Charles and Devlin, my lord," Emily said from the other end of the dinner table that evening. "I am most curious."

"Curiosity is not an admirable trait in a female." Simon surveyed the exotically spiced East Indian curry George had just placed in front of him.

Emily gave him a mischievous grin. "You could hardly expect me to ignore all those loud thumping noises as I went past the nursery door."

Simon was aware Emily was deliberately teasing him. He was equally aware that Greaves and George were listening to every word as they stood watch over the dinner table. "In future, my dear, you will kindly knock before you enter a room in which you hear thumping sounds."

"Yes, of course," Emily said with an acquiescent nod. "I mean, one never knows what one will encounter when one opens a door after hearing a thumping sort of noise, does one? It might be anything. One might even chance upon three men who are not wearing their shirts or something equally outrageous."

"That is quite enough conversation on the subject, madam wife." He shot Emily a severe glare.

The response was an irrepressible giggle. "I refuse to end this discussion until I know what you were doing. Were you practicing a fighting technique of some sort?"

Simon gave up. "Yes, we were. I am not certain how it came about but somehow your brothers managed to talk me into demonstrating it for them. It is something I learned during my years in the East."

"Would you teach me?"

Simon was truly shocked by the suggestion. Emily's charming eccentricities could be amusing at times but there were definitely occasions when she went too far. "Most certainly not. It is not a proper activity for a female and it is definitely not the sort of thing a man teaches his wife."

"Hmm. I am not so certain it would be a bad notion to teach me," Emily mused, unintimidated. "After all, the streets of London are not particularly safe, to say nothing of places like Vauxhall Gardens. One never knows when one might encounter a dangerous villain on a dark path, for example, and be obliged to defend oneself from a fate worse than death."

"*That is quite enough,* madam."

George, the footman who was serving that evening, was suddenly overcome with a fit of loud, sputtering coughing. He rushed from the room. Outside in the hall the coughing turned into a roar of laughter. Greaves, the butler, looked extremely pained.

Simon glowered at Emily. "The dangers of the streets are one of the reasons why you are never to go about unaccompanied in town, my dear. And speaking of going about, my aunt tells me she has received a voucher for Almacks for you."

"She mentioned it," Emily said vaguely as she helped herself to chutney. "But, truthfully, Simon, I have no particular interest in going to Almacks. Celeste says the assemblies are dreadfully boring. One only goes if one is obliged to look for a husband and I have no need to do that, have I?"

"No, but an appearance at Almacks will do no harm," Simon told her firmly. It would be another jewel in the crown of Emily's recent social success. "I believe you should attend next Wednesday night."

"I would rather not. Simon, your chef serves the most remarkable meals. Did you find him in the East?"

"Smoke has been with me for several years, yes."

"Why is he called Smoke? Because he burns the food?"

"No, because he was the bastard son of an island woman and a British seaman. No one wanted him after he was born and he survived by learning to move and act like smoke. Always there, but rarely noticed." A particularly useful talent when one made one's living lifting men's purses in dirty port towns, Simon reflected silently.

"How did you come to meet him?"

"I believe he was attempting to rob me at the time," Simon murmured.

Emily laughed in delight. "What made you decide to give him a position as your cook?"

"He is more than happy to prepare the sort of food I came to enjoy in the East. With him in the kitchen I am not obliged to eat the usual English fare of tough mutton, greasy sausages, and heavy puddings."

"I have noticed we eat a great many dishes with noodles and rice in them," Emily observed. "I must say, I enjoy them. The wonderful spices are very stimulating to the sensibilities."

Simon gave her an impatient glance, well aware she was attempting to change the topic. "You will go to Almacks, my dear," he said softly and deliberately.

"Will I?" She looked delightfully unconcerned about the whole thing. "I shall talk to Lady Merryweather about it. She is a fount of wisdom on how to carry on in Society, is she not? Simon, I am thinking of starting my own literary salon. I attended one this afternoon and, I must say, I was quite disappointed. We hardly touched upon literary matters at all. Everyone wanted to talk about investments."

That comment succeeded in diverting Simon's attention at once. "Did they, indeed?" He took another bite of the curry and watched his wife's face carefully. "Who attended the salon?"

"It was held in Lady Turnbull's house," Emily said air-ily. "There were several people there. I have forgotten some of the names, I confess." She frowned intently. "There was a gentleman named Crofton, however. I do remember him because I did not particularly care for him."

If Crofton was there, Ashbrook would not have been far behind, Simon reflected grimly. He decided to probe gently for more information. "I believe I made Crofton's acquain-tance once on the street in front of his club. I was not im-pressed by him, either. Do you recall anyone else in attendance at Lady Turnbull's salon?"

"Well . . ." Emily shot him a cautious glance. "One or two others, perhaps. As I said, I did not get all the names."

So Ashbrook had, indeed, attended and for some reason Emily was trying to conceal the information. Simon went cold with sudden anger, sending Greaves from the room with a single look. He waited until he was alone with his wife, who was munching enthusiastically on a bite of curry and chutney.

"I would like to know everything that happened at Lady Turnbull's salon today, Emily."

"The thing is, my lord," Emily said earnestly, "I would rather not tell you until I know for certain if things are going to work out."

Simon stared at her in baffled fury. *Bloody hell.* Was she planning to run off with Ashbrook a second time? He could not credit the notion but at the same time the jealousy was already starting to gnaw at his insides. "What, precisely, do you intend to work out, madam?"

" 'Tis a secret, my lord."

"I wish to know."

"If I tell you, it will no longer be a secret, my lord," Emily pointed out reasonably.

"You are a married woman now, Emily. You do not keep secrets from your husband."

"The thing is, this would be terribly embarrassing for me if matters did not conclude happily."

Simon, who had picked up his wineglass, set it down again before he accidentally shattered it between clenched fingers. "You will tell me what this is all about. I am afraid I must insist upon knowing, madam."

Emily heaved a small sigh and darted him a searching glance. "Will you give me your word of honor not to tell a single soul?"

"I certainly do not intend to gossip about my own wife."

Emily relaxed slightly. Her eyes glowed and she was suddenly bubbling over with an excitement that she had apparently been hugging to herself all afternoon.

"No, I do not suppose you would. Well, my lord, the secret is that Ashbrook has promised to read my epic poem and tell me whether it is good enough to be shown to his publisher, Whittenstall. I am so anxious and excited, I can hardly bear it."

Simon felt the cold tension in his gut unknot at the expectant look in Emily's eyes. Of course she was not planning on running off with Ashbrook. He must have been mad to even consider the notion. He knew her better than that. Emily was helplessly in love with her dragon of a husband.

His reaction to the unlikely threat was, however, a clear indication of how powerfully she affected his self-control. Simon scowled.

But now he had another problem on his hands. Emily might not be planning to get herself seduced by the poet, but there was absolutely no doubt in Simon's mind that Ashbrook's goals were not innocent. Emily was fast becoming all the rage and Ashbrook considered himself extremely fashionable. Forming a liaison with the charming, eccentric wife of the Earl of Blade would no doubt strike the poet as an interesting challenge. He was probably wondering just what he had missed out on five years ago when Emily had used a chamber pot on his skull.

Ashbrook, you bastard. You guessed immediately that the one sure way to get Emily's attention was to show an interest in her writing. Simon decided he would definitely have to attend to the poet but in the meantime he did not have to worry that Emily was going to leave.

Even as he told himself not to be alarmed, Simon was obliged to realize just how important Emily had become to him. He was grappling with that uncomfortable notion when Emily spoke again.

"Well, Simon? Is it not the most marvelous opportunity for me?"

His mouth twisted laconically at the hopeful excitement in her lovely eyes. "It is certainly a most interesting development, my dear."

Emily nodded in satisfaction. "Yes, it is, and now you can see why I did not want anyone to know until Richard has given me his opinion. It would be too humiliating if he decides *The Mysterious Lady* is not suitable for publication. I have discovered that the *ton* dotes on humiliating gossip."

"You are quite right to keep the matter a secret," Simon murmured. "And I think it would be a very good notion to establish your own literary salon rather than attend Lady Turnbull's. She is not known for her genuine appreciation of literature, I fear. Her salons are simply excuses for a certain crowd to gather and share the latest gossip. And, as you have noted, here in town the gossip can be quite cruel."

"Yes, that was what I concluded." Emily went back to work on her curry. "I shall establish my salon as soon as possible. I believe I shall invite Celeste and her mother and Lady Merryweather, of course. And there are two or three other ladies I have met recently who are quite interested in the latest style of literature. I hope they will attend."

"You must give me a list of the names of those you plan to invite," Simon said.

Emily looked up quickly, a wary expression in her eyes. "No, my lord, I am not going to do that."

He blinked at the unexpected defiance. "May I ask why not?"

She pointed her fork at him in an accusing fashion. "Because I have finally discovered from your aunt how you go about managing things, my lord. You are apparently in the habit of intimidating people into doing what you want them to do. To be perfectly honest, I would not put it past you to coerce everyone on my guest list into attending my salon."

Simon was at first startled and then reluctantly amused.

"Very well, Emily. Invite whom you wish and I will stay out of the matter entirely."

She gave him a suspicious look. "I am quite determined on this point, my lord."

"Yes, I can see that. Do not fret, Emily. I will not frighten your guests."

"Excellent." She smiled approvingly, her brow clearing as if by magic. "Then I shall get started on the project at once."

"Do not forget you still have to make preparations for your soiree."

Emily's expression immediately turned anxious. "I am working very hard on it, my lord. I vow I am doing everything I can to make certain it is a success. Although I still do not know how we will get everyone inside the house."

Simon eventually tracked Ashbrook down at one of the St. James clubs. The poet was ensconced in a chair near the fire with a bottle of port, apparently taking a breather from the card tables.

"Well, Ashbrook, what a convenient circumstance." Simon sat down in the chair across from the poet and picked up the bottle of port. He poured himself a glass of the dark red wine. "I have been looking for you for the past hour or so. Where is your friend, Crofton?"

"I am meeting him later." Ashbrook flicked open his snuffbox with a one-handed, negligently elegant gesture he had no doubt practiced for hours. "We are planning an entertaining tour of some of the more intriguing brothels."

"Just as well he is not here." Simon sampled the port. It was somewhat too sweet for his taste. "I wanted to talk to you alone."

Ashbrook's fingers tightened around his glass. "I do not see why. I have abided by our little agreement. I have not breathed a word about the scandal in Emily's past."

Simon smiled dangerously. "I have no idea what you are talking about. There is no scandal in my wife's past. Are you implying there might have been one?"

"Good God, no, I am not implying anything of the kind." Ashbrook gulped his port. "What the devil do you want from me, Blade?"

"You have, I believe, something that belongs to my wife. I would like it sent back immediately."

Astonishment lit Ashbrook's gaze for an instant, quickly replaced by an indolent stare. "We are discussing her epic poem, I collect?"

"We are." Simon smiled without any humor. "Ashbrook, do not play games with me. We both know why you offered to read the poem for her. You could not resist trying to seduce her, after all, could you? She no doubt seems far more interesting now than she was five years ago. The more jaded one becomes, the stronger the appeal of naïveté and innocence, hmm? And you think to attract her by praising her writing."

Ashbrook crooked a brow. "You sound as though you are familiar with the technique. Is that how you convinced her to marry you, Blade? By complimenting her poetry instead of her eyes?"

"How I got her to marry me is none of your affair. All you need keep in mind is that she is married to me. I am warning you that if you attempt to lure her into your bed, I shall see that your blossoming career as an author is nipped in the bud."

"Are you threatening to call me out, Blade?"

"Only if it becomes absolutely necessary. I prefer more subtle methods of persuasion. In your case, I believe my first move would be to call upon your publisher, Whittenstall, and convince him that you lack talent, after all."

Ashbrook's mouth dropped open. "You would pay him not to publish me?"

"I would see to it that no reputable bookseller or publisher in town would find it worth his while to publish you. Do I make myself clear, sir?"

Ashbrook closed his mouth and leaned back in his chair. His initial expression of shock was fading to a look of reluctant admiration. "You are quite incredible, Blade. I have heard rumors of how you go about getting what you want, but I confess I had not entirely credited them. I am impressed."

"It is not necessary that you be impressed. It is only important that you do not attempt to tease my wife by dangling the lure of getting her poem published in front of her."

"You do not think her work good enough to be published?" Ashbrook asked shrewdly.

"I have come to the conclusion that my wife's considerable array of talents lie outside the world of literature. I do not mind if she amuses herself by dabbling in poetry and the like. But I will not allow you or anyone else to use her interest in literary matters as a means of engaging her attentions."

"You think she can be lured away from your side so easily?" Ashbrook's mouth curved into a mocking smile.

Simon finished the port. "My wife is incapable of infidelity. It is simply not in her nature. But she can be hurt by promises made by people who have no intention of carrying them out. She tends to believe the best of people."

"You do not think I mean to give *The Mysterious Lady* a fair reading?"

"No," Simon said as he got to his feet. "I do not believe it for a moment. I shall expect to see the manuscript returned tomorrow morning."

"Damn it, Blade, hold on. How do you expect me to explain this to Emily?"

"Tell her you did not think you could give an impartial judgment," Simon suggested. "It is nothing less than the truth, after all. How can a man make an honest assessment of someone else's manuscript when he knows that his own writing career is hanging in the balance?"

"Bastard." But Ashbrook sounded more resigned than defiant. "You had best take care, Blade. You have cultivated a variety of enemies. One of these fine days one of them might decide to try his luck in getting past that lot of villains and bodyguards you fondly call a house staff."

Simon smiled. "Not likely. You see, Ashbrook, I do not have as many enemies as you seem to think. That is because, on the whole, I grant more favors than threats. I can be useful, on occasion. You are welcome to keep that in mind."

Ashbrook nodded, his gaze speculative. "I see now how you operate. You are indeed as clever and mysterious as they say, Blade. Useful favors granted in exchange for cooperation, certain retribution if you are crossed. It is an interesting technique."

Simon shrugged and walked away without bothering to respond. He had completed his business for the evening. It was time to find Emily. She was due to put in an appearance at the Linton's ball, he recalled. He looked forward to another waltz with his wife.

Twenty minutes later he alighted from the carriage and walked up the steps of the large mansion. Footmen in blue livery scurried about, taking his hat and ushering him into the hall and upstairs to the ballroom.

The strains of a country dance could be heard above the din of laughter and conversation. Simon came to a halt in the doorway and glanced around, searching the crowded ballroom for signs of Emily. Lately it was not hard to locate her. One simply looked for a large knot of people gathered around a redheaded elf.

The knot would consist of a variety of Emily's new friends and admirers. Among the males there would be several aging gentlemen who wanted to talk about shares and investments, a group of aspiring poets with tousled locks and smoldering eyes who wanted to discuss romantic poetry, and a cluster of young dandies anxious to be seen conversing with a genuine original.

And there would be just as many females in the flock surrounding Emily, Simon knew as he spotted his quarry and started through the crowd. There would be ladies who were as enthralled by the latest romantic literature as Emily was and a variety of women such as Lady Northcote and her daughter Celeste who found Emily a charming friend.

The group would also include a number of women whose astute husbands had encouraged them to cultivate the friendship of the new Countess of Blade. There would be girls not long out of the schoolroom whose mamas had com-

prehended that an association with the new countess meant
their daughters would be brought into contact with a variety
of eligible males. And last, but not least, there would be a
selection of bluestockings who considered Emily intelligent
and delightfully eccentric.

Simon had just reached the outskirts of the throng that
surrounded Emily when she sensed his presence. A murmur
swept through Emily's crowd of admirers as they stepped
aside to let her husband pass.

"Blade." Emily raised her quizzing glass for a quick look
and then let it drop. She smiled widely in welcome, her eyes
lighting up with pleasure. "I was hoping you would find
time to drop by."

"I have come to beg a dance with you, my dear," Simon
said as he inclined his head over her hand. "Do you by any
chance have one to spare for me?"

"Do not be silly. Of course I do." She threw an apolo-
getic glance toward a young man whose blond hair had been
laboriously styled with a crimping iron. "You will not mind
if we postpone our dance, will you, Armistead?"

"Not at all, Lady Blade," Armistead said, giving Simon
a respectful glance.

Emily turned a laughing, eager countenance toward her
husband. "There, you see, Blade? I am quite free to dance
with you."

"Thank you, my dear." Simon experienced a surge of
possessive satisfaction as he led Emily out onto the floor.
When Emily stepped into his arms, her eyes shining, he was
coolly aware that everyone in the room knew what he knew.

Emily was his.

The *ton* would also know that he would protect what
was his.

Two days later Simon arrived home in the middle of the
afternoon and was astonished to be told by his butler that
his wife was entertaining three ladies in the drawing room.

"Lady Merryweather, Lady Canonbury, and Mrs. Peppington," Greaves said without any trace of expression.

"Bloody hell," Simon muttered as he stalked toward the drawing room door. "What the devil is she up to now?"

"Madam has ordered the best Lap Seng tea to be served," Greaves added in a low voice as he opened the door for his master. "Smoke was asked to prepare an assortment of sweet cakes. He is still complaining."

Simon threw his butler a scowling glance and stepped into the library. He halted at once as he took in the sight of his wife conversing easily with the wives of his two old enemies. Emily looked up and smiled at him.

"Oh, hello, Blade. Will you join us? I was just about to ring for more tea. You know Lady Canonbury and Mrs. Peppington, I believe?"

"We have met." Simon acknowledged both women with a chilling civility. They, in turn, appeared flustered and uneasy.

"Actually, I am afraid we really must be going," Lady Canonbury said, rising majestically from the settee.

"Yes, I have several other commitments this afternoon," Mrs. Peppington said quickly.

"I understand." Emily shot her husband a glowering glance as the two women hurried out into the hall.

When the door closed behind them, she calmly poured Simon a cup of tea and handed it to him as he sat down. "There was no need to frighten them away, Simon."

Araminta Merryweather chuckled. "Simon is good at that sort of thing."

Simon ignored his aunt and fixed his innocent-looking wife with his most intimidating expression. "I would be interested in knowing what you found to talk about with those two particular ladies, madam."

"Umm, yes, I imagine you would." Emily smiled winningly. "Well, my lord, the truth is, we discussed business."

"Did you, indeed?" Out of the corner of his eye, Simon saw his aunt wince at the coldness in his voice but Emily appeared not to notice. "What sort of business?"

"The mining business," Emily said. "Apparently both Lord Canonbury and Mr. Peppington have sunk considerable amounts into a mining project. They now face the prospect of getting the ore to market and have made the astonishing discovery that the canal they planned to use is privately owned. The owner will not give them a firm agreement to use the canal services. He has kept them dangling for months."

"I see."

"The canal is owned by you, my lord," Emily said pointedly. "Nothing moves on that canal without your permission. You have the power to make the entire mining project a financial disaster for Canonbury and Peppington. They are both extremely anxious about the matter. Such a loss could destroy them. They have sunk a great deal into their mining project."

Simon shrugged, not bothering to hide his satisfaction. "So?"

"So, I was just telling Lady Canonbury and Mrs. Peppington that you will no doubt decide to sell the canal to their husbands."

Simon's tea sloshed violently in the delicate china cup. Several drops spilled over the side and cascaded down onto his pristine buff-colored breeches. *"Bloody hell."*

Emily eyed the tea stains with concern. "Shall I ring for Greaves?"

"No, you will not ring for Greaves or anyone else." Simon slammed his cup and saucer down on the nearest table. "What the devil do you think you're doing making such promises to Lady Canonbury and Mrs. Peppington? How the hell do you expect to fulfill them?"

"She is not expecting to fulfill any promises, as she did not actually make any," Araminta said gently, her eyes dancing. "Emily is expecting you to do so, Simon."

Simon shot his aunt a furious glance before swinging his angry gaze back to Emily. His wife appeared serenely sure of herself, he noticed. Obviously he had been far too indulgent with her lately. "Well, madam? Explain yourself."

Emily delicately cleared her throat. "I am fully aware of why you wish to exact vengeance on Canonbury and Peppington, Simon. Your aunt has explained the matter and you have every right to want to punish them."

"I am glad you appreciate that fact."

"The thing is, my lord," she continued gently, "as I talked to Lady Canonbury and Mrs. Peppington, I realized that they have already suffered a great deal and there really is no need to add to their misery."

"Is that right? How, precisely, have they suffered?" Simon demanded through his teeth.

"Lord Canonbury, it seems, has a bad heart. His doctors have advised him that he may not live out the year. He has also had several severe financial losses in recent years. His only joy in life is his granddaughter. You remember her? The one who had a fit of the vapors and collapsed when you entered that ballroom?"

"I remember her."

"Poor chit was dreadfully afraid Blade was going to demand her hand in marriage as vengeance against her grandfather," Araminta murmured.

"Nonsense," Emily said. "As I told Celeste, Blade would never marry a young lady who was prone to fits of the vapors. Now, as I was saying, his granddaughter is Canonbury's greatest joy in life. He wishes to use the profits from the mining project to provide her with a suitable dowry. She will be left penniless if you ruin him, Simon. I knew you would not want the poor chit to be forced to endure the marriage mart without a decent dowry."

"Good God," Simon muttered.

"And as for Peppington, I was deeply saddened to learn that he lost his only son three years ago in a riding accident. His wife says he has not been the same since. All that keeps him going, apparently, is the knowledge that his grandson is turning out to be a fine, intelligent young man who shows a great interest in acquiring land. Peppington wants nothing more than to leave the boy a decent legacy."

"I do not see why I should have the least interest in the futures of Canonbury's granddaughter or Peppington's grandson," Simon said.

Emily smiled wistfully. "I know, my lord. In the beginning I was not particularly interested, either, but then I began to reflect upon the importance of children and grand-children, in general, if you know what I mean."

Simon pinned her with a steady gaze. "No, I do not know what you mean. What in blazes are you talking about now?"

"Our children, my lord." Emily demurely sipped her tea.

Simon was speechless for a moment. "Our children?" he finally managed. Then the most peculiar jolt of exultation roared through him. *"Are you telling me you are breeding, madam?"*

"Well, as to that, I am not able to say. I do not think so. At least not at the moment. But I imagine I soon will be, don't you? Bound to happen sooner or later at the rate we are going." Emily turned pink but she was still smiling.

Araminta sputtered and coughed on a swallow of tea. "I beg your pardon," she said weakly, gasping for air.

Simon paid no attention to his aunt. All he could think about at the moment was the possibility of Emily growing round with his babe. It struck him that until that moment he had not really thought much about the future. All his schemes and plans and thoughts had been focused on the past. Now here was Emily talking about having babies. *His* babies.

"Hell and damnation," he muttered.

"Yes, I know what you mean, my lord. It is something of a shock to think in such terms, is it not? But we must, of course. And I confess it was the thought of how much we shall love and cherish our own children that made me realize you would not wish to hurt Lord Canonbury's grand-daughter or Peppington's grandson. It is not your nature to be cruel, my lord. You are a noble and generous man at heart, as I well know."

Simon just sat there staring at Emily. He knew he ought to be lecturing her on the subject of staying out of his business affairs but he seemed to be unable to tear himself away from the image of his son in her arms.

"Do you think our son will have your eyes?" Emily asked thoughtfully, as if she had just peeked into his mind.

"I can just imagine him running about the place. Full of energy and mischief. You can teach him those fighting techniques you are teaching to my brothers. Boys love that sort of thing."

"I believe I really must be on my way," Araminta said softly as she rose to her feet. "If you will excuse me?"

Simon was barely aware of his aunt taking her leave. When the door closed softly behind her, he realized he was still staring at Emily, picturing her with a dark-haired, golden-eyed babe at her breast. Or perhaps a green-eyed, redheaded little girl.

"Simon?" Emily blinked inquiringly at him.

"If you will pardon me, I believe there are one or two items that require my attention in the library," Simon said absently, getting to his feet.

He had clung to his past for twenty-three years, Simon thought. It had given him strength and will and fortitude. But now it finally struck him that the day he had married Emily he had acquired a toehold in the future, whether he wanted it or not.

Simon was still struggling with the idea of Emily surrounded by his children, still feeling bemused and oddly uncertain of his own intentions, when he walked into one of his clubs that evening.

As fate would have it, the first two men he saw were Canonbury and Peppington.

An image of Canonbury's silly granddaughter fainting in a ballroom and Peppington's serious young grandson studying land management came into his mind. With a deep sigh, he crossed the room toward his two old enemies.

Simon made the offer to sell the canal to Canonbury and Peppington before he could give himself any further chance to think about it. The stunned shock on the faces of both elderly men was extremely satisfying.

Canonbury got to his feet with painful slowness. "I am very grateful to you, sir. I am well aware you had other intentions a short while ago. Intentions that would have ruined both Peppington and myself. May I ask what changed your mind?"

"This is not some sort of new trick, is it, Blade?" Peppington asked suspiciously. "You have kept us hovering on the brink of disaster for the past six months. Why should you set us free now?"

"My wife tells me I have a noble and generous nature," Simon said with a cold smile.

Canonbury sat down abruptly and reached for his port. "I see."

Peppington recovered sufficiently from his astonishment to give Simon an assessing look. "Wives are extremely odd creatures, are they not, sir?"

"They certainly do tend to complicate a man's life," Simon agreed.

Peppington nodded, looking thoughtful. "Thank you for your generosity, sir. Canonbury and I are well aware that we do not deserve it. What happened twenty-three years ago was . . . not well done of either of us."

"We are in your debt, Blade," Canonbury murmured.

"No," said Simon. "You are in my wife's debt. See that you do not forget it." He turned on his heel and walked away from the two old men he had hated for twenty-three years.

As he went out into the night he realized vaguely that something inside him felt freer, looser, less confined. It was as though he had just unfastened an old, rusty chain and released a part of himself that had been locked up for a very long time.

The frantic message from Broderick Faringdon arrived a day later. Emily was in the midst of consulting with Simon's cook. The consultation had turned into a rather loud discussion.

"I do not mind having some of your wonderful, exotic specialties from the East Indies on the buffet table," Emily said firmly to the strange little man who wore a gold earring in one ear. "But we must remember that most of the guests will be unfamiliar with such foreign delicacies. The English are not terribly adventurous in their eating habits."

Smoke drew himself up proudly. "His lordship has never complained about my cooking."

"Well, of course he has never complained," Emily said soothingly. "Your cooking is marvelous, Smoke. But I fear his lordship's palate is considerably more cultivated and refined than those of many of the people you will be serving at the soiree. We are talking about the sort of people who do not consider a meal complete unless they have plenty of boiled potatoes and a large joint of beef."

"Madam is quite right, Smoke," the housekeeper chimed in. "We must serve some turbot in aspic, perhaps. And sausages and maybe a bit of tongue."

"Sausages! Tongue!" Smoke was outraged. "I will not allow any greasy sausages or tongue to be served in this house."

"Well, then, some cold ham would do nicely," Emily said hopefully.

A loud, urgent knocking on the kitchen door interrupted the argument. Harry, the footman, went to the door and after a short consultation with whoever stood outside, he approached his mistress.

"Beggin' yer pardon, madam. I am told there is a message for you."

Emily turned away from the squabble with a sense of relief. "For me? Where?"

"A young lad at the door, ma'am. Says he can only deliver the message to you." Harry raised his hooked arm. "Shall I tell him to be off?"

"No, no, I shall speak to him."

Emily went through the kitchens to the door and saw the grubby little boy waiting for her. "Well, lad, what is it?"

The boy stared at Emily's bright red hair and spectacles and then nodded to himself, as if satisfied he had the right person. "I'm to tell yer that yer pa's got to see yer right away, ma'am. He give me this note to give to yer." A small slip of paper, rather badly stained from a dirty little fist, was dutifully handed over.

"Very well." Emily dropped a coin into the boy's palm, a strong sense of foreboding washing over her as she looked at the paper. "Thank you."

The boy examined the coin closely, tested it with his teeth, and then grinned widely. "Yer welcome, ma'am."

Harry stepped forward to close the kitchen door. The boy gazed in admiration and wonder at the hook and then took off running.

"We shall have to finish planning the buffet menu later," Emily said to Smoke and the housekeeper as she hurried out of the kitchen.

She dashed upstairs, the note burning her hand. She feared the worst. When she reached the privacy of her bedchamber she closed and locked the door.

Trembling with dread she sat down to read the note from her father.

> My dearest, dutiful daughter:
>
> Disaster has struck. Fortune has been against me for the past several weeks. I have lost a rather large sum of money at cards and now must sell my few remaining shares and stocks to raise the blunt to settle my latest debts. Unfortunately, it will not cover the entire amount. You must help me, my dearest daughter. I pray that in this, my hour of need, you will remember the ties of blood and love that bind us forever. You know your dear mama would want you to come to my aid. I shall be in touch very soon.
>
> Yrs,
> Yr. Loving Father
>
> P.S. Under the circumstances, you must not mention this little family problem to your husband. You know well enough he bears a deep, unnatural hatred for me.

Emily felt sick as she slowly refolded the note. She had realized something like this was bound to happen sooner or later. She had tried to pretend her father would show some sense in his gaming but she had known, deep down, that his passion for cards and hazard was too strong. Her mother had often told her he would never change.

And now he was calling on his daughter for help, knowing that in doing so he was forcing her to choose between her loyalty to her husband and her obligations as a daughter.

It was too much. Reality had intruded once more into her world, ripping aside the romantic curtain she tried to maintain around herself.

Emily put her head down on her arms and wept.

Chapter 18

Emily was dressing for the theater that evening when Simon walked into her bedchamber through the connecting door. She gave a small start at the sight of him and then managed a wan smile.

"Thank you, Lizzie. That will be all for now."

"Yes, ma'am." Lizzie bobbed a curtsey and left.

Emily met Simon's eyes in the looking glass. Then her gaze slid away. He was so very powerful and compelling in his austere evening clothes. "You are going out, my lord?"

"I shall dine at my club this evening while you attend the theater with Lady Northcote and her daughter." Simon's gaze was watchful. "But I shall find you later at the Bridgetons'."

Emily nodded quickly and the plumes in her hair danced. She was nervous and she knew she had to be careful or Simon would notice something was wrong. "I shall see you there, then. Did I show you the new pair of opera glasses I bought yesterday?" She reached for her reticule and started digging in it industriously. Anything not to have to meet that too-observant gaze.

"Very nice." Simon nodded approvingly at the delicately designed glasses.

"They give a wonderful view. I was using them to watch a bird outside the window earlier and I could see the tiniest details on its wings," Emily said, valiantly struggling to muster an air of enthusiasm.

"I am certain they are an excellently made pair of opera glasses, my dear."

Emily did not fancy the new speculation in Simon's eyes. "Celeste and her mother have told me that the production of *Othello* we're going to see this evening is one of the best that's ever been done."

"It should be quite exciting."

"Yes, I am certain it will. Did I tell you I had a long chat with Smoke today about the menu for the buffet at the soiree?"

"No, you did not mention it. Emily, is something wrong?"

"No, no, of course not, my lord." She summoned a brilliant smile and managed to meet his eyes briefly in the looking glass. "I am merely excited about going to the theater."

"Emily—"

"As I was saying, Smoke is very reluctant to prepare the standard fare for our guests. He says you prefer his Eastern style of cooking, which I am fully aware is very tasty, but I fear our guests will find it odd."

"Smoke will prepare whatever you tell him to prepare or he will be looking for a new position," Simon said casually. He moved forward and put his powerful hands on Emily's shoulders and seemingly willed her to meet his gaze once more. "Do not fret about the buffet menu, my dear. Tell me what is making you so anxious tonight."

She sat very still and stared into the looking glass with an anguished expression. "Simon, I cannot tell you."

Simon's mouth curved faintly. "I am afraid I must insist. We communicate on a higher plane, so I already know something is wrong, my dear. If you do not tell me the truth, I shall be in torment all evening. Do you wish me to suffer so?"

Emily felt a pang of guilt. "Of course not, my lord. It is just that this is a . . . a personal problem and I do not want to bother you with it." She sighed and added, "In any event, there is nothing that can be done. Fate has dealt its final hand."

But even as she made that tragic statement, her eyes were reflecting a glimmer of hopefulness and she knew Simon saw it. His fingers tightened briefly on her shoulders.

"It sounds as though we are discussing a card game," Simon said gently. "Is that the case?"

"Several card games, I fear," Emily confided. "And the final one was a disaster. Oh, Simon, it is all so perfectly awful and I do not know what to do. I know I cannot ask you for help in this matter."

Simon's brow quirked. "Are you by any chance under the hatches, elf? I am aware that the ladies occasionally play a bit deep among themselves, but I never imagined you as the sort to get into dun territory."

"It is not me who is under the hatches," Emily burst out, "it is my father. Oh, Simon, he sent me a note today saying he has lost everything and more."

Simon did not move but in the glass his eyes were suddenly blazing. His big hands clamped around Emily's bare shoulders. "Has he, indeed? Yes, of course. I should have guessed. It was only a matter of time, naturally, but I had rather expected him to last a bit longer than this."

Emily saw the savage satisfaction in his face and something in the pit of her stomach shriveled and died. She knew then that a part of her had hoped against hope that when the inevitable occurred, Simon would soften toward her father, just as he had softened toward the twins, Northcote, Canonbury, and Peppington.

"Simon?" she whispered helplessly.

"You are quite right, my dear," he murmured. "You cannot ask me to help this time. I have waited too long for this moment." His hands fell from her shoulders. He looked down and frowned at the red marks he had left on her soft, white skin. He touched one imprint gently and then turned toward the door. "I will see you later at the Bridgetons'." He paused briefly, hand on the knob. "Emily?"

"Yes, my lord?"

"Remember that you are no longer a Faringdon."

The door closed softly behind him.

Emily sat with her hands clenched in her lap, telling herself she must not give in to the tears again.

But the truth was she had not felt this helpless and trapped since the day her mother had died, leaving her to assume the full financial responsibility of her father and brothers.

Covent Garden was filled with boisterous theater-goers from several levels of Society. The *ton* glittered in the boxes and promenaded in the lobbies. Lesser mortals filled the galleries and the pits. All were exuberant and fully prepared to let the actors know exactly what they thought of the performance. Many had brought vegetable peelings, bells, and assorted noisemakers to aid in conveying their opinions.

"Did you bring your new pair of opera glasses?" Celeste asked as the small party made its way through the crowded lobby. Lady Northcote had paused briefly to speak to a friend.

"Yes, I have them with me." Emily glanced blindly around, having stashed her spectacles in her reticule. All she could see was a blur of color and movement.

She and Celeste were being jostled about and Emily was about to put on the spectacles to better defend herself when she felt a man's hand on her arm.

"What on earth?" Emily whirled around and saw a vague halo of graying blond hair. Her heart sank. She was aware of Celeste's curiosity. "Papa! What are you doing here?"

"Happened to be attending the performance and spotted you entering the lobby," Broderick Faringdon said with a false joviality. "How are you, my dear?"

"I am fine, Papa. Allow me to present my friend." Emily quickly ran through the introductions, praying Lady Northcote would return and whisk them off to their boxes.

Broderick acknowledged the introduction with the usual Faringdon charm. Then he tugged firmly on Emily's arm.

"If you don't mind, I would like a few words in private, m'dear. Haven't seen you in an age."

"I cannot leave Celeste alone," Emily said desperately.

"Do not worry about me, Emily," Celeste said blithely. "I shall join Mother. Your father can escort you to our box."

"Yes, of course," Emily said, knowing there was no escape. She rallied herself as Celeste disappeared into the crowd. "Well, Papa?"

"You got my note?" Broderick asked bluntly, dropping any pretense of civility at once. It was obvious he was under enormous strain.

"Yes. I am sorry, Papa. You know there is nothing I can do. Oh, Papa, how could you be so foolish?"

"T'weren't foolishness. Just a run o' bad luck. It happens." Her father leaned closer to mutter in her ear. "Listen, Em, I know I can come about with a little financial assistance from you."

"Perhaps, given time, Blade will soften on this matter. But it is much too soon to expect anything from him. You must know that, Papa."

"Damn and blast, Em, I ain't got time. Got to settle my debts."

"Have you truly sold everything?"

"Everything," Broderick confirmed gravely. "The thing is, Em, it don't quite cover my vowels."

Emily was shocked in spite of herself and her knowledge of her father's reckless ways. "Papa, how could you lose the entire amount? I worked years to build up that security for you and the twins. This is terrible. Utterly terrible. What are we to do?"

"No need to panic, m'dear. First, you have got to get Blade to cover my debts, Em."

Emily looked up, trying to make out his expression. "But, Papa, you know he will never do that."

"You have to, Em. Don't you understand? This is an emergency. Emily, m'dear, I must tell you I have made a horrendous mistake. Had a few too many bottles the other night. You know how it is when a man's in his cups. Talked a bit freely, I'm afraid."

"About what? To whom?" Emily was frantic now, trying to understand the note of strain in her father's voice. This sounded worse than just a horrific loss at the tables.

A dark shadow loomed at Broderick Faringdon's elbow. "Your papa made the mistake of talking to me, Lady Blade," said a familiar, sardonic voice.

"Mr. Crofton?" Emily turned vague eyes toward the dark shadow. A sense of dread now gripped her as she made a violent effort to collect herself. "I am afraid I do not understand. What is going on here?"

Crofton moved closer, his voice lowering to a slimy, confidential tone. "Your father and I have become close friends of late. He was most distressed after his defeat at the tables, Lady Blade. I am certain you comprehend and sympathize with how he must have felt as he contemplated how he would pay his debts of honor. He went through several bottles, I fear, and in the end he let slip the news about the rather appalling scandal in your past."

Emily's mouth went dry. She stared at her father. "Papa?"

"It's true, girl," Faringdon said morosely. "God help me, but I told him about the Unfortunate Incident. I was drunk as a lord, you know. And a trifle overset by my losses. I know you'll understand. But the thing is, he's threatened to spread it around town if I don't pay up."

"I fear the unsavory gossip about his wife's past will have the rather unpleasant effect of ruining Blade socially," Crofton murmured. "He will be cut by virtually everyone and will no doubt be obliged to quit town and retire to the country. And I do not think he will thank you for that, my dear."

"He will more likely destroy you for that, Mr. Crofton," Emily said fiercely.

"But the damage will be done. People will talk. Think of the scandal that will ensue, the slur on Blade's title, the humiliation he will be forced to endure. Your husband has fought hard for the power and position he presently holds, madam. But he has made enemies along the way. There are those who hate him and will not hesitate to use the scandal in your past to bring him down. And it will be all your fault, Lady Blade."

Emily felt nauseous but she kept her features as expressionless as possible as she peered up at the dark, hovering blur that was Crofton's face. "You do not value your life very highly, Mr. Crofton?" she inquired coldly.

"Do not threaten me with your husband's temper, madam. It is a bluff. I do not think you will allow things to come to such a pass. That would be letting them go too far and the damage would be done, would it not?"

"Mr. Crofton . . ."

"You will see to it that your father's debts are paid in full, Lady Blade. The whole world knows how much you adore your husband. Not to put too fine a point on the matter, you have a rather charming habit of making a complete cake out of yourself when it comes to Blade. I believe you will do whatever needs to be done to protect him from the scandal."

Emily took a deep, steadying breath. "And just how do you expect me to pay my father's debts? I receive a quarterly allowance, but that will probably not begin to cover Papa's losses."

Crofton chuckled. "Blade is said to be extremely indulgent toward you, my dear. Lord knows why, but there you have it. 'Tis an open secret. He apparently finds you amusing. I do not think it will be too difficult for you to claim the gaming losses are yours and beseech him very prettily to cover them for you. You may say you lost to Lady Malcolm or to Bridgeton's wife. They are both noted for deep play."

"Are you mad?" Emily breathed. "He would easily uncover such a lie."

"If you do not fancy the notion of coaxing the ready out of your husband in that manner, try a more feminine approach. Blade is, as I mentioned, said to be indulgent with you. You may have more success wheedling a diamond necklace or a string of pearls out of him. You can have it copied and sell the original to a discreet jeweler."

"That would never work. Blade would recognize the copy the first time I wore it. He has an excellent eye for such things."

"Then you must be more creative, madam, if you would save your husband from humiliation and scandal. Let me see. Perhaps a simple bit of theft will work best."

"Theft?"

"Yes, why not? I have heard tales of the fabulous collection of jeweled dragons Blade is reputed to have brought back with him from the East Indies. They say he has statues of the beasts sitting casually around his library and that each one is worth a fortune. Who would notice one missing? And even if it was missed it would be simple enough to blame the loss on a servant."

"Dear God. Papa, stop him." Emily turned desperately toward her father, but she knew no help lay in that direction.

"I'm damn sorry, Em," Faringdon said, clearly unhappy about the turn of events but apparently ready to shrug aside the responsibility for them, just as he always had in the past. "None of this would have happened if you had not insisted on losing your foolish heart to Blade. I did warn you, but you had to marry the man."

"Sad, but true," Crofton agreed. "Now, then, Lady Blade, I have a notion as to how you may successfully carry out the theft with no threat of being discovered and blamed. You will wait until the night of your soiree and arrange to remove one of the dragons then. Everyone in town will be there. The house will be packed with people and extra servants. When the dragon is eventually discovered to be missing one of the extra servants can be blamed."

"But you could never pawn anything so exotic as one of Blade's dragons," Emily said quickly. "Any jeweler would be suspicious of it."

"There is no need to pawn the entire statue. I shall simply remove the stones embedded in it and sell them off one at a time." Crofton chuckled. "Yes, an excellent plan, don't you agree?"

"Bloody hell," Emily whispered as she felt the cage door close behind her.

"Such colorful language, my dear," Crofton said mockingly. "No wonder Blade finds you amusing. His tastes have always tended toward the unusual." He bowed ironically to Emily and her father. "Now, then, if you two will excuse me, I must be off to find my box. *Othello* is such an interesting play, is it not? The enraged husband smothering his innocent wife at the end is my favorite part. Of course in your case, Lady Blade, the situation is somewhat different. After all, you are not so innocent."

Emily watched with seething helplessness as the dark shadow moved off into the crowd. When Crofton had vanished, she whirled to confront her father. "How dare you, Papa? How dare you do this to my husband?"

"Here, now, girl, you cannot go blaming me." Broderick Faringdon was righteously incensed at the accusation. "Blade's the one who set up the situation when he dragged you away from the bosom of your family."

"He did not drag me away, Papa, and you know it."

" 'Twas those damn romantical notions of yours that made you think yourself in love with the man. No sensible female would have made such a fool of herself. This whole situation is entirely your fault, Em. I knew there was no way he could keep your soiled past a secret. He should have known it, too. In all honesty, I have to say this mess is as much his fault as it is yours. He ought to be made to pay for it, by God."

"Bloody hell." Emily swung around on the heel of her new green kid pump and walked blindly away from her father.

Hours later Emily lay alone in her bed, staring up at the embroidered canopy. She had not been able to sleep at all since she had come home from the Bridgetons'.

She had heard Simon moving about in his bedchamber an hour ago and had waited tensely for him to come to her as he did nearly every night. But he had not opened the connecting door. It was very quiet in the other chamber now. Simon must have gone to bed alone.

Emily turned on her side and pounded the pillow in frustration and anger. Her mind was in a turmoil. She still did not know how she had managed to get through the performance of *Othello* without letting on to Lady Northcote and Celeste that something was dreadfully wrong. At one point Celeste had been obliged to remind Emily to use her new opera glasses.

When the terrible scene came in which Othello avenged himself on his innocent wife, Emily had watched in frozen horror, Crofton's words burning in her mind. *You are not so innocent.*

But it was not a question of innocence. It was a question of scandal. Blade had married her on the assumption that the dreadful scandal would not follow her from Little Dippington.

And now it was threatening to do precisely that.

Emily sat up and punched the pillow again. Then she shoved back the covers and got out of bed. She must find a way to save Simon from the humiliation and disgrace that would descend upon his shoulders if the social world discovered her past.

Her father was right. This whole mess was her fault. Emily began to pace the floor. She was the one who had talked Simon into offering marriage. She had done so by telling him what an excellent bargain of a wife she was. A built-in hedge against financial disaster.

Emily wanted to cry. Simon did not need insurance against a downturn in his fortunes. He needed insurance against the threat of a scandal in her past.

Emily frowned and came to a halt as a thought struck her. Insurance was precisely what was needed here. Insurance that Crofton would keep silent.

Emily started pacing again, her mind seizing on the first rational, useful thought she'd had all evening. The more she considered the problem, the more the answer became obvious.

If she was to protect Simon from scandal, she would

need to insure herself of Crofton's silence. What was needed was a plan for getting rid of Crofton. Permanently.

Emily sat down abruptly in the chair near the window. *Permanently* sounded so very permanent. Finding some way to pay off her father's debts would not solve the problem. Crofton would always be there, threatening to ruin the power and position Simon had worked so hard to build for himself.

Emily thought about the matter for a very long time and came to the conclusion that there were really only two options available to her if she was to protect Simon from her past.

The first was to arrange to disappear forever from Simon's life and allow everyone to think she had died tragically. The problem was that she knew Simon well enough to know he would search for her until he found her or her body.

The other option was to make Crofton disappear forever.

That last thought took away Emily's breath for a moment. *Make Crofton disappear.*

When Emily was able to breathe again, she began to think logically and clearly. In the end she knew what she had to do.

After a long moment she stood up and moved to the connecting door, opening it with shaking fingers.

Simon's room was cloaked in darkness. She could barely make out the shadowed bed without her spectacles. For a moment she stood there gazing into the room as the fierce protectiveness and the equally strong sense of longing and love welled up inside her.

"I will protect you, dragon," she whispered.

"Emily?" Simon's voice was a husky growl in the darkness.

Emily jumped. "I am sorry, my lord. I did not mean to wake you." She had not spoken to him since he had made a brief appearance at the Bridgetons'. He had not asked her to dance—indeed, had barely spoken to her. He had acknowledged her presence and then disappeared.

"Have you come to plead with me, elf?" Simon asked emotionlessly. "Because, if so, you had better know that you would be wasting your time. I will not rescue your father the way I did your brother. Nor will I let him off the hook the way I did with Northcote, Canonbury, and Peppington. This is a different matter entirely."

Emily heard the implacable chill in his voice and knew he spoke the truth. "I will not ask you to pay Papa's debts, Simon. I know that would be asking too much."

"You might as well be asking for the stars. I have waited too long for my vengeance."

"I am aware of that, my lord."

There was silence from the bed. After a moment Simon spoke again, his voice harsher than ever. "Well? Are you just going to stand there in the doorway all night? You look like a dismal little ghost in that nightdress."

Emily instinctively glanced down at the fine, pale muslin that floated around her body. "Do you really think so, my lord? I have never actually seen a ghost."

"I have," Simon said flatly. "My father's. I swear the damn specter has haunted me since the age of twelve. But at long last it is about to be banished. Go to bed, Emily."

"Yes, my lord." Obediently, she stepped back into her own bedchamber and started to close the door.

"Wait," Simon said with unexpected urgency.

"What is it, my lord?"

"Why did you come to my room, if not to plead with me?"

"I do not know if I can explain it," Emily said softly. "I just felt a . . . a desire to look in on you."

"You are quite certain you did not come here to beg me to forgo my vengeance?"

"I know that would be useless, my lord. You are entitled to your revenge. I only hope it will bring you the peace you seek."

"Damnation, woman. At the moment you are the great-est threat to my peace of mind. You have been all evening." There was an abrupt movement from the shadows of the bed as Simon threw back the covers and got to his feet. He started toward her.

"Simon?" Emily retreated another step in confusion. "Are you angry with me?"

"No, I am not angry." He reached her and scooped her up into his arms before she could retreat any farther. Then he turned and started back toward the massive bed. "I do not know how I feel at the moment, nor do I care. You are here in my bedchamber and I find I want you in my bed. That is enough for now, madam wife."

Emily did not argue. When he settled her gently in the center of the bed and came down on top of her with a sudden, searing passion, she opened her arms and pulled him close.

Simon's mouth closed over hers, relentless and consuming. Emily clung to him as he claimed her and vowed silently that she would do anything to protect him.

A long time later Emily awoke to find herself being carried back to her own bed. She stirred slightly in Simon's arms, enjoying the power and strength in him.

"Will you stay with me?" she asked sleepily as he set her down amid the tousled sheets of her own bed.

"No." Simon straightened beside the bed and stood looking down at her with brooding eyes. "I do not think I dare do that, elf. Not tonight. I am beginning to wonder if the Faringdons have played one last joke on me by convincing me to marry my greatest weakness."

"I am not your greatest weakness, my lord," Emily said softly. "You have no great weaknesses."

"No? I only hope you are right. In any event, I intend to be cautious. I will not allow you to ruin everything I have plotted and waited for these past twenty-three years."

"I will not do that, Simon."

"It will be interesting to see if you still come to my bed as willingly as you did tonight after your father has been forced to leave town in disgrace. Good night, madam wife."

Simon went back to his own bedchamber, closing the door deliberately behind him.

Emily lay awake, dry-eyed and clearheaded, until dawn. The details of her plan began to take shape in her mind. The night of the soiree would be perfect for what she had to do.

The first task was to obtain a suitable pistol, something small that could be concealed in a reticule or under a cloak. Perhaps it would be wise to get two, just in case.

And then there was the problem of the body.

Emily was suddenly seized with an uncontrollable shivering. Her palms were clammy and cold and her heart was racing madly. She felt dizzy at the prospect of what she was planning.

The heroine in *The Mysterious Lady* would not be so weak, she told herself bracingly. And had she not always thought of herself as that brave female who had set out to rescue her beloved? Shooting Crofton would not be a great deal worse than confronting a real ghost or monster.

Emily prayed that her nerves would be steadier on the night of the soiree. She knew that if her plan did not work, she would not get a second chance.

Having his wife arrested would be every bit as much of a scandal for Simon to endure as having the Unfortunate Incident in her past revealed.

Chapter 19

Simon waited for Emily to appear in the library. He had sent for her a moment earlier. He told himself that it would be interesting to see if she responded to the polite summons with her usual alacrity. Normally she came flying through the library door within seconds after one of the staff informed her that the earl had asked to see her.

Emily had not yet learned the fine art of making her husband wait.

But this morning Simon was not certain what to expect. After he had carried Emily back to her own bedchamber last night he had lain awake for hours trying to wrest some satisfaction from his victory over her father. All he had been able to think about was how cold and empty the big bed had felt without Emily in it beside him.

There was a quick knock on the library door and an instant later Emily, wearing a morning gown trimmed with black and gold dragons, whisked into the room. She looked breathless and slightly disheveled. There was a smudge on her nose and a perky muslin cap sat slightly askew on her red curls.

"You sent for me, my lord?" She came to a halt in front

of the desk, pushing her spectacles up on her nose as she gave him an inquiring look.

"I did not mean to interrupt you if you were involved in a task." Simon, who had risen politely as she entered the room, sat down again and motioned her to take a chair.

"I was supervising the cleaning of the drawing room," Emily explained. "The soiree is only two days away, after all. So many last-minute things still need to be done."

"Ah, yes. More preparations for the damn soiree. I should have guessed."

"I want everything to be perfect, my lord," Emily said quietly. "I am well aware that everything I do, including acting as your hostess, reflects on you."

"Do not fret about it overmuch, my dear. My position in Society is solid enough to sustain the discovery of a few stains on the drawing room carpets or a blot on the drapery." To his surprise, Emily paled and sank abruptly into the chair.

"Some stains and blots are especially difficult to hide, my lord. Sometimes one is obliged to take drastic measures."

He scowled at the odd note in her voice. "Emily, have you been working too hard on this soiree? I employ a decent-sized staff and I expect you to make use of everyone on it. If anyone is failing to do his duty, I would like to know about it at once. Greaves will handle the problem."

She rallied quickly at the implication that any of the staff might not be performing properly. "Your staff is wonderfully helpful, as I am certain you know, Simon. Everyone is working very hard."

He nodded, not entirely satisfied with the response. Emily was upset about something and he knew what that something had to be. She was worried about her bastard of a father. "Excellent. I am pleased to hear that. Now, then, I asked to see you so that I could return your manuscript to you."

"My manuscript?" For the first time Emily glanced at the package sitting on the corner of his desk. Her eyes flew back to his. "I do not understand, my lord. Why do you have my manuscript? Did Richard return it?"

"I asked him to send it back. I shall be quite blunt, Emily. He had not yet had a chance to read it and I did not think it proper for him to do so. I do not want you seeking his opinions."

"But he is a published author, my lord. I thought he would be able to judge whether there is any hope of my manuscript being made suitable for publication."

"I do not believe his judgment would be unbiased," Simon said flatly. "You will find he now agrees with me."

Emily flashed him a quick, hopeful glance. "Are you jealous of him, after all, Simon? I told you once before there was absolutely no need. My relationship with Richard is strictly professional, I assure you."

"I am not jealous of Ashbrook." Simon spaced each word very carefully. "And I expect you to have enough sense not to try to make me jealous."

"Yes, my lord. I mean, no. I would not do that." Emily chewed on her lower lip and eyed the manuscript for a few seconds. Then she jumped to her feet and snatched up the package. "If that is all you wanted, I had better get back to work. After the drawing room is properly cleaned I am scheduled to go over the buffet menu one last time with Smoke. Then I want to check the pantry with Greaves to make certain that all the supplies have arrived."

"A moment, if you please, madam."

Halfway to the door, Emily swung around to face him, clutching the manuscript to her breast. "Yes, my lord?"

"If you care to leave *The Mysterious Lady* with me, I can arrange to have it delivered to Whittenstall or Pound or one of the other publishers," Simon said softly.

Something that might have been amusement flashed in Emily's eyes. "I would not dream of allowing you to take my manuscript to a publisher, Simon."

"You trust Ashbrook more than you trust me?" he asked in silky tones.

She chuckled. "It is not that. The truth is, I know you too well. You would probably frighten Whittenstall or Pound into accepting my manuscript for publication or else you would pay one of them to publish it. Either way, I would not know for certain if my manuscript was capable of being accepted on its own merits. I would much prefer to take my chances like every other aspiring author."

Simon drummed his fingers lightly on the desk. "I see."

"In any event, while you may be able to get *The Mysterious Lady* published, you could not guarantee that it would sell to the public. There are some limits on even your considerable power in town, my lord. But I thank you for the offer." Emily whirled about and dashed from the room.

Simon watched the door close behind her and then he exhaled deeply. "Bloody hell."

She was right, of course. Getting the thing published would have been no great feat. Whittenstall or Pound would have been happy to do it for a price or a threat. But getting the public to buy Emily's epic romance would have been another problem.

He was brooding over the matter when the door opened again and Araminta Merryweather was ushered into the library. Simon got to his feet.

"Good morning, Aunt. I assume you are here to offer aid and council to the budding hostess?"

"I have promised to give a last-minute analysis of the plan of battle." Araminta smiled as she gracefully stripped off her gloves and took the chair Emily had recently vacated. "Your lady is determined that the soiree go perfectly so that you will not be humiliated in front of the *beau monde*."

Simon groaned. "I know. I told her not to fret about it."

"She is hardly likely to pay you any heed. The poor chit is so head over heels in love with you that she would do anything for you, Blade. And she feels enormous pressure not to embarrass you publicly. It is a grave responsibility you carry. I trust you are aware of it."

Simon gave her a sharp glance. "I assure you I am fully aware of my responsibilities toward my wife."

"Umm. Yes. She believes you are, too. Thinks you can do no wrong."

"Her opinion on that may have changed in the past twenty-four hours," Simon said grimly. "Her wastrel father has already ruined himself. Several months ahead of schedule, I might add. He had the gall to approach her for help."

Araminta's brows rose. "I see. And she turned to you?"

"She said she knew there was probably no point asking me to rescue him and I told her she was right." Simon slammed his palm flat against the desk and eyed the gaping jaws of a jewel-encrusted dragon that sat on the corner of the bookcase. "I will not do it, Araminta. I have waited too long for this moment. Rescuing her brother from that stupid duel and letting Northcote, Canonbury, and Peppington off the hook was one thing. Saving Broderick Faringdon is another. Emily knew that from the beginning."

"Yes, but Emily is much given to romantical notions and happy endings. And up until now you have generally indulged her."

"If she had false hopes, that is her problem. She has no excuse for them."

"You are quite right, of course. She has no excuse for them at all, except that she thinks you incredibly heroic and the most marvelous husband on the face of the earth."

Simon narrowed his eyes. "You find that amusing?"

"Naive is what I find it," Araminta said bluntly. "But I expect you will eventually destroy her illusions. Emily is too intelligent to remain naive forever."

Simon squelched the surge of anger that went through him. "Do not taunt me, Aunt. This is none of your affair."

"Perhaps not." Araminta considered that briefly and shrugged. "Is Emily angry with you?"

Simon got to his feet and went over to the tea table. He picked up the gold-and-green-enameled teapot and poured two cups of Lap Seng. "To be perfectly frank, I cannot tell what Emily is feeling today. She is in an odd mood."

"How so?"

Simon handed a cup and saucer to Araminta and then stood sipping the delicate brew. "Distracted. Harried. Running around as if she had far more weighty matters on her mind than the fact that her father is about to be ruined. But she does not seem angry."

"Well, I expect you will know soon enough if she is furious with you."

"In what way will I discover such fascinating information?" Simon muttered.

"By her response in bed, naturally." Araminta smiled knowingly over the rim of her teacup. "Has she begun withholding her favors?"

Simon was startled to feel himself turning a dull red. "Damn it, Araminta, I do not intend to discuss my private life with you."

"Of course not."

He shot her a scathing glance. "Emily would not know how to use sex to get what she wants or to punish me."

"You are probably right." Araminta shook her head. "Your countess really is much too naive to use such standard feminine ploys."

"Will you kindly stop saying that?" Simon said furiously. "The fact that Emily does not have the usual bag of female tricks does not make her naive, damn it."

"How about the fact that she thinks you are a paragon among husbands? Does that make her naive?"

"Bloody damn hell." Simon started to say more but at that moment the library door opened once more and Emily blew into the room.

"Excuse me, my lord. Araminta, thank heaven you are here," Emily gasped. "I have just had word that the musicians would like a list of pieces I would prefer to have played at the soiree. I am attempting to make up my mind. Have you any suggestions?"

"Stick with Mozart, my dear," Araminta said as she put down her teacup and rose to her feet. "One can never go wrong with Mozart. Such a sophisticated composer."

"Yes, yes, you are quite right," Emily agreed instantly. "I definitely want the musical pieces to sound sophisticated. After all, everyone knows Blade is a man of the world. They will expect music that lives up to his standards."

"We certainly would not want his image to suffer, would we?" Araminta smiled serenely at Simon as she followed Emily from the room.

Simon stood alone in the empty library and wondered again why he did not feel the heady rush of triumph and satisfaction he ought to have been experiencing today.

Dealing with a blackmailer and planning a soiree simultaneously was really asking too much of a woman, Emily decided grimly the following day as she reluctantly left for Lady Turnbull's literary salon.

As the carriage jounced and swayed through the streets she frantically wracked her brain one last time for an alternative to her plan for dealing with Crofton. But she knew in her heart of hearts there was only one certain way to deal with a blackmailer, only one certain way to protect Blade. The moment Emily was ushered into the crowded drawing room and met Crofton's vicious, mocking eyes, Emily made up her mind once and for all. If she could not convince Crofton to give up his scheme, she would have to take drastic steps. She would find a way to frighten him off so that he would never return.

Emily swallowed hard and met Crofton's gaze as calmly as possible. He waited until the conversation had begun to grow animated before taking her aside. They went to stand by the window. No one was paying any attention.

"Well, Lady Blade? Have you made your plans?" Crofton sipped his claret and eyed her from beneath drooping lids. His cruel mouth was faintly curved with expectation.

"Be in the alley on the other side of Blade's garden wall at midnight tomorrow night, Mr. Crofton. I shall bring the dragon to you."

"The alley is a bit close and the streets will be crowded with your guests' carriages," Crofton murmured.

Emily tilted her chin. "The fact that the house and surrounding streets will be crowded should work to your advantage. No one will notice one more man moving about. I have made the arrangements, Mr. Crofton, and I intend to stick by them. I want this business over and done."

Crofton shrugged. "Very well, madam. The alley it is,

then. It is no great matter where we meet. I shall be watching from a safe point. If you attempt to bring anyone with you—one of your brothers, say—I will not appear. And the next time my demands will be considerably higher."

"I shall be alone. But I want your oath that this will be the end of the matter. I never want to see you again, Mr. Crofton. Is that quite clear?"

"Of course. One of Blade's dragons should be more than enough to cover the unpaid portion of your father's debts. I shall disappear from your life, my dear."

Emily looked straight into his terrible gaze and knew he lied. Crofton intended to come back again and again. He intended to bleed her dry and always the threat to Simon would be over her head. Blade would never be safe.

"Until later, madam." Crofton inclined his head with taunting gallantry and went back across the room to join Ashbrook and a handful of other guests.

Emily stood near the window a minute or two, taking deep breaths to collect herself. Then, chin high with determination, she crossed the room to join one of the small groups exchanging gossip about Byron.

Shortly after eleven that night Simon was still raging at himself for his inexplicable weakness even as he tracked Broderick Faringdon down in one of the gaming hells off St. James. He could not believe the decision he had made, could not credit what he was about to do.

When the notion had first occurred to him that afternoon, he had told himself Emily had somehow worked on his brain, softening it with her silly illusions and naive faith in his nonexistent heroic characteristics.

He had argued with himself for the past several hours, questioning his sanity as well as his intelligence. He had everything he wanted within his grasp. Faringdon was about to destroy himself. This was no time to weaken.

But weaken he had.

Simon located Broderick at a table in the corner of the crowded, noisy room. He was alone, having apparently just finished a bottle of claret and a hand of cards. The irrepressible Faringdon grin flared to life when he looked up and saw his nemesis standing in front of him.

"A bit too soon to gloat, Blade. Still some life in the old horse."

Simon eyed his enemy, astonished, in spite of himself. By rights, the man should have been desperate by now. "I congratulate you, Faringdon. You certainly do not have the air of a gentleman who cannot meet his debts of honor."

"I fully intend to meet my vowels, sir. Never fear."

Simon sat down slowly, wondering how in hell the man could be so confident when it was clear he was facing disaster. "I trust you know better than to expect help from your daughter."

"Emily's a good daughter. Always been able to rely on her." Faringdon hoisted his port and took a deep swallow.

"Not this time, Faringdon."

"We shall see." Broderick scanned the room as if looking for other players who might be ready for a game.

Simon watched him. "Does this mean you would not be interested in a bargain, Faringdon?" he asked softly.

Broderick's head came around swiftly, blue eyes keen. "What are you talking about?"

"I am willing to pay off your debts under certain conditions."

Broderick had the look of a hunting hound on the scent of a rabbit. "Good God. Did she get to you, then? Talk you into doing the right thing by me? Knew she would. She's a good girl, she is, just like I always said. Got a real sweet way about her, don't she? Just like her mama."

"This has nothing to do with Emily. This is between you and me, Faringdon. Are you interested?"

Broderick grinned. " 'Course I am. Always interested in a financial proposition. What are you offering, Blade?"

"To pay off your debts in full in exchange for your agreement to accept a position as manager of my estates in Yorkshire."

"*Yorkshire.*" Broderick choked on his last swallow of wine.

"I am breeding horses there and it occurs to me that your one undeniable skill is your eye for first quality bloodstock. You would have to give me your word that you would not return to London or your gaming habits. This would be a position, Faringdon, and I would expect you to work at it with the same industriousness with which you have always pursued gaming."

"You must be out of your bloody mind," Broderick sputtered. "Send me off to Yorkshire to run some damn breeding farm? Not on your life, Blade. I'm a man o' the world, not a farmer. Get out of here. I don't need your goddamn offer of a *position*. I can take care of my own debts."

"Without the help of your daughter?"

"Who says my daughter won't help me, by God?"

"I do." Simon stood up, disgusted with himself for even making the offer. "That part will not change, Faringdon. Not ever. I will never again allow you to use Emily."

"Bastard. We shall see about that."

Simon shrugged, picked up his hat, and walked toward the door.

It baffled him why anyone was particularly attracted toward the occasional, inexplicable impulse to be forgiving. It was obvious the world did not appreciate such naive qualities and acting on them only left one feeling like an idiot.

Still, Simon was rather glad he had made the crazed offer to Broderick. He made a note to mention his generous act to Emily after the soiree. She would look at him with her customary adoration and tell him how she had known all along he would be generous and heroic in victory. The fact that her father had failed to accept the offer in Yorkshire would be Broderick's problem, not Simon's.

Simon would no longer have to feel the lash of guilt whenever he looked into Emily's eyes.

Yes, he decided as he walked out of the hell, he was already feeling much better. He would like to tell Emily about his good deed tonight but she was frantic with soiree preparations. She would not be able to be suitably grateful and adoring. Much better to wait until the household had been restored to a semblance of calm.

• • •

"Emily can relax," Araminta murmured to Simon the next evening. "Her soiree is a brilliant success. The house is packed with guests, the street is clogged with carriages, the buffet is a perfect combination of the exotic as well as sturdy English fare, and the music is of excellent quality. Tomorrow morning everyone will be calling this a highlight of the Season."

Simon nodded coolly as he glanced around the crowded rooms. Laughter and music and conversation hummed through the townhouse. Emily's soiree was, indeed, a stunning success. "Have you seen Emily recently?"

"I noticed her talking to Lady Linton a short while ago." Araminta scanned the crowd. "I do not see her now. Perhaps she has gone to check with Greaves to see that the staff has everything under control. She has fretted over every detail of this evening. It's a wonder she has not collapsed from sheer exhaustion."

Simon frowned, aware of a vague sense of unease. It had begun a few minutes ago and was intensifying rapidly. "If you will excuse me, I believe I shall attempt to find her."

"Good luck. You might check with your butler. He has been keeping an eye on things."

"I will do that." Simon made his way through the knots of elegantly dressed people, pausing occasionally to exchange civilities and acknowledge compliments on Emily's charm as a hostess.

He eventually reached the hall, which was as crowded as the drawing room. He quickly located Greaves.

"Have you seen Lady Blade recently?" Simon asked.

"A few minutes ago, my lord." Greaves glanced around. "I do not see her now. Shall I have one of the footmen look for her?"

The uneasy sensation was getting worse. "Yes," Simon said. "Immediately. I shall check the kitchens."

"I doubt she would be in there, sir." Greaves gave a disapproving frown. "I advised her it would be best if she stayed with her guests and left the staff to see to the replenishment of the refreshments."

"Perhaps she is taking a short rest in the library. I will try there first."

The uneasiness had turned into a strong sense of urgency. Simon let himself into the library, which had been declared off limits to guests, and closed the door behind him.

It was something of a relief to step into the quiet sanctum. Simon saw at once that Emily was nowhere in sight, however, and the urgency crystallized into a genuine sense of foreboding.

He walked to the windows and glanced out into the gardens. There was just enough light pouring from the house to reveal a flicker of shadow near one of the hedges.

Simon froze as he recognized the swirling hem of a familiar dark cloak.

He told himself it was undoubtedly a guest who had gone outside for some fresh air but even as he tried to reassure himself he knew something was wrong.

Acting on instinct, Simon opened the window, threw one leg over the sill, and dropped lightly down onto the damp grass.

A moment later he was slipping silently along in the shadow of the tallest hedge. He caught sight of his quarry a short time later.

It was Emily, he realized grimly. There was no doubt about it. She was wearing her black velvet cloak.

Even as Simon watched, she unlocked the gate and stepped cautiously out into the dark alley. Simon started forward, his stomach cold with dread. He stopped short as a familiar masculine voice rose out of the darkness on the other side of the wall.

"Well, well, well," Crofton drawled contemptuously. "So you managed to pull it off, did you? I hope you have had the good sense to bring me one of Blade's better specimens concealed under your cloak, my dear. I would not want to have to send you back for another so soon."

"There will be no more, Mr. Crofton," Emily said fiercely.

"Oh, I think there will, Lady Blade. Your husband's wealth is a matter of much speculation, but there is no doubt it is considerable. I do not think he will miss one or two more of his odd statues."

"You are a bastard, Mr. Crofton."

Crofton chuckled evilly. "Remember what will happen if you do not cooperate, my dear. The husband you so obviously adore will be held up to public ridicule because of the scandal in your past. He will be humiliated forever because of you. But we both know you will do anything to protect Blade, don't we? Such a loving wife."

Simon found a chink with the toe of his boot and hoisted himself silently up to the top of the broad stone wall. Crouching on the rough surface, he looked down and saw two figures dimly illuminated in the weak moonlight. His hand clenched into a tight fist as the rage washed through him.

Emily had the hood of her cloak pulled up over her face, her hands buried inside the folds of velvet. Crofton stood a few feet from her, dressed in an enveloping greatcoat and a hat pulled down low over his eyes to conceal his face.

"Are you quite certain you will not give up this dreadful scheme?" Emily asked quietly. "Is there no hope of appealing to your better nature?"

"None whatsoever, my dear. None whatsoever. Do you know, I have grown vastly curious. I believe I would be interested to find out just why Blade finds you so amusing. I think we shall arrange for another meeting very soon, madam. Someplace private, I think, where you can show me how clever and amusingly eccentric you are—in bed."

"You are a monster, Crofton."

"Tut, tut, my dear. Just remember what will happen if you do not cooperate with me. I know you are probably too eccentric to care about your own reputation, but you will do what you have to in order to protect Blade from humiliation, won't you? And I shall so enjoy the experience of bedding you, madam. I feel certain it will be quite a novelty.

Has he taught you any interesting Eastern tricks for entertaining a man?"

"You are correct about one thing, Crofton. I will do
anything to protect my husband."

Emily's hands came out from under the cloak. Simon
saw moonlight reflect off the small pistol she was clutching
and he realized with a shock what she was about to do.

*Emily was about to put a bullet through Crofton in order
to protect him from the scandal in her past.*

Crofton's mouth dropped open at the sight of the
weapon. His eyes widened in stunned surprise. "Damnation,
woman, are you mad? Put down that pistol."

"I gave you your chance, Mr. Crofton. And I hoped
against all odds that I would not have to go to such extreme
lengths to make you disappear. But you would not go away.
There is only one way to protect my husband from you."
She aimed, set her teeth, and started to pull the trigger.

"Bloody hell," Simon muttered. It was a heartwarming
gesture, of course, and one he would treasure until his dying
day, but he really could not allow Emily to shoot Crofton
for him.

Simon dropped straight down from the wall, colliding
with Emily an instant before she fired the pistol.

Chapter 20

Emily felt as though the garden wall itself had fallen on her.

"It's me, damn it," Simon growled in her ear as the impact of his body sent her sprawling along the damp pavement stones. "Don't shoot."

"Simon! What on earth . . . ?" The pistol was knocked from Emily's hands. She heard it skitter across the narrow alley. The swirling folds of her voluminous cloak protected her from the dirt and grit of the pavement but they also blinded her. For a moment she could see nothing.

"Blade! So the bitch told you, did she? I warned her not to say anything," Crofton yelled. "She was a fool. I'll kill you both, by God."

Simon's weight was suddenly gone from her as he leapt to his feet. Emily sat up quickly, jerking the black velvet away from her face. She got free of the cloak, only to realize she could see nothing but the blurred shapes of the two men. Her spectacles had fallen off in the struggle. She groped frantically about and her fingers closed around the delicate metal frames. They were unbroken, she realized in relief.

Emily put her spectacles back on just in time to see Crofton drawing a pistol out from the pocket of his coat. He aimed it straight at Simon.

"No," Emily gasped, struggling to her feet.

But in that instant Simon lashed out with his foot, catching Crofton's hand with such force that something cracked and the pistol went flying.

Crofton's eyes widened in genuine terror as Simon closed in on him. He sidled backward but there was no time to run. He grabbed a stone lying on the pavement and flung it at Simon's head, but missed and hit the alley wall. Then Crofton dove for the pistol Emily had dropped.

Simon closed the short distance between himself and the other man in the blink of an eye. He slashed at Crofton's neck with the edge of his hand just as the man grabbed the pistol.

Crofton crumpled to the pavement and lay very still.

Emily looked down at the fallen man and then raised her eyes to Simon's savagely controlled face. He gazed back at her, golden gaze burning in the pale moonlight.

"I told him I would bring a dragon with me tonight," Emily whispered.

"Go back to the house," Simon said quietly. "Find Greaves. Tell him to send either George or Harry out here at once. Then return to your guests."

Emily shook off the odd paralysis that seemed to have gripped her. "Simon, wait, I had a very clever plan."

"Did you?" Simon came toward her, eyes still glittering strangely.

Emily instinctively took a step back. "Yes, my lord. I was going to make it appear as though he had been attacked by a footpad out here in the alley. I spent a great deal of time working out the details."

"I will take care of the details."

"Is he dead?"

"No. I do not think it will be necessary to kill him. There are other ways of getting rid of his type." Simon's hand closed over her arm and he hauled her toward the garden gate. "You will go back to the house at once and you will do precisely as I have instructed. Is that quite clear, madam?"

"Yes, Simon."

Emily glanced back once over her shoulder and a small shudder went through her at the sight of Crofton lying on the damp pavement. Then she was back in the safety of the garden, hurrying toward the warm lights and the sounds of laughter that spilled from the house.

The last of the guests did not leave until nearly dawn. Just before being handed into her carriage, Lady Merryweather took Emily aside and assured her that the entire affair had been an enormous success and that the soiree would be the talk of the town by noon.

If only she knew just how exciting the soiree really had been, Emily thought as a yawning Lizzie finally finished preparing her mistress for bed and left the bedchamber.

The sound of the door of Simon's bedchamber opening and closing told her that Higson was also through with his tasks. Emily jumped out of bed, grabbed her wrapper, and rushed across the carpet to the connecting door. She had been seething with impatience ever since Simon had quietly returned to the soiree and rejoined the guests.

For the remainder of the evening he had acted as if nothing untoward had occurred and naturally Emily had been obliged to behave in the same fashion. Together they had played the role of host and hostess for the next few excruciatingly long hours. Now, at last, they could talk.

Emily yanked open the door and saw Simon standing near a small table in the corner. He was wearing his dressing gown and was in the process of pouring himself a glass of brandy from a decanter. He glanced over his shoulder as Emily burst into the bedchamber.

"Do come in, madam," Simon said blandly. "I have been expecting you."

"Simon, I have been going mad. Is everything all right? Did you get rid of Crofton? What have you done with him?"

"Kindly keep your voice down, madam. We do not wish to alarm the servants."

"Yes, of course." Chastened, Emily sat down on the side

of the bed. "Simon, please," she urged in a loud whisper. "You must tell me everything."

"No, Emily, I think it is you who should do the explaining." Simon crossed the floor and sank down onto the other side of the bed. He propped himself up against the pillows and stretched his legs out in front of him. His eyes met hers as he swirled the brandy in his glass. "From the beginning, if you please."

Emily twisted around and peered anxiously at him. She heaved a deep sigh. "It is rather difficult to explain."

"Try."

"Yes, well, you remember me telling you that my father was in dun territory?"

"Very well," Simon agreed. "I assume that Crofton was the gamester who held the vowels?"

"Yes. I encountered both Crofton and Papa at the theater the other night."

"Where they had no doubt been lying in wait for you."

"Most probably," Emily admitted. "In any event, Papa said he had gotten quite downcast when he'd realized he'd lost the last of his fortune. He apparently drank too much one night. While he was in his cups he had talked to Crofton and told him about the Unfortunate Incident in my past."

"You refer to the nonexistent Incident, I presume?"

Emily frowned. "Well, yes, but Crofton knew it was a fact, you see."

"Blackmailing bastard." Simon sipped his brandy.

"Crofton said that unless I helped Papa pay his gaming debts, he would spread gossip about the Incident throughout Society."

"I see."

"I did not mind the threat to myself, of course. I long ago learned to live with the blot on my reputation. And in Little Dippington nobody seemed to mind, anyway. But if the truth emerged here in town it would create a dreadful scandal. It would result in a terrible stain on your title. You would be humiliated and it would be all my fault and I could not bear that, Simon. I know you married me on the assumption that you would be able to keep the scandal hidden."

"So you plotted to shoot Crofton?"

"Well, yes. I could not think of any other alternative, you see. He had heard about your beautiful dragons. He said just one of them would undoubtedly cover Papa's gaming debts. So I told him I would bring him one of the statues tonight. I lied. My plan was to wound him very seriously. I wanted to frighten him off, you see."

"You were going to *kill* him in order to protect me from humiliation." Simon shook his head in disbelief. "God in heaven. You never cease to amaze me, madam."

A shiver of fear went through her as she absorbed the odd tone of his words. Emily drew back slightly, folding her hands in her lap. She studied him carefully. "Have I shocked you at last, Simon?" she whispered.

"Yes, Emily, you have."

Emily finally began to realize how the whole incident must appear in Blade's eyes. No wonder he was acting so strangely. He was no doubt sickened and repulsed by her now. She had ruined everything. Emily stood up slowly as tears welled in her eyes. "I am sorry, my lord. I confess that until now I did not consider the matter from your point of view. I can see how disgusted you must be to know you are married to a woman who is capable of shooting someone."

"Not that it matters, but you did not shoot anyone tonight, Emily."

"Not for lack of trying."

His mouth curved faintly. "No, not from lack of trying. You are a tigress when you set out to protect your own, aren't you, my dear?"

Emily stared at him in confusion. "I could not let him humiliate you, Simon."

"No, of course not. You love me. You adore me. You think I am noble and generous and brave, a paragon among husbands." Simon took a sip of brandy. "You would do anything for me."

"Simon?" Emily's voice was uncertain.

"You must forgive me for being somewhat dazed at the

moment. Actually, I have been in this state for the past several hours. No one in my entire life has ever tried to protect me, elf."

Emily continued to stare at him, unable to speak.

"I have taken care of myself for as long as I can remember," Simon continued. "And when I met you, I realized I wanted to take care of you, too. But the notion of someone being willing to risk her life for me, the concept of someone willing to shoot a man to protect me, has temporarily scattered my wits."

"Simon, are you trying to tell me you are not repulsed by my actions, after all?"

"I am trying to tell you that I probably do not deserve you, elf, but I will kill anyone who tries to take you away from me." His golden eyes flashed in the candlelight. "In that way, I believe we must be two of a kind."

"Oh, Simon."

"A long time ago I wrote three letters asking for help."

"You wrote them to Northcote, Canonbury, and Peppington. Yes, I know," Emily said gently.

"When that help was refused I vowed I would never again ask anything of anyone in this world or the next. But now I find I must break that oath. Please do not ever stop loving me, elf. Losing your love would destroy me."

"Oh, *Simon.*" Emily's fingers twisted in the folds of her wrapper as the happiness threatened to explode inside her.

"I love you, Emily," Simon said quietly, his eyes never leaving hers. "I probably have all along. God knows nothing else could account for much of my behavior recently. But when I saw you about to shoot Crofton in order to protect me, I knew it for certain. I also knew I had to tell you."

"Simon." Emily could not stand it anymore. She threw herself across the bed and into her husband's arms.

He caught her close. The empty brandy glass fell to the carpet as Simon crushed his wife against him and buried his lips in her hair. He held her so tightly Emily could not breathe, but she did not mind in the least.

"Tell me you will give me what I ask," he whispered.

"Tell me you will love me forever, elf." Simon tipped her chin up so that he could look down into her eyes.

"Forever, Simon."

"Good. Now, then, there is just one more point I would like to make tonight."

"Yes?" she looked up at him expectantly.

"You will give me your word that you will never again attempt anything so dangerous as that meeting with Crofton," Simon said roughly.

"But, Simon, I had no choice. The scandal—"

He put his fingertips over her mouth. "The scandal does not exist, Emily. How many times must I tell you?"

"But Crofton knew about it. He would have told everyone."

"No, my sweet, he would not have dared to tell anyone. He would have known the price of such gossip would have been his own life. And there would have been no reason to take the risk. He would have realized I could have crushed the gossip as easily as I would have crushed him."

"Simon, are you really that powerful?"

"Yes, Emily, I am. Crofton's only hope of using the information was to threaten you with it. And that is exactly what he did."

"Oh. And I fell for his trick."

"Because you love me. But in future you will also trust me enough to come directly to me if you are ever again faced with such a problem. Are we agreed?"

"Yes, Simon." She smiled tremulously.

He carefully removed her spectacles and then he brought his mouth down on hers with a soul-wrenching hunger that sent shivers through Emily.

She moaned into his mouth and joyously gave herself up to the embrace. With utter abandon and excessive passion, she clung to her husband.

"Oh, God, elf, I need you so much." Simon muttered thickly against her throat. "Love me. *Love* me."

"I could do nothing else except love you, Simon."

Gently, he pushed Emily onto her back. As he undressed her, Simon's hands were everywhere, moving with a tender,

possessive urgency across her breasts and along the inside of
her thighs. The raging need in him sparked her own blazing
desires. Emily shivered again in the grasp of the dragon.

When he settled between her legs and guided himself
into her with one long, powerful thrust, Emily cried out and
clawed at his back. Simon gripped her hips and held her to
him as he drove himself into her.

And then they were lost in the wondrous world they had
created for themselves.

A long time later, Emily stirred sleepily in Simon's arms.
"Well, my lord?"

Simon yawned hugely. He looked like a lazy, supremely
satiated dragon. "Well, what?"

"Would you agree at last that there is only one way to
describe the culmination of our lovemaking?"

"You refer, I imagine, to that immortal line from your
epic poem. We are, indeed, *cast adrift upon love's transcendent, golden shore.*"

"Actually," Emily said thoughtfully as she moved her
toes up and down the length of Simon's leg, "I think our
lovemaking is even better than that. I do not believe the line
quite captures the full magnitude of the event."

"You are quite correct. It does not."

"I shall have to work on some new lines for my poem."

"Perhaps you ought to broaden the range of your sensual experience a bit further, madam poet." Simon's fingers
trailed warmly over her thigh.

Emily turned toward him. She was about to kiss him
when a thought struck her. "Simon?"

"Hmm?" He was busy nuzzling her throat.

"How did you happen to know I was conducting that
dreadful scene with Crofton in the alley tonight?"

Simon's bare shoulders moved in a negligent shrug. He
pinned her leg with one powerful thigh. "I merely had a
hunch something was wrong. I searched for you in the
crowd and could not find you, so I went looking."

"Hah. I knew it."

"Knew what?" Simon drew the tip of his tongue across one nipple.

"We do communicate on the metaphysical level, Simon," Emily said excitedly. "The events this evening prove it. How could you have known I was involved in something terrible tonight unless you had received some mystical message on the transcendental plane?"

Simon raised his head to gaze down at her. At first he looked rather nonplussed. And then a slow, wickedly sensual grin curved his hard mouth. "You are quite right, my love. But in future, I would rather you did not rely on metaphysical communication. The next time you are plotting an adventure of any kind, I want your word you will discuss it with me verbally as well as in the metaphysical realm. Agreed?"

"Whatever you wish, Simon. You know, I am having second thoughts about my epic poem."

"Is that right?"

"Yes. I am thinking of changing the title from *The Mysterious Lady* to *The Mysterious Earl.*"

Simon groaned.

"Just think, Simon. It opens up all sorts of new possibilities for exciting adventures and thrilling scenes."

"Come here and thrill me, Emily," Simon ordered, pulling her closer.

"Certainly, my lord."

Simon sat behind his black lacquered desk and eyed the library full of Faringdons. Broderick Faringdon was occupying the chair nearest the brandy decanter. Devlin and Charles were ranged expectantly on either side of the black mantel, rather like a handsome pair of gilt candlesticks.

Emily, dressed in a dragon-trimmed gown, sat demurely in a red velvet chair near the desk. Simon was not unaware of the significance of her choice of position in the room. She was on his side.

"I have summoned the three of you here today because

the time has come to settle certain matters," Simon said slowly.

"Well, well, well." Broderick Faringdon nodded approval. "Must say it's about time you assumed your duties to your in-laws. I can give you the total of my current losses immediately and let you know how much additional blunt I'll be needing to carry on with until Emily can replenish our finances."

Simon drummed his fingers on the desk, aware that Emily was chewing on her lower lip again. "First, we shall discuss the future of Devlin and Charles." Simon glanced at the young men. "You have both agreed to my offer?"

"Jumped at it, is more like it," Devlin said cheerfully.

"Cannot wait to be off to India," Charles agreed. "Good thing I never got around to offering for Maryann Mathews. Much rather go abroad and make my fortune. India's the land of opportunity and adventure and all that. Bound to come back rich."

"Excellent," Simon murmured, amused at the surprise on Emily's face. "I have spoken to my man of affairs and he has arranged suitable positions for both of you in Bombay. Passage has been booked on a ship in which I own controlling interest. It sails tomorrow on the morning tide. Captain Adams is expecting you aboard."

"We are already packed and ready, sir," Devlin assured him happily.

Broderick Faringdon scowled first at his sons and then at Simon. "What the devil is this all about? Dev and Charles are off to India?"

"They have decided to seek their fortunes on their own, without relying on their sister," Simon said smoothly. "And as their father, I am certain you will wish to do the same. You know how important it is to set a good example."

Broderick sputtered in outraged shock. "See here, if this is another offer to fob me off on some menial employment on your horse farm in Yorkshire, you can bloody well go to hell."

"What offer was this?" Emily broke in to demand.

"Your tightfisted husband came to me the other day with

the crazed notion of paying off my debts if I would agree to go to Yorkshire to manage some damn horse farm," Broderick said in aggrieved tones. "Can you believe it? Me? Working on a horse farm?"

Emily blinked and turned to Simon. "You offered to do this for him? Simon, that was wonderfully generous of you. I had no notion you had done such a thing."

Simon shrugged. "My offer was rejected out of hand."

"Damn right, it was." Broderick was overflowing with righteous indignation. "Cannot expect a man o' the world to bury himself in Yorkshire."

"Sounds like an excellent suggestion to me," Devlin observed. "You've always had an eye for good horseflesh, Father."

"Should have thought you'd have taken him up on it," Charles agreed. "Perfect solution to the problem."

"Now, see here," Broderick yelped, shocked at the traitorous words of his sons. " 'Twas no such thing."

"Your father had another solution in mind," Simon said quietly. "But as it happens, it did not work out." For some strange reason he did not feel like telling Charles and Devlin just what sort of bastard their father had been. Emily had been right. The twins were different from their parent. They had been languishing for lack of a proper example but had been eager enough to grow up when shown the way.

"Did not work out?" Broderick flicked a startled glance at his daughter and then scowled at Simon. "What are you talking about now?"

"I have made some arrangements for you," Simon said.

Broderick nodded, looking somewhat placated. "Thought you'd come through. Told Emily she would be able to talk you into it. Didn't I say that to you, girl?"

"Yes, Papa. That's what you said," Emily murmured.

"Whole world knows Blade indulges you to an astonishing degree. And he don't want any more scandal, o' course." Broderick smiled with satisfaction. "Now, then, Blade. About the matter of replenishing my capital."

"Yes, of course." Simon folded his hands on top of the desk and met Broderick's expectant gaze. "You will want to get started as quickly as possible, as you are, apparently, almost entirely without funds at the moment."

"Quite right."

"I have, therefore, taken the liberty of booking one-way passage for you on another of my ships. This one is not bound for India, however, as I feel your sons should be on their own. Instead you will be sailing for a small island in the East Indies where I have some business investments."

Broderick stared at him. "You've gone mad, sir."

Simon ignored him. "A position in one of my ventures awaits you on the island. Once there, you may choose to accept that position or reject it. I do not particularly care. But either way, you will be going to the island and you will not be able to get back to England unless you manage to earn your passage. It is rather expensive."

"See here," Broderick raged, surging to his feet, "I am not going to Yorkshire, let alone to some bloody damn island in the East Indies."

"You are right about not going to Yorkshire. That offer will not be made again. I want you out of England altogether, and mark my words, you will be on board the *Sea Demon* tomorrow morning when it sails. You have only two options. You may go willingly, or I shall have you tied up and carried aboard. Take your pick."

"You cannot do that, damn it," Broderick snarled.

"I own the *Sea Demon* and every man on board, including her captain," Simon said softly. "I have told Captain Conway that you are to sail with him to the East Indies. Two of his men are waiting out in the street now. They will escort you back to your lodgings and assist you in packing your belongings. You will spend the night aboard so that we do not have to worry about you nipping off to the country."

Broderick's desperate gaze went straight to Emily. "You cannot let him do this to me, Em."

Emily drew herself up and faced her father. "My husband has, as usual, been extremely generous under the circumstances. But, then, he is naturally inclined to do the noble thing. 'Tis his nature. I wish you a good voyage, Papa. Be certain to write when you arrive."

"Emily!"

"I am in need of a good correspondent from that part of the world. I have always felt I lacked sufficient information from the East Indies for my various investment decisions in that area. You can be a great asset to me, Papa."

"Dear God," Broderick said, clearly dazed. "My own daughter has turned against her loving papa. I cannot credit it."

"I myself had a bit of difficulty crediting the arrangements you had allowed to be made regarding the payment of your gaming debts," Simon said, feeling dangerous all over again as he recalled the scene in the alley.

"You . . . know about that?" Broderick asked uneasily.

"I know all. Emily and I enjoy a most unusual form of communication," Simon explained.

"Good God. I never meant . . . never actually thought it would come to that. Thought Emily could talk you into paying the debts. It was Crofton who suggested applying the spurs, you know. Said Emily might need some incentive."

"I would not say anything more, if I were you," Simon warned softly. "You may be interested to know, however, that you will not be alone when you sail to the East. Your good friend Crofton will be with you. Indeed, he is already on board, awaiting your arrival."

Broderick's mouth opened and then closed again as Simon's cold fury finally registered. This was obviously the first time he had realized his opponent knew everything. Whatever he saw now in Simon's gaze must have convinced him that there was no more hope. Broderick turned to Emily, eyes pleading. She returned his glance without expression.

"Goodbye, Papa."

"Banished to the East Indies. Of all the unjust fates. I wish your mama were here. She would know what to do." Broderick got up, walked slowly to the door, and let himself out into the hall.

A long silence descended on the library. Devlin glanced at his twin. Both straightened away from the mantel, looking suddenly much older and far more mature than they had a few weeks ago.

"Time we were on our way," Charles said crisply. "Plenty to do before we leave tomorrow." He leaned down to give Emily an affectionate peck on the cheek. "You'll come down to the docks to see us off, Em?"

"Of course." She smiled at him.

"We'll write to you, Em." Devlin kissed his sister's cheek and grinned down at her. "And we'll send you all our profits to invest."

"Do take care, both of you." Emily jumped to her feet to embrace the twins.

"We will." Charles gave her the charming Faringdon grin. "And the next time you see us, we'll both be rich nabobs." He turned to Simon. "Goodbye, sir. And thank you for everything."

"Yes," Devlin said, giving Simon a straight look. "Thank you. We know we're leaving our sister in good hands. Take care of her."

"I will," Simon said.

He waited until the door had closed behind the twins and then he got to his feet and went over to the brandy decanter. He poured two glasses and brought one back to Emily. "A toast, madam wife."

She smiled with her eyes as she lifted her glass. "What are we toasting, my lord?"

"An England free of Flighty, Feckless Faringdons." Simon took a satisfying swallow of brandy.

"What about me?"

"You," said Simon as he set down his glass, "are not a Faringdon." He crossed the room and locked the library door. "You have not been one since the day I married you."

"I see." She watched his every move with brilliant eyes. "Simon, I must thank you for all that you have done for my family. You have been extremely generous. I have never seen Charles and Devlin looking so excited about anything as they are about going out to India. And as for my father . . ."

"What about him?"

"As I said, you were most generous toward him. He did not deserve it."

"No, he did not."

"You are so kind, Simon," she said impulsively. "So generous and noble and—"

He held up a palm to silence her. "What I did, I did to free myself of Faringdons. It was entirely selfish on my part."

"No, what you did, you did for me," she said knowingly. Then she laughed up at him with her eyes. "The whole world knows you indulge me shamelessly."

"And the whole world knows you are helplessly in love with me, totally in my thrall, and completely at my mercy." He untied the knot in his white cravat as he started back across the room.

"It seems a fair enough arrangement to me."

"What the whole world will no doubt determine soon enough," Simon said as he eased the length of silk from around his throat, "is that I am just as much in love with you as you are with me."

"Does that possibility worry you, my lord?"

He came to a halt in front of her, the white silk cravat dangling from his fingers. "Not in the slightest."

"Simon? What are you going to do with that cravat?" Emily asked.

He draped it sensuously around her throat. "The same thing I did with it the last time we made love here in the library."

"Really?" Then her eyes widened. " 'Tis the middle of the day, my lord."

"Never too early to be *cast adrift on love's transcendent, golden shore,* my sweet." He scooped her up in his arms and carried her over to one of the huge satin pillows.

He settled her on the gold cushion and came down beside her. She smiled at him, her love blazing in her beautiful eyes.

And when she was wearing nothing at all except the strip of white silk, she went into his arms the way she always did—with a joyous, loving passion that was strong enough to last a lifetime.

Out of the corner of his eye, Simon saw one of the jeweled dragons grinning at him. The earl laughed and the laughter became dragon's music and it filled the house.